MRS CLAY

The Austen Expert's Companion

to

Persuasion

by

Dorothea-Sofia Rossellini

2nd edition, 2018

paperback:—

9"x 6"

ISBN-13: 978-0-9953790-0-8

A5

ISBN-13: 978-0-9953790-8-4

Published by:—

The Rabbits of Whisky Creek
PO Box 148 Dorrigo
NSW 2453
Australia

Image sources:—

Front cover: image adapted by author, after details of 'The Loss of the Halsewell East Indiaman', print by James Gillray, after painting by James Northcote, held by the British Museum.

Volume I, Chapter 2: image of the same event as depicted by W.M. Clark. Public domain, via Wikimedia Commons.

Volume 3, Chapter 5: 'Napoleon Escapes from Elba'. Image retrieved from http://content.time.com/time/specials/packages/article/0,28804,2067565_2067566_2067593,00.htmlOriginal source unknown.

Volume 3, Chapter 11: Detail from 'The Dance of Death' by Isaac Cruickshank, after image by George Woodward. Public Domain, via Wikimedia Commons.

Volume 3. Chapter 31: 'A High Wind in the Park!' by J. Baker. Public domain, via Wikimedia Commons.

Volume headings: Volume 1: 'The Fashions of the Day, or Time Past and Present'; Charles Williams, after Woodwardom. Public Domain via Wikimedia Commons. Subsequent volume headings adapted by the author from this initial image.

Paperback cover: —

Clare Colins, after design by D-S Rossellini.

Dedicated

with respect and gratitude

to

Australia's Medicare System

without which neither this book

nor its author

would exist.

Preface

A preface to a work of fiction is, I have always believed, a bad sign. A story should speak for itself. Nevertheless, I find that to readers of *Mrs Clay* I often need to make certain points.

The first concerns the Narrator as you first encounter him or her. Am I, the reader may ask, *supposed* to find this person annoying?

Yes.

The narrative voice of *Mrs Clay* is a twenty-first century voice: dissecting and decrying the past; pointing out where it falls short of us today; rewriting it, to show our long-dead ancestors how to do it properly; even, where it is just beyond all bounds of correctitude, condescending to fix their work with a little compassionate Bowdlerisation.

Now, at the opening of the book, *Mrs Clay*'s modern Narrator has only just found themselves stranded in Regency England. They still have all their own contemporary assumptions intact. Give the poor creature time to encounter that new reality; time to react; to reflect. To blend in.

And don't worry. In Austen, no-one who starts out by claiming Universal Omniscience is going to make it through the book unscathed.

Then there's the occasional accusation that *Mrs Clay*, as a book, suggests that we should marry for money rather than love. Good heavens.

The main argument I am making in *Mrs Clay* is that the culture you are in is a cage from which none can entirely escape.

There are times, and places, and groups— many times and places, many groups— for whom that cage is inhumanly small. Those within it will react like the trapped animals they are. The weak, the gentle, the intelligent, will recognise the impossibility of escape, and do all they can to subdue their tormenting desire for more; they will 'submit', in the moral vocabulary of Austen's time. The best-adjusted will declare the cage ideal real estate, and set about exploiting their fellow inmates and gaolers. Others will be found patrolling the perimeter, with a viciousness in proportion to their sense of humiliation at being trapped within it. Only the most powerfully independent minds can even conceive of escape, and if they try an actual goal-break, they pay heavily.

And in whatever way the caged are deformed in forming themselves to their confinement, popular wisdom of the time will declare to be their natural state— as naturally apathetic, say, or naturally devious, or hysterical— and condemn them accordingly. As being unfitted for freedom.

How quickly we forget! How naturally we assume that the airy expanse Western women occupied in the late twentieth century, with its reliable contraception, its rights to education, its welfare, its health care, and work that pays a living wage, was all our natural state and birthright— not a space hard-won by a generation of women and men of good will, working within a brief miracle of economic and social expansion. This miracle is now passing away.

Mrs Clay was dropped into a very small cage; the one which, in Regency society, confined all but the most financially- and mentally-independent women. Outside its bars lay not only ostracism, but actual death. Inside that early nineteenth-century cage, a gentle soul like Nellie Clay of course had the individuality pressed, crushed, and eventually, punched out of her. She became the only thing someone of her personality could be: a good woman; submissive, as the literature of the time urged, to her circumstances, and to her social and spiritual superiors.

That is to say, she twists her behaviour into any shape these forces demand, to retain the kind of social toehold on which her very life depends.

Mrs Clay does this. She survives. All of those she loves best, survive. This makes her life, in the end, a Regency triumph, or a twenty-first-century tragedy: take your pick.

Alright but— moving on— what of all the nasty things the Narrator says about Anne?

Let us leave aside the point that *Mrs Clay* centres on Penelope Clay, from whose perspective Anne is, inarguably, a cold, critical, unbending, repressive presence. Leave aside, too, the fact that the Narrator is a partial, prejudiced and ignorant historian, one whom readers must often feel goes too far, and one with whom they must, at least sometimes, stoutly disagree. (I certainly do.)

Far more interesting is to argue that Anne is *not* perfect— nor was ever seen, by Austen, as perfect. The Anne we first meet in 1814 is always right in her external behaviour, but in her private reactions she is not always kind. She does her duty, but she never fails to note when others don't. Her resentments are justified; we see her struggle against those resentments; but she isn't all that successful— and sometimes, she simply indulges.

The spinster-cage was a confinement with confinement, a cage within a cage. In her cage Anne is quite simply starving, for lack of love, and lack of regard. The sour satisfactions of conscious superiority are the thinnest of nourishments, but when we first meet her those little acid drops are nearly all Anne has to keep her sense of self alive and I, unlike the Narrator, cannot blame her at all for sucking on them from time to time. Nevertheless. They will end up rotting more than your teeth.

This is the reality which our own recent freedoms have protected us from knowing. A social little-ease, particularly one as small as that which ageing single women then occupied, does far worse than to constrain your behaviour. It also presses its own shape into your very thoughts and feelings, and over time, it warps you. Anne Elliot, offstage, in *Persuasion* proper; Mrs Clay, in the humiliating years before we meet her; Austen, in those dreary years in Bath: all three heroines of this book are intelligent enough to see what is happening to them. I would argue that in showing us Anne's besetting 'imperfections' we see evidence of Austen's own iron detachment; her constitutional inability to fool herself. This is a clear-eyed depiction of what it means to be pushed out of the stream of life, and yet, to live on, in a society that has no use for you.

—pictures of perfection as you know make me sick & wicked—

Austen, March 23rd, 1817.

VOLUME I

The Year (1740) a Lady's full dress of *Bombazeen* — The Year (1807) a Lady's undress of *Bum-be-seen*.

THE FASHIONS OF THE DAY or *Time Past and Time Present*.

Chapter 1

"You may perhaps like the Heroine, as she is almost too good for me."
Austen, March 23rd, 1817.

Anne Elliot, delicate, perceptive and refined, daughter of Sir Walter Elliot (Bart.) of Kellynch Hall, with ten thousand pounds dowry assured her in marriage articles, was also, and above all, a famously lovely person.

For example (and although she herself never complained of it; often, indeed, begged others not to mention it) everyone knew how short of money the ghastly Bart. kept her. Nevertheless, alone of her family, Anne could be often seen performing acts of charity in and about the village: providing slates and chalk and books to the parish school, hiring, overseeing and firing its teacher, and presenting sturdy working boots to the village boys on leaving that school. Stout blankets, too, on marriage; blankets so stout that many are today still extant, mortal flesh being, to these blankets, as but grass to coconut matting— though it should also be said, that whenever the poor of Kellynch were gravely ill, Anne carried– that is, arranged to have carried– so much broth to the family concerned that they were commonly able to set up, for the duration, a little soup kitchen as a sideline.

As you would imagine then, in the village of Kellynch, the name of Anne Elliot was spoken with reverence.

Not always in perfectly grammatical sentences, it is true. And this, in spite of the trouble and expense of the school. But; still— you know.

She was, however, quite violently unpopular at home. This is because Anne Elliot was one of those lovely people who can get very nasty indeed if they feel their loveliness is insufficiently appreciated; much nastier than many people professedly unpleasant.

And she was good at this too. Oh yes, Anne Elliot was good.

Nothing that you could really put your finger on. Nothing you could openly object to. How silly would you look, for example, if you took her up on being such a frequent sigher?

Oh— the sighs!

There were, too, her smiles: inward, discreet, almost regretfully amused, as if chastising herself for how foolishly inflated her expectations of you had been, how foredoomed to disappointment. Ah, she had a speaking countenance, did Miss Anne; and when our story opens, it hadn't said anything nice, to any of her family, for eight years.

Though– perhaps I am unkind?

I would not wish to appear unkind.

This early in the book, too: I really should be putting my best foot forward. As your Narrator, I want you to trust me; to repose upon me, with confidence. To like me, even— which people don't often do. Perhaps I should just shut up about Anne.

I mean, the truth is, she's a minor player in our story! She will be important only at one brief point, towards the end of Volume II; and even then, only for something that she never actually *does*... So it is strange– isn't it?– that she has immediately assumed centre stage like this.

Strange that, while originally declaring herself appalled at the very idea of Austen writing a book about her— insisting that it should be called *Persuasion*, rather than *The Elliots;* managing in any case to escape introduction until page four of that book when set in standard typeface, and evading utterance, even, until halfway through Chapter 3— strange, that in spite of all this, Anne Elliot should nevertheless appear persuaded that a novel called *Mrs Clay* must, necessarily, start with Anne.

Not because of the intelligence, and breeding, and *cetera*. No: Anne knows that the gifts dropped upon us by Heaven's careless hand are nothing of which we can, ourselves, be justly proud. But— her loveliness. Anne is sole author of her loveliness.

It is 1814, you see, and the tide of moral fashion is...

Alright, to most people at the time— delighted with the Peace, Napoleon on Elba, and everyone else happy and busy about their own affairs — it probably appears to be hanging still, or just washing idly about, just as it has for the last ten years or more; suspended between the sun and the moon, the Rational and the Romantic, the easy, flowing Empire line and the kind of corsets that deform your internal organs. At such times, a lot seems to be happening, and nothing seems to happen. At such times, sailors will tell you, the current can still be foaming up the estuary even while at the river's mouth the sandbars, fanged with the ribs of earlier prey, begin to swim back up out of the depths. It's hard to see what might lie ahead, at such times. For most people.

But take a clever woman— a reading woman, perceptive, mature; and living, too, quietly to the side now; playing the pianoforte while others dance; "an old maid (I beg her pardon— I mean a young lady) —... no more regarded in society than a poker or a fire-screen"... Such a woman may well sense, before any of us, the last swirl in the water which signals that the tide has finally turned.

Sense it— and foresee (sitting alone now at her miniature work-table, a book before her), that the years of its flow are over. That between herself and her grave will be only the race of the ebb.

Against which, it will soon become dangerously inadvisable to pull.

So she rests her oars at last. She submits herself to the current, and she is lovely.

For a genuinely superior mind, it cannot be easy.

It *is* not easy.

On the contrary:– As any careful reader of *Persuasion* will recognise, what Anne Elliot itches to do, really really *itches* to do, nearly all of the time, is to take each of her acquaintance severally by the shoulders, and then, *shake* them so hard that their heads snap about on their necks like balloons in a storm.

Still: what can I say? Anne Elliot is not our protagonist.

There is nothing for it but to start again.

*

Mrs Clay, wan, and hollow-eyed, and so obviously failing to make ends meet that strangers quietly doubt that she can be respectable— and when she sees that in their eyes, she is driven to agonies of self-expiation— Nellie Clay, with all her possessions locked in one shabby box at her feet and a vulgar outburst less securely confined in her breast, illustrates some of the least picturesque aspects of Regency femininity, and has spent half her life in a nail-splintering slide down its social heap.

It has been long slide, for she was born to comfort, and culture, and kindly parents. In Paris, too, of all places (though perhaps, in Austen, that's not really a plus?...). Her family history must be reserved for Chapter Two, but in a nut-shell: when the girl was not quite fifteen, the brutal hands of War had stripped her bare of all protections and, having had its wicked way with her, tossed her weeping into the streets of England— whence young Penelope has since been repeatedly required, by the Forces of a rude and uncouth History, to 'move along'. It was all very damaging psychologically– more of that later, as I say– and in addition is a strike against her in itself, as we all know on what distant terms an Austen heroine should be with History. Here on this patch of Ply-mouth pavement, though– nearly fifteen years later, a grey April morning in 1814– Mrs Clay's one overwhelming and distinctly feminine problem is money. In England, right now, it is almost impossible for a solitary woman to make a decent living.

I hope the commonplace of that observation has not dulled you to what it entails. A sudden frailty, especially in the strong, will excite our compassion, but persistent helplessness soon exhausts that compassion, and inescapable, legally-binding, lifelong helplessness provokes only a robust general contempt. "The business of a woman's life is marriage", as a contemporary let-ter-to-the-editor remarked, "and if she fail in it, all that can be said of her is that she has failed in her business."

Look at Miss Anne, after all.

On the other hand: *Mrs* Clay. She can be credited with wedlock, at least. Why, then, is she looking quite such a wreck? —holding back those ugly tears, here on the cobbled apron of a Plymouth post-house?

A coach is appearing, clattering out from the yard where the horses have been changed. As it lumbers to a halt Mrs Clay gasps — and the lumpy, vulgar sobs she has been dreading seize their opportunity and race up her throat. She turns quickly to smother them in the collar of Alice Barratt's coat. Miss Barratt is one of Nellie Clay's two oldest friends in England. The other one is Alice's brother, Mr Barratt. Richard.

He is here too. He has carried Nellie's box down for her.

Now, he is standing about, large and silent with embarrassed concern, for his turn to do the goodbyes; yet Nellie snuffles on, and will not show her face... He flinches, and hoods his eyes. He turns his face out to sea— he is crumpling and twisting the papers in his pocket. (The family washing-bill, oddly enough, and that cursed bill for the poulticing of the chestnut mare.) He is the silent type, is Richard.

One should mention, too, that he is tall for a working class man, and dark, and that his family think him very handsome; but through all the years that this trio have been friends, he and Alice have had thirteen orphaned younger siblings to raise, so Richard has perforce been handsome, each night, in solitude... Nellie's sobs grow louder. She has given up trying to hold back: she is yielding all at once to the most intense physical pleasure available to poor but decent females, which is a really good cry.

... Ah! Here also to farewell dearest Nellie are the Comte et Comtesse du Richelin de Beaufleuri, known *tout simplement* to their few friends as the Count and Countess. They cannot afford many friends, they are too humiliatingly poor; nevertheless they lift the tone enormously as they step, with unsteady precision, up onto the pavement now, to stand beside the tall Barratt and his modestly well-built sister: the Count is flourishing a lace handkerchief so worn that it is more darning-thread than lace. Except when visitors are present, their little breakfast table supports each day only a boiled egg or two and a pint of very weak tea, so the walk to the coaching-house has been a significant tax on their meagre energy.

There is more to tell about this poignant couple too, but— the coachman blows his horn impatiently. Mrs Clay is galvanised, hastens to comply, stumbles towards the... oh good Lord; she has turned back again. She is embracing each of her friends in turn. She is insisting that they will meet again, that they *must* meet again!— which all of them know quite well isn't true— that this is it, this is *adieu*– but one says these things[†]—More weeping... Alice has started up too now... so has the Countess, though she's keeping it to just a few French drops– Mrs Clay is quite *white* suddenly, goodness I hope she's not going to faint! Alice fumbles in her pocket for smelling salts. (The coachman

---

† ...remember the washing-bill, though? It stands a guarantee to any Austenite (who might otherwise judge that the brief appearance of these characters, just here, is so tangential as to be structurally unjustifiable), that we *will* meet them all again— and under more romantic circumstances. Just a heads-up.

rolls his eyes.) A quick sniff and a whoop or two and the danger is past; and now Mrs Clay, inhaling and exhaling in an exaggerated fashion, is finally, and shakily, climbing— Oops!— no!— No, yes it's alright— she's climbed into the coach.

Her father has sent the fares. She feels, desperately, how lucky she is in this: to have a father; to have him able, and willing, to send fares. She is heading for his home in the country town of Dashe, where so many minor nineteenth-century characters spend so much time. It is a town she has never seen, a father whom she has not met for half a life-time, and all two days' hard journey from every friend of that half-life.

It's not all doom and gloom, though; not for everyone here. Perched on the imperial— the top of the coach— are her half-niece Josephine (oh God, what a name; especially in 1814; especially in England) and half-nephew Ariosto (oh God, again...): they are eleven and nine respectively, and they at least are surreptitiously excited, in spite of– well— everything.

The conflict and embarrassment of feeling, beneath the dignity of their black armbands, and the noisy tears of Aunt Clay, that Uncle Clay was *vraiment dégueulasse*. And that grandpapa, though they have never seen him, and in the eyes of the True Church he is not really their grandpapa *exactly* so much as their dissolute dead grandmother's unconsecrated paramour, is almost certain to be an improvement. "My dears, you will–"... Mrs Clay has stuck her head back out of the coach door, and is clinging– hanging, sort of backwards– to peer anxiously up at them... "you will hold on *tight*, won't you?"

"*Yes* Aunt Clay." She has been going on about this all morning.

"You wouldn't prefer–"

"*No* Aunt Clay."

"Well but Josie you could sit in my lap and Ariosto–"

"*Nooo!*" wail the children in unison —oh! but they will be singing another tune the minute it rains! And then, how on earth to keep them warm?... A fellow traveller, already annoyed with her (and sensing, too, with that sweet jab of satisfaction that such people feel at such a moment, that *here* is someone she can dislike with impunity) pokes Mrs Clay firmly in the back with her umbrella.

"You are blocking the doorway."

Nellie quite whimpers in her anxiety as she withdraws herself, with clumsy haste, apologising all the way, into the coach interior, which is dark, and smells of vomit.

— But by now, reader, you will have caught the key to Mrs Clay's sorrowful derangement. Have you not?

And you are right; for– look!— Her garments are stained, not merely by the kind of vintage dinge that no amount of scrubbing can remove, but also by the recent application of a cheap black dye; it is not grime that rings her wrists and neck, but the leakage of this nonfast pigment. Yes: where Anne Elliot is a spinster, poor Mrs Clay is a widow.

*

Over the next two days, during which Mrs Clay will be flung about by the lurching coach, ruthlessly imposed upon by Umbrella Lady, and pinched incessantly by the sleazy attorney whose hams are even now being pressed hotly against hers, we can devote Chapter 2 to the history of Nellie Clay's parents— maybe her grandparents too, if there's time. Only a fraction of it will have any bearing on the rest of the story, and the moral reflections that frame it will be tedious precisely to those who might most profit from them— but this was the narrative tradition of Burney, Edgeworth, Mrs Radcliffe; and who am I to break with tradition?

Before we do, though, I'd just like to complete the contrast between Miss Anne and our own protagonist by ensuring that Nellie Clay shares a few intimate thoughts well before page whatever in Chapter Four. Lean in, then, and eavesdrop with me on her inner monologue.

It's a bit hard to do, isn't it, what with the coach throwing everybody around like this. Here; I'll grab her head– hold it still for you...

...oh God oh God forgive me oh God oh George I'm so glad you're dead. Oh God forgive me, at last you're dead thank God you're dead. Oh God oh God forgive me....

— and so on, round and round.

There you go. Right now, that's Mrs Clay.

Chapter 2

Fashion is amongst the cruelest of Nature's forces. It is as perilous to rush too far ahead of it as it, is to lag too far behind— let alone to scamper merrily aside from its strait and narrow path, like some oddly-dressed Biblical goat. The peril lies, you see, in those poised high upon the proud swell of Fashion's normal curve.

On those heights dwells a strange chimera of sheep and wolf; half herd ruminant, half bloody-toothed hunter. Strange, yes: but— not uncommon.

And the dual nature of these creatures is such as to impel them to swarm down, in packs or herds, upon any outliers that they spot below them— exposed upon the dusty foothills of Taste, the barren plains of Judgement; frisking about in their ones and twos— and rip them to bits.

Thus the low-rise pant, for decades universally flattering, is now discovered to make you look horribly like a mango in an egg-cup. Thus too, I'm sure you can recall— for it was just before Slow Cooking got started— when the Raw

Food approach cleansed us? One felt utterly marvellous!– and yet in just months it was found to be poison. Going up a social notch, there is the *couture* of the mind to attend; Austen's writing, for example, from being the province of social goats, will suddenly came along so nicely that for a while there, even the most discriminating adore her!— and then, in the subsequent several years, sadly yet somehow inevitably, her writing falls off again; falls off so badly that one need not have read a single book in order to know it.

But most thrilling, most high-risk, is the dressing and accessorising of— the soul? ...the mind? Well; the belief system.

Here, transitioning elegantly is trickiest of all. Feminism must yield, in the proper season, to a concern for men's groups, and then to a frenzy of Christian revival— oh, remember that?– when for a few years Jesus, in a stunningly-effective *volte face,* wanted you to be rich? It's still around but the middle class is embarrassed at the memory of what they got up to; it's really gone down-market. (Stoicism, though, is rather interesting; isn't it?– worn with plain clothes and a calm demeanour. Or the hijab: increasingly dowdy in Iran; increasingly elegant in much of South-East Asia.) And then there's the tradwife look, where, on a spotless counter, you meditatively stir the teeny-tiny bowl of batter with which you are making a cake for your family of nine...

Yes, it's all fun and games for most of us; just now, just here. Riding still, as we Westerners are, in the last, fading slipstream of that huge wave of liberal freedoms that the twentieth century won for us. In other places, though— and at other times— failing to keep pace gets you killed.

Is that why we still practise it so strenuously? Why we all feel it, deep down; the grim imperative to keep in with... them?

And the shame, the mortal shame, of walking alone.

*

Penelope Clay's mother illustrates the horrible risks some people nevertheless choose to run. Her scorn of her own time's norms— her determination to dress, feel, think, and even act for and as herself— eventually killed her. Indirectly, it also killed her two youngest sons, and even her one surviving daughter's current situation (wedged now in the swaying coach, counting carefully, through her tears, the small change from the fares into her purse) may be traced to her mother's culpable disregard of Fashion.

For while Mrs John Shepherd– Ophelia Shepherd, *née* Bouscogne– was born a recognisable Romantic, she was born a Romantic, alas, in the *Alps-Maritimes* of 1765, when Romanticism, *applied* Romanticism, was as yet little more than a mad gleam in Rousseau's eye and a few nasty spats with his peers.

Nevertheless the tiny Ophelia, all untaught, doted on everything rugged and untamed in her father's estate on the Franco-Italian border. She ran wild in its woods, befriended its mosses and waterfalls, lambs and eagles, shared lunches with shepherd lads and lasses, befriended *them*, too— oh, yes, roll

your eyes, it's all a cliché now; it was absolutely bizarre back then. Confinement indoors did nothing to regularise her behaviour: she would feed bread to
the carriage-horses, and chocolates to the dogs, and by the age of twelve had
already nursed dozens of perfectly healthy canaries to death with diets of
warm milk and honey.

She became, in short, the kind of teenager who changes your mind about
the value of boarding schools, and it requires no particular historical insight to
understand why her parents packed her off at thirteen to a fashionable
Parisian convent— four years, *vacances comprises*— followed immediately by
marriage with their dear near neighbour, a certain Count Ariosto. His title, her
beauty, and the Bouscogne money would, all three agreed, provide a founda-
tion on which anything might be built.

(Really? Mrs Clay's father, a Count??? Vulgar Mrs Clay, of *Persuasion*– who
by the way has discovered a dodgy shilling in that change of hers, and is turning it helplessly over and over between her fingers, as if hoping, by that process, to find it true coin?

No no; just wait. Just be patient.)

The marriage came as a surprise to more than Ophelia. The Count was
quite old, but in his youth he had generated for the House of Ariosto an absolute embarrassment of heirs both legitimate and natural, and with duty so
evidently done he had long seemed settled into a comfortably slovenly routine
with his cook, in the kitchen of the family castle. Yet... on finding our
heroine's mother, at seventeen, quite as beautiful as her own parents had led
him to hope, he married her out of hand— smiling indulgently at her cries of
"No!– by all that is sacred!" that rent the church throughout the ceremony.
Many of his brides had carried on just like this; and Custom, as Edmund
Burke remarked around about this time, reconciles us to everything.

Well yes; as touched on at the opening of this chapter, it reconciles us to
some pretty incredible things. Most get reconciled quite a lot; a few, not so
much. What custom does *reliably* do, though, is render invisible, to most of us,
the real source of our subsequent diffuse and persistent pain.

Thus, the eighteenth-century commonplace of Ophelia's first marriage
doesn't mean that, back then, deep within a million such young women, a
wan, limp, rather nauseated canary did not lean against the bars of its cage,
and sing softly of ... of what?

Well, go on— what?

Yet still, the soft, fretful plaint. The sex was, in those days, proverbially
unreasonable.

Penelope Clay's mother's inner canary, though, was more in the nature of a
roc, and the battlements of *Casa Ariosto* were soon dark with the storm-clouds
of her wrath, its corridors ringing with the screams of her rage. Even the

nicest women found her tiresome now. There comes a point, doesn't there, when a sensible person ceases to kick against the pricks.

What is emerging, though, is that Ophelia was one of those people who go through their lives without any brakes. They are, of all personality types, the most likely to reach escape velocity from the drag of their culture's mass. It's still rare, and they have to do it young, before some overwhelming collision with social comeback smashes them beyond functionality— but with enough luck, enough money, they, of all people, may do it.

And even the birth of a child failed to make pliant Ophelia's ill-formed character. To his father, her own little Ariosto-the-nth was just another item in the heir stockpile, to be whisked from the castle and agisted with one of the Count's obliging peasant women. A fine milker, her husband assured her; but what consolation is that, to a young mother with aching breasts and an empty cradle, and her husband's withered hand eager on her shoulder? The Classical marriage might have the support of tradition, scholarship, even Rousseau — but screw Rousseau, Ophelia thought, as she gazed from the windows of her husband's travel-splashed carriage, over the filthy streets of Paris, and into the eyes of John Shepherd.

Oh yes.

Mr Shepherd, though known to posterity only as a bit-player in the life of Anne Elliot of Kellynch Hall, was once a Romantic hero too, in his own quiet way.

The day on which his eyes met those of his future wife across that Paris street, for example, the young Mr Shepherd had already risen at dawn to shoot an unfortunate challenger neatly through the heart, breakfasted mildly and self-effacingly at the R— coffee house (so favoured by the King's more trusted ministers), encoded the information he there had gathered into a cipher which only the keenest of English minds could master and, ever the innovator, consigned the resulting document to the leg of a reliable pigeon, which was even now winging its way across the Channel to Whitehall, where it would inform British understanding of France's lingering hopes for the Northwest Territory...

In truth, looking at him, back then— and looking, now, at his offspring Mrs Clay (who is finishing quickly her meal at their fifth coach stop so far, gobbling her food and urging the children to do the same– they were the last to be served, and everyone else is gone, she fears back in the coach already)... well, yes; he scarcely seems a more plausible father for her than the Count.

Young Shepherd had his Achilles heel, though. His lungs, though unexceptionably heroic in *quality*, had never been strong, and after the morning's proto-Byronic[†] exertion, Mr Shepherd was feeling the wisdom of a quiet luncheon and a little lie down. Instead, he found himself gazing back into Ophelia's eyes

---

† —because at this point Byron wasn't even born.

and experiencing, as a thunderclap from clear blue skies, the overthrow of his heart and the disorganisation of all his life's short, medium and long-term plans.

*

Who can doubt what followed? When two young people are determined to elope, they are pretty sure by perseverance to carry their point. Ophelia's dowry consoled the Count for her loss: her parents reflected that, Ophelia being lost now to the Church, she was dead also unto them, and were likewise consoled.

And Ophelia?

Blissfully content.

She'd found the right place, you see: the right person, the right set of reactions to the way she was; she was free to be her true self. It can be as simple as that.

Supported by Mr Shepherd's income as a spy and arranger of English-French legal matters, Ophelia Shepherd was in time the loving mother of three more children: our protagonist, Penelope— now crammed, head-to-toe with Josephine and Ariosto, in the cheapest bed of the cheapest room in yet another coaching inn, and asleep, almost, at last— followed by two boys, John and Charles. Even the French Revolution passed her by with scarce a frisson. Mr Shepherd was in charge, you see; and whilst all about him were losing their heads, and blaming him for it (not always without reason), that mild-mannered gentleman maintained a steady and profitable correspondence with men of business and politics on both sides of the Channel.

*

Now, I realise you may think I've written myself into a corner here. Promised, was a cautionary tale of the danger in being seriously out of step with your surrounding *zeitgeist*. Thus far, however, our protagonist's mother, by means precipitately Romantic, has escaped a life of Neo-Classical horrors, and attained a marriage of such happiness and financial security as arguably disqualify her from being romantic at all. This, too, when Romanticism was finally becoming quite modish!

Nevertheless, the novels of Austen teach us that to impetuously follow your impulses is to court disaster. It makes sense.

Very well, Ophelia's career to this point has been completely predictable within one of our own Historical Romances; a cliché, even: but for someone of her tendencies, in her own time, it has hit a height that is actually about as likely as winning a National Lottery. That is, yes, it happens to someone every week, but at the same time, it happens to almost no-one.

Anyway, the Shepherds hit the rocks. They had snatched but sixteen years of marital bliss before M. Shepherd was betrayed by the carelessness of a sub-ordinate. A pigeon, young and inattentive, bearing north-northwest at Dover instead of west-northwest, flew a stubborn 381 further miles before coming to rest in the streets of Edinburgh, where its coded message was deciphered by a Scottish schoolboy of Radical leanings. By return of mail, our hero was seized and cast into prison.

Not just any prison, either. Sir Walter's future steward found himself in the worst of prisons; the Revolution's own Bastille; the mephitic cells that lay beneath the *île de la cité;*— the *Conciergerie!*

Mr Shepherd had, of course, provided for this eventuality.

His family, in such case, was to flee to England. Established there in a dis-creet location with good amenities, confederates and a solid bank draft would provide for them until such time as Mr Shepherd had explained, to a sufficient number of well-placed people, the embarrassing consequences of a trial: all manner of things, he would remind these people, would be sure to come out. The trial would consequently be aborted, and Mr Shepherd would be released. Any funds or properties seized in the confusion of arrest would next be restored; perhaps, too, a little extra would be restored, in recognition of the inconvenience; that would be nice. His family would sail back across the Channel into his welcoming arms, and everything would go on pleasantly as before.

Obedient to this plan, then, a well-briefed Madame Shepherd summoned her children, packed them a pre-Regency overnight bag apiece, and fled.

They fled via Le Havre to Plymouth; it should have been Portsmouth, but she got her Ps mixed up– it seemed like a disaster at the time, but it didn't make any difference in the end, because at her heels, Napoleon seized power — the *Directoire* was dissolved– French loyalties within and without government reconfigured themselves strangely, the allies and the funds arranged by Mr Shepherd for his family's care all vanished, as into air — ...and, last and worst, the flow of reassuring letters from Mr Shepherd abruptly ceased.

*

The depths of the winter.

The diminished family cower in lodgings in Plymouth. They are living, in the penny-pinching, pound-foolish way of the newly-poor, on Mrs Shepherd's jewellery. Of this, however, there is only what she snatched up in the hour of their flight, and the local pawnbrokers have in any case (they confide to her) little call for diamond pendants, however fetchingly set in gold amongst cabouchons and rubies; they take them from her almost as a charity.

Poor Ophelia does not fight. Not this time. Not any more. She knows that in some dripping cell, her beloved husband has already coughed out his last: his constitution had always demanded all her care. She sleeps, rather than eats—

it saves on food, she explains to her daughter, who is pressing her to take something porridgy the girl has contrived for their supper; she spends her waking hours, too, on the bed, staring up at a small square of cloud framed by an ice-rimed window.

The late nineteenth century would have detected feebleness of will, and killed her briskly with cold baths. The twenty-first century would have diagnosed pancreatic cancer, and whipped out the peccant organ in no time. Left to her own devices, she faded, instead, from the only diagnosis available to her at the time: a broken heart. When the cloud beyond her window at last frayed to wisps of windblown white, Olivia Shepherd, made weightless by inanition, was wafted up on the same March wind, and drifted away.

Yes, convention got her at last.

And thus, at last, was Olivia punished— punished indeed— for her decades of wilful anachronism. What had it led to? her parents asked, shaking their white heads over the pitiful letter in which Penelope announced her mother's death— what but exile, poverty, and death? One husband– ay, and a son!– abandoned in Italy; another disgraced and jailed, and probably dead as well— and three little children wandering, lost, upon the shores of perfidious Albion.

But any satisfaction Ophelia's parents might have felt was brief indeed. They never even got to post the Collins'-worthy letter they composed in response to our poor Penelope's; for war soon visited their small town, too– in passing, on its way to greater things at Marengo– and with it, Bouscogne *père et mère* ceased to be even a theoretical possibility of support for their grandchildren.

In an English naval port, then, the fifteen-year-old Nellie consigns her mother to a pauper's grave, and gathers her small brothers to her skirts. It is up to her now, and her alone, to divine in which direction their future lies. Then she must lead them, these two little brothers of hers, across the treacherous wastelands of Georgian poverty, towards that future. She begins!

That is, she clutches her brothers tight, and gazes, timidly, about her...

Take a good look at her there, with her pretty French child-clothes and her flawless indoor skin; her delicate features, and mild, dark eyes. Here, at the brink of her life, you might easily describe her as 'an extremely pretty girl', say; or judge that she 'united a strong mind with sweetness of manner, a sensibility naturally deep, and spirits not naturally high'. Add to this fluent Italian, elegant French, and a singing voice of purity and promise, and anyone might take her for a budding heroine.

Today, on all this promise, Fate begins the practice of her strange, inverted alchemy. Soon she will trade those pretty clothes (at a loss, of course) for something more practical. Then she will learn to say "Lawks!", and to eat peas with her knife; and eventually she will come to do things, in the pursuit of money, that a Baronet's daughter would never dream of needing to do.

Just now, though, you can see: she could have been a lovely girl.

*

Ah well. Traditional novel construction is all very well, but "what use", as a later heroine will enquire, "is a book without pictures or conversation?" There is a lot more backstory to cover— we have to get Mr Shepherd out of the *Conciergerie,* for example; we have to explain the disappearance of little John and Charles, and the appearance, in their stead, of these two new, completely different children— but while we have been occupied with the last of the sad family backstory above, Mr Shepherd's grown-up daughter and those two new children have clattered and jolted into and down the main street of Dashe, and the horses are already pulling into the White Hart.

Nellie is almost stunned with exhaustion. Her right thigh is black with bruise upon bruise, her spirits wearied, near to death, from two days' ceaseless placation of Umbrella Lady:– but, she has done it! Here they are! Here is *all* their luggage. *There* is Umbrella Lady, lamenting her loss of the obliging Mrs Clay as she is borne away thank God by the departing coach—and here are both the children, beaming and voluble, having remained perfectly dry all this time under the Umbrella.

In our search for intellectual and emotional refreshment, we will skip over the scenes where the waiting Mr Shepherd's eyes, for the first time in fifteen years, meet those of his daughter; skip the bit where he wonders, in shock, if it is really her; skip the tears, the embracings, Nellie's private horror at seeing her father so old and so frail, his, at finding her so feverish of eye, so odd in her grammatical choices, and so easily startled by slammed doors; we will skip the next three months altogether. During those months, Nellie has run up a couple of plain, pretty dresses from the lengths of lovely muslin that her father had waiting for her when he ushered the three strays into the dark (but cosy) cottage in which they all must now crowd...

...Please note his action, dear reader. I expect that you're reading this at great speed— at 21st century speed— so it's possibly you have neglected to think, at this point, "Gosh! How sweet!" (If you're a man you don't have to think "how sweet"; just, think something along those lines.) "How many fathers, in 1814– or even now– would foresee and accommodate feminine needs so sympathetically?"

I'm outlining your response for you early on here, word for word, just to give you the idea. In future, small stuff like this, we won't bother; but I assure you here that (out of respect for your crowded life, and your consequent and perfectly natural stretches of inattention) I will continue to flag the really important things quite clearly. Universal Omniscient Narrators have been unfashionable for over a century: that same century has seen literature of ever-diminishing thematic and moral clarity. *Mrs Clay* will not, I flatter myself, be that kind of book.

...so yes but we skip the actual making of the dresses, as I say — skip the welcome increases of flesh and complexion, and the letting out of those dresses; skip the abatement of neurotic symptoms in Nellie, the gaining of spirits by all three of our wanderers. We skip the warming winds of spring and the children's ecstasy in their first country summer, rambling the blooming, blowsy fields and woods of Somerset; skip the bits where they get into trouble for tearing their clothes in the process, and then, for preserving those clothes by the expedient of taking most of them off as soon as they are out of sight of the last farmhouse; we skip, as well, the dawning of Nellie's understanding that her father, in spite of a definite and growing affection for her — in spite, too, of his pronounced degree of old-fashioned eighteenth-century broad-mindedness— sometimes finds her, his 'restored English daughter', brow-cockingly *déclassé*. (Through those Plymouth years, and as they grew darker and darker, Mrs Clay had been in the habit of rehearsing, just privately, within herself, her history as a French *grande*-ish *bourgeoise* with connections among aristocracy; that last must have come as a nasty shock.) We will skip, too, the initial exchanges between father and daughter about the set-up *chez Elliot*, entertaining though these must have been —

— and light down, instead, three months later, at Kellynch Hall itself; there to re-encounter our Nellie in the combined heat of a July day and an absolute profligacy of soft furnishings.

*

She now looks, you will be glad to see, a great deal better.

She looks really quite nice.

She has, about her, the limerence that you sometimes see in young people who have escaped a dangerous illness; seeming actually to glow as life floods back out beneath translucent skin. She is nicely dressed too, in the most becoming of her new gowns (her father had, for the benefit of all the neighbourhood, back-dated Mr Clay's death to a comfortable distance), and she is doing her vigilant best — while also doing her best to take everything in, and to appear at ease (but not *too much* at ease — she detects already that a *soupçon* of awe is most acceptable to her hosts, here at Kellynch Hall) — to speak nicely too; insofar as she knows, as yet, what that comprises, just here.

For she engaged in conversation with two undeniable ladies. Real ladies: English ladies.

Nellie's first English ladies.

And Nellie is...

Well.

You will see what Nellie is up to, as soon as she opens her mouth. After all that stuff about Franco-Italian borders, and Counts and heirs and dowries, I'm afraid it's going to be quite a come-down.

Nevertheless, the ensuing chapter will have *lots* of conversation— while for those whose need is pressing, a picture is inserted to provide immediate relief.

The Loss of the Halsewell East Indiaman

Chapter 3

"Oh Miss Elliot! How *too* dreadful for you! To lose a mother– and such a mother, such a pagoda of *all* the virtues, I hear it on all sides; and when you were only but..."

"... sixteen!"— with a sigh.

"And poor Miss Anne even younger... just merely..."

"...fourteen." This sigh was a little more perfunctory.

"And Mary; the baby of the family!— Only ten?"

"Nine."

"Oh yes." Mrs Clay narrowed her eyes at the relevant page of the *Baronet-age* and its wreath of inky annotations. "Yes; just *nearly* ten– Oh the poor little infant what a *shame!*"

There was a pause.

"Nothing can replace a mother's love", Mrs Clay apprised them. "The passage of years... La!– but to a grieving child's heart, what is thirteen years? Little more than thirteen days!"

The pause grew longer.

The thing is, (and as you almost certainly know, dear reader, but Mrs Clay is only just learning it), Elizabeth has, with the passage of those years, developed a short fuse for dates. Dates, and ages and birthdays, and sisters and– well, a short fuse for a lot of things; and it was now just about time for Penelope Clay to shut up.

I mean it was all right there in the *Baronetage*. In print; for all the world to see. Who might fancy to look.

Like this Mrs Clay.

Whom Elizabeth had been *beginning* to think was maybe just a fraction less tedious than most women. *Beginning* to think, might be someone one might possibly be able to have around, for a morning at least, without having them go on and on about boring things, other people, and so on. Mrs Clay had struck her, up until now, as someone with a sense of proportion: an idea of what matters, and who doesn't.

(Though it was only papa's steward's daughter. And it was early days yet: Elizabeth would be cautious; would reserve judgement...)

The effect, though, right up to this point, had been undeniably agreeable. Mrs Clay was impressed, yes; clearly very impressed: she made no attempt to hide it. And yet— not to the point of running out of conversation. Not to the point of retreating in confusion, and vowing never to call again, as so many women did.

Yet now suddenly this same Mrs Clay (and in spite of that dress let's be candid, she was fresh out of some dreadful provincial naval port)— this Mrs

Clay, granted what was probably her first sight of the *Baronetage*— just lying there, casually, on a little inlaid table, open (as it would, always, fall open) at the relevant pages of family history— and suddenly she is full of pert questions and arithmetic!

Anne seemed to feel it too. Anne rarely spoke, in or out of any company that her sister might have: now, though, her sweet, reasonable voice was heard from the far end of the drawing-room;–

"You can do the sums for yourself."

That was Anne, being sweet and reasonable.

And yes; there was Anne's familiar sour half-smile, and the half-drooped eyelid which veiled, to a limited degree, the familiar look of complete contempt...

Directed, though, not at its familiar targets— sister, father— but at Penelope Clay!

Elizabeth's feelings, recoiling from Anne, were experienced as a contradictory surge of allegiance for poor little Mrs Clay. (And through her mind, the phrase *human shield* being then unknown, floated the words 'a trouble shared is a trouble halved'.)

But Nellie had heard a great deal about the Elliots, and the observations of the last half hour had only reinforced all that she had heard. So she calculated, just here, that she could afford to look back at Miss Anne quite coolly. Pleasantly: but coolly.

"Yes, of course. What a thinking head you have to be sure, Miss Anne. I can do the sums for myself."

And in truth, Nellie had made the relevant calculations many months ago. On her first visit to Kellynch's tiny church, she had whiled away the sermon in scrutinising first the backs of three Elliot heads, and then, the curlicued dates and inscriptions on the Elliot tombs and memorials which loomed over the pews and crowded upon the aisles, themselves declaring most intelligibly that ostentation was among the first of Elliot traditions.

So yes, she had done her sums. The trouble was they didn't always add up.¶

"And then–" Mrs Clay returned to the elder sister, and her countenance warmed again, "then, you *came out!*– as they say in England. You know I have heard such a vast deal of your successes– past *and* present *may* I say..." Elizabeth smirked: yes, she may; "quite *bowling* the gentlemen over, I hear!– from your first appearance in society!... mmmm?"

Elizabeth turned her head disclaimingly, in the way that displayed the fine length of her white neck. "Oh Lord, don't tell me you've heard that old tale of Mr Atkinson!"

Climbing onto a chair, in his efforts to glimpse Miss Elliot as she passed by (those first years, she had gone about forever hemmed in by a throng of

¶ See Endnote 1.

admirers), and losing his footing– from pure admiration– and falling off: he had had twelve thousand a year. How these stories do follow one about.

"And you only sixteen!..."

And your mother dead only— Nellie Clay did more sums — four months, was it, by then? Party on. "Why, it's a wonder you kept your head! Kept your head and kept you heart! How many motherless girls of sixteen could do that!"

Kept your hand, as well, thought Anne: Elizabeth heard her think it. Kept it, oh so successfully, for the next thirteen years, and counting.

"But not for want of gentlemen asking for it! Or, at least, that is what one cannot but hear!– spoken of, as it is, all about the county!"

Ha! Take that, Anne! Right in the gonads!

And Mrs Clay was smiling at Miss Elliot in a way that managed to be at once roguish and respectful— ah, Elizabeth had not been mistaken. Mrs Clay was a woman of real ability.

"Oh!– as to that, certainly; not for want of a tiresome amount of asking... and by the way, Anne, you *are* lucky to have no idea how tedious the season can be, in that regard— But then", turning to fall in beside Mrs Clay as the latter moved smoothly away from the table and the book, "it is scarcely enough for a man to find *me* agreeable. I must find him agreeable myself, must I not?"

The widow smiled admiringly; deprecatingly: few could afford to emulate such spirit and independence as was Miss Elliot's.

Elizabeth's air of authority expanded: "And I truly *cannot* imagine a situation more replete with comfort, and fulfilment, than that in which I find myself! I could not be more mistress of any house than I am here, of Kellynch Hall; nor more the first in any husband's eyes than I am in those of dear papa! I am afraid Sir Walter does rather spoil me for other men."

"Oh, Miss Elliot!— To leave this noble house, with all its precious memorabilia of your childhood— Perish the thought! To leave these charming grounds– and your own sweet gallery, with all those family portraits, row upon row, why I was quite dizzy with looking! And prodigious handsome the faces are, the family features certainly do run so very true! I can quite see an Elliot *look*; when they ask me, I will be able to say, now, that I can spot the Elliot *look* in just a flash, it is *that* distinct!..." And, thus talking, the two of them wandered out through the French windows that punctuated, spasmodically, the facade of this wing: they were practically arm-in-arm.

Anne could see how it would be. If today's accidental meeting recurred, Elizabeth would consider that she had acquired a friend.

And Mrs Clay would certainly recur.

*

"Is there a woman on earth can marry a–"

— drat, what was proper English for 'girt wallage'?— "who ain't even entirely clear when–" Nellie stalled again; snorted; straightened her dress with a jerk. "(Isn't even.)– which year his first wife *died? –*in?"

Yes of course, thought her father. Millions. Why was she asking?

Nellie herself had seemed amenable enough to the idea this very morning, when for the first time she had accompanied Mr Shepherd on his near-daily drive to Kellynch.

Well... *'amenable'*... mm. Sometimes, when he spoke of the Elliots, Mr Shepherd thought he detected, perhaps, in Nellie, a silent scepticism; a reservation of judgement, that not all his arguments and assurances had yet been quite able to do away with.

Nevertheless, she had fallen in with her father's wishes without demur— as, indeed, she submitted to all his direction. He had found that he could rely on his widowed daughter for that. So: compliant, at any rate.

Very much resolved, too, to comply.

Resolute in compliance.

They had driven across to Kellynch Hall together, therefore, in accordance with his plan; and as per plan, he had released her into the far fringes of its shrubbery. For a solitary ramble. Amidst its renowned glories.

— and Mr Shepherd, glancing back moments later as the gig rolled swiftly away, had felt his heart sink. She still looked so thin. So vulnerable, clutching her skirts uncertainly, as she prepared to brave the first of many ditches. The girl was armed with nothing but his prayers, this new dress, and his stratagem— as clear as stratagem can be, under the fickleness of circumstance– for being surprised by Miss Elliot in the Pine Walk, and there falling into a sustained conversation with her father's employer's eldest daughter on a series of five easily-linking topics which he knew to be near to Miss Elliot's heart, and with every appearance of naturalness — even, a certain modest shrinking.

He had drilled his daughter in those five topics for all of three previous evenings. They had role-played the scene, over and over, himself in the part of Miss Elliot evincing a rainbow of rich-girl moods: consciously kind; consciously cold; bored; coy and elusive... From here on, though, it was all up to Nell.

The joy and the pride that he had felt, therefore, on entering the Hall drawing-room after business to find his daughter in easy possession of the second-best wing chair, and all of Miss Elliot's attention– Well! His face had grown quite hot with emotion.

Was this his little Nell? Was this clever woman — graceful in her simple, elegant gown; subtle, unfaltering; shaping her presentation, moment by moment, the better to support Miss Elliot's chosen *rôle* — was this really the subdued and tentative daughter he had dropped off behind the privet this morning? By the end of half an hour (half an hour!) *la Elliot* had been rolling about on her back, purring like a kettle, and Mrs Clay had departed with an open invitation to spend the morning at Kellynch Hall any time— why, tomorrow– oh Miss Elliot how *kind!*– tomorrow morning, then!– for a walk about the park, and to see the succession-houses; and then tomorrow too perhaps papa, perhaps Sir Walter, would be free of business demands; be able to join them; show Mrs Clay the newest improvements, explain them to her— Heavens Miss Elliot, what a treat that would be!

Yet now, when any other woman might fairly be in a fever of self-congratulation, here instead was–

"I can't believe he loved her at all!" She sounded aggrieved.

On behalf of her co-wife, already?–

But Mr Shepherd reserved his reply a careful minute. They were heading home, threading once more through the grounds of Kellynch Hall; and though he had, as always, departed from its front door and spanked off down its carriage drive, once out of sight he negotiated a tricky turn– he was doing so right now– onto a little-known track, that linked with the service lane, which in turn got you to your destination in a fraction of the time. "...Possibly not, my dear... But he surely loved her forty thousand pounds. And I understand that she herself quite enjoyed being Lady Elliot. I'm sure you would, too."

Nellie was silent.

They all would. Enjoy her being Lady Elliot.

Mr Shepherd, having completed his manoeuvre as neatly as ever, studied her profile briefly; sighed, and tried another tack.

"The story is, that he did respect her. Admired her, tremendously. Right to the end. Everyone agrees on that."

More silence.

"They talk very compassionately, too, of how *she* doted on *him* at first. Quite besotted, they say!"

He sucked his teeth; could not forbear adding, "And much good it did her."

Love was very well, of course; Mr Shepherd was not against love— could not in all conscience be against it, considering his own past. A pyrexia of love may consume the best-regulated mind. And call him a Romantic who will, laugh if you must, but John Shepherd held that when the delirium is persistent then marriage is the condign remedy; probably the only complete one.

To *object* to a marriage, though, on the grounds that on one or both sides there was no particular tenderness– that would be Romanticism run mad! No.

No. His old Nellie— his new Nellie— might have some odd, unpredictable corners (she certainly did), but she could not be, *was* not, an impractical air-head. So what, then, was this about?

Could it be about brains? Already?

When it came to Sir Walter's brains, there was every rational cause for alarm.

Mr Shepherd's business here, though, was to say as much as he honestly could for the man. "It ain't necessarily *he* who got it wrong", he essayed. "It's the Baronetage entry that's wrong. He got it right on her tomb."

"Surely, though, it's him that tells the Baronetage people?"

Mr Shepherd shrugged.

"And in the book, he inked it in himself— the day she died. And the month, too", Nellie persisted. "Why not set the year to rights? — while he had the pen in his hands? My own fingers were just itching to do it!"

"Neither have either of his daughters corrected it, remember. *Why*", with a sigh (and by the way, dear reader, it's a good question) "*why* does everyone always blame poor old Sir Walter for everything? Mm? Why hasn't that pinch-faced little sub-daughter of his run a line through it?– she, with her passion for correctitude."

Nellie screwed up her nose; concession. Wriggled on the wooden seat of the one-horse gig. And then, twisted her head fretfully. Her neck, as usual, was giving her trouble.

"And in any case", pursued her father, "can you be sure he *hasn't* noticed? Mmm? Often enough, vacant minds make for busy eyes. (That's a classic point to overlook, my dear, and a very *dangerous* one to overlook; I hope you don't usually dismiss the threat of the vacuous–)... no: my money says our man spotted the Baronetage gaffe straight away but– his sense of reverence for the tome, you know. It is too great to admit of him openly contradicting it."

Still Nellie said nothing.

Then at last, a little hesitantly—

"Maybe it's just their way. Not to make a to-do about it."

To just let people put their foot in it, and look at them, and smile and say nothing.

Maybe, even when it's just a book, the better class of English gentlefolk don't correct it openly.

"Well, you should know! Fourteen years among the English!" Mr Shepherd was English both by birth and breeding, but he only sometimes chose to trade on it. Other times, as now, he found it more convenient to stress that he had spent the majority of his adult life abroad: Rome; Prague; St Petersburg. *L'île de la cité.*

Penelope sniffed. But only inwardly.

Inwardly, too, she *nearly* reflected that, in her childhood, papa always *would* be saying that me and the— boys and I were too French.

She said nothing, however.

Mr Shepherd rolled his eyes. Nellie wasn't watching, so he made a good French job of it.

But; what the hell. A certain amount of squeamishness was understandable. Everybody knew that Sir Walter, like so many low-hanging plums, was more than half prune. Notoriously unequal even to the arithmetic necessary to keep his expenses within his income, in ten years of boyhood tuition he had acquired nothing but the air of a gentleman and an encyclopaedic knowledge of dress, and he now read nothing but the Baronetage, and the newspapers, which he took for the social columns.

Granted, stupidity need be no vice in a husband, as when softened with ductility, for example, and tempered with silence. Sir Walter, however, was renowned for going, in the face of any uncertainty, on and on, and on, while everyone else nodded and went 'mm' or (if possessed of a comparable natural authority) fell into a light doze. There were people who said it was a nervous tic, but Sir Walter didn't seem nervous. His fondness for his own voice was rivalled only by his fondness for his own face, which brings us in turn to points like, 'vain as a tart with three tits' and, 'even though he was older than Mr Shepherd himself'– who here had his turn to find the gig's wooden seat uncomfortable– where was his handkerchief?– this damned night air was starting to pick at his lungs... And as for those two unmarried daughters!– oh, for the nunneries of France!

So no, Sir Walter was by no means a totally desirable prospect. He was more what later generations would call a fixer-upper.

And what of it? The Shepherds were in no position to be finicky. Considering what Nellie had endured (and he still didn't like to enquire, too deeply, as to how she had survived those first years;` a girl of fifteen, quite alone, in — well— some dreadful provincial naval port. She *seemed* alright. But then they usually did, from the outside)... considering what she'd been through, what they'd all been through in the last fourteen, fifteen years, Sir Walter was a godsend to the house of Shepherd.

And she to him, the piggy-eyed dolt. Nellie would sort him out.

Nellie would sort them all out.

After the marriage she'd been through: merciful Heavens. What his poor girl didn't know about numpty-wrangling could not be worth knowing.

His poor girl was speaking at last, though apparently only to herself. "...Any rate, a deal of what I feared to be difficult, *won't* be difficult.... It's other things... Mm...

"So tomorrow, lest Sir Walter should be by, I'll put some trimmings... on the grey dress?"

She reflected for some time.

Mr Shepherd knew when to be silent.

"Yellow."

She turned to her father. "What hour does Mrs Cummings open the haber-dashery?"

Good girl. Back on track.

Chapter 4

Oh dear. Mrs Clay is being terribly artful, isn't she? No wonder hardly any-body likes her.

Except that father of hers — which hardly seems a recommendation so far, does it? — and those old friends in Plymouth.

And the children: they love her of course, as children do. Though they are inclined to think of her, still, as a bit of a basket case; poor Aunt Clay, always having to be sheltered, always unsuccessfully, from news of Uncle Clay's latest thingummy in town.

So just them, really, and the acquaintance they've made in the town of Dashe, who agree that Mrs Clay is very pleasant, very pleasant indeed. In a gushing, twitchy sort of way. Still far too thin.

But no-one else. No-one of judgement. I mean that really was a quite hor-ribly disingenuous performance we just saw.

Nellie — Mrs Clay — would shamefacedly agree.

Or perhaps, alternatively, she'd agree with every appearance of bold insouciance. It would depend on which attitude she felt would be most agree-able to you at that moment. She has, for many years now, felt a pressing need to be found agreeable, by all her company, all the time: frowns, coldness, even an unreadable expression, especially in a man, especially in a thick-set, muscu-lar man, makes her stomach flutter. So if she thought it would make you laugh, and think her great fun, she would have told you herself that with George dead, her object now was to *marry!*

Only this time, merciful Heavens, properly.

Something to live on.

Sir Walter, and Kellynch Hall and such, was all very fine — (Lordy me! the drawing-room! And, those beautiful windows! As a girl, Nellie would have claimed them instantly for her own future home...) — and Miss Elliot did seem shockingly credulous. But, however, Nellie did still hope that papa was not too set upon it; would eventually let it drop.

For you must cut your coat to suit your cloth. Alice had often told the fif-teen-year-old Nellie Shepherd that, as she guided her around the traps of Ply-mouth. It was obviously true, even then. Later, as Mrs Clay, she'd found she'd had to cut her cloth even more economically.

The consequence was that, these days, Nellie's worn and anxious heart pounded hardest, *not* on her entrance into Kellynch Hall (though it did pound horribly for that as well, of course), but in the presence of an unmarried two hundred and fifty a year. The wages of a post-captain: imagine how comfortable!

A reliable two hundred a year, though, might have her for the asking. One-fifty was an animating prospect if it was a sure thing, straight into the house-keeping. "That, and a few smiles to the children, and he is a lost man. Should not this be enough, for a navy widow?"

That is to say:— After ten years in the stratum where her husband had placed her, what claim did she have to be nice in her choice?

None.

Nellie was no fool. Right now, to her mind— and in spite of any conclusions that Anne Elliot might have jumped to— the Kellynch lot were really only good for one thing: through them, she might hope herself to gain a bit of reflected glamour in the eyes of the locals. And that, in turn, might be something to set, in their minds, against the burden of the two young'uns.

Her father was alone, then, in hoping for something better, something congruous with the blooming, silent daughter, of gentleness, modesty, taste and feeling, that he had last seen; a girl whose elegance of mind and sweetness of character must have placed her high with any people of real understanding.

The horrible gaunt mask that had superimposed itself on that memory— glaring, with pinched mouth, from the coach window in April— had nearly dealt a death-blow to those hopes: but no, look; Nellie was shaping up again beautifully.

She was different, of course... older... but though Mr Shepherd would certainly have asked a great deal more for his daughter at, say, nineteen, nevertheless at twenty-nine he would be delighted to see her so respectably extracted from the snail-shell house and social circle into which he nowadays found himself curled, and removed to the comforts and (once they had fixed up those ghastly windows) the elegancies of Kellynch Hall. A Lady Elliot might not be wealthy; not as the Shepherds had been accustomed to measure actual wealth, in the old days; but, she would be very comfortable.

They would all, once more, be comfortable.

Hesitantly, and only once, did Nellie allow herself to demur.

"Don't you think, papa... I often think this... well I *imagine*— it's a funny thing— but when a man has debts like Sir Walter's, that man is poorer even, properly speaking, than any beggar?"

"Oh Nellie! Where did you learn to think like a— like a religious tract?"

He had nearly said, 'like a shopkeeper'.

Nellie, among the funny little Plymouth dreams she had nursed (just day-dreams, of course), had confessed to her father the one where she ran her own little shop. Quite by herself: not married to anybody. The dream had required a prologue, of course, where someone leaves her a bit of capital... but then, she sets up!— in haberdashery, would be nice... (How much did Mrs Cummings make?)

(What a thing it would be, if one could clear one hundred a year!)

Chapter 5

Yes: wealth is a relative concept.

The wealth of Sir Walter, while not inconsiderable in the eyes of the world — Sir Walter himself, naturally, never considered it; that was the concern of his man of business, of Shepherd; why does one have a man of business, if not to take care of that sort of thing?— the estate of Kellynch, while by no means inconsiderable, was certainly– not— not *sprawling*, or anything like that.

For theirs was an old family. It was an old estate. Kellynch had been the seat of the Elliots for countless generations; five, no less (Sir Walter felt it right, in these calculations, to include the young generation at hand); and the wealth that issued, of itself, like spring leaves from that ancient wood, was of a finer sort than many times that amount in guineas from other sources.

It was a matter of breeding. Anyone could flash about in second and third carriages— it seemed, to Sir Walter, that anybody did, these days; anybody could ride about on a string of hunters. Anybody could do up their drawing-room in ugly little striped spindly-legged furniture that a man with anything of a manly figure could barely sit upon, or throw up ridiculous pre-ruined follies, Italian marble, bang in the middle of the drawing-room view, where everybody would be practically forced to comment on it; virtually compelled to come up with some kind of remark. It was Sir Walter's opinion — just his opinion, mind you— that that was not breeding. A man can tell the difference at a glance.

In short, Sir Walter had far less income than most of those he took to be his peers. Since the death, thirteen years ago, of his very sensible wife, he had also been exceeding that income each and every quarter with the accelerating riotousness of a dog at last off the leash and splashed out especially in the way of renovations and supernumerary carriages — had been checked, on those fronts, only by the irretrievable breakdown of relations with his architects some way into the deconstruction of the Kellynch facade, followed, shortly thereafter, by an unfortunate accident involving the barouche-landau.

Spending on other fronts, however, continued undiminished. The situation had recently become so severe that, this quarter, Mr Shepherd had actually found himself forced to cut into some of his own traditional perquisites, just to shore up the shakiest of Sir's local debt-holders! This, too, at a time when Mr Shepherd's own finances were under fresh strain– It was all becoming thoroughly inconvenient.

In fact it was insupportable and it couldn't be allowed to continue.

"It's not a matter of *incomings*", Mr Shepherd was explaining next morning, over breakfast in their pretty little east-facing parlour; a parlour much the prettier, he felt, now that Nellie and the youngsters were crowded in it with him. (The children, though they had a room called a nursery, did not eat in it, neither was there nurse, nor tutor nor governess; an economy, in the children's eyes, as rational as it was pleasant.) "The Kellynch estate was alway good; and these days, now that so many of my little rearrangements have come into effect, it is better and better...

"...better and better..." murmured Mr Shepherd to himself again, with absent-minded complacency, as he speared another mutton chop. Managing country estates had come to him late in life, and he was pleased (though not terribly surprised) to find himself brilliant at it.

"No, my dears", he resumed, the chop arranged to his satisfaction (and very much to his daughter's; at least he always ate well) across his plate between two eggs and a rasher of bacon (so why did he not gain flesh?); "no; there's *plenty* of money coming in, and there will be for— well, for the future, you know. The foreseeable future. As long as Sir doesn't take it into his head to interfere: steady as she goes, and so on.

"No, it's a matter", and he fixed his eyes here on young Ariosto, as man to man, "of *outgoings*. The man has no discretion in his outgoings." His eyes veered of themselves to Josephine; on the matter of outgoings, he obscurely felt, she was likely to be almost instinctively capable. "He simply spends too much, on too many things, all the time.

"And *this* you must never do–" he waved his knife at the two youngsters to underline the point, and a shred of fried egg landed on the tablecloth between them, rather spoiling the effect. "This, young Ariosto, young Josephine, is what you must never do! Regulate your outgoings to be, at all times, no more than ninety percent of your incomings. At most. The more your incomings, the higher the percentage you should save. And you can do that even though you may also *spend* more. Now: why's that, eh?"

While the children had no regular instructor, Mr Shepherd was determined to see them well versed in the basics, and already he was proving successful here too. By means of constant practical application of theory to the materials at hand their grasp of domestic economy, Latin, Greek, and mathematics was coming along by leaps and bounds, and the household felt quietly confident that the youngsters' handling of the terrestrial and celestial globes, their knowledge of history, and their expertise at code-making and -breaking would soon outstrip that of Sir Walter and all his expensively educated daughters.

Once Josephine had explained, with some eagerness, why she would be able to spend far more on dress while saving 30% of the baronet's income than she could while saving only 10% of their own, Mr Shepherd returned to his mutton. "The extravagance is silly enough when he's down here in the country. And here, you see, I can murmur things in his ear about the vulgarity of display. Murmur like a hive of bl— , of blessed… of *bees*."

"*Blasted* bees" hissed Josephine, extremely quietly, into Ariosto's delighted ear.

Mr Shepherd, who had narrowly avoided using a much stronger term, chose not to hear. "But Lord!– come spring, off he toddles to London and spends like a sailor and it's quite out of my hands. He can't actually sell the Kellynch property— entailed, you know, on this young Mr Elliot we hear so little of— but he's mortgaged every scrap that he can, to the hilt. So that's bleeding interest, too."

He brooded, and an egg-white seized the opportunity to slither soundlessly from his fork.

"And now it's all *my* fault, of course, that he's feeling the pinch! No more easy marks among the local tradesmen. Actually getting a 'not convenient' when he tries to put yet more absolute necessities on credit. All *my* fault!"

Mr Shepherd glared about him, and made the noise usually written as 'pshaw!' "What am I? A nursery maid? (And it'll be eating upstairs in the nursery for you, young Josephine, if you use your fingers like that again.) I'd ditch him— I *will* ditch him, indeed, if you don't– well.

"What I mean is: given time, I could earn more from Atherton than I do from Kellynch. And Rogers is very keen. So there are– other— options... mm..." The children were listening attentively.

"Y e s *indeed* that's one outgoing you should never skimp on, young Ariosto!– if you are ever a steward. Always pay yourself first. The Lord knows they won't." (This was true on both counts. Mr Shepherd, along with its greatest generator of wealth, was also the estate's first and greatest operating expense.) "Now, Ariosto", and he scooped up the peccant egg-white with the swift-slow efficiency of a heron; "can you list for me the sources of income legitimately open to the steward of an English estate? An English estate mind you; I specify English… And in France…?

"… That's excellent, Ariosto, excellent… What was I saying?"

His daughter, who during the disquisition on stewardship had gone back to navigating a tricky section of a kipper, had to think. "… Kellynch. Kellynch; incomings not equal to outgoings; Sir Walter– er—"

She sent her own quick glance at the children.

"… er, *irréfléchi;* possibly not a good prospect for a simple *veuve de guerre*." (They did claim to have forgotten nearly all of their French.)

"Ah: yes. Although— he's still a good prospect, *if well managed*. This is my point. *Incomings*. As I say. Most of that debt could be cleared in three, four years, *if* anyone could really manage Sir Walter."

"But didn't he sell every stick of the woods, at the height of the demand? Surely they could live for years and years just merely on that alone! The Naval Board was desperate!– the Baltic blockaded and no timber to be had, ships falling apart in the water... it was terrible! Then Sir Walter steps in. We heard about it even in– *Deal*, yes we were in Deal then, for only but half a year– the timber from the Kellynch estate."

"Did you my dear? Yes — they built a lot of new boats with that wood, they tell me."

"*Ships*, grandpapa!" corrected Josephine. "They're called *ships*. *Boats* is for a dinghy or a fishing smack or— or something. They built *three* ship of the line and–"

"–a frigate and then with the scraps a sloop and–" Ariosto's legs, beneath the table, began to swing vigorously as he launched a rapid fire of names, ratings, technical features —

"Spare me your ships of the lines", interrupted their grandfather, "spare me your sloops. All that is relevant here is that he *improved* the Kellynch estate — that's what he called it; *improved* it, bare as a billiard ball; nothing I could do about it; ghastly result. But ready money down, yes, he got plenty. Went through it all in five years, dear God, *improving* the Hall out of all recognition and proportion. And he's barely slowed down since."

Nellie chewed her lip and stared at her mangled kipper, the backbone and ribs of which were distressingly evident. (It had suddenly occurred to her — and her skin was prickling with the thought — that perhaps this was another of those things which her father found rather Plymouthish...? Or... but... I mean what else can you do with a kipper?) Fourteen years in naval ports during the Napoleonic wars, first as Miss Shepherd and then as Mrs George Clay, had taught her a lot about things like the cost of timber, good ship-building timber, at the height of those wars. (What if one ever had to eat a kipper in front of an Elliot?) If Sir Walter could get through all that, so quickly, he was worse than she'd realised. Worse than anyone had realised. Did people like that eat kippers? She noticed papa never did.

Mr Shepherd was watching her, with that equivocating grimace he often wore when the topic turned to the Elliots.

Or was it the kipper-detritus?

Think.

"The more of a fool he makes of himself now, on his own, the more it shows a wife could keep him in line."

"Exactly! Seventeen years! She kept him in the black for all but two of them!"

"*And* it was a smaller income then than it is now", Josephine reminded the room.

Could they possibly let such a— prune— slip through their fingers?

Mr Shepherd shook his head at his last mutton chop; jabbed it with all implements. "Between us, Nellie",

"And us", murmured Ariosto to his sister.

"and although I most certainly do not wish to put undue pressure on you regarding this little project..."

"The vamping of Sir Walter!" cooed Josie softly to her brother.

"— a lady's touch. Firm, yet adroit; exacting, yet not exigent: it's their only hope. Or the day I leave— the day *after* I leave— the whole place will go belly-up."

Chapter 6

Mrs Clay, complete with yellow ruffles at wrist and neck, was exhibited to Sir Walter the very morning that followed. The result was such as to confirm Mr Shepherd's calculations rather than his daughter's doubts. Sir Walter Elliot almost instantly discerned in Mrs Clay an acceptable addition to their circle at Kellynch Hall. In spite of the poor lady's freckles, he found her attentive, really very quick at grasping the importance of whatever one was trying to explain, and only anxious to learn all that he, Sir Walter, could impart. If it pleased Elizabeth to take the young woman up, he should have no objection to seeing her at Kellynch again. (But oh!– that projecting tooth of hers. What sad deformities so many women must endure.)

His clear-sighted detection of Mrs Clay's failings, as well as her strengths, did not endear her new find to Elizabeth any the less. She *was* forced to acknowledge that dear papa did have a point, as regards the freckles; and the tooth, too; added herself that Mrs Clay had not the smooth wrist, both plump and fine, that makes of a woman's arm such a beautiful picture as she plays upon the harp, say, or the pianoforte. (Elizabeth had been forced to exercise upon both under her mother's long dead eye, and she still liked to try a move-ment occasionally, abstractly, in the midst of conversation— if a gentlemen was boring her, you know— to run her fair and slender fingers in a swift movement lightly across the shining edge of a dining table, or playfully pluck harp music from a vase of flowers... You could only afford to do that, though, with a really lovely arm.)

This apart, however, Mrs Clay was certainly very deserving. She had had a sad life, and was so touchingly sensible of all that Kellynch could offer; strove constantly, one could see, to improve her manners and her speech; she really seemed to look immediately to Miss Elliot, as her guide!– she deserved encouragement.

It was soon Kellynch Hall with Nellie almost every day. Mr Shepherd could hardly be more ready to drive her there than Elizabeth was to invite, and all was rapidly in better train than even her father had dared hope. This was all the more satisfactory, as a number of other little projects, which he also had in hand, were themselves reaching a crucial stage.

The intrusion of three dependents into the fading glow of Mr Shepherd's twilight years had been a jolt. He'd had George Clay pegged for one of those whom alcohol actively preserves; one whom it pickles, rather than poisons: he'd foreseen his daughter's husband drawing and drinking and drawing and drinking his pension, indefinitely. Suddenly, the man was dead and here they were. All three of them.

And the elderly *pater familias* must shake off his malaise, his creeping debility— force himself to his feet— look about him, if anything further might be achieved for this hapless little trio, before remorseless Death claimed Mr Shepherd at last.

And of course to the fresh eye of enquiry, opportunities will then present themselves.

And then action must be taken; and taken, necessarily, in its proper season. That is to say– and although Mr Shepherd did not normally like to hurry matters– there is nevertheless such a thing as seizing the moment, and—

... oh dear. I cannot pretend to follow the details of all Mr Shepherd's computations. But what it boiled down to was this: if the Elliots could be got out of Kellynch before the next quarter day, it would be convenient on more than one front.

He decided to pull out the big guns.

*

Here in Somerset the largest calibre, as regards Sir Walter, was Lady Russell.

Ah well. It's not merely the size, Mr Shepherd reminded himself– as he studied her form, upright as a pepper-pot, seated on the sofa beside Anne, opposite Elizabeth; she was hinting, to Elizabeth, of the advisability of more conscientious and regular something or other, and Elizabeth was looking bored... When it comes to bringing home the bacon, far more depends on the skill of the marksman. A frisson surprised him, half-hidden as he was behind the newspaper in the Kellynch drawing room. Goodness me. Let us hope the old lungs are still up to it.

Yes— so— Lady Russell.

Lady Russell had been the lifelong friend of Sir Walter's first wife, the late Lady Elliot, whose virtuoso touch upon her husband's strings had achieved so much for so long; and in contrast to her quietly clever friend, the good Lady

Russell might be described as sound, rather than subtle. It was one of the things that Lady Elliot had liked about her; about Margaret: she always took the view one depended upon her taking, and then, she always put that view of hers just exactly as one had imagined her putting it, as one lay in one's chamber that morning, as it might be, drinking tea and planning out the day's events. Dear Madge. So helpful.

It is hardly surprising, then, that since the death of Lady Elliot, Madge– Lady Russell– had never ventured even a single hint upon– well– *expenditure*– to Sir Walter. Good Heavens no: her own husband had been only a knight.

Nevertheless.

If one *could* contrive to draw the old lady into the discussion, John Shepherd calculated on getting a lot of good sense from her. A lot of accurate arithmetic, presented, in her own rather large round hand, with all workings; backed, too, no doubt, by lists of purchases necessary, and of purchases deferrable, debatable, or unnecessary. Lists which no gentleman could thrust aside with a hasty "Take care of it will you?" that a steward might receive. *Had* received. On occasions become too numerous, lately, to mention. Yes. The witterings of his steward may be unworthy of Sir's notice, but the irreproachably-connected Lady Russell's view on the Elliot debt, finally stated aloud, might well be the salutary slap across the face that the Baronet so imperiously required.

And it wouldn't kill the old chap: no no— Sir Walter was in good shape. He owed his figure only partly to corsets, largely to exercise and a sparing diet. Sparing, too, with the liquor (so damaging to the complexion): no, Mr Shepherd declared repeatedly to Nellie, there need be no concerns on that score.

It was the delicate work of ten days to cultivate in Lady Russell sufficient conviction that duty called her to declare her fears for Kellynch Hall; duty to the dead, as well as to the living. That she should sacrifice her own— reservations; her own inevitable discomfort, as being perhaps guilty of some— of appearing, superficially at least, *inappropriate...* yet– were they not, at bottom, selfish fears?— self-regarding fears, at any rate. Yes: that much was clear. And one must place duty before self.

It was her duty, then, to beard the monster, Debt. On behalf of all the dear Elliots.

This point gained, it was then but the work of another minute to inspire in Lady Russell a determination to, say, draw up a full budget, perhaps?— But of course, Mr Shepherd, a comprehensive budget was indispensable! Yes, ah, Lady Russell was absolutely in the right, it was the only way; a thorough-going, *long-term* plan: if Mr Shepherd might be allowed to venture an opinion, seven years should do it. He fed her the necessary statistics and sat back.

It took the old dear a while, but eventually she produced a very sensible document.

Though she tried to baulk, she was next nimbly persuaded to present it to Sir Walter and Elizabeth herself; even, to walk them through it, item by item — while Mr Shepherd, seated inconspicuously off to one side, did not anticipate having to stick his grubby little *sans-culotte* oar in more than once. Twice, at the utmost.

*

The event proved Mr Shepherd right.

The shock was severe, certainly, and while its first full force was felt, it did stagger the Elliots to a degree. There were all the exclamations, all the tossings of heads and flingings-aside of papers, that Mr Shepherd had foreseen. In their inevitable turn came the out-thrust under-lips, and the forceful foldings of the arms, followed by rapid evacuations from one chair to another, and blackening frowns and finger-drummings and hunchings-forward, all culminating at last in a burst of angry tears from Miss Elliot, and in Sir Walter, as he was just attaining the upper slopes of a tirade and within sight of the summit– a sudden pallor– forcing him, by the unsteadiness of his head, to break off and lie on the sofa with his feet elevated.

Just for a while, though.

Just for long enough that, when things stopped spinning about them, they did not enquire too deeply into the process by which they found themselves coming to rest with their backs to mathematics and restrictions and the whole horrid *imbroglio* (and Kellynch Hall too– *that* could be rented out– pure profit!) and facing, instead...

"A nice little resort town, perhaps?" enquired Mr Shepherd brightly. "A town with enough of society to be acceptable! Now, does not Lady Russell herself spend part of every winter in..."

"—Bath", supplied that lady.

"...Bath?" Sir Walter echoed vaguely.

"*Bath!* Why— Sir Walter, what a capital idea! The very place! *Bath* fulfils all your demands, does it not?— reaches all your standards; offers, to you and your daughters, everything most imperiously required of your new milieu. Is not Lady Russell's own long patronage of the city the best possible assurance of all this?" It was a point which no-one could dispute. "A spacious set of apartments in Bath; why, Sir Walter–", who was at this point essaying the resumption, tentatively, of the upright seat, "you have hit upon it immediately! You have trumped us all!"

For the truth is, Lady Russell's budget was excellent, of its kind, but Mr Shepherd knew that real economies were quite beyond the Elliots as things stood. For as long as they remained at Kellynch, in these massive, servant-swarmed buildings and grounds, with the necessity of complementing its country lifestyle with some months in its rented London equivalent every spring; well— *tiens!*— nothing would ever really change.

But you could strip it nearly all away, by moving them to Bath.

Mr Shepherd knew that Bath, to Sir Walter, still spelled fashion, society— *ton*— so no problem there. Miss Elliot, though no doubt uneasily aware that Bath was not quite what it had been in her father's youth, was not, he felt sure, going to oppose any scheme which promised her an admiring public twelve months a year, instead of only three. Miss Anne would dislike it, of course, but Miss Anne disliked everything.

Chapter   7

"So perhaps we are to go to Bath, Penelope. To Bath...or, perhaps, to London. Of course we do know London rather better. One has acquaintance there... Papa is starting to think more of London, I believe." This last was not strictly true, yet— Sir Walter was at that moment slouched over his bedroom fire in his dressing gown, his mind an hopeless blank— but it would be true if and when Miss Elliot chose that it should, so her habit of anticipating his wishes was natural enough. Nellie's heart seemed briefly to stop.

"Oh— dear me— Miss Elliot *yes; everybody* goes to London... *Everybody* has acquaintance there. It is quite the thing! The *Miss Coopers* went to London, last year, with their dear old mother, after their father started to do so well with his shops... But— Bath! Why, I couldn't say, I'm sure, Miss Elliot."

("Be enthusiastic!", her father had urged her. He'd rolled his eyes and held up his hands to demonstrate: "'Bath! Lawks! So fashionable it is to be sure!' Lay it on with a trowel, Nellie. We want them happy, and we want them in Bath."

(But Nellie, with a better understanding of her role in Miss Elliot's life, knew that too much familiarity with Bath, by such as Penelope Clay, would not endear the place to Miss Elliot. (She also felt that her father should know that she would not say 'lawks'. That was completely behind her; had been for weeks.) No, her father's aim would be best achieved by evincing a little ignorance of Bath. It was knowledge not pleasant in its tendencies, but Nellie held it— and in what was clearly the interest of all, she put it to good use.)

"*We* know little of Bath; at least, we in Plymouth— is it not rather exclusive, perhaps? That is what the *whispers say!* I hear so much more of London. We all feel that we quite *know* London! All the young ladies of Plymouth are wild to go to London; and a vast many do, these days."

"Very likely, Penelope. All the world may go to London for the season.

Bath is rather quieter, I suppose; one meets largely one's own type there."
(Which, increasingly, was true: impoverished gentility was a booming occupation in Bath.) "But retirement suits me, you know, Penelope. Few people realise just how little I enjoy the endless round of balls and dinners one endures in
London. Crushed!— one is positively crushed at some of those balls! And the
men!— so demanding of one's time! One must dance every dance, and even
then, some one or another will absolutely accuse me of neglecting him."

Oh absolutely, indeed; there was little that Mrs Clay didn't know of
crushes, and importunate men, and the dangers when the two were combined,
as in for example the maelstrom of a Plymouth market day. Nellie fought a
bizarre urge to suggest that Elizabeth solve the problem by choosing a third
option, frantically though of course hopelessly supported by Miss Anne, of
retiring to a small, a *very* small house, in the country about Kellynch, where she
would meet only herself and the odd housemaid, and thus free herself at a
stroke from crushes and demanding men.

These odd little urges swept her— like fits— sometimes, and it vexed her.
She was perfectly accustomed to behaving with vigilant hypocrisy. A wife-time
(as she still liked to put it to herself, at that stage) of hiding practically
everything: the handful of coins that made up the housekeeping kitty; her few
bits of portable property; the odd personal opinion that she might still hold—
towards the end, even a glimpse of happiness, in her, could be perilously pro-
vocative. Yes, Mrs Clay had all the reason in the world to regard herself as a
tolerably adept dissembler... She pulled herself sharply together, tossed out a
reflection on the temptation to incivility that Miss Elliot must represent to
headstrong young men, and returned to the emergency-shoring-up of Bath.

"Oh, but I do seem to remember something... some remark... about its
being always *the season* in Bath. Which seemed so strange to me, Miss Elliot;
for how can it be *always* the season? I know the Miss Coopers were a full five
months in London, and they went to ball after ball!— but they said it smelled
quite horrid towards the end. Summer, you know. *The drains.*"

Nellie paused, ostensibly to rethread her needle with a deep blue. They
were embroidering cushion covers together. Not for Miss Elliot the usual
drudgery of ladies: the hemming of household garments; the calico smocks in
the charitable poorbox.

"And at the last, nobody there at all, they said. Well, working people, of
course; folk like that." She slid the needle with careful precision into the fabric. "The merchants and beggars and so on in the streets became very self-assured, they said."

Again a little silence, while Miss Elliot contemplated this awful picture.

"Because London is *out* of season for most of the year, is it not? (Which
must be rather difficult for the people who just live there all the time, how *do*

they manage, I wonder?) So how can possibly it be *the season* in Bath, *all* the year round?"

Miss Elliot let her embroidery drop. "Why, Penelope, they mean that Bath is never quite abandoned — as London is, through the shooting season, and the hunting and so forth. It is a healthier air, you know; indeed Bath is quite delightful in autumn. One takes the waters at any time of year."

"New faces arriving every week, I suppose? Parties and balls from one year's end to the next, then?" It was not quite compatible with the retirement that Elizabeth had been seeking a few moments ago, but it was nevertheless a happy direction in which to wander. "How delighted your London acquaint-ance will be to find you in *Bath*; for in London, you know, it seems that *every-body must* go there; and yet, then, nobody has any time to visit anybody! For did not you mention that the Honourable Mrs Coussins visited you twice in London last season—? And one cannot but think — in the whole of the sea-son! Certainly I know she is *much in demand (!)* but– such a crushing place Lon-don *must be*, where such old friends, as you and the Honourable Mrs Coussins are, can cross paths so infrequent! Now, Bath sounds rather different: it sounds the kind of place where there is always time for *true friends*."

... And thus, with a little ignorance, and a little knowledge, with a lot of flattery, and the occasional innocent-seeming reminder of the ease with which one may sink from sight in the ocean of humanity that is London — for she found that Elizabeth could be made to glance, just quickly, under lowered eye-lids, at her comparative insignificance there — Mrs Clay steered her patroness away from London, and towards Bath, and solvency.

∗

"That was the trickiest part of the whole business."

A fortnight later and Mr Shepherd, sitting over the evening fire with a newly-signed lease for Kellynch in his lap, was relieved and grateful. "That was a knife-edge. If Miss had completed that sharp-about, and suddenly plumped for London, it would have been the end of the Elliots. I'd have had to find myself *imperiously* demanded at Atherton as soon as possible; hand this lot over to old Hardcastle; look about for someone else for you. I mean it's a good property, but there's still a limit to what the Kellynch set-up is worth. You've saved their bacon, young lady!– As well as giving us another shot at the hog ourselves."

He sighed himself out of his armchair: it had been a ticklish few weeks. By no means without its gratifications– but now he felt rather tired, and, at times, not a little breathless. "And as they'll never say thank you, *I* will" — kissing his daughter firmly on her forehead. "Bless you, my dear. On behalf of all con-cerned. Now I must lock the lease in my desk and then I'm off to bed." He poked the fire — unnecessarily — Mr Shepherd was death to fires — and bent to light his candle directly from it as usual, which process is harder than twenty-first century readers might think, and that is why everyone else in the household was perfectly happy to use the spills sitting right there on the mantle for the purpose. "...mm yes. They may be a tiresome lot, those three, but nobody deserves... what they were heading for.

"As we know pretty well. Don't we, eh, Nellie." He faced her, his candle now lit, though at some cost to his wig. She'd have to tidy those singed hairs off it in the morning.

"Oh papa! We're happy now, aren't we?"

Mr Shepherd pulled a *moue*. "We're— snug."

"And snug is alright, isn't it?"

Another *moue*.

"Well, *I* like it here. It's so lovely, papa. It's exactly like I've imagined Heaven."

"Really? I would have fancied Heaven as roomier."

"Heavenly", Nellie reiterated. "So calm. Each morning the day comes along, and you wake up and you know just what will happen today; and then— it does! And then at night you go to bed, and drift off, knowing that tomorrow will be just the same; so green and peaceful. You take care of us so well, papa. We love it here. The children are growing wonderfully."

Which reminded them both: new sets of clothes, now the cold was drawing close. "Merino. Your mother always insisted on merino, God alone knows why. (What is merino?) Does Mrs Cummings carry merino?"

"Oh but could we not get something secondhand at the market?"

"Oh— yes. Second hand. Yes indeed why not."

Nellie blushed so hard it hurt. "Yes they do grow *so* fast I never found any point in... And so I just *suddenly* though, out of nowhere— 'oh, *that* would make a good saving'."

Yes: well that was true. Saving was important now. And investing, and above all *gaining*, that was the thing....

The law. He could help Ariosto in that profession at least.

And, half running over in his head yet another permutation of those long-determined calculations of the interest on... what capital sum?... needed to support the lad for how long?... and a dowry for Josephine, large enough to attract a man of comfortable circumstances, who could provide a home for Nellie as well; though then, a little extra too, a small investment for her, in case of difficulties... Oh dear.

And perhaps five good years left, to achieve all this.

After that, he could well start to be a burden himself.

Mr Shepherd kissed his daughter again, and turned and felt his way towards the door, waving his candle gently to conjure from the gloom the reflection of the brass doorknob. "...Still. I would be happier, my dear, if I felt that you were all, once more, really *comfortable*."

Mr Shepherd was speaking apparently to the doorknob, as it winked out of the dark at him.

"Because, looking back, it was a lot of fun."

Chapter 8

Yes, for the comfortably-off, eighteenth-century Paris could be a lot of fun. It's easy to overlook that, in the light of subsequent events.

Nellie and her brothers had been raised on the romantic story of how, for true love, their mamma had cast away title and fortune both together. Pre-revolutionary society had cracked its paint-glazed face with gaping, powdered wigs shook upon mercury-raddled necks when the Countess Ariosto, so young and beautiful and (here mamma's eyes drifted sideways) so universally popular, had flung all aside for love in a Parisian maisonette. And with an Englishman!

Nevertheless (went the nursery lore), there, in the little house of their married bliss, mamma had sewn the seams of his plain shirts — pricking her finger many a time in the unaccustomed exercise, and leaving a touching trail of red dots along each hem in consequence; she had tripped off to market with a plain basket of woven rushes over her arm, had told over the copper coins in her pocket, and bargained with the plainspoken stallholders for their freshest and best, for dear papa; with this, had cooked the simple meals of their married life; and in all this simplicity mamma had, at last, found happiness. *Enfin*, my dears!– What need have we to drag about us the purse of heavy gold, when the heart is light with the treasure of love?

So the story went, and very charming it was.

It was true, too, that in the first flush of her new life, Ophelia had indeed tried out sewing, and shopping, and on one never-to-be-forgotten occasion had even attempted to mop the floors, ruining any number of heavy Turkey carpets in the process. Enchanting though they were to the friends whose ears they reached, Madame Shepherd's efforts were nothing but an annoyance to the battalion of highly-trained maids and men engaged to run M. Shepherd's marital home. Do you have any idea how difficult it is to get bloodspots out of a dozen silk shirts?

Her new husband, though, merely sighed, and signed the receipt for a dozen more.

Ophelia, who really had been very worried about the shirt thing, was overwhelmed with relief at this; wept, at her new husband's patience and generosity. The shirt episode, the whole Turkey carpet *débâcle*— these were the kind of peculiarly Ophelia-like disasters that would have triggered days of high-volume Italian at Castle Ariosto, a reaction incomprehensible to Ophelia. Oh, the Count had been so exasperating!– forever crying poor! Especially at any little impulse of her own. Yet look: far greater poverty had not hardened John Shepherd's plain and simple heart. Ophelia had never had it so good in the way of undergarments.

The attentive reader, though, may have spotted a couple of points which always slipped Ophelia by.

Prime amongst them: while, post-dowry, the more conspicuous luxuries of life had been once more on display about the Castle, beneath the surface conditions had remained harsh in any sense of that word. Ophelia's flight into the arms of the common man, on the other hand, happened to have landed her in the midst of some very fine bourgeois *matériel*.

So while Madame Shepherd had certainly been in the right (at the time) in holding up to her daughter her own life history (to date) as a shining example of true happiness consequent upon *"le suivre du coeur"*,[†] nevertheless the reader may join me in thinking that her fresh-minted happiness was as much the dependent fruit of Mr Shepherd's exceptionally comfortable circumstances as it was of his mild and equable character, his unobtrusive skill at intercepting his wife's zanier moonshots, and his humorous and loving acceptance, so rare in a man of that time, of the fact that he couldn't, always, actually, keep her under his thumb. And in regretting— for regret it I think we must— her advice to young Penelope; the advice which always concluded and summed up the tale of 'your father and I':– to "follow zee 'eart, only zee 'eart", in matters matrimonial.

For it was those words, echoing in young Penelope Shepherd's ear, which tipped the balance: that fateful day, years later, on the battlements of Plymouth. That day, when, with the sun shining about them, and a fine southwesterly (25 knots and backing) bringing roses to both their cheeks, Penelope gazed down at the handsome, brilliant Captain George Clay as he knelt (publicly! so romantic!) at her feet, and said—

"Yes!"

*

Because her fellow boarding-house-dweller and dearest friend, Miss Alice Barratt, had very nearly persuaded her to say no.

Or— not 'no', *exactly*; but, at least— 'Not yet'.

Captain Clay was only just made commander, you see. And Miss Barratt insisted and insisted— oh but she was such a cautious old stick!— that if George truly loved her– that is, loved with a manly, and not a boyish love— he would be happy to wait for the other step. That crucial next step in rank. *Post*. Post captain.

---

† *followeengk yr 'eart.*

The pay. The half-pay. The guaranteed steady promotion, in rank *and* pay! The widow's pension.

A commander's salary may be all very well for young love, but you have to think of the children.[†]

Well and of course George's heart was indeed true as a— as a– as— Nellie's devotion at this moment vacillated between "the Bible" and "the Nautical Almanac"— but– and– so there could be no doubts *there*—

Nellie owed her dear Miss Barratt such a lot, you see. Mr Barratt, too... though here, respect almost overwhelmed affection. The brother was nearly a decade Nellie's senior in years, vastly more so in experience, wisdom, judgement; the head of a teeming household, and its ultimate authority; calm, unwearying, unbending. For some four years— ever since those dreadful early days of orphanhood, in fact— this man and his sister had protected and guided young Penelope (as if their own swarm of dependents had not been enough!)... and really, when you think about it, without them— without dear Alice and dear, dear Mr Barratt— what would have become of little Penelope Shepherd?

Instead, at nineteen, Miss Shepherd has a circle of keen and talented students of music hanging on her every word; and a waiting list, positively a waiting list, of more!

She was really quite the thing in Plymouth in 1804, was the so-very-young Mam'zelle Shepherd. So sweetly pretty, so elegantly French– and yet, with that enchanting dust of freckles, and that child-like little tooth, pouting her upper lip, and quite charming away any awe which the accumulated superiorities of her quiet foreign assurance, beautiful voice, impeccable dress sense, graceful carriage, knowledge of languages, meltingly beautiful movement at the dance, and almost overwhelmingly romantic background might otherwise have inspired. Many papas dreamt, at night, of kissing that innocently pouted lip; of comforting and succouring that little romantic castaway. By day, they did all that they could for her, by extending the singing lessons throughout their family.

And make no mistake, their daughters really did learn to sing. Fired by a romantic spirit genuinely her own, Mam'zelle Shepherd strove to make nightingales of all the heterogeneous brood of hatchlings that she could gather under her own barely-fledged wings. Her candour, her fervour, her enthusiasm for her young charges— these were not the least of her charms.

So George Clay, kneeling on the cobbles at her feet that fated morning, felt very much as he did when going into action. That is, so insane with excitement he was near to piss.

Which brings us, at last, to George.

---

† That's a good point, actually. Austen's two naval brothers had some eighteen children between them. (Two wives died in the process.)

Oh dear.

Oh dear oh dear. *Zut. Zut alors.*

Flûte alors.

Bon sang de bonsoir.

Madre de Dios.

We have come to a long chapter in Nellie's life, and a darkening one.

Chapter 9

In 1804, the man known to history as Lieutenant George Clay was just returned from the West Indies at the helm of a prize— his first command. So while technically he was not *exactly* Captain Clay, but just *Commander* Clay, tradition required that everyone *called* him Captain Clay. It was high time they did. He certainly felt every inch Captain Clay.

Captain Clay was now at a loose end in Plymouth — fledgling commanders being harder to accommodate with a ship, naturally, than lieutenants, and English waters in any case being healthier than West Indian ones, and commanders in search of commands thus being, here at home, much thicker on the ground (I use the term 'ground' advisedly) than in the torrid climes from which Captain Clay had so recently sailed.

Temporarily thrown ashore as a result, George Clay had found a home, for the nonce, in the same lodgings as Miss Shepherd.

He and Nellie had skipped the acquaintanceship stage. There really isn't room for one in a crowded boarding house. Instead, from almost the instant of meeting— on the narrow stairs which Nellie had been descending, as George later told her, like an angel stooping to earth, and George contrariwise ascending from the Stygian gloom of the hallway, and they had met halfway up, and had had to squeeze past each other in a manner both embarrassing and thrilling— from that moment, they had fallen rapidly and deeply in love.

George Clay had no fortune. He had been lucky in his profession; but spending freely what had come freely, had realised nothing.

But he was confident that he would soon be rich; full of life and ardour, he knew that he would soon have a ship, and soon be on a station that would lead to everything that he wanted. He had always been lucky: he knew that he would be so still. Had he not as a mere midshipman, in charge of a re-watering party forsooth, captured an enemy fishing smack that transpired to have over a thousand pounds' worth of French gold smuggled in its hold? The very day that he was old enough, he had been made lieutenant; made, without a smidgen of interest to aid him; promoted, purely from recognition of his shining parts— and he had gone on to see more action (as he liked to say) than most other lieutenants had had hot dinners! (a novel expression that soon gained circulation among his many friends). Above all, had he not, as a result of those overwhelmingly successful actions, raked in the prize money?

And spent it like a– like a sailor?

Yes. He had.

And now here he is; twenty-three years old, and already master and commander!

Which is practically a captain.

Quivering, therefore, on the rank of post-captain.

Post!–

– and a place, at last, on the mighty Naval escalator that would lift him ever upward, past the corpses of his superiors (for it was death that powered this machine; the death of those above you on its steps) to an Admiralship! The blue pennant; the white; the red— his genius and ardour seemed to foresee and to command his prosperous path.

Such confidence, powerful in its own warmth, and bewitching in the wit that often expressed it, was in the end enough for Nellie. That morning, on the battlements, she followed 'er 'eart— trusted in Providence and exertion— trusted, more specifically, that two courageous souls, united in love, ability, and vigour, could ultimately command Fate.

And George Clay rose from his knees, with yet another prize to his credit.

"Quite the greatest prize yet, eh George?", his friends had insisted repeatedly (overlooking, in their gallantry, that French fishing boat when he was no more than a mid). The flow of drink made the witticism wittier each time it was repeated throughout the congratulatory dinner, and evening, and night and morning, that followed on the news that Golden George, Lucky George Clay, had won the enchanting Miss Shepherd, the toast of Plymouth town!– won her, heart and hand and all attached parts. Those twenty-four dizzy hours slapped the capstone onto George Clay's self-approbation, and cemented him forever in all his views and ways.

I mean, why wouldn't it?

Look how incredibly well he was doing!

He was soaringly conscious of this, his splendid trajectory, as he wound his arm about his fresh-minted *fiancée's* waist and swung the two of them to dance the length of the sun-swept pavings. Each, in after years, would often recall that day; the day when Captain Clay had danced with his beautiful bride-to-be in a brilliant chase of cloud-shadow and sunlight, high along the windy battlements. Everyone had turned to look. Everyone had smiled at them. Passing ship-mates had cheered, even; and the future was an open book, written in golden ink, by Mars, the God of War; and Captain Clay was His favourite son.

"Let's duck in here and just grab a jug to take home with us, to celebrate!"

So they did.

And while we wait for them, you and I — to complete their purchase, and make it two jugs, no, three, because there will be visitors aplenty, and then arrange for the return of the jugs and so on — let's stroll over here and lean on this sun-warmed battlement... ah...!...and enjoy the view.

Nice, huh?

Mmmm.

Mind your hand there on the balustrade. A lot of bird shit about.

And — in amongst all this beauty, and on this joyful day — you might allow me to draw your attention to one of the numerous sheer hulks, rotting away, down there, in the harbour below us.

No, not the one with the crowd of circling gulls; nor the one next to it, with the remains of blue trim. The smaller one, somewhat behind them — yes; as you say: the one with, where the masts should be, just dark, ragged holes in the deck. That is (is? was?) the *Justinian*.

And, *did* you know, that it was in that very ship! — in her masted days, and under the inaptly named Captain Keene — that George Clay's father once sailed? First stepped aboard as a young Lieutenant; the famous Clay family hair, near-white, shining like flax it was, in a sunlight very like today's. Hopeful, eager, intense; half-embarrassed by his dreams of glory.

With time, he became an anxious Lieutenant. Later, a desperate one. Years later still, a resigned one; humbled, or broken, depending on your take on these things. Decades more of undistinguished service, and at last the longed-for letter came, promoting him to half-pay invalid. After that, he moved into some place in the lanes behind us and lived there for a bit, the prey, we are told, of "dysentery and boredom".[†]

Well, dysentery does not go with drink.

That's not always a bad thing. Although the income of a lieutenant is relatively small — too small, the service always held, to maintain a wife and children (and Lieutenant Clay had both) — nevertheless the man managed to drink himself to death on it with, at last, something approaching proper naval promptitude. The first impulse of George and his brothers, on leaving their father's deathbed, was to nip out for a celebratory drink.

And then Mrs Clay, the old lady: she died, too, not long after that. Nellie never met either of them; either of George Clay's parents. It is a pity.

From those elders, you see, Nellie might well have learnt enough — even without a word spoken — enough, when combined with the vocal pleas of

---

† Parkinson, 2005; xxxi.

Miss Barratt, and the voiceless constraint Mr Barratt, to furl a bit of sail before it had all gone this far.

Though she was only doing what mamma had always so feelingly urged!

Though, maybe Alice Barratt had a point, about just waiting just a *little* bit... wasn't it prudent? — or but then, wasn't such calculation, of risk and so on— wasn't it properly the masculine preserve? to think things through like that?— and if so, was it even womanly for Nellie to engage in it... albeit on the very edge of her consciousness, like this... wasn't it heartless? Compared to mama, who had so eagerly risked her all, without any calculation whatsoever.

All the best Austen heroines go to the altar looking forward to the education they expect to receive at their husband's hands. Perhaps it is fitting, then, that in the end it was left to Commander Clay to teach Nellie how very unwise it was of her to marry him.

*

For if Nellie was a prize to George Clay, she was his last real prize; indeed, we may say, the last notable action in which he ever took part.

To start with, the Admiralty did a Hornblower on him: they refused to confirm his command. Two weeks into his marriage he found himself a Lieutenant again.

It could have happened to any one. (You know, I can't stress this enough. A hard blow of bad luck, just like this one here, could have happened to absolutely any newly-made commander. Fresh back from the West Indies, say, and flying high on his success; already launched, in his mind, on the brilliant career that lay way beyond the trivial formality of that little letter of confirmation.)

— But it happened to George Clay! And he resented it, bitterly.

Heavens, who would not? Thus thought the very young Mrs Clay, awaiting still her husband's return from wherever it was he had gone this morning. "What would you like for dinner, George dearest? And when— when shall I tell Annie to have it ready for us?– for you?" Annie was their servant, eight weeks on the job and still very keen: it was her first posting, too.

George's nerves— made acute by suffering— could already interpret this as "when will you be home?" He responded with a grunt.

Then a "My dear, whatever you've got will do. Annie can ruin anything it seems. May as well let her loose on something cheap this time"— a reference to the spectacular loss of a goose, bought to celebrate their sixth month of marriage. After that, George had tugged his coat straight and gone out; and that had been twelve hours ago.

Nellie had known there would be difficulties; a few difficulties, to be struggled through, together. She was not disheartened.

There were, in any case, many who felt that Lieutenant Clay continued to do well enough, as these things are judged by the cold dirty waters of the

Channel. After a few years of nothing-much up and down the coast, there was even a little stretch where he had the luck to be assigned, just briefly, to the *Laconia*, under the new-made post-captain Frederick Wentworth — a predictable co-incidence I admit, and perhaps an ill-advised one, but truth is often stranger than fiction— and on the *Laconia*, as we all know, George Clay could, if he had stuck it out, have raked in a tidy pile in prize money.

It was all different, though, this time around.

For one thing, Wentworth raked in so much more.

Albeit never serving together until now, Clay and Wentworth had of course heard of each other. They had been lieutenants both in the West Indies, where they had both the reputation of keen young officers, conspicuous even in that little clutch of keen and bold young officers whose doings and sayings tended to be repeated around the fleet. And perhaps they had kept just a little bit of an eye on each other, that clutch of bold, keen, rising young officers. Who would be promoted first?– *Made!*— and given his own ship and set free!– free to...

There in the West Indies, though, waiting on Fortune, studying for being a legend, George Clay had never felt the need to distinguish Frederick Wentworth, particularly. The man was a good enough officer, by all accounts. Several years his junior in the service.

Now, that junior gave him orders–

It could not but gall.

Moreover, for every shilling that George Clay won in prize money, he knew with naval certitude that Frederick Wentworth was pocketing six.

There was a third thing, too, which George never admitted to anyone; not even himself. Though he might be sailing, there on the *Laconia*, in a steady drizzle of metal, both grey and gold, people no longer spoke so very much of *his* luck; of the luck of Golden George Clay. When he spilled a handful of his prize-money onto the tables of Plymouth, their golden roll triggered in the men around him, not hearty slaps upon the back (well only a few) and demands to hear details of the action (well, not for all that long)... sooner or later, the talk of the room would turn, from him, to tales of the Captain in those actions: to lucky Captain Wentworth; brilliant Captain Wentworth, and his dashing, his darling *Laconia*.

–but, *he* was Lucky George, *he* was Golden George Clay! Good God. In the West Indies, Wentworth had gone by the well-earned sobriquet of Bare-Arsed Fred.

Yet— in that, too, his new Captain was transformed.

No outward sign now, of the Lieutenant Wentworth who had sworn to drink every man under the table at Admiral Trowbrough's take-leave dinner, and had so memorably failed; of the man who had showered prize money in a golden rain on the delighted ladies of Dominica, Bermuda, Saint Kitts; had gone into action, too, many a time, with a foul-smelling rash in his groin. Captain Wentworth of the *Laconia* got drunk only when convention required, and even then, as far as possible only on other people's wine.

Of the cup of debauchery too, he now sipped economically. Sipped discreetly, as well, if not downright cagily: when they got to port he'd just pad off, and then, a bit later, he'd pad back, and no-one the wiser who he'd been tupping. Rumour had it that, in the quiet of his cabin, he had even taken to reading Cowper. And he was quite definitely seen, from time to time, trying to draw diagrams of unusual fish and stuff, and making notes about the customs and dress of the native peoples.

Above all, Captain Wentworth now flouted both naval tradition, and his own, by tucking nearly all of his prize money under the mattress.

When a man acquires a wife, such a sharp-about towards prudence is understandable, even sanctioned, in the service. But Captain Wentworth had no wife.

It was unaccountable.

And a bit repellent.

That was what George Clay thought.

Others though differently.

"Ah, promotion has certainly changed young Wentworth!" senior officers began to say amongst themselves, when they sat late over dinner in some spacious stern cabin, or in nearly equally pleasant surroundings ashore. "It can do that to a man. It can sober him: it can make him steer a steadier course."

And seeing that, with his assumption of maturity, young Wentworth retained all the brilliance of his youth — added to it, indeed, a rather cold-blooded mercenary cunning that was also new, and highly lucrative — seeing all this, as I say, they rapidly and in turn made him post, placed him in one of the handiest frigates of the navy, and entrusted him with a string of independent missions of the kind to bring even more of fortune, as well as fame, to the brave, mature, ruthless, determined, and lucky (and his Admiral) (and any other ship of the navy that happened to be within sight at the time of the capture).

Yes: the Wentworth of late '06 *et passim* was changed indeed.

But no-one changed Lieutenant Clay.

Not even back to Commander.

It was bitterly unfair, George reflected, staring into his freshly-brimming glass of something-or-other. He was denied the opportunities that Fred had gained (and *how*? Who had he sweet-talked? Whose arse had he caressed? — If George only knew, he would have caressed it too). So George downed the glass of something-or-other and reached for another.

Wentworth was only too happy, then, to swap Lieutenant Clay for– well, for anyone; for a Lieutenant Benwick, as it turned out– as expeditiously as could be contrived.

George, for his part, was thoroughly delighted with the change. Sanctimonious blue-light prig that old Bare-Arse had become; prissy Molly; book-sniffing wanker... There were plenty more fish in the sea.

The ship that Lieutenant Clay next boarded, with a light foot and a brisk cheery wave to his young wife, was bound for blockade of the French coast.

It wasn't a brilliant appointment. The Powers-that-Be had, for a moment, hesitated; wondering if it was really the best possible use of a man of Lieutenant Clay's admitted talents. "Should we not give this place to someone else? Hold off with young Clay?– in the hopes of being able to offer him something better, in time– another command, perhaps? Eventually?"

It was rather hard, the way Clay's first command had been knocked back like that.

"Ah, but the man now has a wife to support."

Thus responded a second Power, who was lying back in an armchair, waiting for his friend to finish up and head off with him to dinner. "Sat opposite you at Lawson's dinner, didn't she?— pretty thing, eh?"

"Mm. I thought she looked a bit worn... Well, that changes things of course. Let us hope it has not pleased God to start blessing them with a child." In the matter of children, God's pleasure could be relentless. Aye me. Likewise, well-a-day.

"A bad business, married life on a lieutenant's income." You see? Even the clerk is putting his oar in.

Afloat, Lieutenant Clay would stand a chance of— some sort. Promotion, who knows; a scrap of prize money. "And if there *should* be any kind of big fleet action, ever again..."

"True."

"— a second Trafalgar!—"

"— and Clay stuck ashore for it– Lord! How a body would curse!" They are kind enough men, when the needs of the service allow.

So the Power sighed, and signed the document, and pulled on his coat and went to dinner; and Golden George took ship.

And there, on blockade, George Clay wasted out the rest of his life afloat.

Year after weary year aboard the same ship, with the same captain, and officers, and men, beating back and forth, over the same stretch of sea. Can you imagine being aboard such a ship? Your world, just so many square feet of wet oak decking, repeated, below you, in two or three contracting, darkening lower decks, to finish in the black stench of the hold. Down, up, all about you, no escape: the exact same commands, the identical series of bells, and watches, and duties, day after identical day, heaving endlessly over the same cold grey sea. Not one action to stir the blood, and thin out that of the ranks above; not one capture, to fatten the lean purse, and give a chance to run in to England— home— beauty— somewhere, anywhere, else. Tack, after identical tack, over the same identical waves. Walking your given set of oak planks up and down, watch after watch. After eight months, George Clay could recognise every one of those planks. And he kept on walking them, into years, as the ship slowly rotted beneath his feet, and his eager spirit, gnawing ceaselessly in his breast, ate him alive, from the inside out.

Oh yes. With his marriage, his famous luck vanished.

In later years, he took to pointing this out to Nellie. This was when he was ashore again; invalided, ignominiously, from the effects of a falling block and tackle. George frequently referred to that block as the final, crushing example of post-marital bad luck.

This time, though, luck was blameless. One could have traced a perfectly clear chain of causes— running up the descending trajectory of the block, as it tumbles through the Channel air, gaining momentum at 9.8m/s^2 — over and through a top-man's slippery, skilful hand— and down again— back to George himself. His vivid energy, compressed to harsh temper; his eagerness, curdled, to an impatience vicious in its desires and its expression... No, Lieutenant Clay was by no means so popular, in those years on blockade, as Lucky Golden George had been, long ago, in the West Indies. And in a disaffected ship, its crew almost as frantic with boredom as any of their officers, blocks will fall, from time to time, upon unpopular men.

By the way— I cannot find it in me to deplore that block as much as a nice-minded person should. At least it was consciously selective.

Consider, in contrast, the fate of Nellie's brothers. Do you remember?— Charles, and John?— probably not. Nellie does. A cannonball sweeping the decks does not pause, to deliberate, and choose, which to reduce to a premature rag-bag of flesh. Let's see: *that* thickheaded, unfeeling, unprofitable lout? packed off to sea because his relatives cannot manage him ashore? Or this one; this young John Shepherd, the clever, hardworking friend of all the ship? —No.

No, today it will be his little brother, Charles.

That was the Wars for you. So many embryo heroes, smeared on so many decks, or rotting half-buried in the soils of Europe. Their music unwritten; their discoveries never made. The daring rescues and last stands for which they were once destined, instead a note in the newspaper: Child drowned; Five die in house fire; Battalion lost. And themselves only a moment of memory, from which their sister (an old lady herself now, caged in black bombazine, far away at the other end of the nineteenth century), flinches and turns away.

Thus Nellie came down to earth. Down, from that perfect day when they had floated high on the fragrant hot air of love... down, down... and down some more; to two dark rooms in a noisome back street, and the wearing, anxious, youth-killing dependence of trying to make an inadequate income, and the sympathy of her neighbours, stretch to the next half-day.

As the war went on, and their income shrank again in buying power, Mrs Clay came to play quite a bit on that sympathy. She was aware that she did. Her neighbours became aware of it, as well.

How else, though, to join the ragged ends of the half-year, that suddenly gaped so much wider, now that the injured George also lived ashore? How else, now that she had these two as well; her half-brother's children.

Josephine. Ariosto. Though during his life never able to find out, for her, that half-brother's address, at his death his lawyers had had no difficulty in conveying the man's two orphans, all the way across a war-torn continent, to the Clays' front door.

Never would she cast *these* two innocents upon the waters, trusting— with, oh, what fatuous confidence!— in futurity, exertion; in Providence: in bugger-all.

But— then how? Back again to the daily, hourly question, how to make ends meet? George would not let her teach again. George said that they got along fine on his invalid's pay. Did she not put food on the table before him every day? Did she not always secure the thread to mend?– the cloth to patch?– the board, to fill a broken window?

True. She did. Pledging, negotiating, scrounging; never quite begging: if graft was not in her original nature, it had become second nature. Among those who had once known her, the blooming, happy Mam'zelle Shepherd of Plymouth was rumoured to have died: and indeed, by now George Clay's wife was so diminished that on meeting her again, those who had known the girl of nineteen must have exclaimed— Can *this* be Nellie? Can *this* be Miss Shepherd?

'Why, she is so altered, I should not have known her again.'

*

Ah, how eloquent could Nellie Clay have been!— how eloquent, at least, were her wishes, on the side of demanding, from a suitor, concrete demonstrations of early, warm application, and a cheerful acceptance of conjugal duty!

As opposed to mere sanguine temper, and fearlessness of mind.

Nellie did not blame her mother for her advice. (Frankly, it never occurred to her to do so: I only mention it because Anne Elliot, under oddly similar circumstances, often touches, in a free-indirect kind of way, upon her own magnanimity in not blaming others for her own unfortunate decisions.) Nellie did, however, blame herself, for having been overly influenced by that advice.

She had been nineteen, for heaven's sakes! Her feelings had been strong, but so was her head: it had, even then, pointed out to her a perfectly practical way of being romantic. Practical, and quite wonderfully romantic, and time-honoured too. Had she only demanded of George that he go forth and slay, on her behalf, that Dragon which is a Regency lady's very natural misgiving at the near-total dependency in which a wife must live! — Why had she not laid it upon him, as a Quest, that he should get his post-captaincy?

Perhaps, too, win back once more that modest little fortune in prize-money. And bring it home this time, and lay it at her feet.

(Rather than pissing it up against a wall, eh, Nellie?– heretofore your naval hero's only attested skill with money.)

Surely it was a strange lover who would object to proving his capacity to preserve a wife and children from the pain of actual want!

Nellie blamed herself, in short, for having too easily yielded to George Clay's persuasion.

He may have blamed her, too.

No-one could have blamed him if he had. After all, a little modest reluctance, a little feminine equivocation on her part, a few womanly stipulations– it could only have steadied him. Strengthened. Tempered him. Made of him, through their challenge, the man that he had been destined properly to be.

Good God, man!– was it too much to expect?

Instead, had not her eager yielding distracted him from his duty? Distracted him, too, at a time when his career was quite obviously at a crucial point. And her easy capitulation had then charged him with the demands of a household. At a time when he could least afford it. Barely a Commander, he had been. So young.

Oh, he had been so very young, back then...

So the speed with which she had closed with his offers had at once added to his exigencies, and undermined his capacity to contend with them.

And here, at last, was core of his wife's faults. A woman of a certain stamp may lack the foresight to control, for her *own* advantage, her appetites. She must yet, if she truly loves, be capable of prudence, and self-denial, for her lover's sake.

Chapter 10

"So you choose to *abandon* us, Aunt Clay, and follow the Lady Elizabeth to the fleshpots of Bath."

Fleshpots?— and, Bath?— "(She's not the 'Lady' Elizabeth) I'm not *abandoning* you please take your sleeve out of the butter–" (they were eating again: it seemed, to her father, that since the children had arrived, everyone was always eating) — "where *do* you get this kind of thing, Josephine?"

"Stealing Byron from your library and listening at the door."

"*Ariosto!*" hissed Josephine.

"Byron!— *Stealing!*—"

"Listening at my door!" exclaimed Mr Shepherd at the same moment–
"and *don't* punch your little brother, Josephine!"

"But he revealed sources, grandpapa! You *said* that *sources*–"

"Yes and now you're finding out what happens when my advice is ignored.
You will stay in half an hour after your brother this morning and parse that
Virgil. Ariosto I'll speak to you later."

There was a short, resentful silence.

Nellie broke it—

"I am certainly not abandoning you, children. But we can't always pick and
choose in this life. We must submit sometimes to circumstances. And to the
guidance and decisions and so on of our parents. And guardians. And so perhaps, I might go to Bath, just for a while. You know it is because I love you
and I want the best for you."

"But if you go and stay with Mrs Wellington, why should we not come
too?"

Nellie and her father exchanged a glance: goodness, that listening at the
door had been thorough. "Mrs Wellington doesn't want a brace of brats with
their ears glued to her drawing-room door, that's why", explained Mr Shepherd. "And you'll cramp Aunt Nellie's style."

"*Mais non*— " Josephine was ardent, "I could be her accomplice! I could
gather information for her", ("You certainly could", interjected her grandfather.) "because nobody notices children *grand-père* you said so yourself!"

"I'm sorry Josie darling but–"

"Oh Aunt *Clay...*"

"–but it's out of the question dear, so please just put it quite out of your
mind. And, don't listen at doors. It's really very— well it's vulgar. Miss Elliot
would never do it, would she?"

"Miss Elliot wouldn't have to", pointed out Ariosto. "I bet, when she was
little, she listened like anything. Now, everyone has to listen at *her* door."

Josephine sighed admiringly.

"How divine to be The Lady Elizabeth. If I were her"— (The subjunctive!
noted Nellie. How had Josephine picked that one up so quickly? Nellie herself
had had to check it in Louth's, over and over; she had bought the *Grammar*
shortly after her first dinner party in Dashe, and she had been reading a section every evening, and getting to the end, and starting again. But the children
were shedding Plymouth effortlessly. They already spoke far better English
than her. Than she. Did.) — "*main dfer dans une gant velours!*" finished Josephine.

"*de, fer;* please enunciate *both* words!", snapped her grandfather. "And it's
un gant. *De velours*. Clearly we must see to your French, and right quickly."

"But the Latin lessons...." Ariosto was very keen on Latin. He sensed its significance, here in England.

Their grandfather savaged his hair. "In winter then. When there's nothing else to do. We'll add French. Knock that back into shape by– by... *pfffft!*" he concluded. Anglo-French spy rings had always had genuine meal-breaks, even during the worst of the Terrors.

"So why isn't Miss Elliot married?" demanded Ariosto.

But here, his elders were as baffled as himself.

Nellie and her father had often speculated together about it in private (they hoped, and believed); the apparent unmarriability of those Elliot girls. Ten thousand pounds each. The bigwigs in this little patch of Somerset; to all the gentry about, the Baronetage must count for plenty— and it was clear to everybody that Miss Elliot had only to stretch out her hand to pick up some man or other.

Strange, then, that she risked the censure of the world for being unmarried for so long.

"She is nearly thirty!" Nellie exclaimed now.

"As long as it appears a *choice* though my dear, the world doesn't revile a single woman quite so much", pointed out her father.

"But *thirty!*" repeated Nellie.

"Thirty!" reflected Josephine, a little uneasily. "How ashamed of myself I should be if I were thirty, and still unmarried!"

"It's because she's such a *squeezed*-up lady", Ariosto stated. "Bad-tempered, and squeezed." Meanwhile– "As for The Lady Anne, all the world knows the tragic tale of her seduction and loss!" Josephine was confiding sorrowfully to her plate of eggs. "But the cold proud heart of The Lady Elizabeth is a mystery that not even Cookie has fathomed."

Ariosto nodded. "Cookie and I were discussing it only yesterday."

"Yes Cookie is one of Ariosto's *sources*", remarked Josephine spitefully–

She had danced, at last, too close to the brink.

"It is true", responded her father to Nellie, as he bundled both children out of the parlour, "that the world's tolerance will probably be soon exhausted in Miss Elliot's case." He slammed the door. "There are certain watershed dates, after which it takes very considerable sums indeed to avoid the label of 'spinster.'" He opened the door: Josephine fell in. "Young lady, there will be no further significant conversation in this room until I see you, *and* your brother, playing on the lawn." He slammed the door once more. "As you have no doubt noted, a title, or something that sounds like it, helps one to evade censure for this as for so many other social transgressions..." he padded across the room and peered out of the window— Josephine and Ariosto were already hurrying enigmatically towards the foot of their favourite elm, the russet head and the dark in close confabulation— "...money title and *lovers* yes—

for those women whose single state is extended to a degree that defies the social contract (and I don't know *why* they sign it, poor things, I'm sure I never did myself) a lover makes a good red herring; although by the bye and on the subject I would not–... is Josephine taking something out of that hollow in the elm?... not advise lovers just at present; England is not France, things are delicate enough as they are around here at the moment, and Miss Anne has the eyes of a Hydra and judgement of a shrew."

Mrs Clay meanwhile was blushing at the thought. She had absorbed the profound social value of virtue in the dirty end of Plymouth, and swore to herself, indignantly, that she would never take lovers — Her father misunderstood.

"It's just that, as we are placed, here in England, we are neither rich enough nor thank Heavens poor enough for you to get away with it... Ah. They hide food there. That's why cutting meals holds no power any more. So yes it *is* possible for a woman to die at fine old age without ever having married *or* been a spinster; it happens all the time, in the better circles, given huge quantities of money and superb connections and an open mind. But our Miss Elliot will soon have worn through her supplies of all three. And when she finally does, things will get very nasty very quickly: that is what I anticipate. So whatever her problem may be, we must *get* to the root of it, and *get* her married, as soon as ever we can. Get her, in short, out of your hair."

"Oh yes papa. That would be when I am Lady Elliot, would it?"

"Well of course."

Nellie smiled, and did not reply. Side by side, the two gazed from the window at the cloud shadows that swept across the lawn, chasing the children, chasing autumn leaves in the wind.

*

You will notice that Mr Shepherd does not build upon marrying off Miss Anne. Nobody, nowadays, could get much mileage out of making up matches for Miss Anne; except, with a sort of anxious hopelessness, poor Lady Russell. To everyone else it was obvious that Anne Elliot had embraced spinsterhood as a nun embraces a vocation. It was one of the many ways in which she annoyed her family.

You'll also notice— and it may have startled you— that the ill-regulated child Josephine declares 'all the world' to know of Miss Anne's unsuccessful love! Austen, on the contrary, has always asserted[†] that scarce a soul knew of the Anne's brief, ill-fated romance with Captain Frederick Wentworth; no-one, save her father, her sister, and Lady Russell and all of us.

"How can this be?" attentive readers have cried, down the centuries. "What about the servants?"

Indeed. Did no-one, resplendent in butler's uniform, open the front door

---

† (or has, perhaps, allowed Anne Elliot to believe?...)

on the Captain's knock; to let young Frederick, red and conscious, into Kellynch Hall? Did no footman — sucking hard on his cheeks to hid his grin — pace, stately, through the corridors, to announce the visitor's presence to a nineteen-year-old Anne? — nor observe, as he spoke the glorious words "Captain Wentworth!", the sudden agitation of those slender limbs, the fine colour coming and going in that delicate complexion? And did Miss Anne Elliot have no maid? — or was she already, at nineteen, so refined a soul as to be the first woman in Creation to fall in love without exhibiting a whole new level of obsession about her hair?

It's unbelievable.

Be it known, then, that in the few short months that so altered the lives of Frederick Wentworth and Anne Elliot, both were passionately fond of a quiet early morning ramble, so most of their encounters took place accidentally, while out walking, at half past eight in a secluded little dell on the southern side of the park. Captain Wentworth visited the Hall itself only four times, and after all one of these was for a ball, and in any case the Kellynch butler was old and short-sighted, and the footmen (brothers) each as stupid as an owl, in spite of their magnificent legs. Anne's maid did indeed see the lie of the land; but she had been Lady Elliot's maid, and was consequently so correct that, far from blabbing it all in the servants' hall, she died without ever having touched a man's hand.

Under these circumstances, then, Anne was only half a fool — or perhaps nine-tenths of one — to imagine that no-one else knew a thing. The details, at least, remained very largely a matter of speculation.

Between old Mr and Mrs Musgrove for example, at Uppercross Manor, the understanding was that Miss Anne had once shown a little fondness for a young man in the army or navy way, a poor penniless creature, but luckily it had all come to nothing. The drama of the story gained geometrically, however, with geographic and with social distance, as well as strengthening as an inverse of the age of the teller. Thus, among the old ladies of the county, it was known that Miss Anne Elliot had once been engaged to an officer of the Marines, who drank and swore and spat tobacco juice upon the stately floors of Kellynch Hall. Their daughters, further, knew that the Marine had only departed the country after Miss Anne had found him *in flagrante* with her elder sister, while among the servants of the same establishments it was equally well known that Miss Anne, for all her lovely ways, had once attempted to elope with a foremast jack *and*, that the seduction had been foiled only at the very door of the chaise, when the jolly tar was persuaded by a weeping Sir Walter to accept Anne's dowry in lieu of herself, upon which the Heart of Oak had thrust Miss Anne fainting into her father's arms and driven off in a triumphant cloud of dust along the turnpike road until he had reached Warminster, where he had bought a public house, and was currently doing very well.

It would be more accurate, then, to say that not a soul knew the *full* story of Miss Anne's sad romance, save those first mentioned.

Plus, of course, John Shepherd.

*

Nevertheless the main point had always been clear to everyone.

"Not enough money on his side."

"How much is 'not enough', then, for the Elliots?" enquired Nellie.

"A naval commander's pay."

"Oh!"

Nellie instantly translated this into pounds *per annum* during wartime and during peace, and then took a moment more to calculate it as a percentage of the income of Kellynch Hall.[†] "Oh; that *would* be tricky. No prize money at all?"

"Several thousands, I understand; and all of it spent. Which for a man mostly bobbing around in a boat, miles out to sea, argues a real talent for profligacy. Naturally enough then, her father declined to pour Miss Anne's ten grand into his eager lap. They'd have had to wait for Sir Walter's death."

"So he pulled out?– or did Miss Anne turn him down?"

"No no; *she* was besotted, they say. Perfectly ready to go ahead, give him her all and all that. And he was still willing to take the gamble; Sir Walter can't live forever, you know. It was a very near thing."

"Heavens! But then how...?"

"Lady Russell stepped in; managed to talk her out of it. Luckily."

Nellie was sober. "Luckily indeed, for the poor *ingénue*.

"Gosh.

"Though–" she chewed her lip... "...She did have the sense to *listen* to–... Miss Anne I mean. Had the sense to recognise a responsible advisor. You have to give her that."

"...mm..."

"Well. Poor old Miss Anne."

*

It was on Lady Russell, too, that Mr Shepherd relied for the eventual disposal of Anne Elliot. Even now, Miss Anne often stayed with her, at Kellynch Lodge, for weeks together; it seemed of all things probable that when Sir Walter married Nell, Miss Anne would take herself off and settle there permanently. A bit tough on the old woman, perhaps...? — but Lady R. seemed truly fond of the girl; treated her a great deal better than Miss Anne's own family did– Anne returned the favour– it would be a win-win, decided Mr Shepherd.

---

† About £176 a twelve-month; £143 if peace were declared. Kellynch brought in over three and a half thousand a year. I said I'd be clear about important things, didn't I?

And then those two could go to London together; concerts, public lectures; they liked that kind of thing.

In all that, they might even end up, too, with a husband for Anne! Who knows? Lady Russell was a competent old bird, in her way.

Chapter 11

There remained one person of whom, as yet, Mr Shepherd's plans had not comfortably disposed. This was a certain Mr Elliot.

Young Mr Elliot, that is. Great grandson of the second Sir Walter. Heir presumptive to Sir Walter's Baronetage— and to every last scrap of the Kellynch estate.

Sir Walter's father had been a cold man, but no fool. Long before Austen, long before any of us, he had taken the measure of his son— and come up grimly short of the full yard.

Oh, the boy had been given ample opportunity to prove himself. At seven, though, the future fourth Baronet remained defeated by the most simple Latin, and in spite of regular beatings, still wet his bed. At the child's 364th weekly viewing, as it yet again squealed and pranced about the drawing room, flourishing its mother's fan like an ageing tart making her last bids for custom — "*Look* at me Pappa! *Look* at me Mamma!"— the father had finally, decisively, rung for his steward.

"Mellars?— A new will. Tie up the whole estate, tight as the law allows, and entail it, heirs male, for as long as my will can reach."

Once come into the Baronetage, therefore, our own Sir Walter had been unable to flog the silver or fritter away the ancient medes; his hands were largely tied.

He had failed, though, in such ways as were left open to him, such as running up debts and raising girls. (A solitary male infant *had* made a brief appearance between Anne and the youngest girl Mary— but on finding itself snatched up, yet slippery and bloody, into its father's lace-encrusted arms, it had gagged, rolled up its eyes and died.) By now, then, this remote cousin — this young Mr Elliot— must be feeling tolerably secure of the inheritance.

True, the young Elliot was already rich in his own right. He was also estranged from the family, and had never visited Kellynch in his life. But none of this, Mr Shepherd knew, was likely to lessen a man's eagerness to insert 'Sir' in front of his name, nor soften the hostility with which he must, therefore, view the womanly figure of Nell.

Such a pity, Mr Shepherd thought at times, that word could not be made to reach the young Mr Elliot; just to reassure him, as regards Nellie, and babies.

But no. It was risking too much, over-egging the pudding. Let things run their course. If the man turned up; if the man objected: then it might be time for a quiet hint. Mr Shepherd sighed. "Now... *now!*....

"Now. The most important issue is, how to get you to Bath. I have a few ideas— And don't smirk at me like that, child, for this is a crucial juncture. We don't want anyone else swooping in on the good Baronet, now that we've finally got him thinking, again, along the lines of *lerv.*"

"I really can't think he is thinking of *lerv*, papa."

"As I so vulgarly put it."

"As you put it. If he was— were— then, surely, Miss Elliot would notice?— I can't imagine she wouldn't notice. I think it's better, really, if he doesn't think of lerv at all until..."

"Until you are well dug in?"

"Oh I believe *that* one is dealt with, papa."

"Mm? Still with the smirk, Nellie. By the way."

"Well—!"

His daughter put down her work.

"*As* it happens, papa: this morning, Miss Elliot asked me— and by the way it was 'for six weeks at least, dear Penelope'—" Her father's eyes suddenly goggled, and Mrs Clay's voice rose in triumph— "'to *accompany* us, to **Bath**, *both Sir Walter and I, **feel**, that it would be so, **delightful**'!*"

"Nellie!!!"

Nellie tossed her head.

And bridled, too. Pertly. Ah, one must forgive her the relapse, in such a moment of victory.

"How in the name of— *all* that is marvellous— did you manage it?"

Nellie had initially been trying to manage it by dwelling on the quantities of dreary labour that the Elliots would face, setting up in Bath — and at the same time, bringing before them her own rich experience in moving between— well— lodgings. For example, thus:

"If you will allow an old widow woman to just *hint*, Miss Elliot— you know we old widow ladies are forever making *arrangements* about such things, for our *friends* if not for ourselves, and I know that *I* would take *great care* to take a *good look about me*, once I were in Bath!— and, not *settle*, you know, for the first thing that comes my way. Which is such a *temptation*, of course, when one has not yet found permanent lodgings, and *everything* is at *sixes* and sevens... oh! so unpleasant!— but it has always been my *rule*, (because I *know* from *horrid experience* what *dreadful* mistakes one can make!), to look at, and *into*, at least a *dozen* apartments, *very* carefully, before I make a choice."

"Oh but I believe Sir Walter has already found a suitable place. He saw it in the paper. The Bath Chronicle; Shepherd— your father, you know— has arranged that we begin to take the Bath papers too, which is so useful, one gets an idea of the shops already, and this morning Sir Walter noticed that there is a place coming free in the Crescent which we both feel it is very suitable."

"Ah."

It was all that Mrs Clay could manage, for a strangled eight seconds. Then–

"Is not the Royal Crescent a little, ah, *dear* perhaps?"

"Well certainly some of the finest places in Bath are found there", confessed Miss Elliot readily; "but then, one would not want to live in anything too confined. One is apt, after Kellynch, to resent confinement; one feels it, in London, among the apartments of friends, really sometimes to an extraordinary degree; one wonders that they can endure it! But I suppose it is a matter of what one is used to. And with all the sav- the ec- well in Bath you know, we will be so *free* of all our previous drains — maintaining an estate, a country estate, the farms and tenants and poor of the parish and so on, church repairs, endless obligations — that papa and I do agree that, once in Bath, we need no longer restrict ourselves. A pleasant house, you know: it is the least we owe ourselves, after all this."

"– Oh dear *God!*" Mr Shepherd had shot out of his chair. "God give me strength, will there be no end to the-the-the-the-the-*silliness* of these Elliots?"

He flung himself the short length of their parlour— pulled up— flung about and hurtled back again. "After all this!!"

"I am at my wits' end—

"What is the point?

"Is there really any point at all?

"–And how on earth have I stood it? all these years? Six— no *seven*— *seven* years and more with these maggot-brained–"

He pitched onto the sofa beside her. "But my dear", (steepling his fingers and tapping them savagely), "I apologise for ever entertaining the idea of Sir Walter for you— it would be like marrying navel lint. We've exhausted the efficacy of Lady Russell I suppose?"

"Oh very much so. Miss Elliot has altered the time of her morning walk these days, especially to be out at the hour of Lady Russell's usual visit."

Mr Shepherd gnawed viciously at the side of his finger. "Miss Anne?" Nellie rolled her eyes. Mr Shepherd grimaced. "Alright– so– What did you say next? to this over-dressed dust bunny?"

"*Well!* I talked about *agents*, and how useful it is to have someone on the *spot*, who really *knows Bath*, and I mentioned Mr Wellington, as you had suggested, but—"

"Oh I fancy we know Bath well enough Penelope", interrupted Miss Elliot. "We were there for much of the winter of– I cannot exactly recall, but all the principal areas of the town are tolerably well known to us."

Mrs Clay bit her lower lip— added an earnest nod, in order that any flavour of frustration conveyed by that bite should be transformed, under its influence, to attentive deference; sank her needle (she brought her own work with her to Kellynch now, such was the intimacy between Miss Elliot and herself) firmly into the cloth and unfortunately got her finger as well. Ah. "Do tell– *dear* Miss Elliot– do tell me, all about it. What is Bath like? You know it is all a complete novelty to *me*." And as Elizabeth strayed among the Terraces, Circles and Crescents, Mrs Clay watched the dark blood flow, a wet gleam merely, onto the dark cloth of Ariosto's new winter coat. No problem. That would come out with just a rinse in cold water.

"I thought you were over this stabbing yourself with the needle lark", interrupted her father in his turn. "Clumsiest needlewoman in the south-west, I thought, when you first arrived."

"I am not indeed!" responded Nellie, with a show of indignation. "I'll have you know my stitching is widely admired; among those who understand the matter. Fine, and regular, and firm. I just do miss the material sometimes. And I'm always quick with the handkerchief when it's a light coloured cloth I'm working on. With a dark colour it's better; you can just let it flow."

Her father eyed her; but did not really see how or where to take the conversation. In any case it is of no account— "So then?"

"Well what came to mind, so powerfully at this point, was poor Tom Adams."

"Good Lord!" exclaimed her father with fresh alarm. "I trust you didn't say so!"

"Well I sort of did, actually."

"*What?*"

"Do just listen, papa."

By now Miss Elliot is feeling that Mrs Clay should be saying something. Nellie— Mrs Clay— sensing this, squeezed her bloody finger gently, and commenced.

"My goodness, Miss Elliot— what a great deal there is to choose among, to be sure! My head quite reels with it all! I am not surprised that you should settle for just the advertisements in the Bath Chronicle— in your place (although of course I could never be in your place but) I can quite see that for people in your position of life, it would be perfectly common to do the same. It *is* a shame, really, how these tradesmen do grab and take any advantage of their betters whenever they can, such as yourself and the good Sir Walter; *so* liberal; *so* trusting. So unaccustomed, too, to worry over the expenses that— well!— that the rest of us think so much of! But I do think it is a shame, such prices as they put on these places, when people such as myself, you know, in a more *retired* line of life, all see at a glance that they are not being quite... well — not meeting *your* liberality with anything like an equal *return*."

This raised only a cool eyebrow in Elizabeth, who always exhibited a fine carelessness when it came to being overcharged. There being, you understand, so much more where that came from.

But Mrs Clay had more, too.

"And of course, they cannot imagine the great difference *this* time: they cannot conceive of how much you wish and hope that your so *very* many dependants of your good self and Sir Walter will benefit, *just* for this little while, in securing more *reasonable* terms, more *usual* terms may I say (!). After all— rather than lining the pockets of *these people*, your intention in putting *yourselves* to such *inconvenience,* in all this, is to oversee the *well-being* of your *tenants*— your dear good folk— such a multitude of dependents!— the tax of greatness!— to arrange their affairs in strict *regularly*, as expeditiously as possible."

Elizabeth had made a couple of small hasty movements in the last clauses of this peroration, indicative of a desire to change the subject, so Nellie punched straight (almost) for the solar plexus: "They do— the good people here do— speak *so* respectfully of your consideration in this move to Bath. Especially after what poor silly Thomas Adams— well. I hardly like to mention it, we all know he was quite lacking in his wits, poor man, but — And when people will take it into their heads to do that kind of thing— And the response of the *family*, you know, in this remove to Bath and various things, I hear it spoken of, on every side; how *kind* they feel you and Sir Walter to be, in taking it upon *yourselves* to— the generous sacrifice, of such comforts and prerogatives, and *birthright* and so on— they feel it very acutely, I assure you Miss Elliot. Their respect for the family is greater than it ever was. If such a thing is possible, of course!..." Mrs Clay laughed, uneasily. "... and so... it would be quite *shameful*, of those Bath people, I should think— to just calmly step in!— between you and your noble *intentions* in all this. With their hands held out, my goodness!— imposing! Upon you! Oh, but wouldn't this old widow lady give them *what for!*"

Mr Shepherd had his hand pressed upon his chest by this stage; was sitting still, hunched over and staring at Nellie. "My God!"

Nellie arched an eyebrow at him.

"My God Nellie. How did she take it?" He was rigid, even, about the lips and jaw.

Which almost never happened to papa. Nellie hastened to soothe. "Everyone knows it wasn't your fault, papa. The baronet borrowed it back in the year 05, for Heaven's sake, and Mellars never making a record of it, never even *hearing* of it himself probably; everyone knows that." (Mellars had been the previous steward.) "So how could you possibly have known? It was entirely up to Sir Walter. To keep track. And to pay it back. Everybody says–"

— but Mr Shepherd, the picture of irritation, was already testily flicking through a volume he had snatched up from the cushions between them. "Of course it was! Wasn't, I mean, *my* fault, was Sir's business— to repay what he'd levered off the poor sap. It's just a shocking cock-up, that's all. If I *had* bloody known... well the man needn't have paid a penny of rent for the last nine years, that's all. One expects to have basics like that at one's fingertips, what's owed and what's not. Hardly my fault but it makes me look utterly unprofessional and ignorant which is– I mean there's a limit. I actually pressed him– Adams I mean– for the last lot of rent. Thought that he must be holding out on me, given what I knew he made each year— absolutely damned disgusting. Excuse me, Nellie. But it makes me sick to think if it, that's all."

"Well imagine borrowing money from his own tenant!"

"Repeatedly."

Nellie stared. This was new to her. "Repeatedly?"

"Yes. Adams was slow but he was such a hard worker, you know, and really very good in spite of that funny thing with his speech. Systematic too: orderly to a fault. So he kept on scraping by and putting by a bit more, and now I find that Sir, and Miss too I suspect, kept lifting it off him."

"Good *Lord.*"

Mr Shepherd nodded; though he was gazing at nothing by now, somewhere in the middle of the room, book askew, forgotten, in his lap. "All astonishment, was dear Sir, when he heard they'd found him like that. Didn't believe it could be the money, at the bottom of it. *'But it didn't amount to more than a few hundred pounds, Shepherd!'*"

"Oh dear God."

"*'Man told me he was honoured to oblige! Couldn't really turn him down, you know, after that.'*"

For a moment they both stared, at the nothing, in the middle of the room, hating Sir Walter: hating them all.

But what can you do.

That's life.

I mean it's not like the French Revolution had turned out all that well; certainly not for the Shepherds.

Her father heaved a massive sigh, and slapped the violated book back onto the cushions. "Well I'm amazed young Miss didn't throw you out, after that."

"I'm quite surprised myself, to be sure. She did sit a bit. But I was dealing with the sewing, you know, and wrapping up my finger, and that absorbed me rather. To– *tell* the truth papa, I know you have your heart set on this, and of course I'm quite sure that you know how to do things with Sir Walter, and all that, and of course I don't for a *moment* dispute your... your... but for myself I really can't see that Miss Elliot would let me get away with it. It seems a bit... fanciful?... to me...? — though of *course* I'm not disagreeing, or *objecting*, or anything. But just at this time I found myself, perhaps, feeling a bit careless."

"Mmm?"

"Oh– So, then, she excused herself and went out, and I told myself it was for the usual reason, but she was away rather long; so I was beginning to prepare myself for the worst, and just looking about me as to where all my things were, in case she came back you know, and said she had suddenly remembered an appointment— but then, *in* she came, smiling like any thing, and came right up and sat down beside me and said—

"Now, Mrs Clay; what do you think I have been doing?"

"Why Miss Elliot, I can't for the life of me imagine!"

"I have been speaking just this moment to papa— to Sir Walter— about a scheme that I have had in my mind for some days now; and he concurs with me completely, in feeling, that it would be quite delightful if we could persuade you to visit us in Bath— to *come with* us, that is, to Bath– when we set off from Kellynch– for a nice long visit. Six weeks. To start with; though, I expect longer; though of course one can never... For I will be quite alone there, to start with, you know, except for Anne. And with so much to do, and so many demands ahead of us and so forth, papa and I both agree that you would be tremendously– your clear head, that is, and all your experience: it would be of such assistance, in all the business that lies ahead."

(What Sir Walter had actually said— after a moment's astonishment, a moment's reflection— was: "An excellent scheme Elizabeth. After all, she need not always dine with us.")

"And I trust that we can *amuse* you—", Miss Elliot smiled archly, "what with the resources of Bath, I trust there will be enough of *novelty* for you, that it will not all be hard work! There are the balls, public and private; the Rooms of course. Concerts; Mr Shepherd tells me you are quite the *musician*! — so the many concerts we always attend are sure to be of interest to you; Bath is quite as good as London in that way; also too for shopping, although naturally more limited in some ways but the quality and the fashion is all you could desire. Then we could go to the library, the libra*ries*, I should rather say, for there are several, and—

"and *oh* Mrs Clay, one is so independent!

"I mean, in Bath, one can just *step* out of the door, in any weather almost, and walk anywhere, on the lovely pavements! Instead of always being shadowed about by the dreary carriage, and having to go home when you said you would, because Papa needs it next. The snugness of drinking hot chocolate— in *Mollands* you know!— while the rain comes down outside, and it doesn't matter a bit, and nobody knows where we are—!"

But Nellie remained bent forward over her work, scrubbing counterproductively at that mark.

"So... That is to say; I feel that you too can anticipate much enjoyment, Mrs Clay."

It's not that she wasn't happy to raise a face stained with what Miss Elliot would take to be tears of gratitude. And it was, wasn't it?— tremendous relief, that was making her so woozy inside— to be invited, good Heavens, by a Baronet's daughter, to live with a Baronet's family, in Bath– indefinitely!– Well–! Well it absolutely proved, once and for all, how wrong everyone had been, these last years; how wrong everyone had come to be, about Mrs Clay!

So... but... the tears were politic, and by all means she should display them.

Still, there was no need to admit them to papa, she felt.

Miss Elliot was getting confused.

"If your father can spare you, of course— and your... your friends... your domestic ties..."

Then she leant quickly closer to Nellie on the sofa– put a hand, even, on her arm— "Please, Mrs Clay. Think how much fun it could be. The two of us."

"And what did you say to that?" Mr Shepherd's face was a picture of admiration, without shadow or reserve.

"I spat on my palm and I said, 'Done, Miss Elliot, and here is my hand upon it!'"

"...really?"

"Yes and then I pumped her hand like mad and bussed her on both cheeks."

"Really."

"And then I tore about the Hall, screaming '*I'm going to Bath! I'm going to Bath! I'm going to Bath!*' Josephine would have been proud of me."

"*I'm* proud of you, Nellie."

His daughter blushed with gratification.

Chapter 12

The 22 September.

Dear Papa,

At last I am writing, and in English too as you see because I must practice or I will never learn, tho The Dictionary is goodnesse knows where, still on the carts I suspect, but of all people I hope you will forgive me erreurs. A week I see and scarsely I had time to sit, let alone write. But your lovely letter has smote my conscience, and I have told Miss E I must have an hour free now. Not in so many words of course.

So nice to hear the children are happy and go on well, tho without me. I cannot say the same for me I must say. In spite of all the busyness I have time enough at night, I find, to miss you all very very much. So you must not think this silence is neglect. I think of you all every day, and miss you so much sometimes I coud cry. Alas. How are aunts forgotten. You see I am sorry for myself alredy. No,

every thing is most exciting. The first thing to say is that we have taken appartements!

They are very nice indeed and not too expensiv I having followd your avise
before hand and spoke to Mr Wellington a great deal about it all and made the
situation quiet clear. We looked at four appartements and this one is by far the
best, at least in the public rooms. A little confined in the servants ~~kort corter~~
quartiers which I hope will not make for trouble later but it brout the price down
a lot and was worth it I hope, as I have a little plan regardent the servants, being
that we should have only the fewest to live here, and hire the rest when we need
them. Footmen, and so forth, for dinners, such a saving! You can imagine how
estrange Miss E. thought the scheme and yet it was clair (once I pointed it out to
her) that there was no room for more than a few servants being the butler, cook,
ladysmaids etc etc valet of course and housekeeper (tho I do all that now and do it
rather better than Mrs Collier and a great deal more chepely not to say honestly.
Which by the way reminds me has Mrs Croft ~~given her the boot~~ let her go yet? For
blind daylight robbery there is nothing like her I think, tho all the Kellynch servants were that way inclined to some degree. What she ~~coud~~ could do with a huge
fat cold ham would bring teres to your eyes and I could say nothing being but a
tolerated sort of upper servant then. Things will be different here.

the 24th September

I find that the Es look to me more and more for their arrangementes and it
goes well touch wood. I am interviewing servants tho Miss E must of cours give
the final decision when I have determined who it is to be. She is very pleased I
think I can say, does not really like busyness affaires; houshould arrangements;
financiel calculations; but this has always been evident, no? But it will not be
much longer before I have things ~~thurily thurr Thurol~~ properly en train. (The Dictionary is unpacked at last, but it is astonishing how many words are not in it.)

the 30th September

The furniture begins to look lovely in the new rooms and you can imagine
what a day we had of it trying every piece first here and then there, and there, and
then here again. The furniture men were almost mad with exasperation by the time
Miss E had finished trying out all the different possibilites; see sketch enclosed.
Sometimes she does enjoy herself, you see.

We yet go out very little. Miss E. is waiting for new dresses to be finished
before she ventures too much in public, her old dresses being it seems quiet countri-
fyd or so we heared a lady kindly remark within our hearing when we were about
some business regardent the curtains for the breakfast room. I had to pretende not
to have heared anything but she suspected enough to be I am sorry to say ~~quiet~~
quite cutting in her remarks for the rest of the day. She and Sir W. both are really
very easily brout down, which you wold not think in people so confiente of there
superiorite, and then she always gets very unpleasante. On the bright side Sir W
at those times is very glad to have me around I can see.

I could hardly tell you how many cartes de visite have been left so far which
is in short very many indeed already and I could list them all for you in a variete
of orders—rank, income, alphabetical, size, thickenesse— but I leave that activity to Miss E who does so several times a day and it cheers her up no end.

3rd October

We begin to go about town now which is such a relief. Sometimes she is excited and plaisante, talking of the things we will do in Bath and the people we will see every day, and sometimes still tired and disagreable wondering I think if she has made a mistake, will not pull it off, being the grande lady here in Bath. Sir W. wonders the same for himself, at times, I can see.

It is her last throw, I ~~shoud~~ should think. She is thirty next June, according to the Baronetage, and he is 54!! but you know this of cours— did you? People tell me all sortes of ages for him, and hint that they are both so very much older than they look, but it is mostly just malice I think, and envy even to be fair, his skin and figure being so good still, it is almost unnatural in a man. Hers too but when she thinks I do not attende she looks much, in the glace, at the edges of her mouth, which are starting to droop, you know how it happens, and I see her push- ing at her eyelids. I could tell her myself that your face does not realy fall off overnight when you turn thirty, being in a position to judge freshly of this myself of course, but such a liberte I cannot yet take, but every day I heartily wish her a nice fat baronet all to herself. I will look out for one for her, you can imagine how keenely.

Well my paper reminds me to conclude, which is very ennuyent. Je t'em- brasse très fort, papa, et gros bisous aux enfants,

P.

*

A month later, and Mrs Clay had the domestique arrangements every bit as en train as she had calculated. However, the Elliots, father and daughter, were now at their lowest ebb.

It was a progression only too familiar to Nellie, she having endured so many removals since that first great removal, from home and childhood and security all at once. Amidst a new scene of life there is, at least, the stimulus of novelty, and the liveliness of mind induced by hopes as yet undisappointed. Some four or six weeks on, however, the spirit inevitably begin to flag. New occupations have lost their freshness, and revealed themselves as the old occu- pations, exercised in different rooms merely. New acquaintance prove very like the human beings you thought to have left behind. The new crimson cur- tains, so rich with possibilities when Elizabeth first oversaw their hanging, must already be beaten to get out the dust. And — the walks of Bath yield no prince.

The church, attended now for six weeks (and with what bustle, what delight; knowing oneself the new face and figure, uppermost in all minds) is known, now, together with its congregation: in its gloom, there is no hand- some single man between thirty and forty, bending gracefully at prayer. The libraries yield no studious Baronet, intent on the latest publications— his white hand brushing her own as they both reach, at once, for the same slim volume of poetry (Miss Elliot would first have had to start reading poetry, but this too had been confidently envisaged, another miraculous power of the waters)... "Madam! I apologise profoundly! How could I..." and then his eyes, meeting hers, continue to speak— though his lips– breathless– no longer can...

Yet while nothing is new, neither is anything in the least bit comfortable or familiar. No, it is all strange, hard, and it keeps going on and on — until at last what sweeps over one is a yearning just to be sitting in one's old winter parlour, looking out over the long-despised lawns of Kellynch, while Mrs Collier stumps up the hall bringing in the tea things... As a small November rain blotted the windows of Camden Place, blurring the hurrying figures of Bath shopgirls, Bath errand boys, Bath carriages, Miss Elliot leant her head slowly forward onto the window pane, losing ground against an overpowering desire to weep.

Many was the good cry Mrs Clay had had herself, under very roughly similar circumstances. She too had sighed, in yet another unfamiliar set of lodgings, in yet another naval port, and gazed out at the same English rain. She knew it, too, for a humiliating state — containing, as it must at some level, an acknowledgement of defeat.

And we can guess how badly Elizabeth reacts to humiliation. Nellie slipped out of the room and crept upstairs, to fetch a reel of thread which she knew would prove particularly hard to find.

What she did find was Elizabeth's new dress, cast aside and waiting for the renewed attentions of the dressmaker: it had proven a little too wide about the bust, a little too... something... about the neckline... Half an hour's quick stitching and snipping solved the first problem and removed the lace from the neck, and Nellie took the dress downstairs with her.

At first, to be sure, a little reluctance, a little ennui; but with the most delicate of coaxing, Nellie lured Elizabeth back upstairs, and installed her in front of the mirror; and from there on her spirits began to improve. The fit about the bust was now delightful, so becoming, indeed with a figure like Miss Elliot's it was a miracle of tailoring that could have disguised it in the first place. And perhaps with the neck just *so*—

"– Or no, perhaps like *this*, Penelope— what do you think?"

"It certainly shows your shoulders to advantage."

"Not too much, do you think?"

"Not too much for prettiness, but perhaps too much for Bath..." Sunk deep in the profundities of dress, Nellie pulled a small grimace that might have struck an informed onlooker as surprisingly sophisticated. "How was *la Tarrington's* daughter wearing hers last week?"

Together, in silence, they examined Miss Elliot's image; each trying to conjure the exact set of the Honourable Miss Finlay's gown, about her shoulders, in the candle-lit gloom of last week's concert room.

Nellie spoke. "Perhaps not, then."

And, by proving for some time a little problematical and then suddenly quite promising, and then again– not completely satisfactory– though yet showing *clear* signs of yielding, under truly *vigorous* attack– first the neckline, and then the bust, and the sleeves, too, drew Elizabeth back to happiness.

Or to the best approximation of it that an unmarried Regency lady of nine-and-twenty, with Sir Walter's Baronetage to live up to, and only ten thousand pounds to achieve it on, will feel as happiness: that is, to hope. Once more, it begins to seems probable– to seem almost certain– that, any day now, Miss Elliot will drift elegantly through a crowded room in a beautifully-cut gown (this very gown perhaps– perhaps the gown is already manifest!), buoyant on wafts of admiration... and the crowd parts and there, bowing before her, will be...

Lord, thought Nellie to herself, gazing up at the ceiling of the second-best spare bedroom. Poor old vestal, in her hopeful dress. At least if you've *been* married, nobody can divert themselves by reading, into your best ballroom smiles and civilities, all this. (And then glance at each other— as it is done, over the shoulders of crêpey-armed virgins still presenting in freshest muslin, 'never say die, dear!'— and share a smirk.)

Rain sighed against the windowpanes. How lovely and quiet it is, in rich people's houses.

... and you know, the first years of marriage— the first three– two or three — had been happy... quite often... there had been happy times.

Heavens— She could remember being blissful!

And happy, yes, too.

And Nellie had at that stage seen her husband a lot, for a sailor's wife. Three, even four times each year. For as much as ten days at a stretch. It had been enough, each time, to convince her that she had not imagined his perfections: just enough, and no more.

Certainly, he had always spent every night beyond the first surrounded by a crowd of ever-changing friends, all of them thoroughly lit-up; certainly, each time, he had cleaned out her little store of savings, a few months' worth of feminine economies. After his departure, up until the next half-day, it had always been rather nerve-racking, financially.

But what can you expect? They were just glad to be alive.

Personally triumphant, in the way of young men after danger, at being, themselves, still alive.

And you were so glad, too. There they were!– and still with all their arms and legs and eyes and so on. Of course shore leave was one long party. It ought to be.

Chapter 13

Nellie had not, she hoped, been too understanding— and yet, apparently Elizabeth had understood. Understood, and reflected: and perhaps even made some resolutions.

For she came down to breakfast next morning with a thoughtful air, and her behaviour from that point changed distinctly.

Pettishness diminished. The frequency with which Nellie was plucked from her work, or her book, or the instrument, to do, for Miss Elliot— nothing in particular— a small nothing-in-particular, rich in potential humiliation to someone less determinedly agreeable than Mrs Clay— it diminished; and then, allowing for a few unavoidable outbreaks, it even ceased. Silence and sighs there were still; but these were cut short, now, by conversation from Miss Elliot herself; or reflections, in Miss Elliot's clear tones, on some recent diversion provided by their Bath acquaintance, their Bath activities.

Towards her father, too, Elizabeth became positively attentive. Sir Elliot's own silences, and quarter hours of vacancy, and vague heaviness, and half-formed musings on Bath, and Kellynch, and the differences between their life *there*, and their life *here*, were increasingly interrupted by bright suggestions for a walk, or a visit to the library, or... cards?

Also— and now that the role of housekeeper was passed on to a professional— Elizabeth declared an intention to learn to sing, and Mrs Clay found a new occupation in training her voice. Nellie had always loved teaching. She found that she still did. Elizabeth's voice improved almost by the day, which is not uncommon in the early stages but nevertheless was very cheering for everyone, and it became a Camden Place project; the development, the unfolding, of Miss Elliot's voice. Sir Walter declared himself in a state of high enjoyment as he listened to their warblings in the drawing-room, and Elizabeth's hours of private practice began to give Mrs Clay some respite from the business of being her companion.

Most astonishing of all, Elizabeth coped with the revelation of Nellie's own voice with almost no detectable resentment. Only a week into the lessons — on yet another grey Bath morning, which Nellie had spent feeling her way through a number of new pieces that might be suitable for Miss Elliot— she had looked up from the piano to find her patroness standing silently by the door, stilled by nothing less than the *sotto voce* singing of Nellie herself.

"Goodness, Penelope. I'm not surprised you could teach singing", was all Elizabeth said; but she said it with no more than a hint of curtness.

And two days later, she added– "Penelope, you do sing very beautifully".

I wish I could also say that Miss Elliot henceforth took the opportunity to bring her friend forward, and display *her* talents, too, at those regular semi-public performances that were the drawing-room entertainment of so many evenings— but no: Elizabeth's heroism did not reach to this. Nellie's own singing remained tactfully in the background.

Still, Elizabeth knew that Mrs Clay's voice outshone her own as a lamp is outshone by sunlight; and she, Miss Elliot, knew that Mrs Clay knew this; knew, furthermore, that Mrs Clay knew that Miss Elliot knew this; and yet, Miss Elliot harboured no serious ill-feeling. It was a substantial change.

Elizabeth, in short, consciously set herself to make the best of things in Bath. And as Elizabeth's sensations and desires must always sway any establishment she graces, her efforts very soon came to infuse everyone, from Sir Walter to the scullery maid, with the conviction that number 10, Camden Place, was the nascent hub of Bath fashion— and that for Miss Elliot herself, a Lord was just a matter of time.

It was with a little jolt of apprehension, then, that Nellie, noting the day of the month on her latest letter home, perceived that mere weeks remained between their growing good cheer, and the cool eye of Miss Anne.

All this time, Anne Elliot has been back in the country. There was some complicated arrangement by which she bestowed herself, now upon Lady Russell, now upon some cousins— a little distance from Kellynch, there were whole litters of cousins, of different sorts, and degrees, and Miss Anne was forever staying with them.

The New Year, though, always brought Lady Russell to Bath. This time, her carriage would also bring Anne Elliot to Bath. It would deposit Miss Anne at the door of 10, Camden Place; and then, it would drive off.

And Lord, how long before that same carriage— or any carriage, God love us— came to take the sourpuss away again? Nellie counted on her fingers: five months; four, at best; oh *Lord*, thought Nellie again. Just when everything was starting to shape up really quite well! Poor Elizabeth. Poor old Sir Walter.

Chapter 14

In the intervening weeks, however, the Camden Place project for heightened good cheer and self-consequence got a boost from a source which no-one, within its walls, could possibly have foreseen. An unlikely source indeed: and at first intimation it appeared, to our trio, as more likely to be a lien on their little hoard of good spirits.

They had been out all morning; out, not merely at, but *in* the Baths (oh *come* on Papa, *do* let's try it, Mrs Coussins went and she tells *such* tales!)... so they were all in excellent spirits when they tumbled through the front door, gasping and giggling at the macabre indignities they had seen and endured!—

— and awaiting them, engraved upon an ivory card, in script at once striking and discreet, was a single name:

William Walter Elliot, Esq.

The heir presumptive.

The future Baronet of Kellynch Hall.

The man who could, on Sir Walter's death, turn Miss Elliot out of doors — aye, and Miss Anne too— with only a shabby twenty thousand pounds between them.

Sir Walter and Elizabeth had fallen silent; drawn close. They were staring at the card as if hypnotised.

Then Sir Walter reached out and touched his daughter's shoulder.

I would like to prolong the mystery at this point, in the interest of suspense: but it is of no use concealing from the reader— from any reader worth the name— indeed, from anyone with the slightest acquaintance with English literature— that Sir Walter and Miss Elliot had had previous passage of arms with this young Mr Elliot. That Elizabeth had 'liked the man for himself, and still more for being her father's heir', as Miss Austen cattily puts it. Which is to say:– Elizabeth, at just sixteen years old, embarked, alone, on her first season in London, had there met young Mr Elliot; and had fallen resoundingly in love.

She had never seen a man to equal him since.

This, in spite of his having spoken slightingly of them all: of her father, of Kellynch, of herself; in spite of his well-known *bon mot* (made in strictest confidence, to a close mutual friend), to the effect that he, Mr Elliot, *would* have married Elizabeth, if he could have taken with her a fifty-thousand-pound dowry in lieu of Elizabeth's already famously-beautiful nose. In spite of the image which had then begun to haunt Elizabeth, and still did, of herself in bridal dress with a great ragged hole in the middle of her face, like the syphilitic beggars which no lady could completely avoid seeing on the streets of London... in spite of all this, Elizabeth's heart was still, twelve years later, a slave to her cousin.

Mrs Clay knew none of this. Nor did almost anyone else. Even Austen seems to have largely overlooked it— and I do suspect, dear reader, that you have done the same.

I wish, too, that I could say this near-universal ignorance arose merely from the servants of the London house being mostly hired on the spot, and Elizabeth's maid in any case leaving at the end of the relevant seasons to marry the London butler. (When the chief gossips, in that teeming city, considered Miss Elliot of Kellynch Hall, Somerset, they soon established the routine of scrutinising her figure and dress and air of self-consequence, and her paltry ten thousand, and then, of reassuring themselves by laughing amongst themselves at the contrast. Had she but known it at sixteen, she was lucky to be thus determinedly dismissed. Without a socially-canny adult to work the sidelines for her at balls, silencing disparagement with an icy presence, things could have been a lot worse: the child was offensively beautiful, and they had to get back at her somehow.)

In truth, though, Elizabeth's brief season of hopeful love for her cousin had been founded upon so very little— a dinner or two, a few chance meetings in the public London haunts— and had been, at each meeting, so comprehensively unrequited, that, at the time, there were really no grounds on which suspicion might have been built.

Only papa knew. Dear papa. Who had shared her hopes for Mr Elliot, she now realised; though she'd never said anything to him, and she knew he would never say anything to her. Bless him.

And, Anne.

Anne, then at school.

Anne, to whom the sixteen- and seventeen-year-old Elizabeth had poured out her feelings in a series of utterly humiliating, utterly self-revelatory letters. Even now, a woman of twenty-nine, Elizabeth writhed when she remembered those stupid, stupid letters. Compared to her– to Elizabeth– Anne's little fling with that naval captain, a few years later, had been a model of good taste. *That* romance had come to nothing, too; but it had done so rationally, elegantly, and very very quietly.

Also: however much Anne liked to moon about Kellynch mourning her lost love and so on, the truth is, *she'd* rejected *him*. Nobody, thought Elizabeth bitterly, could say that the perfect little Anne had made a fool of herself.

Nobody ever said, of course, that Elizabeth had. But if they'd known, they would have.

Because she had.

And of course, Anne didn't say a word because she didn't need to. Mamma's pet.

There had been, as they now say, a lot of water under the bridge since then, and Elizabeth, by dint of constant practice, had learnt not to think about Mr Elliot that much.

Instead, she'd gone on to turn down a string of perfectly satisfactory offers; and then, in her twenties, she had perfected a technique of haughty flirtation that forestalled any others. A certain kind of man loves to worship an unavailable woman, extravagantly, but from a distance: Elizabeth liked to have such there, at that distance, worshipping. For the man it is proof, where proof might otherwise be lacking, of his masculine susceptibility: for Elizabeth, it daily reaffirmed her worthiness for the man who must, eventually, come for her.

It enabled her, in other words, to dream on.

At times she could see him quite clearly, that future groom of hers. He was going to be a sort of super-Elliot; very like the original in looks and manner, and breeding, and wealth too (for the middle-aged young Mr Elliot was now, by means of an early and fantastically fortunate marriage, and an even more fantastic recent widowing, very wealthy indeed) — very like him, yes, but— much, much more so.

Oh, incomparably more so!

So much more so, on every score, that the original rough sketch, gazing up at the couple as they knelt at the altar, would look at the man beside Elizabeth and swallow nervously.

Would look, too, at her— at Miss Elizabeth Elliot, radiant in young love, the object of superElliot's open adoration— and choke again; this time with envy.

It is a strange thing, but Elizabeth saw Mr Elliot at her wedding with greater clarity than she saw anyone else, even herself. She dwelled at length, in her wedding plans, on that vividly-remembered countenance- ran it through all the possible contortions significant of torment, and yearning, and loss. If Anne had loved in solitary hopelessness for nearly eight years, consider this: Elizabeth had loved, or something of the sort, with an equal fervour, and a more than equal hopelessness, for all of those eight years, and five more besides.

This, too, with a sense of humiliation that Anne never endured. Though— why should Elizabeth, why *did* Elizabeth feel, that her cousin had degraded her a second time, through his disgraceful marriage? It was he, married to that disgusting vulgar woman, who was degraded! Did he but realise it.

Yet he didn't seem to. Not a bit.

And after a certain amount of delighted gossip, neither, it seemed, did any-one else. More time, and Mr Elliot and his beautiful, vulgar wife became rather the thing, in a certain set. (Not the Elliots' set, of course: Brighton; places like that.) So no; no shame attached to him. Or to his wife. (*To them*).

The shame had somehow, mysteriously, fastened itself wholly upon the palsied heart of Elizabeth Elliot.

Chapter 15

In the face of all this, it is understandable that Austen does not even attempt to record the first meeting between Elizabeth, Sir Walter, and the middle-aged young Mr Elliot.

How to reconcile them convincingly puzzles me too. That remark— and though Austen was too discreet to repeat it, she must have known of it— that remark about the nose was really unforgivable. Yes, Elizabeth and her father have, after intense (though barely-voiced) discussion, agreed to admit him; but now, on a wet December evening, gloomy as only Bath can be, as the middle-aged Mr Elliot himself emerges from behind the butler and the footboy, who are moving to solemnly bracket him, there in the arch of the drawing-room door of 10, Camden Place; as the two Elliots currently in possession, both standing, braced, themselves bracketing the fireplace which is filled with a fresh inferno-let, turn to face him— as Mr Elliot, now, begins to advance, across the polished floor—its double length (that Miss Anne will, in a couple of weeks, lift her eyebrows at and sigh over) seeming quite, quite wide enough, to everyone here, at their various posts about the room, as his footsteps echo at painful, almost ridiculous length across it— now, as he tries to vary and to distract from that semi-ridiculous slow, clear, light, click, by including a tiny opening of his arms towards them as part of his smiling advance— now— Elizabeth's hand moves unbidden to her nose; and Mr Elliot, while gazing frankly into her eyes and softly smiling, curses, internally, that one about the nose and the fifty thousand quid.

Though it had been bloody funny at the time.

Twelve *years* ago! Nearly twelve years ago. How on earth could he have predicted, back then, that twelve years later he would, once more, be approaching– and yes, he is still approaching– these two again, across this not-quite-the-best drawing-room in Bath; assessing their faces, their stance, their dress, none of it anything near as glossy, he noted, as it had been back in '03– more jowls on the old man– Miss had a little pouch that appeared on either side of her mouth when she allowed her chin to drop, as she had now — her hand was still up at her nose.

"Miss Elliot, Sir Walter— We meet at last! I feel as the salmon must feel when, after struggling against a thousand miles of rushing, contrary cascades in all the wilds of the mighty American rivers, it finally reaches that heavenly spot which, for so many wandering years, has been its goal!" Coming at last within hands-grasp of them at the close of this peroration — which had taken an awkward half-second less than the remaining stretch of floor required of it — he tenderly enveloped the hand that Miss Elliot had held out towards him (as much in instinct to hold him off as anything else: there had been a flash of, perhaps, terror in her eyes), and bowing low to meet it, he lifted it gently to his lips. "A thousand thanks for your condescension in allowing me to meet you again! Sir Walter!"— he turned to Sir, and after giving it two and a half beats, burst forth, with an unmasterable spontaneity–

"— Come!—Let us shake hands!"

And while Sir Walter's own mind was still darting about after the scattered fragments of his own little piece of theatre, he somehow found his hand enclosed– found that he had held it out to Mr Elliot, in what must have been a manner as open and liberal as Mr Elliot's own, for Mr Elliot was thanking him warmly for just this, as they shook hands for the first time in twelve years — "Such openness, such liberality! I know not the offence that for so long has necessitated you keeping me at arms' length– but when I heard that you were in Bath, Sir, I determined that, whatever my folly *was* or *had been*, I would cast myself upon your mercy and beg the opportunity to expiate my wrong-doing! The timidity of youth, that feels itself condemned by the head of his ancient and noble house; feels himself, as I have felt myself, cast off for– I knew not what–! — well, it has its rightful place–" (he extended both his arms some 40 degrees out from his side, then let them fall; now he placed his right hand upon the centre of his chest as he continued) — "who was I? a youth of scarcely twenty summers! to question the head of that ancient and noble house? (loosen the hands...) — to demand an *accounting!* (let them move a little forward in a gesture of helplessness...) — for such as I, to demand explanation from *you*... (and now fully throw them forward...) Sir, was an impertinence which I could not approach (let them fall to the sides), feeling as I did — *and do!*— that the House of Elliot owes that favour to no man! Let alone to myself — young and untried as I was then!

"...Yet in those long and may I say dark twelve years, while I have waited — hoped (clench the fists, etc etc— oh you get the picture)— I heard on all sides, wherever company of distinction gathered– congratulations would flow in on me for my connection with you, with one ever held forth as a model of liberal, generous conduct, as much as a model of good breeding.

"You can imagine how this worked upon my feelings! That such a man should no longer wish to communicate with the young scion of his House, was proof indeed of how grievous my unknown fault must be: yet still those very qualities of openness and liberality, each time I heard them praised, led me to ask— 'cannot *I*, then, cast myself upon this bountiful magnanimity, and beg an explanation— or rather, beg *the opportunity to explain myself,* in whatever my fault may have been?'

"And now, you see, Sir Walter, Miss Elliot— that hope has triumphed over fear, and– well— here I am!" (Smile.) "Trembling at my reception; yet heartened already, heartened! may I say, by the open countenances I see gazing benignly upon such a prodigal as I, all confounded, yet feel myself to be! I beg you, Sir Walter, to let me know in what way I have offended you for so long, to let me know why I have deserved to be cast off (for surely I *have* deserved it; your character speaks its own probity; the fault *must* be mine)— let me know, and let me, at last, make amends."

This was going at it pretty hard, and also laying it on pretty thick. Moreover— and although the evidence of contemporary novels shows that in the past, people didn't hesitate to talk uninterrupted for a chapter at a stretch — in actual articulation this speech of Mr Elliot's, at a page and a bit, felt, even to him, like pushing it.

You may be sure, though, that he had at least blocked out and run through a variety of other approaches, as well as the one where he acts as though there never had been a problem– outside his interlocutors' own silly heads– his perennial favourite with people who could fancy themselves slighted by him — This time, however, he judged that the Elliots could perhaps call to mind too many individual instances of rudeness, and neglect ,to allow of sweeping the lot under a carpet of breezy assurance. His judgement, then, as well as his own impatient character, led him to resolve upon the frontal assault you see here.

*

Did it work?

Of course it did.

Or should I not rather say: Success crowned his endeavours!— in a way that brought to mind that fellow Bonaparte's coronation at *Notre Dame de Paris*. That was how his friend Colonel Wallis put it to him, later that evening, as they drank Mr Elliot's triumph in the Colonel's best Madeira; Mr Elliot always drank the Colonel's best Madeira.

They drank quite a lot of it, that celebratory night, and they talked late: of Sir and of Miss ("Lord, Wallis, if you can echo that stuff about her being the new beauty of Bath, you need another trip abroad"); of Mrs Clay ("tasty, yes; but hardly 'handsome' as I use the word 'handsome', Wallis'"); of Mr Elliot's past successes and future triumphs, of heirs and inheritances, cabbages and kings... and when the Colonel's conversation, dazed by fumes of Madeira, eventually wandered off to his wife's condition, and their own imminent hopes for an heir to the Wallis fortune, and how much he loved the gel dammit, and after all it was her first, and who could know, one never knew, they were just dead in an instant, just gone— his darling Fanny... Mr Elliot, who in spite of having downed a great deal more of the excellent wine was not nearly so drunk as his friend, lay back and, gazing into the fire, fell to arranging in it little scenes illustrative of the future of himself and his friends at Camden Place.

Elizabeth's beauty was still considerable, and the fever of admiration into which she threw so much of Bath gave it still greater *cachet*. Perhaps he would take her, after all; launch out upon the role of Baronet at once. In the flames he saw himself installed at Kellynch: riding out, surveying farms and farmland; giving orders to the steward; Sir Walter deferring to him from a corner by the fire... Very nice.

Yes and opening balls in the ancient Baronial Hall!– Elizabeth shining on his arm— while a long line of ladies of his acquaintance, assembling below them in the dance, bit their lips until the blood came: another delightful scene!

But then... He glanced from the London harpies to his chosen wife's triumphant face... Elizabeth's looks, though striking, were of the old-fashioned sort. One was a little tired of the eighteenth century, wasn't one? All that feminine expertise.

Besides, Elizabeth had imposed upon him. This evening she had clutched at her nose, averted her eyes; necessitated him dancing an extra little dance of conciliation, especially for her.

And this, not once only, but several times throughout the visit. It seemed that practically anything one said reminded the damned woman of either noses or dowries.

Once married, things of that nature could be corrected: nevertheless when Mr Elliot, gazing into the fire at Marlborough Buildings, sipping the Madeira, recalled how importunately he had been forced to pay this evening for his spontaneous little witticism of 1803 (*et passim*), ire could not but rise in him—

— and the scene in the Kellynch ballroom gave way to that of the altar of– what was that lovely cathedral Montford had been married in?– where he stood watching some bride— gentle this time, pious, delicate... you know— all the new stuff... treading shying up the aisle towards him.

Flanked by a positive hydra-bed of jealous eyes of all sexes! Oh ha ha and yes!– Miss Elliot, prominent, right at the front, decani side! Yes yes, sulky mouth trembling, countenance projecting poison at the slim, veiled figure of his bride...

And, trailing behind the slim veiled figure; buckets of money?

Or perhaps— he shifted slightly in his chair— with no money at all! How would that look?

I mean it had been charming, and of course necessary, to marry such an amount of it in his first wife; but once it was in the bag, her remaining assets had been almost solely revolutionary.

Revolution had been very fashionable at the time. After all, it had looked, for years there, as if Bonaparte— prevailing as he did everywhere upon the Continent— would eventually prevail here too. So in many circles the new Mrs Elliot, handsome and vulgar, with her grazier father, her butcher grandfather, had been quite the thing. Quite one of *les marveillueses*, as he liked to hear his friends say. Quite a force of nature, by God.

That was over now, of course. The moral style of England was changed.

It would a great deal more fitting, these days, for him to marry, quite simply, for love. *Coelebs in Search of a Wife.*

..."Yes, without a penny to her name!"

"And *he* has made her Lady Elliot!" Elegance, sweetness, delicacy, modesty: everyone talks of nothing else but Mr Elliot's choice! She quite worships him— oh yes!— they are so very much in love!... For some time he mused, studying himself in this new light.

It would be hilarious, of course, if he were to marry Mrs Clay.

Well she was penniless enough.

Quite pretty too.

Clever as well— That dress!

Yes: but the point is, one has had enough of clever women, in what is so nearly 1815. They should have the brains, by now, to hide it better.

A snort from old Wallis.

Asleep, against the wing of his chair, in an attitude that would leave him with a cricked neck in the morning. Must get Townsend to speak to him about that transfer. Before Wallis minor turns up— if he does turn up— and perhaps gets them messing about, re-ordering their affairs...

A sleepy servant has fed and stirred the fire, and in its reawakened flare Mr Elliot empties the last of the Madeira into his glass, drains it, and stands to go. Really, it is probably easiest to stick with the original plan.

Have Sir Walter marry Mrs Clay.

Given what they said of her in Plymouth, that would solve the whole thing.

*

Mrs Clay's musings, as she, too, stayed wakeful late into the night, were quite distinct. With what dread had she viewed Mr Elliot's visiting card!— and then, his second card. And then his third.

The person whom her hoped-for marriage to Sir Walter would seem most to threaten, she could not expect Mr Elliot to be anything but her enemy. Her father's information (her father always gathered information: it was a reflex) had been oddly conflicting; but at least some of it had suggested that Mr Elliot might do a good job of being her enemy, and so, back in the Kellynch days, the exact degree of his estrangement from the family had been a matter of much anxious calculation.

In Bath, though, Mrs Clay had forgotten to think of him.

Then— they had come home to find that bit of pasteboard, engraved with that name, lying in the middle of the salver in the hall; and over the coming days, as she listened to the fragmented conversations of Elizabeth and Sir Walter— and their silences too— in response to his series of cards; as she detected their inclination to give him the meeting increasing with each card left on them; so she had seemed to watch her own fortunes wane. It seemed impossible that this Mr Elliot could be as strangely blind, as easily, even gratefully deceived, as his two cousins! Should a meeting take place, she decided, her course must be to resume the subfusc skin which she had begun to shed so thankfully, and hope that he would, after one astonished stare, discount her altogether. If Miss Elliot had a plain and rather commonplace companion, what of it? Many pretty women liked a foil.

She had made her preparations accordingly, and made them well: surely no-one could say that Mrs Clay didn't know how to vanish from a room!– and without even leaving it. Yet in spite of her diligence, so great had been her dread that she had felt, as Mr Elliot was making that long, echoing progress across the drawing-room floor towards them, positively sick; positively faint.

And then, after all that, the man had been charming! No pretension, no reserve! No hint of suspicion. Every sign of taking her at face value: Miss Elliot's dull companion.

Perfectly the gentleman with it, too.

And that, very much in the new style, rather than the old; an extra few degrees' inclination of the head, if anything, for 'my companion, Mrs Clay', rather than the usual perfunctory nod.

Mr Elliot was quite of the new style altogether, in that plain, superbly-cut dark coat, his hair falling in rough, natural curves, innocent of powder or scent. Simple, full-length pantalons in modest black. All of it wordlessly, rue-fully deprecating Sir Walter's piled finery and tight stockings.

Intelligent, too, in his conversation! He was as urbane (allowing for the little differences of the English ways), as urbane as her old friend the Count. The obvious quickness of his perception had sometimes brought her father to mind, to a degree.

— Though, he had seemed genuinely struck by Miss Elliot.

Ah well. Men.

And then too, his manners were so well-bred.

Which is to say: who knows what he really thought of any of them.

    Elizabeth, now...

Interesting, that she, in particular, had seemed so shaken by the meeting. There was more here than met the eye, perhaps?... Elizabeth's determined silence on the topic of Mr Elliot began to take on a new complexion!

Which raised a charming possibility...

(It didn't do to anticipate) —

... but– still!...

... the charming prospect that— what with *Elizabeth* being single, and Mr Elliot being no longer a *husband*— well: why should not the two of them marry?

A baronet for Elizabeth! A whirlwind romance, a honeymoon on the con-tinent, a house in Mayfair; two birds with one stone.

And Sir Walter, then, left behind alone. Wandering, lonely as a smog-patch, along the streets of Bath...

Whence Nellie saw herself being ordered back, once more, herself; ordered back very soon. Urged, by the Dashe apothecary, to take the Bath waters again. For her health!

As she sketched out this pretty picture, in the darkness of her room, Nellie could not entirely repress a small, anticipatory, rather self-conscious, and to that degree guilty, smile.

*

And what of Elizabeth?

What were her feelings, that December night in Bath?– having stood face to face, after all this time, with the man who, thirteen years ago, had looked her up and down from the height of his twenty-three years, and his independence, and his place in the masculine world— and found her worth no more than a cruel and clever joke? For two centuries, the feelings Elizabeth harboured on this pivotal night have gone unrecorded.

Perhaps that is because they were, right now, so formless, so chaotic,indistinct.

After all, things had ended very badly for her last time.

Oh, certainly, all those intervening years of playing the field had bred in her a marble confidence that she could play her field. But the one time she had stretched out her hand towards love, that hand had been burnt to the bone. She could remember *that,* even if she could not reach to any further self-analysis.

So tonight, she did the best that someone of her caste of mind can do — which is, to continue strenuously not formulating, on the subject of Mr Elliot, any clear thoughts at all.

...and yet...

... if we look very, very closely into her mind tonight, we might glimpse, amidst the tumult of scenes half-formed and ever-dissolving, adrift in the whirling darkness— there!... You saw it?... — Somewhere in there, a Chagall-like bride is floating in the embrace of a shadowy groom.

And the groom, while still a superElliot in general form and air, has about him, tonight, a touch of the nutcracker; a touch of the underhung jaw that juts, more firmly than ever, from the middle-aged face of young Mr Elliot.

Poor Elizabeth.

Chapter 16

In the following fortnight, Mr Elliot called repeatedly at Camden Place. He dined with them once; and seemed gratefully aware of the distinction offered him, for in general the Elliots gave no dinners.

Bath life is also rich, however, in opportunities for chance encounters in public places, and the Elliots happened across their cousin almost every time they ventured out of doors. In one such meeting, in the Upper Rooms, they came upon him in close conversation with a military man of most gentleman-like appearance, whom he introduced to them as his most particular friend, Colonel Wallis. Mr Elliot subsequently gave them to understand that he felt himself to be under considerable obligation to Colonel Wallis; that Colonel Wallis had seen him— had seen Mr Elliot— recently— through some trying scenes, and difficult times. In such a manner, as to win to himself a deal— a *great* deal— of Mr Elliot's esteem. And gratitude.

This of course engendered in them all a host of good feeling towards Colonel Wallis, and a lively desire to get him alone and pump him about Mr Elliot. The chance of doing so presented itself promptly, at dinner with mutual acquaintance. Here Elizabeth and Mrs Clay found themselves, after a certain amount of breathless finessing (quite unnecessary, may I say), seated on either side of Colonel Wallis; and here, by the despatch of the last course, they had wrung from him more than they had dared to hope, regarding their prodigal's first love; one Miss Cork's famous passion for Mr Elliot, and his awakening, his responding... his burgeoning passion for her.

(Colonel Wallis had creased his brow at that point in his instructions. "Is that wise, do you think, Elliot?" But Mr Elliot— who knew quite well what he was about— had lifted his own brows at old Wallis. "Why not? Are you suggesting that I married my wife without feeling anything for her?" And Colonel Wallis, who could certainly comprehend anyone feeling all sorts of things for Mrs Elliot, of beloved memory, was silenced.)

So:- Mr Elliot's smouldering passion!- which had burned like wildfire in the first months of marriage (be clear about that, won't you, Wallis?) and then, slowly...cooled. Into hollow disappointment.

"Better not say exactly what about, when you come to that bit, old boy. If they ask, just look into your glass and remember that it's wrong to speak ill of a lady."

So Colonel Wallis did; and Elizabeth and Nellie felt rather, or very (respectively), conscious of having made a bit of a gaffe in having enquired in the first place— and then went on, as ladies will, to each reflect upon the possible, the plausible, the *probable* sources of poor Mr Elliot's mysterious disappointment; and then, to furnish the specifics of the case from their own imaginations, to the complete satisfaction of each.

And though their conjectures turned out to differ wildly (as they found on comparing them, with many giggles, later), still– each remained privately convinced of the accuracy of her own intuitions. The truth was written, after all, on Mr Elliot's pale low forehead; written clearly, for all who could look with the eyes of discernment; to look, and accordingly, to pity him.

Colonel Wallis, then, did Mr Elliot proud with the ladies. Next, on the departure of those ladies to the drawing-room and Speculation, and Sir Walter drawing near— ("Just sit tight, Wallis; and for God's sake don't ogle him like some tart hoping for business. Just stare into space and drink. Wait for him to come to you. He will." And he did. Elliot was bloody marvellous that way— how he does it, nobody knows— it's like he has a crystal ball) — on Sir Walter drawing near, and striking up a conversation, and leading that conversation around to Mr Elliot and his marriage, *just* as Elliot had predicted he would, such a fellow as he was— at this, Colonel Wallis had expiated to Sir Walter on the further charms of Miss Cork, these charms including (but not limited to) her gigantic, her really *enormous* dowry; that and her beauty, of course. She had been a stunner.

And to top it all off, absolutely besotted with his good friend Elliot. "Like a cat on hot bricks!"

Though— Elliot, God knows, had shown her no signs of favouring her above other women. In fact, from the first, he had tried to avoid her!

(Exclamations of disbelief, at this point, from his growing audience; and one slurred cry of "Tally ho, Miss Cork!")

"No— absolutely *shunned* her!"

Gave her reason to understand that, however poor his purse might be, his connexion with Sir Walter, of Kellynch Hall his future there, possible future, and thus, his responsibilities, in regard to that ancient family, gave him a right, and indeed a duty, to look quite a bit higher than a Miss Cork, dragging a trail of lucre— and that in any case he would not marry where he could not feel, and feel *strongly*. Begad!— (don't blame me. There really were people who said 'begad!' in 1815; otherwise why would Regency romances be so free with the word?), begad! (you see? he said it again) — he had led her a merry dance!

And then, in response to a question from the far end of the long, dim room (which had fallen quite silent by now, entranced by the fabulous tale of Mr Elliot's bride) Colonel Wallis had spoken the words: "Ninety-two thousand pounds."

All about the candlelit darkness, a sharp intake of breath.

Then, silence; while each man gazed— this one solemnly, that thoughtfully, another wistfully— into his wineglass; or drank of it deeply, according to his habits.

By God, Wallis.

Yes.

And this woman, *this* woman, had had to hunt Elliot— oh damme, yes! all over London!—and then, on through just about every drawing-room in the Home Counties!

"The poor creature didn't stand a chance."

Chapter 17

Poor, rich, handsome Mr Elliot: so romantic; so disappointed in love. Lured on, by that hussy, into a debasing union; and now by her abandoned. Abandoned, too, with no child to attach him once more to life, nor heir to bear his blood! Twelve years of tumultuous, tortured marriage; and of it, nothing left to him but ninety-two thousand pounds.

Could any woman hope, now, to step into the void in Mr Elliot's breast, and with the balm of true feminine friendship, lead him– slowly, gently– to understand that not all women were ill-bred designing trollops?– lead him back to hope– to life... to love?

It was an interesting question, and one which exercised the ladies of Camden Place a lot. They often discussed it at length together; and each reflected upon it often, at length, when alone.

They were nevertheless coming to different conclusions about the answer.

After two weeks of nameless agitation, Elizabeth finally acknowledged to herself– on the first day of 1815, as the bells rang out from the churches of Bath (it was a Sunday)– that the answer to this fascinating mystery was not only '*yes*', but that the woman destined to do all of it was, at last, herself.

It wasn't a self-delusion, this time. No. She wasn't so childish as to yield again to love before she'd been given good grounds to do so. This time, it was coming from Mr Elliot: matured, as he often hinted, by the years and by his suffering, he was showing intelligible signs of seeing his cousin Elizabeth in a clearer light. Universally courteous he was, yes: yet, her own hand received, when it lay in his on greeting and (especially) on departing, a certain soft, lingering pressure that she did not see him bestow upon anyone else. His eyes sought hers, a little more each day; and whenever she and he were, briefly, a little apart, those eyes looked into hers with a soft insistence which Miss Elliot– veteran of so many dinner parties, balls, so many scrimmages in so many primitive Regency conservatories– could by no means misinterpret.

Nellie had come to a similar conclusion as regards the resuscitability of Mr Elliot's heart. Only, Nellie could not repress a growing suspicion (incongenial though it might well be, to her own plans) that what Mr Elliot needed– what he *sought*– in his next wife, was an intellectual and a spiritual equal. The Mr Elliot of today, she tended to suspect, might well demand more from a wife, now, than mere position alone could offer. "No; nor grazier's fortune neither!"

Elizabeth was quick to agree. "Heavens, yes! Has he not shown, throughout his marriage, that fortune alone has no power to capture his heart?"

They smiled at the picture.

"—Still. No sensible man can be totally inattentive to breeding; that goes without saying."

"Of course not, Miss Elliot."

That would be too much to hope.

Nellie's judgement is unclouded, you see, by any particular attentions towards herself. Universally courteous Mr Elliot certainly was; even her own hand received, when it lay in his on greeting and (especially) on departing, a certain soft, lingering pressure... and his eyes, when they turned towards her, often held a quiet intensity which tended to rather thrill a woman. Nellie had not been thrilled, *really* thrilled, for at least half a decade— so on the occasions when she and he were, briefly, a little apart from the others, and those eyes gazed into hers with a soft insistence, it was really quite disarming. But one could see that he did it with everyone. Mr Elliot distinguished himself from the bulk of English gentlemen in this, too; this savouring, restrained yet keen, of the feminine in all women. It was another aspect of his near-Continental level of cultivation.

One was happy to leave it at that.

Though it grew on Nellie, that Mr Elliot was the first English gentleman she had met who was not, to some degree, a disappointment. He was the kind of man whom, as a young girl, she had always deep-down expected to meet one day. And now she was a mature woman and— here he was!— In England! Right here in this lovely drawing-room. Where the two of them were sitting, both at their ease, and beautifully dressed. And speaking so nicely.

Still. Happy to leave it at that. As I say.

Mrs Clay had no objection, though, to indulging Elizabeth's fancies when they began to show themselves. What with Mrs Elliot dead only six months, it would be next summer before the man's real feelings must be brought to the proof: there was no point, then, in making oneself unpopular now, by being niggardly with conspiratorial winks and smiles. As for Mr Elliot himself; of mature intelligence and self-command, and well past the age of youthful infatuation that had resulted in the first Mrs Elliot, one could have no fears for *him*. *He* would not be led on to feel more than was wise, or find himself beguiled, by anyone's old-fashioned wiles, into an unpropitious marriage. No indeed. Mr Elliot was more than capable of deciding for himself when and who he should marry. (Whom.) ('Deciding whom he should marry.')... in which, how unlike the rest of his kin; how unlike Elizabeth. Or Sir Walter! Dear old Sir Walter, who had told her that morning that her skin was as fresh as a girl of twenty's. He meant fewer freckles, of course, and had been attributing the miracle to the application of Gowland's, which he himself had recommended; had seemed so pleased with himself, the old stick, rabbiting on about it for a good ten minutes, all the while gazing at her complexion with a gratified and proprietorial interest— Mrs Clay (smiling and saying 'ah' intermittently) was sensible that her freckles had not at all diminished. These days, too, when she forgot herself so much as to smile openly, he didn't even quickly look away from her teeth and start talking about dentists. (Though his eyesight could well be deteriorating. He asked her to read things for him more and more often these days. Even letters of business. She could ask papa to tell his clerks to write with a larger hand, but that could only solve part of the problem. Should she persuade him to visit the spectacle-maker? — but no; of course not, Sir Walter in spectacles, what an idea. (Anyway no need, while she read things for him.)).... Yes — Yes, how unlike Mr Elliot: how unlike his nephew Sir Walter was!

Much easier to handle.

No-one, Nellie suddenly felt sure, would ever 'handle' the young Mr Elliot. The folly! — even, she obscurely felt, the peril — of attempting to work upon the judgement of such a man. She shuddered; though she could not have said why. For did a woman really want to be married to a man whom she could handle as briskly as an experienced housemaid tosses a bulky eiderdown?

(YES, you fool! Of COURSE. What are you thinking!?)

...and perhaps, after all, he really did favour Elizabeth. Simply as a woman, that is. Rather than as a soul.

Because when you think of it: how else to account for the amount of time he seemed eager to spend in her company?

*

A rift, in short — as yet, thinner than a hair; as yet, imperceptible — had sprung within that lute upon which the Camden Place trio had been making increasingly acceptable music over the past months.

Before it could make itself evident, however, a new and far more obvious disharmony announced itself. Miss Anne Elliot drove into Bath, to resume her place in her father's house, and darken the lives of all who lived in it.

VOLUME II

The Year (1807) a Lady's undress of Bum-be-seen.   The Year (1840) a Lady's full dress of Bombazeen

THE FASHIONS OF THE DAY or Time Past and Time Present.

Chapter 1

Anne Elliot arrived in Camden Place as the last icy trickle of the midwinter light was draining from its paving-stones. She had, no doubt, written to Elizabeth, giving her sister more than adequate notice of the day and hour of her arrival, together with a calculation of the margin of error for such things as the state of the roads, the condition of the horses, and her own tendency towards coach-sickness– but Elizabeth had mistaken the day— or had forgotten— she was not given to close reading of Anne's letters— and the household was as yet feeling no more than a vague apprehension. Mrs Clay had run up to the bedrooms on an errand for Miss Elliot, and had just regained the lower landing when that small, erect figure, dressed in shadows, whispered into the hall below.

Seized by instinct, Nellie found she'd frozen, clutching the newel post, hidden in the darkness, at the turn of the stair. Anne did not glance up. Hadn't heard. For once, the watcher was watched.

The new footboy, breathless with alarm, was struggling to trim into more respectable flame the solitary lamp with which her father's house welcomed Miss Anne. In its slow blossoming, Mrs Clay saw that Elizabeth's sister had improved in vigour and plumpness. She usually did, at Uppercross.

No but– improved quite strikingly, this time. Her face seemed different.

Pale, of course; sad.

But she also looked– that most important thing, at her sad age– almost youthful, there in the lamplight, waiting calmly for the servants to get it together. Her gaze was directed inward, it seemed; eyes wide and dark, and still— as if looking upon scenes of memory... In this dim, uncertain light, she could have been the heroine of a romance. About two-thirds of the way through; at the point where all seems lost.

The footboy was bearing away her travelling cloak; the butler, surreptitiously and with desperate haste buttoning his waistcoat (*he* wasn't counting on any change in Miss Anne) strode towards the drawing-room door— yet, still, Anne hesitated. Almost crouching behind the thin copse of bannisters, Mrs Clay saw her shoulders droop.

Across the marble floor, the echo of a sigh.

But the butler was at the drawing room door— a burst of light— Anne lifted her head with something like determination, and stepped forward, and out of sight.

*

Mrs Clay's own quiet entrance, a moment later, went unnoticed. Anne was by the fire. Miss Elliot stood to the right of her, relieving her of her bonnet: on her left, Sir Walter was enquiring after their shared acquaintance in

Kellynch. Each, father and daughter, wore an air of almost rigid embarrassment.

As the evening went on, Mrs Clay divined it to be the result of an unprecedented desire to make Anne feel that she was welcome! (They must have
talked it over it in private; just the two of them. When Mrs Clay was out some
time.) (That was quite understandable.)

As they had never made any effort before towards Anne, in all Mrs Clay's
experience of the family together at Kellynch, it was also understandable that
they should remind Nellie of a pair of stiff-stepping, determined late learners,
sticking it out through their first public performance of the minuet.

Anne, however, was able to respond to the oddity with all her usual self-ef-
facing confidence. The strong public light of the drawing-room revealed nothing, now, but her habitual expression of cool superiority. In her succinct
replies— and yet without approaching anything that could be called brusque,
or dismissive— she made it clear to Elizabeth and Sir Walter that they were
not being missed at home: not by their cousins in Uppercross, nor by their
dependants in Kellynch, nor by any of their neighbours, for a score of miles,
in any direction around it. "Oh, they all go on much as before", was her quiet
reply, repeated, with slight, polite variations, in response to their clumsily persistent questioning.

Even her journey from Kellynch to Bath had been "much as you would
expect".

"Ah yes at the time of year, eh? Dirty, I suppose?" Mm, yes. "And wet?"
Miss Anne inclined her head. "Horses tired towards the end, I suppose?" She
believed so. "Hard to get along eh, with tired horses. Makes the last part of a
journey the hardest to bear, eh?"

"Ah but 'to travel hopefully...', you know..." replied Anne (it sounded like a
quotation, somehow— though of whom?)— and that topic, too, seemed
closed.

A short pause succeeded it.

"*Well!*" exclaimed Elizabeth, jumping to her feet. "*Here* we are, sitting
about, and we haven't shown you the house! You'll *love* the house! We *adore*
the house, don't we papa?"

This was better: this was firmer ground. Elizabeth had traversed it many a
time with many new acquaintance, and a few old ones too, and none of them
had failed to be *charmed* by the house; *delighted;* even, in particularly gratifying
cases, *overwhelmed!*

How much more, then, might Anne be supposed to relish it! Each airy
room and nobly-proportioned window, each pretty table and tasteful drape of
fabric into which the ladies had put so much thought; each careful arrangement and rearrangement and *re*arrangement of pictures and ornaments,
presenting them to their best advantage: this delightful totality would now

reflect its radiance on the sister too; would form the domestic and the social setting, of comfort and elegance, in the midst of which Miss Anne would now live and move.

And as for society–! "We see more people in a *day*, Anne— visit, and are visited, more in a day than in a *month* at home, I declare!— why look at this card– and this one– and half the time I swear to you I don't even know who these people are!" Elizabeth tossed the handful of cards back into the salver and turned to face her sister with eyes bright and glowing cheeks: just at that moment, you could see that she, too, could have been a heroine, for a while, to someone. "*So* different from Kellynch!"

"Yes. Very different from Kellynch." And Anne sighed. It was one of those short, hard sighs, that are perilously close to a snort.

"I see that you live very differently here."

*

Dinner was awful.

Sir Walter did make one last venture. "Nice to have the table *balanced* again, eh?"

And in response to Miss Anne's quizzical gaze—

"Four around a table, don't you know? Eh?— Feels *right*, doesn't it?" He beamed about him hopefully.

Anne received his beams, in silence. Elizabeth's mouth twisted. Nellie made a particular effort to smile back at him warmly, and had the pleasure of receiving a more natural smile in return.

But Sir Walter, really, had had enough. He was defeated, already; and he felt himself to be defeated. For the remainder of the meal the conversation was carried entirely by Miss Elliot and Mrs Clay.

Elizabeth indeed became almost too talkative— accelerating, as the evening progressed, into a rattle that left little room for anyone else to speak, had they found anything to say— with a bright, hard edge to her voice, that spoke of hurt feelings beginning to find their usual refuge; in anger, and then, dismissive contempt. Oh dear. Oh dear oh dear.

And they had all been doing so well.

*

The evening took a turn, however, that Nellie had not foreseen.

In the drawing-room after dinner, she steered the conversation around to Mr Elliot. It would surely cheer them up, she felt. And with their cousin only two weeks in Bath himself, and Miss Anne fresh through the door, on this subject, at least, Anne surely could not exhibit her superior discernment.

Oh, the fascinating Mr Elliot!— It was indeed a topic that animated all three once more. As they rehearsed amongst themselves the details of this so tremendously satisfactory development in the life of Camden Place, everyone's spirits rose... "Could you have *seen*, Miss Anne, how *vigorously* Mr Elliot set about re-establishing the connection!– such decided persistence, such wholeheartedness!–"

Which had, slowly, persuaded Sir Walter (somewhat *against* his own judgement— *he* had felt no anxiety to meet the young man: felt no need of still more company than they already had, pressed upon them, in Bath; applications on all sides)—persuaded Sir Walter, at last, to give the young man audience: prove himself, you know.

"And then!– O Miss Anne, his *candour*, when all met!..."

"Oh indeed Penelope, yes Anne his *eagerness* to do away with all misunderstanding and restraint amongst us!"

To set them all on the footing of family intimacy, may Mrs Clay say... ?

— Quite!— as instanced by his flattering insistence on introducing, to Camden Place, those boyhood friends for whom he himself most cared; the anxiety, indeed, of those friends to meet the Elliots, "his *first and oldest* friends", as he had styled them, on introducing them to Colonel Wallis. So nicely put, Sir Walter felt...

And now– Mrs Clay prompted– his obvious delight in their company!

"Anne, you will find that we go everywhere, meet everywhere, with Mr Elliot. People begin to talk of him as part of our circle: people began to talk of "the Elliots" and to mean Mr Elliot, as well as ourselves."

"Such a handsome man, too", Nellie reminded them.

"Oh, absolutely!" chimed father and daughter as one; and laughed.

But it was not just the natural family prejudice, they assured each other, no mere blind partiality, such as one does tend to feel for those of one's own blood. No: they heard *that* on every side; praise of Mr Elliot's figure and face. Sir Walter waxed eloquent on this point, was generous, to a degree... and now they were romping freely, in familiar, happy territory; the Elliot looks. Almost, Anne was forgotten.

Nellie, though, was beginning to flag. It had been a stressful evening. There was still an hour at least before anyone but the traveller could decently leave the room, and...

– oh thank Heavens; a diversion. A knock at the door.

"Ten o'clock! Surely, Elizabeth, we cannot admit–"

"But Papa, who would call so late?"

"Who would *dare*", declared Mrs Clay, mustering a bright archness, "but a member of the *family*?" She saw Anne's nostril curl. Lord she was tired.

But it was he: it was Mr Elliot.

From the moment of his entrance, fatigue lifted from the room, the house, the street— the whole of Bath, probably, stirred, and felt its mind clear and its spirits lift... and Mrs Clay, suddenly light-headed with fatigue, was able to draw back at last, happy to be quiet, free to observe, with complacency, the harmonious family group developing before her.

Its centre was Mr Elliot. Supple figure, bright countenance; easy, complaisant air; all fresh from some stimulating engagement in the upper part of town. Now he was bending forward over Anne, now, throwing out an appeal to Elizabeth— here turning, with a half-laughing deference, to entreat Sir Walter's authority on some playful point of order or masculine right. Everyone was talking, the conversation bouncing about across and between them... it was quite an Elliot *mise-en-scène*! (Oh, she must remember to say that to Sir Walter... he'd like that... What was *mise-en-scène* in English?...)

And— Anne Elliot was charmed!

Not just when her penetrating intelligence had pierced to the core of this new element within her family circle, tested its consistency, and essayed its worth: hell, no. She was charmed from the first. Mr Elliot had been in the room but a breezy half-minute, they were still standing about, and Sir Walter had drawn Anne forward to make the introduction— and lo! Miss Anne was simpering and blushing like a maid with a new footman. Instantly, Mr Elliot had claimed a relationship– some acquaintance– leading her on to accounts, explanations, descriptions... and Anne's usually set face was softened. Her usual soft drawl picked up pace, to a lilt– smiles and chatter, exclamations and rising above it all now an absolute trill of laughter— from Miss Anne!... and Elizabeth quirked a smile, expressive of surprise and— goodness!— tolerant amusement, even— at her father.

Who beamed benevolently back, clueless as ever; ah, the domestic joys. Hearth and home, as... Plato... as the Ancients said...

Nellie's admiration of Mr Elliot had been growing, as we know; but watching Anne Elliot, too, being twisted deftly in, weft to his warp, she felt that she had never before done even half-justice to his abilities.

                                        *

Mind you, he had really been laying it on with a trowel.

Thus reflected Nellie, later that night, in the privacy of her room.

Goodness knows, one may safely suppose that a trowel is what it takes with Anne. For the Elliot women, the Elliots generally, an atmosphere of silent admiration only just sufficed for their comfort: to raise their spirits any higher, you had to really slather it on. Nellie had just never seen anyone slather it onto Miss Anne before, that's all... Anne had been describing something, some accident, that had befallen a young Musgrove on a recent pleasure-trip to Lyme— and Mr Elliot's face, and gesture, and manner as he listened, could have formed the study for a stage-book exemplification of 'Compassion'. His questions, so insistent! his concern for Anne's sensations on the occasion, so feelingly expressed! You'd have thought he had the interest and rights of a Lady Russell. It was—

...well I suppose it is charming, really?

To assume the rights of an old friend like that?

Because after all, they were all cousins— second cousins or— something. Perhaps this was what the really well-bred English did.

Mrs Clay had followed Elizabeth into some reasonably good English society in the past few months, and yet, she had seen nothing like this.

Still. Mr Elliot's assurance, his graceful assurance, carried its own warrant for the correctness of his behaviour.

And Miss Anne had smiled. Miss Anne had *laughed*— Oh!— Who could have supposed it possible, that Anne's first evening at Camden Place could have passed so well!

Chapter 2

But where was Nellie wandering, allowing herself to be distracted all night by the gifts of Mr Elliot? Miss Anne's arrival in Camden Place signalled a new crisis in her own affairs. Mrs Clay must act!— and act swiftly.

Anne had been installed in the best spare bedroom, kept vacant all this time especially against this day. Nobody could see any impropriety *here,* then: nobody could fancy slights, on self or on dear young friends, as far as accommodation went.

Nevertheless, now was the time when a visitor, having been as useful as possible for a full and rather extraordinary four months, would be expected to retire— leaving the sister, the genuine family article, to assume her place by Miss Elliot's side on those walks to the library, Mollands, the Rooms. For this occasion, Mrs Clay had scripted and rehearsed her own little performance, by which she hoped to yet retain possession of the second-best spare bedroom. Its success would either open a new act for her, here in Camden Place, or see her exiting, downstage right, in the public coach.

*

Nellie felt more nervous this time around than she had on giving her first such little oration, shortly after shoe-horning Sir and Miss into their new quarters. Silly of her; because had not Miss Anne just reminded everyone, vividly, in the earlier part of last evening, exactly why her sister needed a friendly face about the place?... After the strains of last night, Nellie had been slow, and clumsy, on rising, and a sketchy review, while dressing, of main points and phrases, was all the preparation that Nellie could give to this, the second pseudo-valediction. Greek and Latin compounded, Nell, you pain me inexpressibly. Ersatz valediction, then, papa.

Factitious. Mock.

Simulated, specious, spurious.

Fraudulent. False— the white fichu for this, or the blue?

... Brummagen.

Meretricious crock of shit... O God. Was that a pimple starting? No, she was not worried, really, that was just... Again her father manifested somewhere behind her ear (her left ear, I am sorry to say, where your evil angel traditionally dwells)... "it always makes sense to be careful, and also to *display* care." Admiration is the unguent with which you pay your way with patrons. Your practical assistance is welcome, of course; a non-negotiable; but the sensation of your tongue gently caressing their arse at the end of a difficult day is what you're really for. Don't ever cut back on the saliva.

Yellow frills, then, or— ? no. It had been some time since Elizabeth had last shown satisfaction at the way her companion's little imperfections subtly set off her own superior grace, and two weeks back, when Nellie had entered the drawing-room tricked out for Mr Elliot's arrival, she had even protested at the reappearance of the frills. "Are you sure about those, Penelope?"

"Oh! but, Miss Elliot, I felt, that with your cousin arriving, I just looked at myself in the mirror and thought *oh* dear, this dress really is *too* Quakerish now that I've taken the frills off— and though my taste is all for plainness as you know—" (clean lines, sculpted into quiet elegance; which those little scribbles of yellow then artfully shattered); "well I thought; oh *dear* oh dear, I must not *embarrass* Miss Elliot by looking *too* much the Quakerish widow-companion!"

"But Penelope I cannot think yellow the best colour for you. It seems to me that it brings out your— it is not the best complement to your complexion. And most women, you know, must be very careful as to emphasising the wrist. Very few women can afford to do that; and you'll notice, if you really *look*, that when the frills are *this exact* length that you have here, it is not flattering at all in your case. I really think you would be wiser to take them off."

"Of course, Miss Elliot."

Just a slight tucking-up of this sleeve? maybe?— subtly exposing the wristbone? There.

A searching stare into the mirror.

Then she must slide it back down again, over the course of the day. I mean, here in Bath, the standards are much higher than in Somerset. To even slightly overdo the drabness, before Miss Elliot, could also be fatal.

Nellie sighed.

And braced herself, and turned towards the door.

*

She need not have worried. The ensuing performance had all its calculated effect and more; this, even though Nellie felt herself to be off-balance, and fudged one key phrase after another, extemporising, haltingly, instead, on how much she had enjoyed, experienced— ('widened my understanding so greatly dear Miss Elliot, never could I have *conceived...*' etc, was how it should have gone)... As Mrs Clay's little speech stumbled on, the faces of her audience developed into a picture of family dismay.

Hadn't they been expecting this? For goodness' sake?

"...and so, with Miss Anne here, I cannot suppose myself at all wanted..." Nellie stuttered to a halt–... but Elizabeth, all critical faculties suspended, seized Nellie's arm and almost shook it. "Indeed, I consider that *no* reason! She is *nothing* to me, compared to you!"

Oh the poor girl. Miss Elliot in Bath— like Miss Elliot in London, in Kellynch, in Uppercross, Miss Elliot anywhere— had no female friends. Men, of course: but men are not friends with women. Nellie placed her own hand– the free one, the one not getting a Chinese burn– on Elizabeth's, and felt her eyes begin to prickle— but thank God: Sir Walter had caught up with the action. He had a speech to make.

"My dear madam. This *Must Not Be...*" Nellie focussed on the reflections in the silver tea pot, and breathed, slowly, and deeply."...As yet, you— you have seen nothing of Bath! You have been here, only to be *useful*. You must *not* run away from us now. You must stay; stay to– yes, to be acquainted with Mrs Wallis. The beautiful Mrs Wallis!— for to your fine mind" (Nellie choked) "I well know, and how well I know it, the sight of beauty is a real gratification..." at which point a half-laugh, half-sob verily blatted out of Nellie, into the breakfast parlour, oh *no!*...— She ducked her head, turned her confused face away from their open and pleading ones– and there was Miss Anne. Poised in the door frame, motionless.

Suspense. Tableau.

How much had she heard?

All scrabbled through their scrambled wits, searching for what they might have said or not said about Miss Anne in the last two minutes.

Sir Walter, whose wits could be most expeditiously passed in review, was the first to recover.

"Ah. *Anne. Anne*, my dear. Do come in, and join us."

And time resumed its flow.

Chapter 3

Sadly, Mr Elliot could not drop in on them every evening: Anne's presence in Camden Place continued to make itself felt.

Nor was there only Anne to contend with. Lady Russell was now in Bath as well; Lady Russell who, whatever she might politely insist to both others and herself, was at bottom not at all fond of Elizabeth, and quite detested Mrs Clay.

Neither Elizabeth nor Nellie were early risers, and the very next morning, when, arm-in-arm and chattering noisily, they at last waltzed into the drawing-room, it was to find Lady Russell and her *protege* arrayed in full possession of the room. Anne was poised, her spine perfectly vertical, on the edge of the sopha into which Elizabeth and Nellie were expecting to fling themselves to plot the day's activities. In the neighbouring wing-chair Lady Russell had appropriated, to support her own irreproachable uprightness, the same fat cushions that our two friends liked to tuck about themselves late each night as they crowed, on that same sopha, over the day's successes, or bewailed its failures. The very furniture seemed astonished at its new occupants.

Though– of course– the light was best on that side of the room. Anne always had work in hand. She was always sewing; or writing, or reading; or tatting for the poor; and even now she lifted her head from — God knows where she had found it— they had certainly never left it in the sewing-box— some vast, charitable, calico object that she was hemming with rigid precision.

The two couples stared at each other.

"My dear Elizabeth. How delightful to see you."

Elizabeth should have spoken first. If the hostess is remiss, however, a visitor must bridge the gap as best she may: and Lady Russell swayed forward in the seated, dowager equivalent of a courtesy. "Mrs Clay."

"Lady Russell! What a pleasant surprise!" ('...*pleasant surprise*...' echoed Nellie, in weak parentheses.) "I– I should have waited on you today myself— we were about to leave for... for Rivers Street— were we not, Penelope–? But you have forestalled us! So pleasantly. Of course, you keep such early hours!"

"No, my dear. Not in Bath. In Bath, I keep town hours."

Anne smiled secretly into her calico.

"Ah. Well–"

— Elizabeth fidgeted a little—

" I am afraid Penelope and I tend to keep hours that not even *town* life can really excuse." She dropped herself down on the sopha nearest the door: it exhaled the slightest puff of dust. No-one had sat in it since it was placed there four months ago.

Nellie eased herself carefully into an adjoining chair. Collecting her wits—

and seeing with less than half a glance that Elizabeth was in no mood to fulfil her social duties– was, rather, all ready to plunge into a Kellynch-worthy sulk — Mrs Clay herself commenced the series of well-mannered enquiries as to neighbours, travel, lodging...

She became pleasantly aware, as her voice rang back to her in the silent room, that she was doing it all in excellent Bath style. In the face of Lady Russell's dismissive civility, she felt— *not* disoriented— but at first, a little resentful; and then, even, a growing amusement. A tone almost of condescension crept into the smooth flow of her voice as she recommended fresh-stocked drapers, recently-advertised lectures, musical performances current and forthcoming; meanwhile studying the comic effect of last year's lace on Lady Russell's shelf-like bosom. Fashions had changed enormously in the preceding months. These two had a lot of catching up to do.

"Thank you, Mrs Clay. Pleasant to find that the same concert halls are still open; that my customary shops, as you tell me, continue in business. And now I must leave you, I am afraid. Anne, my dear?"

Anne secured the hem of the calico marquee with a competent number of overstitches, folded it in a few swift movements, and placed it, soundlessly, in the sewing basket.

All stood.

"Anne and I have some shopping to do."

They certainly did. As Lady Russell and her young companion disposed their various accoutrements about themselves, Nellie pinched delicately at the lace of her own collar, and slid her eyes to Elizabeth — then rolled them at Lady Russell's dress.

There was a frozen moment.

Then the cold hauteur of Miss Elliot's Kellynch countenance melted — rippled. So sudden and acute was the giggle attack that Elizabeth was forced to wish good-day to her newly-arrived sister and their oldest family friend with her face buried in her handkerchief, and the drawing-room door had scarcely closed before the two friends had to spin about, charge to the far end of the room, and fling themselves face-down into the muffling still-warm cushions to laugh and laugh and laugh until their flushed cheeks were smudged with tears.

"...my customary shops...!" (What is so funny about that? I don't understand. But Elizabeth was laughing too hard to continue.)

"In Bath I keep— *town* hours!" ... and they were off again.

Shared mockery of others is a great cementer of friendships, isn't it.

Not the most durable friendships, perhaps: as a social glue, its hard, glossy surface belies its brittle composition. Nevertheless, laughing openly at last, like this, at Anne and at old Lady Russell, set the capstone on the alliance of Elizabeth and Mrs Clay; and for a while longer they went on very happily together.

Chapter 4

Secure afresh in her position, looking about her with new a degree of ease, Nellie began to perceive that even the grand Lady Russell could fall foul of little Miss Anne's exacting standards.

She first spotted it at the commencement of Camden Place's Campaigns of the Third Coalition. In those of the First Coalition– Camden Place versus Bath– Camden Place had long assumed the laurels. The Second still had Mr Elliot in the peculiar position of both ally and campaign object, but it certainly seemed to be going swimmingly. When it came to the third challenge before them, however, our seasoned campaigners felt a trepidation as great as ever: the territory was strange to them all; the opposing forces' strengths, unknown; the outcome, anybody's guess. Elizabeth and Nellie were giving it almost every waking moment.Lady Russell was in a tizzy, and so were all the servants. Sir Walter, in speaking of it, would slowly grow quite pale with his nervous excitement; it couldn't be good for him, and the ladies of the house even tried, sometimes, (though unsuccessfully of course), to interrupt him.

It all turned on the arrival, in Bath, of the Dowager Viscountess Lady Dalrymple, and her daughter, the Honourable Miss Carteret.

Now, Sir Walter's own grandmother had been a Dalrymple. A real Dalrymple; fifth of the first Viscount's ten daughters. So these Dalrymples — *bona fide* members of the peerage– and not even the bottom rung of it, neither– were also— oh! an almost agonisingly delightful circumstance— cousins of the Elliots.

The agony bit, was how to introduce themselves to her notice.

Sir Walter had once been in company with the late Viscount, but had never seen any of the rest of the family, and the difficulties of the case arose from there having been a suspension of all intercourse by letters of ceremony ever since the death of that said late Viscount— when, in consequence of a danger-ous illness of Sir Walter's at the same time, there had been an unlucky omis-sion at Kellynch; *no letter of condolence had been sent to Ireland!*...

... This much, Austen tells us: and one is left to infer that the omission stands testimony to the warmth of Lady Elliot's heart, the strength of her attachment to her husband, and her disregard for anything else during his time of danger.

Well I'm sorry, but it seems improbable.

We read that Lady Elliot, married to Sir Walter, was 'not the very happiest being in the world herself'; we see that when death approached she turned, not to her husband, but to her good friend Lady Russell for the continuance of the good principles and instruction which she had been anxiously giving her daughters; we cannot entirely avoid the suspicion that, as she did so, it was she herself who dismissed Sir Walter as *a conceited, silly father.*

She can deny it of course. Where are the quotation marks?

And she's right. Or more accurately— her position is unassailable. There's really no way anyone can be *completely* sure whether that incisive bit of nastiness about her husband was just narration, or whether it was in fact free indirect speech– where stretches of narration take on the voice of the character described, and the views expressed should therefore be ascribed, *not* to an Omniscient Narrator such as myself, on whom you can rely implicitly, but rather to that same fictional, fallible character. Austen's skill and inventiveness with free indirect speech is one of the ways she was a century or more ahead of her time.

One of the many ways. At the end of the 1900s, for the second time in two centuries, a taste for Austen began to adorn the minds of the cutting edge offashion (they mistook her for someone whom no-one had heard of)— and then, of the people who read reviews so that they know what to like— and then into films, and then, to television (abig step down, that one) and so on, through to people in shopping malls— which is always the death knell, isn't it, because who dares to share a taste with them?— and so then she must quietly be divined, among the truly hip, to be tiresome. And then there is a lull; and then the whole cycle begins again. But Austen remains as she ever was: infuriatingly, elusively brilliant.

I'm not saying she was nice; that's a completely different argument, which I'm not going to get involved in. But any writer of any ability, is... *exasperated...* by her ear for dialogue. And any reader with any knowledge of eighteenth- and nineteenth-century literature nods at once— and sighs, too— when someone-or-other says of Austen that she is 'a writer without forebears, and without descendants'.

Nevertheless, when it comes to free indirect speech:–as the Duke of Wellington remarked (and around this very time, although in his case not about the use of free indirect speech as such, so much as about the use of poison gas in warfare)— "*two can play at that game!*" Backed into a corner over a slanderous bit of free-indirect, a character can always shrug, and point the finger back at the narrator.

Which is exactly what Lady Elliot has always done.

Very successfully, on the whole.

And yet... and yet!...a lingering uncertainty, as to exactly how lovely the first Lady Elliot really *was,* has has occasionally tugged, here and there, at the mind of the odd solitary reader of Austen.

Now that all involved are beyond the reach of any hurt it might cause, I feel the time has come to reveal the truth. It is this:–

Even beneath the gauzy veil of infatuation under cover of which she had married him, Lady Elliot had always held, towards her husband, the attitude which one sees still, to this very day, amongst other women who on principle embrace a role of submission towards men.

Many of them are truly lovely, of course. You'll notice the odd one or two hundred million, though, who in the process of honouring and obeying their husband scrupulously, both in public and in private, and submitting unto him as the Church submits to unto Christ, with the imperishable beauty of a gentle and a quiet spirit, still enjoys a settled inner certainty, never articulated, that her own far greater...

... *well*...

(and highlighted, as it is, by the very fullness of her submission)

... cannot go unnoticed by those about her.

That people will come to say, often, amongst themselves, "Oh, he is nice enough. But really, what a pity *his wife* is not in charge! Of course, she wouldn't think of it (1 Corinthians 14:34). She is too good."

Much too good.[†]

So, no: Lady Elliot's well-regulated spirits, and her calmly remarkable organisational powers, were quite up to the task of scribbling a letter of condolence to Ireland, that long-ago morning when she saw, in her breakfast newspaper, the announcement of her husband's second cousin's death.

But Lady Elliot was feeling particularly tired of Sir Walter, that morning. We are told that his illness was dangerous: the danger was, above all, to his temper. Also, his monologues always lengthened in proportion to his discomfort. Furthermore, Lady Elliot had not set foot out of the house for a week; had scarcely left Sir Walter' apartment in all that time; had not so much as refreshed herself with Mrs Collier's respectful sympathy for almost a day.

It was too much.

She shook out the newspaper, and turned the page. The Bible tells us that the unbelieving husband is sanctified by the wife, and this is of great support to her mind as regards Sir Walter, of course– but—

Really! The best thing, for Walter, would be to dwell a little less on his position in this world, and a lot more on how he was likely to fare in the next.

*

The neglect, however, had been visited on the head of the sinner. When Lady Elliot died herself, no letter of condolence was received at Kellynch. Consequently, there was but too much reason to apprehend that the Dalrymples considered the relationship as closed.

And how to have this anxious business set to rights, and be admitted as

---

† But notice that she *could* think it, if she chose. When submission is no longer optional it loses these strange powers — a consideration never entertained by its earliest enthusiasts. Thus, by 1850, or perhaps 2050, a Lady Elliot has to get her kicks some other way.

cousins again, was the question which now exercised everyone in and about 10, Camden Place!

Everyone except, *évidemment*, Miss Anne. In spite of her ceaseless industry, the calico piano-cosy was still unfinished— or perhaps it was the next, in a series?— and, while the Elliot household hammered out its plans, Anne sat apart, as ever, beneath the light of the windows, and worked steadily on her hems. When Sir Walter and Mr Elliot pooled information on the Dowager Viscountess's known tastes and habits, Anne did not raise her head from her work: only, she ever-so-lightly compressed her lips. When Elizabeth and Nellie sighed in mock-despair over stories of the Dalrymple coterie of young, handsome Irish cadets (Lady Dalrymple was said to appreciate a fine leg– as who did not?), Anne's needle kept a steady tempo, even while her nostrils flared as if smelling something that should be, but was no longer, edible. But when Lady Russell spoke of 'regrettable fallings-away', Anne actually paused in her work, and lifted her level grey brows *one eighth of a contemptuous inch*.

Nellie was astonished.

— Oh! but who can be bothered with Anne at a time like this? A time when the Elliots might *finesse*, my God, a decisive leap, up, (up), and away— into the stratosphere of Bath society!

Instead of forever fighting off the attentions of strangers jostling to get their own great splay plebeian feet under the Elliot's drawing-room table. (All those dodgy cards, from people they had never even heard of. When they had first arrived it had been flattering, exciting— until they discovered that they had been doing the equivalent of taking Nigerian emails seriously. *"Dearly beloved Sir— "*)

All this is not to say that being Baronets isn't wonderful in its own right. It is. Baronets are the flower and crown of the gentry, and be the company Nelson himself (until the end of 1798), a Baronet walks in to dinner before him. But the Dalrymples are actual peers. Nobility. *Viscounts*.

And cousins, cousins– Oh God in His Heaven...!

It had to be a letter.

Everyone had suggestions: everyone had points, which they knew, with agonising certainly, must be made, in that letter— or the letter would fail. Nearly everyone, too, had thought of some telling turn of phrase which they felt would be particularly efficacious in reaching past Lady Dalrymple's social fortifications and touching her noble (yea, Viscountly) heart. The drawing-room was a storm of point and counterpoint as Elizabeth vehemently, Lady Russell deliberatingly, Mrs Clay anxiously proposed sentences and paragraphs, or even (in Mr Elliot's case) carelessly sketched out entire letters, off-the-cuff; really rather good ones.

Here, however, Sir Walter at last showed his strength. Through all their clamour he stood motionless, straddled before the fire. His hands remained locked behind his back. His gaze fixed, at times, upon the wall opposite, where the serried portraits of his forefathers stood reminders of his duty to the Elliot name (he had brought them along from Kellynch; no point in leaving them for the Crofts to goggle at): at other times, brow furrowed, he turned his eyes upon the floor and withdrew into himself; and then their voices flew about him as light as the cries of starlings while, within the tower of his soul, he meditated upon his path. He heard them all out; heard, without speech or — or other response. It was impressively atypical.

Then he lifted his head.

"I have determined that which I shall write."

And they fell silent.

With firm and measured tread, Sir Walter left the drawing-room. He entered the room they had designated the library.

They heard him call for a new pen.

And fresh ink.

And then, he sent out for a quire of paper better than anything the house had previously held. Then...

nothing. For thirty, then forty, then fifty, tense, ticking minutes: nothing.

Nellie wondered how his eyes were holding up.

When the hour chimed, she crept to the library door, and knocked, softly. "Sir Walter...? Can I help you at all?"

Another half-hour. Surely his eyes must be aching by now; the winter sun of Bath was scarcely a sun at all. She sent in a servant, with more candles.

After two hours, Sir Walter emerged, looking haggard: in his hand was what appeared to be an entire ream of paper. "Check that over for me, will you, Mrs Clay? Then write me out a fair copy." Eagerly she seized it — Elizabeth at her side, there in the corridor, they began at once to read — while Sir Walter, staggering slightly, trode the proud length of the hall to the drawing-room, and a brandy, and a sopha to lie down and drink it on.

The letter, considered as a composition, was more or less shite of course. Nevertheless, and long before she had reached its end, Nellie saw that it would do. She would fix the spelling, the grammar too (Ha!– these days she could mentally correct even Lady Russell, on occasion), and certain expressions would need to be smoothed– turns of phrase made a little more elegant, the tone lifted. And some two thirds of it cut. Then write it out in a really pretty hand; she could do all that.

The main thing was, it was an almost irrefusable grovel. Whatever Lady Dalrymple thought, or felt, or expected, or deplored, Sir Walter had also though of it and deplored it, too. He'd explained everything, apologised for everything, promised everything: he'd stopped every earth. When it came to stuff like this, thought Nellie, with a swelling heart, he was not nearly as brain-less as people thought.

Clutching the slippery pile, she entered the library, the air and chair of which were still pungent with the warmth of Sir Walter's labours, and began to transcribe.

Chapter 5

Never having been in contact with the nobility of these islands before, Nellie was at first obliged to acknowledge herself disappointed. In Lady Dalrymple she found no superiority of manner, accomplishment, or understanding; no knowledge of the world, nor even much interest in it; no cultivation of the mind to enhance or– let's be frank– counterbalance the rural Hibernian cultiv-ation of that lady's dress and deportment. And as for the daughter!— little Miss Carteret was so plain and so awkward that in truth she would never have been tolerated at Camden Place but for her birth.

Still: as those who would collect good company around them, they imme-diately began to deliver full value. Through the Dalrymple connection, the Elliots at once began enlarging their acquaintance among those with whom Nellie could most wish them to associate: the comfortably-moneyed, respect-able minor nobility and upper gentry; men and women neither too high in their rank to despise a baronetage, nor too well-off to discount the value of Kellynch and its rents.

Nor, indeed, too decayed to attend to matters of expense and economy. Sensibly attentive to them, on the whole, in a way that Nellie grew to hope might influence Sir Walter; might show him, by regular example, that a man could be of significance in this world, even merely with two new coats a year.

It was Elizabeth, though, of whom they were all most thinking.

Elizabeth.

Surely, *now*, in this widening, brightening social expanse, the beautiful Miss Elliot was destined, soon, to find...?

Let's hope so.

And the Dalrymples, in themselves, were— there is no other word for it— pleasant.

It was a calm sort of pleasantness, an undiscriminating acceptance of people as they chose to present themselves; a placidity, even, which usually found them, in any new place, quickly accumulating a tail of hangers-on: the Elliots, to their unspoken discomfiture, were not the only poor cousins in their train. But after all it was Bath, and the Dalrymples had only just arrived, and the Elliots at least found themselves pretty much at the head of the queue

— where, calmly and pleasantly, Lady Dalrymple seemed content to keep them.

*

Barely a fortnight later, and there was no longer a single morning on which Nellie and Elizabeth had to set about thinking of things to do. Getting Sir Walter out of the house was no difficulty now either. Every day brought him– brought them all– appointments to walk, to shop, to meet at concerts; even, once or twice, to drive to such surrounding attractions as are afforded by Bath in winter, and they formed many eager plans of doing more when the summer arrived.

The choice of men, too, had expanded wonderfully. At the moment Nellie's working list was topped by a red-letter three:

There was Mr X: allowing the income of Kellynch to be p, Mr X has $0.5p$.

There was Mr Y: only $0.2p$. However, Mr Y, God willing, would be a Baronet himself one day, at which he would rise to $0.45p$ — *and*, whoever he married would be called 'Lady Y'.

Then, there was Mr Z, currently at $0.3p$. He was only a remote prospect, Mrs Clay would have thought; perhaps a poor bet, too. The son of a Lord, yes, but, the second son. Though, the elder brother *was* rather sickly. But, Nellie felt, really not quite sickly enough: between chronic illness and its merciful release may stand the gulf of many decades. Though the brother *had* been ordered to take the waters. And the family *was* gathered about him, here in Bath... Plenty of other people, these days, were discovering the cadet Mr Z to be charming; far more charming than his manners might suggest. Miss Elliot sometimes wondered if she did, too.

She was still disinclined, though, to come to a firm conclusion. After all, these days, there was the rest of the alphabet to play with!

Furthermore, what of p itself? Mrs Clay's algebra may well shock us. Can we expect Elizabeth to marry an income less than her father's?

Well yes. I mean the others gaze; but they do not propose. This is the point.

See it from their perspective:–

Miss Elliot's dowry would add only three to five hundred pounds, annually, to a husband's income. To the men she liked to move amongst, this was smallish change, it was the income of one's student days. It went without saying, too, that Miss Elliot had no further expectations: everyone knew that the Kellynch estate was poised to leave debts, not inheritances. Granted, she was dazzlingly handsome still, especially by candlelight: nevertheless, she *was* nearly thirty. Apart from not being so squishably delicious any more herself, at nearly thirty, she might not even produce an heir.

Elizabeth really needed to lower her sights.

Yet, how to make the respectable Messieurs X, Y and Z palatable to her? Miss Elliot, of Kellynch Hall; whose tastes had long ago been formed upon the sweet expectation of something many times more splendid, and with a Baronetcy to boot. To end, after all, as a Mrs X, on contracted receipts...

Mrs Clay sighed. Could she, perhaps, persuade the poor girl to fall in love? It makes a seemly cover, for this frequently-humiliating business of relinquishing one's dreams. Many a dawning realisation of social insignificance, many a gut-wrenching drop in a girl's hopes, can be made acceptable to self, before all others, by simply falling hopelessly in love.

...But by now, the reader may be wondering about Mr Elliot. We seem to have lost sight of him over the last few chapters.

Elizabeth has not.

And yes: you are right. Mr Y bores Elizabeth, anyway– that stupid laugh. Mr X is just as bad. Mr Z has a certain *something* about him, at least. None of them, though, can hold a candle to her cousin. Her feelings are perfectly logical, her calculations unimpeachable: some 1.3 multiples of p; a future Baronet; her cousin: it stands to reason.

Besides. She's in love.

Nellie has not lost sight of Mr Elliot, either.

She finds, though, that the more she studies him, the less secure she is, as to her own judgement of the man. She only continues to feel— with increasing conviction, increasing diffidence— that there is so very much more to Mr Elliot than meets the eye. His bright exterior; those superb manners; his ready cheerfulness and his complaisance... yet, there remains something further, too. How to put it? (Nellie has been wondering, increasingly, just how to put it...) Oh... he is a man with a great deal of private, inner life. This is what Nellie now feels.

For most of Mr Elliot's relations at Camden Place, the inner life is those inchoate discontentednesses which bubble up when one has had, say, a morning without visitors. Nellie is aware that she, and she alone, has noticed that Mr Elliot is a thinking man; a watchful man.

If one could share his thoughts; how interesting that would be.

Lady Russell shared at least some of his thoughts.

And how, by the way, did Lady Russell score that? She was fifty if she was a day, and as far as Mrs Clay could determine, had enough only to keep her carriage and rent in Rivers Street each winter.

Yet there they sit, those two, in a quiet island of privacy amidst the throng here today in Laura Place: Lady Russell solemnly perpendicular, Mr Elliot loose, easy, yet poised, gazing at her with a quiet intensity. They were talking, Mrs Clay detected, of the Elliot girls: Elizabeth, Mary; Anne... Of family, and family life; of the duty of children to their elders — yes, and of their elders to the young!— Mr Elliot, softly and soberly insistent, was not afraid of taking a stand here!... From these particulars, the conversation segues to wider questions: the duty of each of us to God; and thence, that of man to man and—

— but the delicate murmur is lost under a burst of hooting.

It is Mr Y.

At the card table. Losing, with his usual gormless volubility, to a genuine actual Baron. Elizabeth sits among the men, her fair shoulder turned to Mr Y, and her smile, Nellie is sorry to see, to the Baron: the Baron is flirtatious and shrewd and quite out of the question– *when* will the girl learn?

Mr Y has offered another remark. Now he brays again, a little less freely this time; he is looking hopefully at Elizabeth's averted cheekbone. Oh, he would be a push-over! A bit of a– (the justness of the comparison would be lost on him, but not on us)– a bit of a Bertie Wooster; foolish and functionless, pleasant and presentable; presentable enough, anyway, when not unmanned by the warmth of Miss Elliot's bare skin just inches from his own. All Nellie's short-list were presentable enough. A perfectly good prospect. Yet still, Elizabeth's smile was all for the Baron, nearly: a little of it, as always, kept for someone just out of sight.

... Mr Elliot had altered his position a touch, and now she could hear his voice more clearly. He had moved on to... yes... to the duty, yes, of man to man– *as mediated*, necessarily, by the paramount duty of Man to his Maker– Oh dear! Alone on the sopha behind them, Nellie sighed; laughed at herself; blushed, and shook her head. Nothing like these topics had formed any part of her vulgar English experience, nor yet of her formal French education–

"Come now, Mrs Clay. We must not have you sitting neglected like this!"

"Oh Sir Walter— No, do not trouble yourself, I beg you Sir Walter— you who have so many demands upon your– your company..."

It was too late; he had sat down beside her. "No demands so important as those of family and friends. Of old friends. You are our oldest friend in Bath, Mrs Clay! Do you realise that?" ("And you mine", replies Mrs Clay, with automatic pleasantry.) "Here, surrounded by the throngs of connection... our noble blood... and in the midst of our— our social sphere— it is comfortable, is it not, to turn for a moment to old friends."

Well true enough. Nellie pulled herself together; made an effort.

Sir Walter had been piqued, it emerged, by the elder brother of Mr Z., who was amongst them this evening. For a wonder. Usually this embryo Lord and his amorphous lady walked only their prescribed lengths of the Pump Room each morning, finishing up with a glass of the rather disgusting water, and then went home to be unwell, for the rest of the day, in comfortable seclusion before a good fire.

They were here now, though; looking about the room with a jaundiced air.

Sir Walter had seized the moment!– had got an introduction; had made himself civil... had found his civility met, he felt, with less than equal good breeding. "It pains me, not for myself, but for Elizabeth. And of course, for them. An alliance between our houses is not perhaps unlikely— should Elizabeth choose to allow his brother's attentions— and really— well he struck me as a disappointment. I am as liberal as the next man, I hope; but negligence in courtesy is something that I cannot easily overlook."

"Goodness! So he is *here*, is he? And his wife too? Which are they, Sir Walter?... Oh! *surely* not that *maggotty*-looking man–" Mrs Clay's hand flew, delicately, to press close her own lips, but a noisy burst of laugher had already erupted from Sir Walter. Heads turned– and they turned their own towards the protection of each other— "Oh Heavens, Sir Walter! We must pretend we are talking—"

"Rhubarb rhubarb rhubarb!"

"Rhubarb!– but– you took me aback! He is not what one expects of a *Lord?*– surely? Sir Walter? Or is that– that *face*–" ... they giggle again, this time behind discreet fingers; "is it *normal?* In London, perhaps? Of course *I* cannot know– yet *surely*..."

It was silly, but it cheered him up. Five further minutes, and she saw him on his way, looking once more the complacent Sir Walter; feeling, once more, every inch the Baronet.

The reader may have remarked, at this, that Sir Walter is changing: that our Baronet, all unbeknownst to himself, has learnt to accept not only Mrs Clay's freckles, and projecting tooth, and clumsy wrist even, but also, by now, her innocence of superior society.

The acute reader, however, will have further noticed that what he is accepting here is not necessarily her innocence *as such*, but rather, Mrs Clay's droll self-deprecation of it. They may even suspect that she knew quite well, all along, who the maggoty-faced gentleman was. A promise was made that important points would be flagged clearly: it is important, then, to realise that Mrs Clay is by now sufficiently accepted within the upper-Bath set to appear to embrace her past; can, in this way, even make capital out of it. If people laugh at it, she is confident that she can out-laugh them. She envisages a future, even, in which she laughs at them, laughing at her; thus turning the tables of humiliation. So great are the strides she has made.

As to Sir Walter, however– whether *he* has altered in essential points, your guess is as good as mine. Though I would guess, not. But then I am cynical– perhaps unduly cynical.

Meanwhile, back in that drawing-room...

Nellie, once more alone on the sopha, is leaning back as far as she can, ears flapping like Jumbo's.

It is too late, alas. Mr Elliot has moved. Just a step away; but he is silent. It is now Mr X who is seated beside Lady Russell: he is trying to pump her about Miss Elliot's preferences in music. Lady Russell does not know; regrets. "You are musical yourself?"

O yes, Mr X is a great lover of music. Of the voice, in particular.

"Then it is the *sister* you should meet: have you met Miss *Anne* Elliot?— I could tell you a great deal of *Miss Anne's* musical tastes. She is extremely musical you know. She plays beautifully: the piano, is her instrument. The ideal support, of course, to the voice; to those who sing. Do you sing yourself, Mr X?"

But he does not. He soon moves on; and though Mr Elliot has seated himself once more by Lady Russell (they are speaking again of Anne, her tastes, her talents), Mrs Clay feels her duty. She rises to walk, casually, after the monodic Mr X: she must consult his wisdom on something to do with voice production, Miss Elliot's voice production... 'she is learning that beautiful duet from *Don Giovanni*...' actually yes, she should, what a good idea.

For herself, though— as she goes about her duties in this elegant, crowded room, smiling and schmoozing— there is a gnawing small something around and above her sternum, which she identifies, after a while, in between chatting and laughter, as– regret?

Today is not the first time that Nellie has come across Mr Elliot deep in a certain type of conversation with a certain type of woman; a type with an earnest and an intelligent eye (well; earnest, anyway); a type that Elizabeth had always steered them both well clear of. At such times, that bright, light air of his– that manner of charmingly self-conscious frivolity, with which he enlivened any circle into which he stepped— it dropped away from him, shed as an actor sheds his mask, and she saw a different man.

On this more private stage Mr Elliot, assuming a simple gravity of manner all of a piece with the simple gravity of his costume, could be heard to range with easy familiarity across an impressive sweep of literature, from the most-respected of the ancients, right up to the cutting edge of today's moral fashion. Problems of philosophy, social and moral; thinkers, engaging with the great questions of these tempestuous days; authors whom Nellie, often enough, had never even heard of. Sometimes nobody else had heard of them either, but Mr Elliot could talk eagerly of them for ten, fifteen minutes together: only a sense of his social duty to others could call him away.

And plenty of these women were quite plain.

Which just goes to show. Doesn't it.

The educated English man; the morally sensitive, thinking, reading man; the new English man, in fact: what did Nellie Clay know of such men?

What *could* Mrs Clay have learnt, in her fourteen— no, *fifteen* English years — of such minds? Such souls?

Yet Mr Elliot remains unfailingly courteous to her. Smile just a little wider, as we say, bow a little deeper, recognising their common humanity. Nellie saw it all; found in it now something more, and less, than gratification; wished, gratefully, that he would not.

Chapter 6

Mr Elliot's perceptiveness here, his part in this tacit agreement with Nellie regarding her inferiority, was all the more impressive because, as I say, everyone else these days seemed to be overlooking the woman's dubious provenance. More and more their set seemed to behave, in day-to-day matters, as if Nellie was pretty much one of them. And she had, for a while there, recently, as we also saw, began to feel sometimes that they were right. —She *knew* that they were right, of course; *obviously* they were right; look at her *ancestry* and her *upbringing*, and all that—... but sometimes, recently, she had begun, a little, to feel it as well.

It helped that she was becoming a bit of a favourite with their local empress, the Dowager Viscountess. Dear Lady Dalrymple, truly well-bred as she was, had a smile and a civil answer for everyone, of course. When it came to Mrs Clay, though, her instinctive civility was warming to appreciation, even candour. For the Dowager was an aristocrat second, a mother first; and Nellie had won a place in that sedate heart by her own instinctive kindness to little Miss Carteret.

Miss Carteret was the only daughter of Lady Dalrymple's middle age:long-chinned, long-nosed; a 'late lamb' straying, on spindly legs, many years behind a riot of tempestuous and expensive sons. Her sheep-like features of face and form were complemented by a sheep-like timidity of manner and a habit of bolting off in unexpected conversational directions, and it was soon everywhere said, in Bath, that the mother had taken her daughter into society so early in the hopes of securing an establishment while the girl still possessed all the charms that extreme youth could give because, God knows, she evinced no others.

The truth was wildly different however, and far more fraught.

Plain though she was, little Miss Carteret had demonstrated charms enough to attract the attentions of a penniless lieutenant of the Marines– and he, in the winter wastes of an Irish seaside town, charms enough to attach the child's solitary heart. The intrigue had been discovered before any irremediable mischief had been done, at least to Miss Carteret's virtue; things had not reached the stage where a marriage– and such a marriage! thought Nellie, in all its degrading, anxious, youth-killing dependence!– would have been the only resort: but it had compelled a rapid decampment to England, and this early 'coming out' amidst the staid glories of Bath. Nellie heard the whole story, on only the second evening spent with the Dalrymples; heard it while, Mr Elliot leading Lady Dalrymple in the talk on one side of the room, it fell to Nellie's lot to be placed rather apart with Miss Carteret, and the impulse of her nature obliged her to attempt a conversation. The girl was clearly shy, and disposed to abstraction; but Nellie knew how to project an air of interest, mild yet sincere, that children found deeply flattering,in those far-away days when adults rarely paid them any attention at all.

She was well repaid the first trouble of exertion— for, though shy, Miss Carteret did not seem reserved: it had rather the appearance of feelings glad to burst their usual restraints; and having talked together of books, and trying to ascertain whether *Marmion* or *The Lady of the Lake* were to be preferred, and how ranked the *Giaour* and *The Bride of Abydos*, and moreover, whether the *Giaour* was to be pronounced suitable reading for an unmarried girl (Miss Carteret was in the affirmative, her mother for the nays) — and then, how the *Giaour* was to be pronounced at all— by the time they had covered all this, Miss Carteret had shown herself so intimately acquainted with all the tenderest songs of the one poet, and all the impassioned descriptions of hopeless agony of the other; she repeated, with such tremulous feeling, the various lines which imaged a broken heart, or a mind destroyed by wretchedness, and looked so entirely as if she meant to be understood, that Nellie ventured to hope that Miss Carteret did not always read only poetry; and to say, that she thought it was the misfortune of poetry, to be seldom safely enjoyed by those who enjoyed it completely; and that the strong feelings which alone could estimate it truly, were the very feelings which ought to taste it but sparingly; especially Byron, on the subject of whom Nellie was forced to admit herself of Lady Dalrymple's opinion; his effect on the unformed mind is rarely good. (Everyone else just tends to laugh like a crow.) Above all, though, Nellie dwelt on her surprise— her consternation, indeed!— that Miss Carteret, so tender in years as she was, should yet have plumbed such depths of suffering...?

It was enough to open the floodgates. For the next half hour, Nellie gasped through the white-water ride that was Miss Carteret's misadventures in love. Side-by-side upon the sopha and, as the story progressed, at times even clutching hands, they navigated a veritable Niagara of calamities, through cataracts of passion that burst on black rocks of betrayal, with scheming relatives and designing rivals looming up in abundance, raging fathers– weeping mothers– heroes, villains— and above all and most distressingly the difficulty of telling these last apart!– for the Lieutenant of Marines, after swearing undying fealty to her in a last-ditch effort beneath her bedroom window and on a frighteningly chilly night, she had been sure he would catch his death, but he was so fired up with adoration for her, so near incoherent, so legless with love he seemed to feel it not at all, though it struck Miss Carteret to the bone even wrapped in all her bedclothes as she leant from the third floor window, hour after tormented hour, she had yet seen, as she was borne away in her parents' carriage-and-four galloping headlong for Bath, and exile, and *misery*, entering a public house on the High Street, his arm around the waist of Another... I've completely lost track of my sentence structure, so great is Miss Carteret's bewilderment and distress.

In short, Miss Carteret– her first name was Catherine — well no it was her middle name, but it was more elegant than Fiona, don't you think Mrs Clay?– was in dire want, first, of being listened to upon this subject, by someone who *did* listen, instead of interrupting her at the first word she uttered with exclamations of how froward and silly she had been, more trouble than all the boys put together, and would bring her father's grey hairs in sorrow to the grave —

Listened to; as I say.

With an attentive, and a sympathetic air; and then, with an imperceptibly smooth segue moving to something more cheerful, better calculated to restore an unmarried girl's belief in life, and herself. Which is to say; the deep-down, body-tingling, overpowering intuition that someone, any day now, was going to fall in love with her.

As a first measure, Mrs Clay reached for the therapeutic properties of fashion. Its action on the young, and the young at head, is panaceaic: it is at once soothing and invigorating, styptic, yet vulnerary; demulcent and depurative at once. A case as severe as that of Miss Carteret cried out for a complete makeover, but they would start with her hair.

"And he stole a lock of it, did he — *quel diable!* oh!– and did he leave a nasty chopped-off end? Let me see... well you know we should trim that– *feather* it (as we say in French) — then, it will not be so obvious an injury to your poor dear hair, such lovely hair too, my dear Miss Carteret if you will forgive my praise, but— I cannot but admire! *Any* other girl, here in Bath, with hair *half* so lovely as this, would... well!— but have you ever *thought* of putting it up, more, on the *back* of the head?— and allow those curls, then, to cluster by the side of the face; do you know the style?... and then, if you cut them at just *this* length *here*... they will also draw attention to your beautiful eyes." Miss Carteret's hand began to stray towards her front hair, Mrs Clay's, to drift out towards a copy of *La Belle Assemblée* that graced the table before them...

Half an hour of increasingly technical discussion, and the conversation had moved, as of its own accord, to range freely across all matters of dress and personal adornment. The Carterets were not familiar with Bath at all: beyond Ireland, they knew only London:– "Oh but you will find that Bath is a little outpost of London in the West, you know, many of our shops display the fashions almost the very day after they appear in London"; and on being requested to particularise, Mrs Clay mentioned such Bath dressmakers, such Union Street collections of the finest jewellery, such eminently-patronisable *émigré* milliners of worth and suffering, as occurred to her at the moment as calculated to rouse and fortify Miss Carteret's spirits.

It was a skilful and a difficult business, and Lady Dalrymple nearly wrecked it all by unexpectedly adding her voice, from the far side of the room; that voice, usually so gentle, now suddenly fretful, monotonous, wearing; a meno-pausal dove on an endless airless summer afternoon: "Now, there, Fiona, you see? Mrs Clay is quite in the right. I didn't bring you here, *all* the way here, to sit in the drawing-room, and mope. Oh, *dear* Mrs Clay, there's been any dreary amount of mooning about the house, but shopping, I tell you, and I tell you, Fiona, but you never listen to me, puts everything else, *out* of your head..." – Drat the woman!

But the last forty minutes of sustained emotional First Aid held good. Miss Carteret— though with a restrained shake of the head, and renewed sighs, which declared her little faith in the efficacy of any shops on grief like hers— noted down the names of those Mrs Clay recommended, and promised to visit them. She would buy something, too, if... perhaps– Mrs Clay *might* be kind enough... to come with her...?— and help her in her choice? For Mrs Clay, someone had mentioned to mama, certainly knew how to dress, and Fiona— I mean Catherine— well, she really did not. 'Understated elegance', was what they had said. That was perfect, surely; for mama was all for under-statement, until Fiona was seventeen. While Catherine was quite interested, as a matter of fact, in elegance.

Mrs Clay was *delighted* to help... she hesitated.

"Not if you haven't the time, of course." Miss Carteret was tomato-red in an instant.

"Oh my dear, I will *make* the time, because it will be such fun— you will see what fun we will all have."

"Oh so Miss Elliot too, then?"

"Miss Elliot too of course—" (Miss Elliot was the problem)— "nobody loves shopping more than Miss Elliot; and shopping with *you* we will have all the fun of it, without having to wheedle another penny out of her papa, so think how Sir Walter will be pleased with us all!"

Miss Carteret smiled again, tentatively; her cheeks faded to a more attract-ive hue, and Mrs Clay snagged the passing Mr Y and left him to entertain the girl, while she slipped off to re-arrange Elizabeth's understanding of her Monday schedule.

And in the end, it *was* fun: even Miss Elliot, with address, could be per-suaded that it was a lot of fun, directing a young Honourable in the choice of her first decent wardrobe.

In fact, after she and Penelope had taken the girl in hand, Miss Carteret really became quite a credit to them! So much so that, from this time, people often saw the happy trio strolling, in picturesque formations, about the fashionable streets of Bath: the handsome, dashing, high-born Miss Elliot, Bart.ess, with the sweet little Honourable Miss Carteret; and that clever Mrs Clay.

*

For Nellie, too, there was another benefit of the Dalrymple connexion. This was the introduction, afforded by it, to another sphere of existence; a sphere which, while strictly speaking novel to her, she yet found bizarrely familiar. Lady Dalrymple, it transpired, had acquaintance among those other fringe dwellers of Bath; the *émigré* community.

It had something to do with Lady D. being Irish. She had explained it all to Elizabeth, once; something to do with them all being Revolutionary— or, all being *not* Revolutionary, and fighting Revolution together— Secondhand, through Elizabeth, it had not seemed to make much sense... and anyway we have seen by now how undiscriminating she is, the good Lady D.

The consequence, though, was that the Elliots soon found themselves being introduced to one sharp-faced French midget after another.

After so long in exile, Bath's little flock of French fugitives was a well-defined, self-conscious group. They rented in certain favoured streets; they had their own promenading area in the Pump Room, subtly more elegant than the surrounding space; in the Octagon Room there was a particular fire-place at which they all congregated, to exchange news, make arrangements, and eye each other's dress with the tightly-contained resentment that does duty, between French women, for admiration. To outsiders they were overwhelmingly gracious— with the not-unexpected consequence that almost everyone else in Bath tended to slip, discomfited, down the slick surface of all that Frenchness, and off onto the floor. So it is telling evidence, of Lady Dalrymple's supra-national niceness, that they seemed genuinely to like her!– Sir Walter and his daughters were in an awkward position.

And Mrs Clay came to the rescue. Mrs Clay made herself invaluable yet again. Each time they came across the French *mêlée*, Mrs Clay would excuse herself, just for the necessary moments, and spend a mere few quick minutes with the Chevalier and his dear family and *cetera*... for, after all, the man *was* a Chevalier— whatever that might signify— and, they *had* been introduced to him by their cousin: by the Dowager Viscountess. And so, if they bowed agreeably, while Mrs Clay conveyed their respects, well: Miss Elliot was spared the bother of speaking much French. Any French.

So Nellie would be forced to slip off...

— and Mr Elliot, who on principle did not allow anyone to give him the slip, slipped after her once or twice.

It proved well worth his while.

Right now, in the early darkness of 1815, England's *émigrés* were a-clamour with the massive agitation of a million starlings in autumn. The talk was of one thing— migrating back, at last. Who has gone? Who is planning to go? What news returns?

Above all, the news that returns.

Tales of brilliant success stir the throng to frenzy:– "Walked straight back into their chateau!" "... embraced him with tears–" "–rang the bell, and who should come but his majordomo of twenty-five years ago!" "...touchingly eager to give him his back-rents..."

— but others report, sickeningly, only the French shrug, the Gallic *moue,* the Continental *bras d'honneur.* "But my cousin writes–" my brother says– "I have heard at last from an old friend in Paris who assures me–"

Should we go?

"— No no no, remember the Peace of Amiens!"

But Bonaparte is abdicated! Confined on Elba! Imprisoned!

"– and my aunt avers that to delay is to risk losing all!" "And she would know."

Or perhaps not—

Yet I feel we *must* go—

Oh! But, *remember Amiens!* — and around and around wheels the flock. And there, among them...

Why!– it is Mrs Clay!

And doesn't she look different, moving with this flock? Doesn't she look almost exactly like the rest?

Yet only a moment before, when she had smiled deprecatingly at her Elliots, regretting, with them, the necessity of this courtesy— and then turned to do, with these Frogs, her British best; well, one would have felt sure that she had no hope; sure, just from the set of her fichu.

Mr Elliot is startled; intrigued; fascinated.

Surrounded by foreigners, that annoying habit which Mrs Clay still has, of waving her hands about sometimes... in French, it has reconfigured into a gift for elegant gesture.

To which, it becomes evident, her hands and fingers are ideally suited– being (as one suddenly realises) long, intelligent; refined.

Yet... and at the same time... that ugly wrist of hers becomes unaccountably hard to pin with the eye. Any portrait of her (taken, that is, in the French language) would have been forced to depict, between her forearm and her hand, a sort of unseeable area; a gap.

Then, her lingering tension is really poise. That air of hers, which even the most candid English mind– take Anne Elliot's, just for a wildly-random example– might well judge to be gratingly self-satisfied, and at the same time, ingratiating, in a way so utterly typical of that class of woman— No. In French, indisputably, that air unites self-possession with a gracious attention to social demands.

Most bizarre of all, her attention to social advancement— so risibly obvious to Mr Elliot— is transformed.

Right up until the Revolution, eighteenth-century England doesn't seem to have objected to people trying to wriggle up the greasy pole of class. Laughed, most heartily, at the individuals— the Miss Steeles, and so on– but... One thinks of the citizens of Rome, watching some feisty little scoundrel slogging it out in the arena for his first and last time. His efforts *are* hilarious, you can't help but laugh; yet who, in his situation, will not at least *try* to– oops!– did you see?– there he goes!...

In 1789, though, the funny little men climbed out of the arena and started on the audience, and social climbing lost its comic innocence. Do not think of it, Jack, Tom, my dear good very thin men with hands like horn hooks. God has placed us where he wants us.

Dear old God.

Given how poorly their placements served the majority of people at that time (sorry God but– You have to admit...), the independently wealthy might have found themselves dangerously isolated, just at that point in history, if God hadn't also become– after a century or two of toying with more liberal ideas– suddenly so conservative again. Through pamphlets and from pulpits (well, the kind sold to people like Dr Grant), He spoke resoundingly in support of the landed classes, and their moneyed equivalents in town. Indeed, such was His preference for them that He almost always relied on these very people to channel his views. From the year 1500 to today, the word 'submission' was never as popular as it was in these decades after the French Revolution, the Napoleonic Wars.[†] Usage reached an all-history high just at these years in which Fanny Price is eagerly, Anne Elliot forcibly, seeking to submit herself to His new, updated will.

And yet, in spite of God's fundamental re-think of his views, more and more these days, popping up next to you at the dinner table, there was Tom Hod. Or at least, his son; and his grand-daughter too.

Tricked out, usually, in clothes more expensive than your own! Faced with industrial fortunes, it seems even Heaven wavers; starts to grin ingratiatingly.

Though vulgar clothes. New money, you know. Among the truly well-bred (one comes to realise, just at this point in English history), one does not *become*; one simply *is*.

Or, in Mrs Clay's case: isn't.

In French, though, a determined ability to fight one's way up through the ranks of society—well, it can be just a little bit attractive. Rather admirable. Like physical bravery, and lively ambition, in a young army officer.

So Madame Clef's flawless classic courtesy to the Marquis, for example: a little stiff, a little doll-like perhaps at the very first moment of introduction;

---

† It's coming back in now, of course.

and yet so charming— was it not?— to hear the old phrases, produced with faultless tone, a moment there I believed myself young again, awaiting with anxiety my own turn to present myself before the great man... Yes; wry admiration: that was the French consensus on Madame Clé.

Mr Elliot found it intriguing.

By the way:– It would be nice to think that our heroine's continental refinement, here revealing itself at last, to Mr Elliot and to ourselves, was an irreducible quality of her soul. It would be heartening especially because, beyond regaining her good looks after years of poverty and distress, so far Nellie hasn't revealed much in the way of heroic qualities at all. But no: the reality was simply that all this Frenchness had of course been intensively cultivated from infancy by Nellie's mother, whose duty it was so to do. Subsequently it had been kept up to scratch, and lifted way beyond scratch, through her friendship with the *Comte et Comtesse;* once renowned even at Versailles for their superb French polish.

There had been a periodic wash, too, of others; refugees from the later socio-temporal strata, that were forever being furiously poured down, and then, gouged out, by the shifting torrents on the Continent. Each type, when its time came to be washed off and out, shot a fresh splatter of human waste across the Channel and into the Count and Countess's reception room over a dancing master's studio. There— as the shouts, and the smells, of the streets below filtered up into the bare, cold, unaffordable space; sipping with horrified civility at the unaffordable coffee— they had added layer after layer to Nellie's Continental self-image (as well as to her exquisite sensitivity to humiliation). Successive glazes, building depth and luminosity. A patina laid over her own natural intelligence and grace.

Unlike most people, Penelope had become more adaptable as the years went by, more and more plastic. Or maybe it's just that when your sense of self is eaten out of you, so much of you lies empty that anything around is welcome into the resulting vacancy.

Anyway it's not all bad. With the Plymouth grime hosed off, what emerged at last, here in the Octagon Room, was by no means contemptible. "All of the *ancien régime;* and yet, withal, a refreshing assurance with the modern!"— that is what the Chevalier's eldest son said to his brother.

At least, Mr Elliot was pretty sure he'd said that. His countenance did, quite clearly.

A tragic waste. Thus it seemed to Mr Elliot. Could not one put this– all this– to some use?

Chapter 7

There had been a period in his life when Mr Elliot had given the French situation a great deal of thought. It would not be untrue to say, even, that there had been a period when Elliot had had the most tremendous hopes of the Revolution. More baldly: as a stripling law student, penniless among his penniless friends, William Elliot had revelled in the most extravagant Radical visions.

In subsequent years, newly-married and freshly-rich, with his dashing grazier's-daughter wife in tow, Mr Elliot had found that he could continue the same cutting-edge conversations in far finer surroundings, with a fresh selection of much richer friends. It might seem counter-intuitive, but one sees it all the time: when change seems unstoppable, and kingdoms are toppling and heads rolling and limbs and severed trunks fly and thump merrily all about the Continent— well: what man of fashion, or woman either, flails against the current? Mr Elliot's own prospects, as second cousin once removed to a childless Baronet, he had frequently and freely sacrificed— what was the line?– *If baronetcies were saleable, anybody should have mine for fifty pounds, arms and motto, name and livery included.'*

Ah, that Elliot!

Oh yes, don't you know?– he will be a Baronet some day.

Quite a pretty property too, I hear!

Poor chap. How it will rankle.

Even when the Revolutionary Republic's First Consul suddenly Jack-in-the-Boxed (*boo!*) into an hereditary ruler with absolute power, Mr Elliot had defended the man magnificently: alone, armed only with his wit, he had persuaded many a vacillating drawing-room to give the dear Emperor another go...

For all that, Mr Elliot was aware that he had never been able to penetrate the secretive centre of the movement. In a decade of Radical fervour, he had received not so much as a single morning call from a known revolutionary: no; not even during the Peace of Amiens, when all his friends seemed to have had at least one sight-seeing Napoleonista dropping in and sleeping over on the sopha.

It had been due, he had ultimately determined, to the poverty of his wife's French. She could not translate the simplest sentence for him without provoking smirks from his interlocutors. Oh!– Eugenia's incompetence had cost him heavily!...

Still.

That it was all in the past, wasn't it.

Which is to say, dear reader:– two decades had France, a monstrous canni-bal, devoured its neighbours: then in as many months the bloated Empire had convulsed, spewed forth its prey and collapsed. Now, the Emperor of Europe ruled a goat-picked island off the coast of Tuscany. It was a humiliating reversal.

To be fair to oneself; perhaps, yes, one's Republican certainties *had* waned a little, lately, as Napoleon's difficulties grew. I mean he'd embarrassed himself badly in Russia, hadn't he. Not a good look. Put the onus back on his support-ers, didn't it, to try to keep up the tone... But.. and... on the other hand Buona-parte *was* the genius of the impossible victory. Famously so. And, Elliot was nothing if not staunch– and, in the end, it all happened so fast... it was not until last March that Mr Elliot could bring himself to repudiate the man entirely.

He had been cutting it very fine. Over the ensuing month he had changed his haircut, his wardrobe, and most of his close friends; he had even swapped his chaise for a closed carriage. Then Eugenia, too, had passed on...

By the time our own Elliots met him again, therefore, almost nothing remained to tie Mr Elliot of Bath to the past.

A few exceptions; and only a few. Among his intimates, Colonel Wallis was worth retaining. So was Mrs Wallis, his pretty, complaisant wife. So too was a certain Dr Mills, who had treated Eugenia in her final illness; the good doctor didn't always seem to appreciate it, but Mr Elliot felt that, in that anxious time, he and Dr Mills had grown close. Dr Mills was now in Bath at Colonel Wal-lis's expense, having brought Mrs Wallis safely through her time of danger: Mr Elliot was looking forward to seeing him again.

But no-one else. No-one.

... withal...

... once peace was declared, and the dust had settled a bit... matters stabil-ised... Mr Elliot himself had been at the very forefront of those adventurers who raced across: toured the country. Viewed the situation first-hand.

He had felt it a duty, almost, in these tempestuous times, to bear witness to History.

Again, though, one encounters the damned language problem. He'd hired a man, but it's not ideal. They jabber away and jabber away, and after a while you wonder what they're finding to talk about— surely it doesn't take that long to arrange a *chambre* for the night?

Mr Elliot had returned as he left: disappointed, empty-handed; piqued, to spitting-point, by the sensation of something, hanging, just out of reach.

I mean— defeated– humiliated!– yet still the French dominated fashion! What *was* it?

Now here he was in Bath, moving in new circles, a budding Baronet.

Upright in his new clothes and his new manners, his fresh sentiments and fresh convictions; a new man altogether— and what should he find, but the whole compelling tease, dangling before him again.

Chapter 8

While Nellie, and Mr Elliot too, thus strayed a little, amongst the exotics of Bath, the Elliots remained true to their cousins. They visited in Laura Place, they had the cards of the Dowager Viscountess Dalrymple and the Honourable Miss Carteret arranged wherever they might be most visible, and when they could not be with their new friends, the Elliots could still talk of them, and 'our cousins in Laura Place'—'our cousins, Lady Dalrymple and Miss Carteret', were talked of to everybody. Mrs Clay was amused.

Amused and just a little bit— what, exactly?

I mean the Dalrymple connection was a tremendous *coup*. It was beneficial on a daily basis, and there was still more to hope from it in the future. And she liked the Carterets, too. She sincerely liked them.

But, *en vérité*— and *en fait* as well— Elizabeth, and Sir Walter also, did take it all a bit... well... seriously?

Not, of course, that it *wasn't* serious. And yet... watching Elizabeth, at the other end of drawing room, explaining the antiquity of the Irish peerage to a credulous new acquaintance... Nellie could be amused by her friend's enthusiasm— but she found that she was not exactly proud of her.

And that new gown of hers. There was something not quite right about the length of the arm in relation to the waistline and then, to the drop to the hemline... Mrs Clay sighed. Elizabeth clung, her companion was realising, to a subtly old-fashioned style.

After all, she was nearly thirty.

If she wanted to charm Mr Elliot, though, she had to get things like that absolutely right. The man had a quick eye, and a quicker taste.

... Whereas the Carteret girl was coming along very nicely! A sense of style, in spite of a face like a horse poor darling, such a challenge... They had been looking this morning at an engraving of Annabella Milbanke's portrait— Byron's new wife— what a fool that woman must be. And really very ordinary-looking. But– "Look at how she (well, no; it is the artist; but if she is clever she will see, and she will now do this herself): look how she tilts her head— that angle. Now you think the jawline is pretty, don't you?— but– look! Really look!– You could equally well say her jawline was ugly, could you not? Mm?... but then, she tilts— *so*— and, now the hand— *thus*— This is very very good."

Mrs Clay turned to Miss Carteret, and spoke with serious urgency.

"Like *this*, the model does not acknowledge you; if you look at her straight; according to your own tastes. The artist chooses, the artiste says, you must look at me *this* way. Any other way— *pah!*— so then you are irrelevant to her! *Poise.* This is poise. And you, my dear, are the artiste, and your subject is your-self."

Miss Carteret looked dubious. But Nellie was transported with intensity: she was practically channelling her mother. "Oh yes!– these grave Englishes, these Miss Annes, and these Lady Russells, they do not trust the poise– the artist, within a woman's soul. But— my dear! Do you really want to be *quite* so English as them?"

Miss Carteret had tilted her head— and smiled.

Mrs Shepherd had taught her daughter some valuable lessons, when you think of it. Along with all the nonsense.

Dear mama. There had been a refinement about her, a harmony of line and colour, voice and feeling, that made her a joy to be with; even when she was just stuffing chocolates into her mouth, and everybody else's, after dinner.

All an act of course. An artistic presentation of herself, conscientious and consistent... the Frenchwoman's primary duty.

Though— perform the role, every moment, every day, in every situation... When you can keep it up, even while giving birth— what is the person, where the role? When you method-act your way through your life?

In just a few years, Nellie would be older than that sweet silly lady had ever been.

... '*Silly.*' In English only: it cannot be complimentary in French; it had been one of their father's favourite endearments, in speaking to his wife.

Yet, you have to admit:– right up until that last pigeon, things had mostly worked out pretty well for Ophelia.

There is luck. Yes.

But there is also, in some, a quickness of perception, a nicety in the dis-cernment of character... and in this, Ophelia had indeed been gifted.

More gifted, certainly, than her daughter. Even in the miseries of her brief Countess-hood, Nellie reflected, mama's heart would never have been stirred by, say, little Catherine's Lieutenant of Marines. Or Commander Clay...

And then, look at Elizabeth, posing away there; "... in— er— *Ballimena*– I believe. Quite the finest property in the county..." Bah! *Quelle maladroite!*

— No.

No. Elizabeth was alright.

Nellie was not going to start privately mocking her patroness.

And anyway none of this was Elizabeth's fault– "You are abstracted, Mrs Clay." It was Mr Elliot, leaning over the back of the sopha.

Leaning over *her!*

At the sudden consciousness of his proximity, Nellie's bosom heaved. (These low-cut high-waisters were good that way. He would be sorry to see them go.) Nellie felt his eyes dive into her cleavage; but in little more than an elastic instant they had bounced away towards the figures at the far end of the room. "Oh..." and Nellie gazed about her– What had she just been thinking of?

"Our friends are happy in their new acquaintance?"

As she tilted her head back to answer him, arching over her as he was, she saw a wryness in his smile, and a certain deep returning gaze... He held the gaze, and the smile. "They should be grateful to you, Mrs Clay, for securing it... Mmm."

The smile deepened.

"I saw the letter my dear cousin proposed to send to our Irish relatives. And I saw what you made of it, when you *copied* it out..." He raised his eyebrows a little, intensifying the shared joke.

"Sir Walter and Miss Elliot owe you a considerable debt."

The extraordinary directness of his words!

The frankness, the intimacy, of his whole manner as he spoke them! The placing of himself, and herself, on a level together — and apart, too, from the pair in whose company they sat! — the pair to whom she must be thought, by all the world, to be herself the indebted!... "Oh... Oh I did nothing— or, only a very little..."

"Come, Mrs Clay; you are too modest! Too modest for the world in general to be aware of half your accomplishments —" and he cast a meaningful glance towards that part of the room which held the piano. It stood open, upon it the simple duet that she had that morning been teaching Miss Elliot, "and too highly accomplished for modesty to be natural..." Mr Elliot was sliding lithely around the sopha's end as he spoke these last words, and now he slipped onto it beside her and leant in. "You do not sing for us, Mrs Clay."

"Oh!– no. No I leave the singing for Miss Elliot. *She* is the performer in our household."

"Yes; I have heard Miss Elliot sing. She *improves*, I think, almost daily." Now Mr Elliot's nearest hand was describing small, languid circles on the silk of the sopha. (Absolutely Continental circles, Nellie's thigh asserted, with unexpected heat.) "Perhaps she has a little help...?"

"Perhaps I *have* helped, just a little. Her voice has never reached its full potential."

"Ah. And your voice...?" The circles grew larger. "What is its potential?"

Mrs Clay laughed. "That is not for me to say, Mr Elliot!"

"Pity."

Again he held her gaze; that deep, probing regard... the almost conspirat- orial smile.

"I have an *intuition,* that you sing very well, Mrs Clay."

Yes. She did.

Nellie leaned back on the sopha; crossed her arms; tilted her head at him. "What can *possibly* lead you to think that, Mr Elliot?"

"Ah, Mrs Clay. An intuition, as I say...?"

"Well:– No—" he wriggled a little closer. "It is more than that"

– and the circling finger began again on the silk; closer too, necessarily, to Nellie's increasingly flustered thigh. "It is a firm belief of mine, that when a woman has a throat like that, she cannot sing ill." And now that overwhelming gaze slid lower.

Mrs Clay swallowed.

"Perhaps, too, I have heard whispers of your past..."

Music, that had been playing— from who knows whence — a soft, strange, deep, languorous air (surely it was Barry White?)... faltered. Fell silent.

After a little while Mr Elliot's white finger, too, slowed its circling.

He seemed to pull himself together.

Sat upright once more.

"Ah... Well... That is—" Directed, at her, a searching, puzzled look. "We must perhaps, agree to disagree whether *you*, Mrs Clay, should add to our pleasures in Camden Place, with your voice."

(His look was tinged, perhaps, with hurt...?)

"In one point I am sure, at least, that we *must* feel alike. We must feel, that every addition to Sir Walter's society, and enjoyments, may be of use in divert- ing his mind from those influences which would depress it."

He looked, as he spoke, to the seat which Miss Anne had been lately occupying: a sufficient explanation of what he particularly meant; and although Nellie still felt a small cold sickness within her (the colder, of course, for its sudden transition from heat and light)— still, she could be pleased with him for not liking Miss Anne.

Because everybody else was so quick to congratulate Elizabeth on the return of her sister to Bath. Everybody assumed that Anne's presence must be a boon to them all! Everyone wanted to cry up Miss Anne's refinement, and her mind, and seemed to think that Anne must be lifting the tone, within their little society at Camden Place, and enlarging their evening delights no end. Little did they know.

Mr Elliot, though. *He* knew.

It was something to hold on to, through the further contradictions and inequalities of the night, for Mr Elliot was soon off at the other end of the room, dutifully electrifying a string of new visitors, and he scarcely gave her another look all evening; he might, almost, have been avoiding her.

Now, how was this to be read?

The strangest, the happiest interpretation (though it had, of course, its own distress) was that Mr Elliot was shaken. Stumbling, unprepared, upon that precipitous view down onto the warm skin of her breasts, he had found himself roughly seized by those animal forces within any man and torn — a helpless prey— by sensations foreign to his character; even, to his principles.

The sophistication of the former; the counterbalancing seriousness of the latter: both were at war with the urges of the flesh to which he had been forced, momentarily, to yield mastery. And thus, now, now he quarrelled with himself. With that inner self, that so few were permitted to glimpse.

The touch of Mr Elliot's hand at the close of the evening seemed to confirm Nellie's most agitating speculations. The pressure was forceful– more masculine than gentlemanly– an intense gaze– the brow– puckered, a little, with... bewilderment?... Then all was cut short, and Mr Elliot spun about and swept down the hall and out into the black of night.

Mrs Clay chastised herself, all the rest of the evening, that her blatant physical charms had shaken that beautifully poised, self-assured man's *sang-froid.*

In the privacy of her own chamber, the self-chastisement went on well into the night. In between regretting his perturbation— and yet pointing out to herself that there was *nothing* she could do about it— that she was quite as helpless, in all this, as he could be himself— Nellie also found time to marvel on a something else, that she now realised– to her bewilderment– had always existed between herself, and this man. She, and Mr Elliot.

What was it, that they shared?

What was it, that made for an unspoken concordance between them?

There was something. In spite of the gulf that seemed, in worldly matters, to be set between them; there yet was something.

Though— and in all justice to herself— if things had gone as they should, if they had never been forced to leave France, then a young Nellie Shepherd could well have matched with a young Mr Elliot. (What had he been like then? she wondered; Mr Elliot, as a very young man...) And now, here, on the other side of the Channel, of the War; and still, something in him rang in harmony with something in her.

Now that she thought of it; didn't she always feel it, when, in a busy room, she and Mr Elliot, for all their common liveliness of speech and manner, found themselves both silent?— both watching, listening. Both within the company, yet not entirely of it.

What was it?

— and their very isolation was leading their souls, then, to turn each other. They were natural confidants.

Even about rather intimate things; no doubt; in time. His judgement of Miss Anne Elliot!—that had been a profoundly intimate confession!

Going over each detail of all this took a couple of warm hours, after which Nellie began to experience a desire to meet Mr Elliot's confidence with a confidence of her own. How would he react to that, do you think? Such marks of confidence as he had given her— and this was not the first, she realised now — though it was the strongest yet (that look, at her throat... Nellie flushed all over again, and thrashed in her bed like a fish on a line) — these marks of confidence, they *demanded* a return...

It was a cooling thought.

Because, when one then looked at her life, from what might be a gentleman's point of view– searched it for confessable intimacies... her past, in Plymouth. Her father's poky house in Somerset. Her position in Camden Place, lying here, in the second-best spare bedroom, a guest of nearly half a year's standing... What grew on you was, that there wasn't a great deal that she could afford to confide to Mr Elliot.

Chapter   9

It is a happy circumstance, then, that Mr Elliot has no need of Mrs Clay's confidences. Locked in his writing-desk is a long report that details all of her publicly-known life in Somerset and in Plymouth, and all that is hazarded (he particularly likes the hazarded bits) about her private life there as well.

Nevertheless. He'd have thought, at the rates he was paying, that they'd have taken the trouble to mention how brilliantly she could work a roomful of Frenchies. It was his own discovery of this last which had inclined him to step things up a bit with Mrs Clay— with the rapid success (mortifyingly rapid; I had expected better things of Nellie's good sense) that we saw above: he is making up for lost time, is he not.

Tonight they are all to meet again in the Upper Assembly Rooms, and Mr Elliot is looking forward to it. He anticipates the results of his little experiment on the sopha two days ago, with eager confidence.

Nellie, too, knows that she will see him here tonight. She has thought about it a great deal all day. She wonders how he will be.

As for herself, she has determined to be sober, rational, restrained.

She has collected herself, you see. Since that shattering hour when he had leaned right over her, and slid beside her, and caressed the silk of the sopha, speaking of the things that only the two of them understood— she has got a grip. Whatever Mr Elliot might feel for her, a grave response is the wisest. Restraint, decorum, gravity: considering the delicacy of her position, it is prudent.

Gravity is becoming, anyway. These days, she is coming to understand that.

Mr Elliot, though gay, is also grave.

Meanwhile, though, here we are in the Upper Assembly Rooms, waiting for Nellie and her– lover?– to meet again— and everyone is scattered everywhere and no-one has met anyone. By the entrance to the Concert Room, the Dowager Viscountess pays unassuming court to a Dowager Countess; with flushed cheeks and wandering eyes, Mrs Clay frivols by the French fireplace; in the seclusion of the old Card Room, Mr Elliot is speaking in low tones to a short man, and Elizabeth's voice projects beautifully from the centre of the Octagon Room– "Now, you mention *Ireland*–". Sir Walter and his other daughter stand by the main door; he is waiting, too, for everyone.

And now, barrelling through the crowd towards him, Sir Walter recognises Dr Mills. Anne inclines her head– the man has been introduced in the course of– but Elizabeth has actually turned and greeted the little doctor, and Dr Mills must stay his flight, ensnared by the gravitational mass of Sir Walter and his daughters. Poor little Dr Mills, looking harassed and worn (thrice-daily attendance on Mrs Wallis and the baby); yet it seems that tonight he 'could not forbid himself the treat... is such a lover of music'—

But Elizabeth has another topic in mind.

"Ah. Yes: if I make myself clear, Miss Elliot; an access of black bile. That was the root of the problem. In poor Mrs Elliot's case. Weakness of the lungs — and bile. Responded well to laudanum; tincture of..." Dr Mills' voice trailed off. He seemed hypnotised by the crowd in the entrance hall beyond them; rubbing his hands together, he gazed blankly into its noisy swirl.

"Tincture of laudanum, eh? Wonderfully tonic", Sir Walter assures him.

"Yes— yes. Anti-tussive too– completely appropriate; normal treatment. Twenty drops in a glass of water twice a day. Three times the absolute utmost; absolutely normal. Efficacious for her migraines, too— nervous spasms— all, much as one would expect in her time of life."

"And pray, how old *was* Mrs Elliot?" This from Elizabeth.

"Ah– well, advanced in ...ah.... — a little older in *health*... than in years, one might say. Yes. Yes one might say that. London life, don't you know. Some of my patients do make the very best of London— and London *life*. Candle at both ends, you know."

"Yet Mr Elliot is as fine a man for his age as one could hope to see", counterposed Sir Walter, feeling that the conversation touched him nearly.

"Ah yes. The men!—"

The doctor raised his eyebrows at the night out there, beyond the entrance hall; sharing with it a well-known secret. "It doesn't catch up with men nearly as quickly, that kind of life."

"What kind of life would that be?"

Glancing back, to find himself suddenly pinned by Anne's gaze, the doctor's hands begin once more their rubbing. "Well– *London*. Don't you know."

"No I am afraid that I do not know London. I myself have never been there."

But Doctor Mills had rocked onto on his toes and, rubbing his hands and bobbing like a robin, was dipping his head to a figure approaching— to Mr Elliot.

The doctor and Mr Elliot were great friends! Mr Elliot addressed him, before them all, as his trusty guide; called him his adept, and his paraclete; announced to the little group that, without Doctor Mills, his dear wife would have surely been lost to her husband and friends many, many years before the sad events of last July. "Dr Mills was my oracle. I followed your instructions in everything, Dr Mills; scrupulously and exactly, confident that in so doing, there could be no error; no harm to my wife's health. Could I have persuaded dear Eugenia to do the same..." and Mr Elliot's free hand was now passed across his eyes. The other was on Dr Mills' shoulder, pressing it; with powerful feeling, as appeared evident from the good doctor's sinking somewhat under it. Sinking under it, and quite away; for it seemed that Doctor Mills, though delighted to see Mr Elliot and to see him looking so well– to see no lasting effects of the sad events of last July– had had his alarms at the time — feared an excess of phlegm— but clearly in excellent... pressing duties, Mrs Wallis, must return...— and Doctor Mills had bowed himself out of the group, the room, the building and their lives.

(An odd little episode.

(Probably put in to pad out a chapter.)

...and as they all turn back, to each other— here is Mrs Clay, hurrying up, breathless. She has missed it all; missed everything. "Where *have* you been, Penelope?"

"The Chevalier renders you his regards, Miss Elliot, Sir Walter; his wife, also, requests to be remembered to you." She lowers her eyelids before Mr Elliot as she says this, and then– of their own accord– they flash up again and stare straight into his with an irresistible, knowing, eighteenth-century smirk.

He smiles politely back, as if he has never seen her before in his life.

Now his smile twists; his head recoils from her a fraction. The corner of his nose contracts.

Nellie finds she has turned away. The room booms around her, five fathoms under a heavy sea. Her skin crawls, there is a prickling along her hairline and she feels her cheeks burn into that unmistakeable blotchy red which signalsintense shame. Looming up larger than life is the Dowager Viscountess, and a hand plucks at her arm — she is being jostled by people in movement.

Because it is time to enter the concert room. Everyone is moving towards the Concert room. Mr Elliot...

Mr Elliot is talking to Miss Carteret.

Now he is talking to Anne. Now he is bowing to Miss Carteret— Nellie finds that she has turned towards the exit.

"Mrs Clay?"

Mr Elliot is standing, right here, in front of her. He is smiling. Politely. Still.

He is offering her his arm.

Mrs Clay's spirits flounder like a Great Dane trying to get to its feet on a polished floor. She has instinct still to glance about for Miss Elliot— but no, she is gone— everyone is gone, into the Concert Room, on the arms of each other: she sees only backs.

She looks down at her own hands, arms— but they seem clean.

So Nellie takes Mr Elliot's arm.

Walks, beside him.

Her fingers are at rest, with every appearance of legitimacy, on the fine, warm broadcloth.

The nap tickles her palm; and her heartbeat flounders still, but now there are additional convulsions. His biceps necessarily brush her muslin-clad breast as they are pressed together in the crowd, and she feels her pulse bubble into her throat. Someone bumps into her and she bumps into Mr Elliot and he puts his free hand, steadying, on her hand, and now her heart is doing things that would earn it a respectable score even in the insanely competitive world of modern gymnastics. She can't think of anything to say.

She tries—

"I have great hopes of the concert tonight."

Mr Elliot looks sideways at her; lifts an eyebrow; inclines his head. Nellie's blotched face mottles up some more–

"I mean— the *singer*— I hear great things of this voice."

Again the sideways look; the inclined head, this time a little deeper. He knows what she means.

"I hear he is..."

... Mr Elliot, with Nellie on his arm, gazing easily about him, as they inch their way along the crowded aisle.

He does not speak.

He speaks!

To an acquaintance already seated. "Half your luck, Travers."

"Ah Elliot! My wife—"

The procession has slowed to a stop. Travers and wife glance at her. A conversation is carried out across her body.

Now they are edging forward again— Thank God— It gives her something to do. She makes a show of gathering her skirts, protecting her new gown. Elizabeth's old gown.

The bench! The edge of their bench is in view! Everyone else is already seated and deep in conversation.

Mr Elliot eases her politely onto the bench; sits down, himself, on the very end of it.

"That must be so uncomfortable for you, Mr Elliot."

"Not at all, Mrs Clay."

"Oh but you are exposed to all the people bumping past—"

"No no, Mrs Clay; I am quite comfortable here", he repeats.

She glances at him; just a quick glance. Mr Elliot is smiling slightly. She knows she should drop the topic but she can't think of what else to say. "Let us swap places— do!"

This time he only smiles.

It goes on, like this, all the way through to the interval.

After the first... twenty minutes perhaps?— who can tell, Nellie is in a place where time, and light, and even gravity are all acting a bit oddly— and as time expands further— longer and longer intervals between exchanges— she comes to feel that she has been silent, this time around, now, so long, that she— The silence has grown more substantial than she is. She can't intrude.

They sit silent, for the rest of the half.

*

You would have hoped, wouldn't you, that Nellie would cope better with being tossed up and down and twirled about `like a yoyo a few times like this. You would have hoped she would have stood up to it a bit better. A bit longer. Why so sensitive, my dear?

Especially considering that, in the last year or so before people simply stopped inviting them out at all (the Clay's own house having been off-limits, for the wife's acquaintance, long before that)— in that last phase of pretence at social normality, events like, say, the projectile vomiting at Admiral Boyce's had occurred— goodness—how many times?

Well maybe not that many, really. The word had spread pretty quickly.

After all, it had been building up for a long time; this thing with Lieutenant Clay.

But it had seemed to Nellie that she'd dropped, there, into an infinity, where things were suddenly gushing out all over someone's snow-white damask— ejaculations of disgust— recoiling figures, the scrape of chairs flung back...

(Meanwhile a smaller part of her is vividly engaged in the scene of the Concert room. Mr Elliot's cheekbone. The flicker in a corner of a mouth; the lower eyelids, the upper. A glance here. A glance away. How should she be?

(But Mr Elliot is imperturbable; marmoreal. She can get no lead at all.)

*

At last: the interval!

He takes himself off in pursuit of tea.

Mrs Clay droops on the bench. She is utterly bamboozled.

*

And after all, the alternation of heat and frost will crack even marble — let alone badly-broken, recently-glued porcelain.

Perhaps it's fanciful to even invoke Nellie's miserable, humiliating marriage. Its precariously-maintained pretences; all those years.Or that final series of public, spectacular collapses; one crash after another, like a drunken dancer at last losing his footing, and falling, in several instalments, off the stage...

The truth is, Mr Elliot got most women to this point, sooner or later.

*

Bells: and a tide of silks and fine wool, odour mixing with that of over-heated bodies, rolls back to fill the seats again. Mr Elliot is the last to return.

He comes in with Elizabeth on his arm.

It is a relief.

But no— Elizabeth, a gift, is passed to Colonel Wallis. Mr Elliot is free. Mr Elliot looks about.

Mr Elliot sits down next to Anne. *Anne!*

For most men of their set, an hour next to Anne Elliot is an hour of penance; an hour, if God is just, that will be lopped off their time in Purgatory.

("Let me swap— O *do!*")

They are directly behind her where she sits, alone, on the front bench. She lifts her spirits and diverts her mind by endeavouring to catch, through the noise about her, as much of their conversation possible.

She can hear them only in snatches. The Peace. The moral tone of England, at this critical juncture in her history. The character of her common people...

Spiritual and intellectual improvement! Anne is eager, candid—*Leadership!*...

Ah!– but to whom can England turn, to so lead them? Mr Elliot is grave.

And Anne sighs– understanding, acknowledging; deprecating...

Nellie's mind starts to blank: which is sad, because the two of them are now starting to share some very insightful and cutting-edge views about the bearing and obligations of England's clergy, and Nellie might have learnt something worth knowing.

But, you see, for herself— and apart from naval unemployment— Nellie had always just though that the Peace, whatever it was, was always a good thing that meant that now everything could all get back to normal. Whatever that was.

She needs to attend far, far more carefully.

To Mr Elliot's meanings, and feelings.

And above all, his judgements.

Dear God. She'd thought he liked her tits.

*

One spot of brightness. As they are leaving the concert, hemmed once more in the aisle, cheek-by-jowl with each other, Lady Russell drops a cool enquiry: she is wondering; how long *is* Mrs Clay going to stay? "Because Mr Shepherd (so busy as the man must be, without Sir Walter's direction, does not retain a housekeeper, does he?"

Nellie turns to Elizabeth — she is exhausted.

"Why!" interposed Elizabeth, positively, "Penelope will be staying with me for as long as her father can possibly be persuaded to part with her! As long as I can possibly arrange for it!"

As she spoke, she drew Nellie's cold limp arm within her own, and squeezed it; and then pulled her about, so that they faced Lady Russell, side by side.

Nellie looks back for Mr Elliot.

He is there: he is watching.

She lowers her eyes.

When she dares to look up, he is still watching her. And his smile is broader.

One bright spot.

Chapter   10

Dear Penelope,

The generosity and the liberality of Sir Walter and the beautiful Miss Elliot continue to overwhelm me: each time I feel that I have the full compass of the Elliot soul, you write of something that opens up to me yet new vistas. Your wonderful news, that Miss Elliot feels that you can continue to add to her enjoy-ment in Bath, until at least the beginning of May, has convinced me that the time has come to venture back to our old haunts, to see if there is anything left there which might perhaps add to our little store of comforts here in dear England. Sir Walter, whom I have of course consulted before all others, kindly urges me of the advisability of such a journey: Sir Walter counsels me to scrape together whatever sad fragments might remain to us, and secure them, where possible, from the further rapacity of the French ~ though God knows that, for every day that I will spend on my own concerns abroad, I cannot but anticipate a night filled with solicitude for the ancient seat of Kellynch! ~ and all who sail in it. Only the knowledge that my dear Penelope is so delightfully placed, among those whom I have learnt most to trust and to reverence, will comfort me in coming weeks, as I struggle with the perfidious wop.

— and on a separate enclosure, for her eyes only—

There is no other way, Nell. Letters achieve nothing, I must go in person. Lefarge did not make it, as you know, but young Bovary is still at his old place, and a letter to his address should always reach me.

I leave within the fortnight, then, hoping to return by the end of April; should plans change, I will write. Beckwith (Chancery Lane) has a sample of your hand and will honour promptly any request in £20 increments; he also holds my Will. Hardcastle steps in at Kellynch and will be renting the house too, pro tem., which is a good saving. The children go to Mrs Mortlake's and Mr Lithgow respectively.

~ In preparation for which, we have been refreshing our French! The little doves have forgotten a great deal of it, of course: and yet, what they can still come out with, every now and then, is quite eye-opening. It is evident that, somewhere, somehow, they have had considerable exposure to the demotic. We offer the following exercises enclosed, as specimens of their progress.

Bless you my dear. The well-being of the children and yourself is always my foremost concern. Now, it must be yours.

— and— yes, here were the inclusions from Ariosto and Josephine; demanding exercises indeed, being both in French and in cipher, and it took Nellie a full hour to decode the children's scribble: Mr Shepherd's ciphers had grown a great deal more complex, since the bleak day of the Edinburgh pigeon. Ariosto: *Grandpere says Bath is full of retired clergy so if you cannot get the Baronet you should branch out...* Josephine: *I do not see why school must be Bristol when Bath is just as close, but grandpere says Bristol people have far more actual cash, so in the intervals of study I will look about me for someone satisfactory myself...* Oh Josephine.

She had been used to laugh at such cheerful rapacity. She: Nellie.

Perhaps, her primary duty, now, lay there...?

If she were there, the children would not be banished to school. She could save them that expense, that upheaval. And then; quiet, regular employment... it was what they all needed. Josephine's sewing had been shamefully neglected!

That lovely little house. The empty fields.

Oh, God! What was she doing, alone, far away?

*

Being a true friend, a helpful companion; a useful member of the Elliot's little circle, here in Camden Place. That should be enough.

It *was* enough.

Mrs Clay, these days, was a very different woman from the poor creature she had been!

*   *   *

Nellie reminded herself of this, as she entered the lofty rooms of Laura Place for another evening *chez Carteret*. As they went through the routines of greeting, the background tremor in her spirits quietened somewhat. Lady Dalrymple's pleasant smile grew wider when she got to Mrs Clay, and Nellie smiled eagerly back— and, *here* was dear Miss Carteret!...

The evening improved for others, too. Sir Walter announced his younger daughter's absence: charitable sickbed, urgent case; desolated, very; but when social duty calls, he knew neither of his girls would be found deaf.

Lady Dalrymple perked up immediately; smiled, even through the effects of a heavy head cold, and observed that in that case they would seize the opportunity to play cards– because Miss Anne did not seem to enjoy cards– "and I find, with this cold, I am not up to any kind of, well, *real* conversation at all– I simply can't concentrate I'm sorry Lady Russell — though that latest play was very nice– wasn't it my dear?"— Miss Carteret nodded— "and I did enjoy the concert last night, that nice pretty Italian boy, and his dear sweet little friend on violin, such nice tunes, but... and Lady Russell we do have some *lovely* books for you on the little table by the fire there — But otherwise, indeed, why don't we all just sit down to a nice comfortable game of lottery tickets."

So they did.

*

It was a delightful party.

That Sir Walter and Miss Elliot could play at lottery tickets might not have occurred to you. To tell the truth it hadn't occurred to them, either, for over thirteen years: yet, time had been when Sir Walter, a young father, had regularly found himself astonished!— as he remarked— to be granting this girl of his— all these girls— still another late-night game before the fire, in his study, though how they contrived to be downstairs anyway at such an hour of the evening is anybody's guess, their mother absent of course[†], otherwise Lizzie, young lady, we would never be allowed– Oh pappa *do* stop talking and shuffle the deck, it's your turn to deal.

How it came flooding back!

So they all played lottery tickets for a while. Then Elizabeth and her father,

---

† Probably visiting the sick somewhere.

with some argument, between them reconstructed their own ancient Kellynch
Hall version of the game, in rules and spirit more competitive and more
bloodthirsty, as had befitted that simpler time; and they all played *that*. It was
even more fun, and under its primitive sway the party became almost too bois-
terous– hands waved, heads bobbed, a lot of laughing– really quite loud...

and any passing stranger, glimpsing them through the street windows perhaps (in the all the dim uncertain candle-light), might have taken them for nice
enough people, as people go. Might even have fancied that little Miss
Carteret– flinging herself back in her chair with her legs stuck out, crowing
with triumph at wresting a fish from Sir Walter– seemed rather a lovely girl.

Now the long evening was drifting to a close. Lady Dalrymple, worn out
with coughing and laughter, had fallen into a doze in the corner of a sopha,
one crumpled handkerchief balled in her hand, another peeking out of her
sleeve. At the other end of the long room, Miss Carteret and Elizabeth were
burrowing through piles of library books and neglected needlework in search
of a novel, the nicest novel in the world, by an Irish writer, Miss Carteret was
quite sure that Miss Elliot would *just* adore it... By the fire, Mrs Clay and Sir
Walter, gazing sleepily into the embers, wait patiently on their charges.

Mr Elliot's voice acted on her smelling salts.

Nellie hadn't even noticed him come in!

She was wide awake again. Her scalp crawled. She actually felt her ears
move.

He was sitting with Lady Russell, at her isolated table.

His conversation was giving her relief from such volumes as Lady
Dalrymple had been able to supply; no doubt the first such relief the poor
lady had had all evening. And their topic?...

It was yet again, quite simply, Anne.

"Ah, Lady Russell. How we miss her, on an evening like this."

"Indeed we do! Every minute."

"I must confess: delightful as is a party like this — a quiet party, a strictly
family party— still, one must feel something lacking, without the presence of
Miss Anne's calm intelligence; her quiet, yet piercing commentary. One cannot
imagine *Anne Elliot* content, the whole evening, with a round game!"

"Certainly not–" Lady Russell hesitated. "Or, not since she was *quite* a
child. Anne is of a serious turn of mind. It excludes her from many small
pleasures, I am afraid."

"But opens, to her, many more! And many, let us confess it, larger in their
nature; more lasting in the benefits, and the satisfactions, that they can give.
Pleasures", and he sounded rueful, "that may not be counted *among* pleasures,
perhaps, by the sort of mind more often met with! For I tell you freely, Lady
Russell (knowing that *you* will understand it correctly, as nothing more than

the plain truth, plainly stated): Miss Anne strikes me as a very remarkable young woman."

"So she must, to all who know her."

"So she *should*, to all who know her, Lady Russell— But forgive me! I speak hastily. And yet— if you will allow me to presume on our acquaintance — and I am afraid I already have!... speaking plainly again— (perhaps a little too plainly!)– It puzzles me, at times, to see Anne Elliot so overlooked in our little society. Yes; it puzzles me exceedingly."

Lady Russell only inclined her head: but she was listening.

"She is, in objective judgement, a most extraordinary young lady. When I look at my cousin I see, in temper, manners, and mind, a model of female excellence. This compassionate visit to an old school-fellow, this"— Mr Elliot leant back, folding his own arms in a tight self-embrace— "this Mrs *Smith*, I think you said that was the name?"

Lady Russell inclined her head again.

"Mrs Smith—! How many Mrs Smiths must there be, in England!— in Bath alone, even! And Miss Anne heard of her, here, simply as *Mrs Smith*? Heavens!–" Mr Elliot seemed diverted. "Without the aid of a Christian name! — how is one to distinguish one *Mrs Smith*, by report, from another!— without a Christian name..?"

How indeed. Lady Russell was no help here.

"And yet, here in Bath, our Anne finds— ill, and reduced— her own particular Mrs Smith! Once a young girl; a vigorous playmate; in Bath itself!– I think you told me?... that *Bath* is where Miss Anne first met Miss Hmm— *hmm*— this Mrs Smith-to-be... Ah— *Miss* Smith?– shall we call her then...?" Lady Russell had no alternative to offer. "...Here, in Bath— where the young Anne went to school?"

"Yes indeed. After the death of her mother, you know. Dear Lady Elliot was my greatest friend; an excellent woman; when I tell you that Anne is Lady Elliot over again, in looks as in disposition, you can imagine what a loss it was to us all, for–"

"—oh indeed! A terrible loss! Such a loss one might imagine could scar, could wound, an affectionate, gentle girl forever— thank Heaven she had you, Lady Russell. Were you yourself in Bath, at that time? Did you ever meet this old playfellow of Miss Anne's?"

"No; never. I never knew of her existence, until Anne approached me for my advice in the matter of visiting the unfortunate woman."

"Once so vigorous— and now, stricken– it is a sobering picture! It is sobering in its tendency. A rheumatic fever, I think you told me."

Lady Russell, concluding that she must have, inclined her head.

"And— *how* many years a widow?"

"Two or three, I believe Anne said."

"Two, or even three... It is an affecting picture, is it not. One to move the gentle heart of our cousin. Husband gone, health gone— and quite poverty-stricken, you say."

"Unable to even afford the comfort of a servant, Anne tells me."

"Indeed. That argues a degree of poverty, which— And yet, Anne has visited her repeatedly?..."

"At least once each week, my carriage conveys her as close to Westgate Buildings as Anne cares to be taken. She would not wish a carriage to draw up quite at the door, you understand.'

"Of course not! Of course!" Mr Elliot sat back in his chair, gazing upwards at the smoke-dimmed ceiling, its scarcely-visible painted cherubim, as if committing to memory something up there; perhaps their fat and vaguely outdated bottoms. You must remember that all this was lit only by firelight and candles. "...Of course; Anne has a delicacy, to feel... And– but then— This *Mrs Smith!*– they talk over old times together, I suppose! They must have much to talk of, if Miss Anne visits every week. *What* do they talk of, do you think, Lady Russell?"

Lady Russell gave him an encouraging smile.

"Our elegant, neat little Anne Elliot— and the broken Mrs Smith! I think I see her, almost; our poor Mrs Smith; wrapped in some short, old-fashioned pelisse, some old favourite perhaps, snatched from the sale of her effects, green silk now long grown shabby... It is an affecting picture, two such oddly-assorted figures. A picture to draw, and to intrigue a man! What *do* you think they talk of— the long-time friends— for so many hours together?"

But Lady Russell could not help him; had no idea. Anne had never mentioned... and in the end Mr Elliot had to give up this particular point.

"... But you know, Lady Russell; I could almost love my cousin Anne! I have seen ten thousand women, in ballrooms from Cornwall to Scotland, but none to rival my remarkable cousin. All around me I see pretension and paint, cunning and calculation: the spirit of the eighteenth century still haunts us, Lady Russell; we cannot shake it off, it seems. But— Anne Elliot! Anne, with her candour, and her modesty; her self-effacement; her principles, so firmly yet so quietly held— Anne is of the new Century, one feels, and hopes. She is of the new world."

"Perhaps you should discuss this with Anne herself."

"Ah!— Can you imagine the scene? How my cousin Anne would smile, and blush, and gently shake her head?... no: Miss Anne would not accept praise from an old reprobate like me! *You* must plead for me, Lady Russell. *You* must try to persuade her, that I am a good kind of man. As for being good enough for *her,* we both know that cannot be— but then, what man is? And I must look about me, since *you*—" and he took Lady Russell's dry, cool hand in one of his, and patted it snugly into place with the other, "have rejected me so *crushingly*."

At which Lady Russell threw up her long face, and laughed as she had not laughed since Marie Antoinette, too, was young; and herded sheep, their neat hooves clicking, across the marble floors of Versailles.

*

Damn. I had meant this— this evening here, at Laura Place, when Lady Dalrymple had her head cold, and Anne persisted in visiting Mrs Smith— to be the point at which Mr Elliot gives all the ladies in the room a lecture on the new century, the new woman. As they listened, they were all going to tuck their shoulders in; and then, start to droop their heads a little to one side, and simper, Evangelically— as all women sensitive to fashion *would* be doing, in ten or twenty years.

A lecture on the nineteenth century ideal. The Anne Elliots. The Fanny Prices— all her delicate feelings, all that finespun cloud of sticky pink floss; of more weight, in the end, than the one iron coin of truth her family needed. Lord, what a self-absorbed little wimp she was.

No; alright. That's not fair.

It's not fair.

Fanny, of Mansfield Park, really was constitutionally incapable of girding her loins and slaying the serpent that had entered her family home– I mean, she wouldn't even have had loins, would she? She was, quite simply, so maidenly that she truly couldn't so much as indicate that serpent's hiding place (in Mr Crawford's trousers). She is so enchantingly frail that she cannot choose but to shrink away to the East Room— while the happiness, the honour, the very social existence of the family which had brought her up in comfort and health, all went to hell in a handbasket. Can we blame her, for leaving undone that of which she is absolutely *required* to be incapable?

No.

Sorry, Fanny. I was thoughtless: I was spiteful. I take it back.

Then, too; in that case.... Perhaps I'm not being entirely fair to Anne Elliot?

Because, whatever she might have been like at nineteen, once she's reached a Regency twenty-seven— which is pushing forty-five, in our terms— no woman of any sense can keep up a Fanny Price act. Even to a man (especially to a man!) a pushing-forty-five-Fanny Price, stranded by the receding tide of oestrogen, would lie horribly exposed as a great saggy burden. When he grabs a handful of *that* flesh, it yields, not with the satiny springiness, the huge puff of pheromones (that intoxicating cloud!) with which teenage flesh yields. No:

its yielding is flaccid, slack. In his palm is cold, loose skin; sagging muscle; a sinew twangs beneath his finger. A tang of anxious sweat reaches his nose.

I think this is Jane Austen's problem, in *Persuasion*. If Fanny Price is the new model of the female— then, ten years on, how can this perfect woman *be*, if no-one marries her? Male authors assumed it impossible that such a situation could arise; but Jane Austen knew better.

So– look: she must, at least, start to drop hints.

And this is what Anne Elliot does, isn't it?

She's a great one for hinting.

If I'm to be truthful, Anne Elliot does sometimes speak out, too. If she thinks it her duty. Her authorised duty.

Strict veracity does, at this point, compel me to acknowledge, too, that Anne Elliot also acts. *Seizes* opportunities to act, when the action is compatible with her sex and station.

It's just that such opportunities— they don't come often.

And it gets more and more iffy to go out looking for them. With Hannah More on one side of her, and Dickens (at this point not even three years old, being shuttled up with the family effects to London, but —) eager to grow up and use his pen, acid-dipped for the purpose, to score out Woman's efforts even in her traditional sphere, of charity!— well.

What more can a dried-up passed-over spinster aspire to, now?— but to close her lips; fold her hands; pin, to her face, that faint, objectless, conciliatory smile, that so many single middle-aged women still wear when they are alone in public. Sit, in the coffin-sized space left to her, in silence.

Self-respecting silence.

Year upon year.

Upon year. The blockade of France is dynamite by comparison. (And over so soon!) The lack of a third volume in *Persuasion* stems, I begin to think, less from the onset of Addison's Disease, or whatever it was, than from the author's realisation that her Anne— "almost too good for me"— was forbidden, by virtue of those virtues of hers, from *herself* smashing out from this glass coffin in which she finds herself, so unexpectedly, locked. In the midst of this briar forest that surrounds her, suddenly. And which grows, every year; grows wider. And wilder. And more desolate.

And now we can only wait, there, with her: pray, with her, for rescue.

We must pray, specifically, for the blithely, superlatively imperfect man to hew a path back through that forest— back, to her.

Or at any rate, to get over his hissy fit. Which is all I really see Wentworth doing, myself. To get over himself, and come sailing back in at last, colours flying, and scoop her up and make her his wife.

Fat chance. Only in fiction, babe.

And she's already done it— self-regulation, patience, submission— she's done them doggedly, unremittingly, for two volumes! By Vol. III there is a danger it would grow tedious to more than just Anne.

So— ...

So yes:– We were remarking– with surprise, and annoyance– that Mr Elliot has failed to deliver that thematically-pivotal lecture on how to be a woman, in this new century, going forward. Instead— and once more— he has been frying fish of his own. Damn.

Maybe he'll do it later?

I hope so. I was counting on that speech.

Mr Elliot is starting to get a bit out of hand.

Chapter 11

Listening to Mr Elliot enthusing to Lady Russell about Anne– putting this together with his interest in Anne's opinions about the role of the clergy and the state of the nation– overlooking all the evidence, once obvious to her, of his habit of flirting like this with every thinking woman he meets, and in other ways, with every other kind of woman– Nellie is roused, by forces beyond her control, to a perturbing degree of not *anger*, no. That would be hopelessly unwise. Not jealousy either; that would be ridiculous. But— concern.

She is confused; confounded; concerned.

Could it be– surely it could not be!– that Mr Elliot was transferring his attentions to Anne?

But– what of Elizabeth?!?

Nellie's heart beat fast, when she thought of the possible implications for Elizabeth. Her cheeks flushed; her fists clenched and unclenched— tut tut, Nellie. She twisted her handkerchief with agitation, in the holy cause of friendship. She realised, as a third handkerchief disintegrated in her hands, that it was her duty to her friend— and to her patron too, Elizabeth's father, dear Sir Walter— to ascertain Mr Elliot's intentions in relation to–

"... Miss Elliot."

"Miss Elliot?"

Mrs Clay, alone in the Camden Place drawing-room with Mr Elliot, and bent low over her work to fire this sniper's shot, now risked a startled upward glance. Was that a trace of amusement and— could it be disdain?— in Mr Elliot's voice?

"I thought–... well we all thought... many *amongst* us thought, (though of course not Miss *Elliot*), but *some* have wondered, that perhaps you have had a

preference...?" The topic was suddenly coming to seem way outside the conversational remit of a Mrs Clay, no matter how fired by friendship's flame. She
blushed for her own indelicacy.

Mr Elliot seemed to feel it, too. He was silent; and she dared not lift her
eyes again to his face, to seek more understanding of his feelings. (Notice,
under Mr Elliot's influence, how tremendously Austenian she's becoming!)

For once, though, it would not have been a waste of time. For once, Mr
Elliot's true feelings were displayed openly upon his countenance, various
though those feelings were.

Mainly, he was feeling charmed at how beautifully people do fall in with his
wishes!

He had meant them, of course— the original inhabitants of Camden Place
— he had meant them to believe that his object was Elizabeth (why not?);
while at the same time ensuring that Lady Russell and her little *protégée*, and by
now half of Bath, believed it to be Anne herself.

And he had had no real doubt that everyone so believed that which he had
severally set them to believe— but– so pleasant to hear it, just the same. He
was human, after all, and we all need a bit of positive feedback from time to
time.

Then, as a result of luxuriating in that feeling— and yet, somewhat at war
with it— there grew the urge to disabuse Mrs Clay, as one might put it.

To see her eyes grow round with astonishment, while her jaw slackened
with awe.

And then he would see, wouldn't he, that little cringe, that little shrinking
and recoil as someone grasps, with a sudden plummet of their certainties, that
the person they are talking to is vastly their superior, in some whole, new, and
unimagined sphere. That would be nice too.

But there was no need to tell her; and, more importantly, some risk in
doing so.

But then Mrs Clay was coming along so quickly! She deserved a little
reward of some sort.

Here, too, would arise the opportunity to point a particular moral lesson;
one she would need to take on at some stage; so why not now?

He chose to indulge the urge.

*   *   *

I leave out the next bit, because it was so unsatisfactory and unproductive
on both sides. There was Mr Elliot, civilly, skilfully insinuating that Elizabeth's
air of command and consequence were, regardless of what the self-consciously virile population of Bath says, quite chilling to the discerning male–
while in contrast Anne's modest displays of duty and deference, her pose of

submission to her father, Lady Russell, and himself, were as a blow-torch beneath the male loins— Mr Elliot was insinuating all this fit to bust, for fully fifteen minutes; yet nary a twinge of guilty self-reflection did he elicit from Mrs Clay; so satisfactorily prone though he had found her, to date, to self-reflection of a guilty sort. The woman was silent. Her face showed only confusion.

Actually, she was thinking that Anne was only too given to judgement, so what was Mr Elliot talking about? It was odd.

Of course he couldn't know her so well. He didn't see her in unguarded moments at home.

Still. Was he really so clueless as to her character?

Yes: he was, actually. It is a pity Mr Elliot had only skimmed More's *Strictures on the Modern System of Female Education*. Right after '*They must even endure to be thought wrong sometimes*' it went on '*when they cannot but feel they are right*'. Sadly, you can't teach a woman to follow every rule in the Bible (even accompanied with its exegesis by yourself) and expect her never to notice that you don't: no, that takes actual brain trauma, the results of which may affect how well she performs her other feminine duties like rising early and cleaning the house. So it was this bit— '*cannot but feel they are right*'— which explains why, then as now, those who have been successfully moulded in youth into an eagerly-yielding helpmeet and a conscientiously submissive spirit nearly always develop, over the years, for men generally, and their husbands specifically, somewhere deep within them, a diamond-hard chip of contempt.

Another reason to prefer females young.

Younger and younger.

Just as they did, over the coming decades; until the Dickensian ideal was so youthful of mind as to be practically imbecilic– verging on the infuriating, even to her creator– and, yet, somehow inescapable, returning instant and insistent in his books again and again like a sheep-fly sticking itself back and back to the corner of your eye— and educated men were falling in love with twelve-year-old girls; fathers, the length and breadth of the civilised world, molesting their daughters— to the tremendous benefit of hysteria-doctors everywhere and ultimately of Freud in particular: who more popular, to those aficionados of the yielding feminine, than the doctor who asserts, as a matter of medical *science*, that their fainting, weeping daughters are just making it all up? Making it up *because*– here's the best bit– *because, deep down, they're hanging out for it!*

Jesus wept.

What an idea, to father a discipline.

Yet again, though, I seem to have charged off from the immediate point: which is:–

Such women, in later years, when they start to get long in the tooth and just a little bit smelly– that bit: *"Cannot but feel they are right"*.

Yes: so obviously Anne, at twenty-seven, was way over the hill. She could not but feel, in relation to those around her, that she was right almost all the time.

But Mr Elliot was, as I say, a great skimmer. Be it of books, ideas, people; his keen and active mind was quick to extract just those aspects most germane to his situation, richest in potential to grow his wealth. So he hadn't read that last little bit. Or if he had, he hadn't thought through the implications. Skimmers must be happy leaving implications to sort themselves out, or for someone else to sort out, or, just, to leave them... Mr Elliot is quite modern, isn't he. He did well back then, but he would do even better now, in our times.

After another ten– fifteen— nay, twenty minutes of strenuous and masterful hinting, Mr Elliot began to feel, with some impatience, that his morning could be better spent elsewhere.

"Perhaps you will allow me to recommend, to you, a little book—?" He ran through his mental inventory of possibilities. There was *Strictures,* of course: since he had cut his hair, he had recommended *Strictures* to a great many women, and their husbands too. Fiction might go down more easily here— *Mansfield Park,* then, and... what was that other good one... *The Misfortunes of Virtue*...? Oh, and *Hints Towards Forming the Character of a Young Princess*– (though didn't that go on rather a lot about learning history? and German? God! Who wants a German-speaking wife!) — and all of it much too late now, of course, to form anyone's character; these women here, or the princess in question—

But any of those books would do, really. Any of them was calculated to foster that self-doubt; that *distrust of her own judgement* (to quote More), that *submissive spirit* (Edgeworth), which of all things ensures a happy home life. Yes. Though Mrs Clay had given but a poor return, this morning, to his energies; still, he would not allow it to be too late.

Not for her.

Elizabeth was hopeless of course. Show her that book and she would... Well:– she would simper and coo, for a couple of days. Then she would get bored with it; and then, she would forget all about it.

But, Anne! Reading, thinking, sensitive Anne! For her, Mr Elliot could see; self-distrust, self-vigilance, self-correction were daily habits. Married to Anne, a man could act as he saw fit– confident that whatever he did, his wife would shut up and submit. Honestly, he didn't understand why all his friends were not Evangelicals.

*

Bearding the smooth Mr Elliot about his intentions, then, hadn't turned out anything like Nellie had hoped.

She toddled down to the library: they only had *Strictures,* but that was bad enough. Such a dreary volume, it seemed to Nellie— and so badly written! No structure; no logical articulation of ideas. Just endless reiteration, in strings of loose sentences, running, one after another, and banging on, and on, about her pet ideas—[†]

Nevertheless, the very reiteration, unreasoning unhearing singleminded reiteration of its premises, gave Nellie all the sinking feeling Mr Elliot had calculated on. Like a Jew reading her first Nazi pamphlet in 1932, like a feminist reading a men's movement manifesto fifty years later: the author saw a great future– a wonderful future, a glorious future!— Just, to reach it, they must purge from among them all that resembles Mrs Clay. Nellie. You.

That night, drifting off to sleep, she thought... or rather, felt... the next thing, which so many think (or rather, feel) at these turning points: when they see, for the first time, that *this future has no place for them...*

If she were to purge *herself;* quietly, of course, but comprehensively. And then, drop little hints about it. (Or even put up an Instagram thing where she's milking, with small white clean hands, a perfectly clean cow; and do a voice-over about how she makes her own cheese, for her family.)

Would Mr Elliot admire her, then? As he admired Anne?

Would Nellie, the new, transformed Nellie, be allowed into this future of theirs?– this future, which she glimpsed, now, suddenly so unnervingly close at hand?

There's often a lot to be gained, being among the first to submit.

Chapter   12

February draws on. In Dashe, the little household is dispersed.

Nellie receives one last letter from her father, dated the morning of his departure for France, and telling of the children off to tutors and school: evidently enthusiasm had withered as the day approached. On the morning itself, Ariosto was quiet from first to last: he probably wonders how he will go; will he be teased, yes of course, will he be bullied, who can say... *I am more struck every day by his resemblance to myself at that age. While I often catch glimpses of your dear mother in both the children, it is odd, surely, that Ariosto could not seem more my own grandson.* Mr Shepherd hesitated; censored the next bit — ('I have some concerns about his lungs.') *Josephine cried torrents, which is strange too, considering how she sang about the house on first hearing of the plan. She flung her arms around me ~ around*

[†]   — So? What's wrong with that? Nellie's a critic too now is she?

her brother ~ around Cook, and the maid and the gardener and of course and repeatedly the dogs ~ said that she would pray for us ~ begged us to pray for her ~ declared that she would never forget us (on which point I had had no concerns. Only early senility could expunge us from her mind completely by May? surely?) ~ waved us goodbye from the carriage window and blew us kisses for as long as we remained within her sight ~ We may have to start censoring her reading. I am sorry to say Handel reports that the tears, after some intermission, returned in good earnest for the first stage or two of the journey, but he put her down at Mrs Mortlake's Academy completely recovered and able to greet people at the door with her usual magnanimity. She writes that her room is darker, and the teachers not all of them as well-informed, as she could have hoped: I do not doubt, however, that she will soon have things in good train; and it is a comfort to think that if this French journey does not yield us return, and if Bath too should disappoint, we can probably go to Bristol and help Josephine run the school.— And the house in Dashe had been sublet.

That was that, then. For a few months.

On those nights when the weather was drear at her window pane, and the fourth-best bedchamber of Camden Place felt indifferent, and Bath, hostile and difficult, Nellie would no longer be able to warm her own spirits by thinking of them all snug together at home; occupied, and happy, and independent of the world; wanting only for her, for Nellie, to walk in... and how they would jump up, astonished!— and embrace her; draw her to the fire, settle about her; show her, by their joyful faces, that her arrival had made their happiness complete—

Just for a few months. Then papa would be back, and everything would be as it had been.

*

"So your father is in France, Mrs Clay!"

Nellie smiled agreement to Sir Walter— folding her letter quickly. That was the only way to head off, without offence (she hoped), any request for the common public reading.

But Mr Elliot was at once alert: "France! Mr Shepherd in *France* how interesting...

"but, he will have plenty of company by now! I hear that, by now, the whole of the Continent is quite overrun with visitors."

"Hardly touring weather surely", protested Sir Walter. "Depths of winter."

"Ah! but *France*, Sir: really something to be seen, now that the Peace is here at last. I dashed across myself, as you know, last year; just as soon as was possible; or rather sooner, perhaps!— I felt I could not deny myself that experience![†] An interesting country, Sir, experiencing interesting times."

[†] Mr Elliot had been in the process of returning from that very visit, back in November— landing from a friend's yacht at Sidmouth, and thus famously meeting Anne Elliot in Lyme, while on his journey back to London. Just so you know.

The conversation turned for a while to the modes, politics, and tone of the newly-humbled France; which Mr Elliot's tales made clear was not nearly humble enough, considering the circumstances.

"Well then, Mrs Clay", resumed Sir Walter— once Mr Elliot had finished describing, yet again, the spirit of Paris and its fashions up to an including the morning of the 28th of October, 1814— "Mr Shepherd wrote to me of hoping to chase up some old investments? In France and... and so on?"

"Oh; yes..." Nellie hesitated. "He hopes, perhaps, to reclaim some of what our family lost in Bonaparte's time. And it may be— there are friends, who may still be alive. Relatives too."

"In Paris, mmm?" Mr Elliot again. "Any particular *quartier*?"— and he lifted his eyebrows, casually; Frenchly.

"Papa will visit his offices there, but you know that when the dreadful business first began in earnest– I was quite a little child– he removed us to—" She mentioned a town of such insignificance that, just as Mr Shepherd had calculated, Revolution had overlooked it: indeed it is so obscure that I myself do not know its name.

"Your father supported the Bourbons, of course", Mr Elliot offered.

It sounded like a statement.

His gaze, however, lingered on Nellie's face; until she began to feel that her assenting smile must be, somehow— as a response— insufficient.

Into the expanding hiatus Miss Elliot, and then Sir Walter, turned their attention towards her, with a vacuous limerence that might be the early dawning of inquiry...

Nellie spoke:–

"Yes. Yes of course."

Mr Elliot's gaze did not leave her face, however. Sir Walter and his daughter were now looking from him to Nellie, and back again. "My father — It is a matter of *public record*—"

Nellie collected herself.

"Naturally, with the return of the *legitimate* regime, papa will be able to seek out his friends, at last; risk a return to that unhappy country— where he spent so long a *prisoner,* of the Corsican Upstart— and seek out yes his friends, and acquaintance; his friends among the *legitimate* regime. It is for this, that he returns to France. At last."

She was afraid that she may have spoken, by the end, with too much emphasis. In the face of Mr Elliot's unwavering gaze she felt the need to be emphatic; though her judgement, perhaps, was poor; she felt that perhaps her perceptions these days were unduly sensitive; though, at other times she wondered if perhaps she were not blind... But it seemed that indeed she must have been too emphatic.

For Mr Elliot's brow was just faintly puckering...?

*

Mr Shepherd had indeed supported the Bourbons, as a matter of course. He had also supported the Jacobins, the Montagnards, the Thermidorians and the *Directoire,* as each in turn had appeared necessitous of support. Unfortunately, deep in the chill of late '94, he had not supported an angular morose youth of Corsican extraction who, fresh out of house arrest, had spent an unhappy half-hour in John Shepherd's offices, trying unsuccessfully to arrange a loan.

History has not dared accused Buonaparte of having a petty tendency, of the kind to seek requital for small slights,[†] and in any case, he was subsequently too tied up most of the time slaughtering faceless millions in his quest for world domination. However, revenge can be outsourced, like anything else, and Mr Shepherd was to find that he had fallen foul, not so much of the larval Corsican Brigand himself, but of a— well not a *friend*— the C.B. was a friendless youth— but, of an acquaintance of his. Who, being similarly placed financially on that unlucky winter's day, had chanced to accompany the foetal French Devil to Mr Shepherd's offices; and with similar lack of success.

In later years, disqualified from a post in his dear old acquaintance's vast armies by a crippling cowardice, this gentleman had taken it upon himself to arrange, for the Notorious Impostor's delectation, strings of the heads of individual, personal enemies; a fresh string to be presented, a congratulatory garland, on each of Napoleon's returns to Paris. The Corsican Pygmy didn't seem terribly interested each time. Nevertheless, neither did he actively object: so the acquaintance beavered away at his war-work; and over the years, he got through a lot of heads. Mr Shepherd's had chanced to be one of the first.

Not here in England, Nellie would assure herself. In England, even the middle classes felt themselves too human for the law to risk subjecting them to such grossness. Here, now, things like the gibbet were reserved for the working class, and down— tinkers, tailors; shopkeepers, and suchlike.

The Barratts, for example.

Not that the Shepherds were all that middle class any more.

*

After this, Mr Elliot enquired after her father's progress in France regularly, and minutely. His interest in Mr Shepherd's route, intentions, connections, and history was ever alive: he often pressed Mrs Clay for details which she was then obliged to declare herself unable to supply.

How long is it, now, since Nellie has had a really sound night's sleep?

---

† Yes yes the cardinals, the Black Cardinals, who boycotted his wedding: but a slight is small only in proportion to the man; by then, he was the biggest man in Europe.

Chapter 13

All events, no matter where they began, seemed to end these days in Mr Elliot.

There was the morning when Cubbins tapped, very quietly, on her chamber door, a full two hours before breakfast. In response to his whispered communications Nellie hurried downstairs through the shadowy pre-dawn halls; to encounter, in a drawing-room still chilly from the night— wrapped in a massive pelisse, and sobbing inelegantly— Miss Carteret. Catherine.

"My *dear!* What has happened?"

Followed a tense, blubbery two minutes; Fiona Catherine Carteret, along with all her other misfortunes, was one of those whom tears render adenoidal, and Nellie had time to imagine a great many frightening things. Eventually, though, she pieced it together. Mr Y had spoken to her mother; to Catherine's mother. Mr Y had proposed. To Catherine.

"Oh!" Nellie laughed, buoyant with relief. "How wonderful!"

"— *not* wodderful!" was Catherine's muffled protest.

"Your—" (your second proposal) "...and you only just turned sixteen! But of course my dear, it's delightful; such fun!"

Another muffled wail from Catherine. Mrs Clay saw further.

"You don't have to *marry* him."

This brought Miss Carteret's face out of Nellie's dressing gown collar at last.

"Yes I *do!*" she howled with sudden and horrible clarity— my God she would wake the house! "Mother says I *do!* She says, this is what she came to Bath *for!* She says, if I don't marry him, she'll give up on me *entirely!*"

"Well— Mr Yates is alright, isn't he? Hm?"

Catherine gulped.

"Hmm? Even Miss Elliot thinks he's—... he's a nice man. He has a good property; good prospects. What's wrong with Mr Yates, for the Honourable Miss Carteret?"

Miss Carteret pushed out a lumpy lower lip. "Well he's just a Baronet. He's not even a Baronet *yet.*"

Nellie gaped; ostentatiously.

Catherine remembered herself. She flushed even redder— and they both glanced towards the door. "Oh you know what I *mean*", Catherine whispered.

"No I don't!" hissed Nellie. "Plenty of girls in your position marry lower and less!" (Miss Carteret had only eleven thousand pounds. Those brothers.)

"But 0.2p!"

"0.45, once he's the Baronet."

Catherine thrust out her jaw, and stared down at her screwed-up handkerchief. (Heavens! — and had that Lieutenant of Marines been a Lord in disguise?)– "Alright. Tell me. What else is wrong with him?"

"He has the most ghastly *hairs* up his nose. It looks like a– like a——" Miss Carteret cast about for an adequate simile. "Like a horrible bunch of *hair*. Bristly *hair*. It looks like a torn-up doormat."

Nellie had never noticed the bristles. Miss Carteret was so very young, however; still with her last growing spurt to do: she would have a different perspective.

So. Severe nose hair. This is bad: every woman knows how bad.

"Well what's the worst thing about him? The Baronet, or the 0.45p, or the nose?"

"Oh the *nose!* "

Nellie probed a little longer; but Catherine just shrugged. Apart from a general sense of ickiness, natural in a girl contemplating a man twice her age, there was nothing further: they had come to the root of the problem.

In the end, Nellie managed to persuade Lady Dalrymple to calm down.

Well— She persuaded her not to pressure her daughter. We all know what Miss Carteret is capable of, for love. Let's not put to the test what she might do for... dis-love? Disinclination. Distaste. "We do *not* say, 'No'. Rather, we ask him, just this: to give her *time*. To give *himself* time— Time, to engage her youthful heart." And Mrs Clay had smiled, persuasively, at Lady Dalrymple.

... Oh, but Lady D. was miserably anxious! Like Sir Thomas Bertram before her, she couldn't believe her luck— this instant she wanted to seize it in both hands and, while it was still dazed and smiling, hustle it up a church aisle. Like Sir Thomas too, she felt that Mr Yates' constancy might best be supported by not testing it for too long. She allowed herself, however, at last, to be persuaded. ("How *much* time, Mrs Clay?... do you think it might need?...")

Catherine was ecstatic— and then, ready to put it all behind her. To fifteen, 'not until you can feel you can be happy with him' means, of a man who has a doormat up his nose, never.

Of the three, Mr Yates was the most rational.

"I suppose she is only a slip of a thing, isn't she?"

"Full young indeed! Too young to feel anything but bewilderment, at the sudden, overwhelming offer of a man's love! Give her time." Mrs Clay smiled– a knowing, compassionate smile this time– this time, she was the mature widow. "Be gentle with her." And Mr Yates had brayed, eagerly; uneasily.

How very fortunate that Catherine hadn't taken a dislike to that laugh. One can do little about a laugh. Mrs Clay had already spoken, privately, to the man's valet, and he in turn had secured a tiny pair of skissars.

Then there was Miss Elliot's reaction to manage, her feelings to soothe, her understanding to reconstruct. Elizabeth herself had no use for Mr Yates as such; but one of her train has defected. Possibly two: possibly they would marry (probably, they would marry), Mr Yates and little Catherine. The Honourable Miss Carteret. Then she would lose them both.

Which was not unserious.

"Well I for one am happy for the poor man", declared Mrs Clay boldly. "He was *so* miserable, seeing— as we all did— that you were not in the *least* struck by him, in spite of *all* those things he tried! Now Miss Carteret is lovely, of course– but just perhaps rather a plain little thing one must confess: he must have felt safe, proposing to her."

"Is that what people say?"

"Oh yes. That's what everyone is saying. I heard Mr Elliot speak of it."

Elizabeth thought of her cousin, and was comforted.

Furthermore, and despite the nose hair, Mr Yates had his strengths. Mrs Clay felt none of Lady Dalrymple's concern, for example, as to his constancy: she sensed in Mr Yates a modesty and a susceptibility of heart which, with only the slightest encouragement, would attach him to his beloved object like ivy to an oak. Let him only sit in the same drawing room with Miss Carteret as she felt her way, with many an earnest frown, through her latest piano 'piece'; let her elders only sit by Mr Yates the while, and smile upon him, and speak to him, at intervals, of her girlish heart; let Catherine only, and especially, chew her lip sometimes in his presence, and seem to feel a little for his predicament, as well as for her own— and the gangly, bashful Mr Yates would endure with a steadiness, a steadfastness, to leave many a more manly man for dead. Nellie felt, at any rate, that it was so.

Contrast those diffident eyes, for instance, with Commander Clay's flashing orbs! A man like Clay wouldn't have tolerated this palaver– *he* would not have suffered to be put upon probation! Not for a moment! — Let alone indefinitely; like this.

No, George had had a heart above prevarication. When all was said and done; if Nellie's own submission had not been so prompt, and so complete, then George probably would have buggered off and never clapped eyes on her again.

Unless by sheer accident. Any number of years later. Brought together, almost against their wills, say, by some newly-shared common acquaintance.

The insight should have startled her, shouldn't it?

But it didn't. It simply drifted across her consciousness, one day— trotting across Union Street, with Miss Elliot leaning heavily on one arm, and Miss Elliot's purchases, slipping, under the other— that George had always allotted his own *amour-propre* a higher place, in his scheme of things, than his love for Nell.

They make it sound good, these men: *I could not love thee half so well, loved I not honour more:* but that's what it boils down to.

Probably— thought Nellie, gaining the opposite pavement and hitching her various burdens into place— that's why she hadn't held out, really. Hadn't put a higher price on herself. Any price.

Hadn't stipulated, first, the head of a dragon.

*

But I said the whole thing was going to lead to Mr Elliot, didn't I?

*

So, as you can see then, around this time, Nellie was busy as a bee. Planning, arranging, persuading; outwardly, at least, Mrs Clay reached here the zenith of her influence. Her smooth swift transformation of the Yates-Carteret *fracas,* from ticking gossip-bomb that all Bath was going to shriek and cackle over, into a sweet sentimental secret that did the rounds to hushed applause— it was masterly. Everyone involved was terribly grateful. Even Lady D., once she'd calmed down, recognised the necessity, the wisdom, of the strategy of Mrs Clay.

But this is all the more impressive for the fact that Nellie was giving it only half her mental powers. Even while, a benevolent Mme de Montespan, she reconfigured everyone's understanding in everyone's best interests, her newly-awakened consciousness writhed distractedly within her. It was impossible, she was realising, to square everything she needed to do, in this case, with all those Evangelical principles laid out in the reading matter that Mr Elliot had prescribed for her. In broad outline, maybe. In intention, yes. But not in detail. And as the early Evangelists knew— as Nellie was discovering— the Devil is in the detail.

Her self-doubts were sincere, and correspondingly painful. In the face of comparable challenges, future generations would keep their spirits up by developing an intricate system of self-deception, hypocrisy, and corruption; long-term, it is the way that inhuman standards are always maintained. This is of no help, though, to our poor little Nell right now. In the first breaking wave of ideological change, those of clear head and sincere heart must pass *un mauvais quart de siècle.*

On the other hand...

Nellie did also feel— and with a thrilling gravity— that this issue, which she faced, here, was exactly the kind of moral problem which Mr Elliot would appreciate. It would surely be wise, in her perplexing circumstances, to consult their valued friend?

There seemed little doubt, really, that they would need to talk it over at some length. That he would need to listen to her, as she laid her perplexities bare before him... listen, with that soft, intense gaze, that attentive stillness of his. (When he did this, she no longer stared back at him avidly, as other women did: she kept her countenance mostly a little averted, her eyes lowered, paying his words the compliment of the same thoughtful attention that he was awarding her. She sensed that this pleased him.)

Then, on her plea, he would respond.

He would lean in, closer; a pensive hand, perhaps, would be supporting his temple... he would speak... and she would hear from him that quiet, reflective tone that he had reserved, until now, for people like Lady Russell, Miss Anne.

Perhaps— given the subtlety of the issues, the delicacy of her situation— he might even display a thoughtful hesitancy, that no-one else had ever elicited from him before.

∗

The event nearly fulfilled Nellie's hopes; especially at the beginning, before Mr Elliot got a bit bored.

"Those of us who work behind the scenes, those who 'seek to do good in secret', must often walk these thornier paths."

Oh yes Mr Elliot. But—

"Saint Paul himself, you will recall, found that he must 'be all things to all men'."

Oh yes, Mr Elliot... yet– Were not the Jesuits, now, thought to be...?

"For the Lord rewarded the good steward, remember, who put his master's wealth out to– er– usury."

Nellie remained conflicted; so conflicted, that of itself, her nose screwed up. "But doesn't the Bible say..." She hesitated again. But, surely the Bible condemned usury?

Mr Elliot laughed merrily: reassuringly. When it came to Biblical justifications of usury, he was on home turf.

Oh; yes, Mr Elliot... But...

Mr Elliot was patient, open; only his ring finger began to tap, woodpecker-swift, on the stem of his cane. "I suspect, my dear Mrs Clay — if you will forgive the liberty– from a man, and a scholar — perhaps, if I may draw a bow at a venture:– You are, as yet, of the many who know *of* the Bible; **yet**, do not really *know the Bible?*"

Nellie gaped.

"For example; have you yourself actually read the Bible all through? Starting at the beginning and going all the way through to the end?"

"Well..."

"'*Well*'— " laughed Mr Elliot. "It is '*well*', indeed! Perhaps, when you have done that...?"

Nellie gave up. She was a good steward, at any rate; if Mr Elliot said so. Personally, she felt more confused than ever.

Mr Elliot observed it all in her downcast face... Yes; on balance, another twenty minutes well-spent.

As for Nellie actually reading the Bible all through, he felt tolerably secure! She would get as far as Chronicles at best, and then she would have to admit herself unequal to the task. Everyone gave up by Chronicles.

(Whereas Mr Elliot, moved by the spirit of the times, had recently bought his first Cruden's. A Concordance wasn't something one would want to see in just any hands— but he could already divine what a splendid investment he had made on his own part.)

With one gloved finger, gently he lifted her chin.

"Be of good heart, my sister. Be of good heart."

Then he was gone.

*

How crudely George would have spoken of it! How he would have laughed!

So would most of her Plymouth acquaintance. They would have laughed her to scorn, and shot out their lips, and shaken their heads — until she was ashamed to own this feeling.

Even papa might have laughed.

(He would, indeed, have laughed like a cat. He and the children would have laughed her out of all this, in no time.)

There was a fineness, about this man, that none in her past could have recognised.

Chapter 14

By the end of February, the fineness of Mr Elliot had become an obsession. The mysterious quality he exercised, of making every interaction painful — easily taken for a drawback in a lesser man— was revealed in him as a bizarrely magnetic power: it compelled her to seek counsel with him, again and again, as she strove to surmount her own irrational weaknesses. And confusion. And her confusion and her irrationality increased almost daily— So the matter was of some urgency.

A few conversations were almost too much, though, even for Nellie. Consider, in particular, this one, which followed a morning's visit to the Cravens, neighbours and good friends of their cousin the Viscountess Lady Dalrymple. The Cravens had taken Number 3, Laura Place— actually adjoining their cousins!– such a coincidence! They lived in comparable style, and Mrs Craven spoke, too, of sending, when the weather was more favourable, for their *third* carriage, a phaeton; the better to explore the surrounding country.

In spite of all of this, Miss Elliot could not judge that today's visit had been enhanced by the presence, actually in the drawing room among them, of Mrs Craven's seven children. No: in this matter, Elizabeth was decidedly in the negative.

Sir Walter, while pronouncing that as a general rule a child's place was the nursery, or the school room, except and allowing for purely family occasions, and etc and etc... nevertheless alllowed that Mrs Craven herself had made a charming picture with the sleeping baby (a bundle of expensive lace) nestled in her satin lap. The brief appearance of a quiet and pretty child might well be permitted, as and while it contributed to such graceful domestic scenes. The others had been unnecessary.

Mrs Clay wasn't sure what to say. Normally, she liked everyone's children, as a matter of policy. She also liked several of Mrs Craven's as a matter of personal taste; and she had, after all, just been seen spending almost the full quarter hour with the two eldest girls, far more absorbed than she should have been in their enumeration of the merits of Blücher, their pug, and in speculating about the possibility that Blücher may, in spite of his rather obvious sex, be— as he indeed fully appeared in all other respects *to* be— on the point of his confinement; and if so, what kind of infants might be expected to issue from Blücher, and finally, whether she herself might give a home to one— so now she was in some small difficulties. As if instinctively she turned, seeking the guidance of Mr Elliot...

...who was drawing a paper from his waistcoat. "Without wishing any reflection on Mrs Craven's little brood— and my cousin's feelings are understandable!" (a quick, complicit smile to Elizabeth), "yet there is, as you say Sir Walter, a feminine sweetness in the very blindness of Mrs Craven's affection for her children. A woman's doting upon a helpless infancy always has something of charm, to a man; does it not, Sir Walter?"

Yes, Mrs Clay would definitely need to talk over the Craven visit with Mr Elliot.

"And it is not only the gentle sex whose parental feelings can rouse our minds to admiration. I have here—" (unfolding the paper as he spoke), "the memento of just such a touching little tale. Mmm.

"What, for instance, might you judge *this* to be?"

He held out on the palm of his hand a tiny curl of something, tied about with a scrap of faded ribbon.

Miss Elliot, who was seated to his right, took his hand in both of hers to draw it closer:– "Why, it is a lock of hair!"

"And whose hair?— how old would you judge that person to be?"

They were all, in those days, far more experienced with locks of hair than we are now. Not quite so grotesquely expert as the Victorians were to be; but pretty dab hands all the same. "Clearly it is child's; from its fairness, I should have guessed, an infant's", replied Elizabeth on their behalf. The lock was fine as silk, and almost pure white.

"Indeed: an infant. A little boy. The child of one of our heroes of the sea, our officers of the Navy. English, as you can see"— pulling the pale shining strand through his fingers, so that it caught the light. They all nodded, and *"non— non Angeli sed Angli"*, murmured Anne.

Mr Elliot turned his head a fraction, so that his turned eyes could look into hers: they shared one of Mr Elliot's small, intense smiles. Mrs Clay's hands tightened. Elizabeth shifted in her seat.

Mr Elliot's smile deepened.

Eyes still on Anne, he held the lock out to her. "And now? Where is that child?"

From the others, baffled silence— but Anne, the eager pupil, bent over the object. His hand was in both of hers.

"Observe the ribbon", said Mr Elliot.

Her head was leant in, close by his.

"No English weaver conceived this pattern..." said Anne slowly; "no English dyes produced this— this shade of pink..." Mr Elliot had quietly turned. He had tipped the coil towards Nellie. Slithered it right into her lap.

That ribbon.

Nellie had been more struck by the ribbon, all those years ago, than by the hair itself. Save for its fineness, the hair could have been George Clay's own; it could have been a girl's; ridiculous, that anything male should be so fair...

The ribbon, though, would have been chosen by her. By the boy's mother.

She found that she had picked the thing up, between thumb and forefinger. Lifted it to her nose. Through the apple-wood fire, that scented the drawing-room of Camden Place, she sensed again the old smell; unwashed, rum-soaked skin.

But look. The hair was clean. So extraordinarily clean. She had never seen it so clean, not for years and years.

Had somebody washed it?— had he washed it?

Mr Elliot?

Everyone was staring at her.

She pushed the grotesque little relic back to Mr Elliot; whose hands remained folded, in his lap.

Too urgently, Nellie thrust it towards Elizabeth— who recoiled slightly. Nellie twisted the other way... and here was Sir Walter leaning forward to relieve her of it. "Ah–! And— this little lock of hair—" He made a show of examining it, turning it this way and that. Probably only Nellie knew that he could barely see it. "...You have some tale to tell us, Mr Elliot? Some tale of naval derring-do?"

With an obvious effort, Mr Elliot tore his wondering eyes from Mrs Clay.

"Why— yes Sir Walter— yes..."

(Was it even the same hair?)

"...Er— yes. It is a sad little tale: a tale of—

"But really, Mrs Clay, are you quite well?" — the attention of the room, which had followed the hair and its story across to the other side of the circle, swung violently back and fastened on Nellie again.

"Perfectly well, I thank you", she managed.

But Mr Elliot could not look away.

And now Elizabeth was hastening to her side. Sir Walter was ringing the bell— calling out for smelling salts, brandy...

Anne— who had, during all the above, more than once inhaled audibly while lifting her upper body and tilting her head, in the way one does preparatory to certain speech (preparatory, in this case, to presenting the room with her deductions, as regards the little puzzle Mr Elliot had set them)— sighed, and passed Elizabeth the smelling salts from her pocket.

Once, George had sent the woman all their money.

It had been half-day; long awaited half-day. In the relative sobriety of that portentous morning, George had put on a clean shirt. Nellie had brushed and sponged his coat and his hat, smartening them up, too, to the best shape the now-shapeless garments could hold; and thus made as much like his old self as his current self could now shape up to be, George had skipped out down the dirty alley, towards the room off the victualing yard that did duty as a Navy Office. Just for a moment, watching him hurry eagerly away, she could recognise in him the remains of the man she had married.

It was better when she couldn't. Watching him hop over a puddle with a bit of a spring to his step, it was like catching the flicker of a ghost in daylight; like watching a man whom you know is walking to his death. He swung around the corner and disappeared.

Off to collect his fifty-four pounds twelve shillings.

It would clear away all their current debts, if George brought it straight home.

Even if he didn't— even if he detoured, on the way back; and of course, he would detour on the way back— still there would be heaps left, relatively speaking. Oh, the joyful relief of half-day!– For a while, Nellie would be able to put things on tick again with reasonable ease.

This time, though, only an hour into his detour, George had met an old shipmate... dear old someone-or-other... there were many such— but, the killer is, this time, that old Someone-or-other had just been made commander. He was come to Plymouth this morning, to join his ship.

His ship.

And then he, the Commander, was to sail with all possible expedition... to sail, as it happened, to that very port where Lieutenant Clay's long-lost lady lay —. Commander Someone had been a midshipman, once, under George. A pissy mid.

George had looked down, at his hands on the table before him; at the lace on his wrists, which wear upon so many tables of so many public houses had still not entirely removed. He had looked up, at dear old someone's dismayed and smiling face, and reached into his pocket and handed over his half's pay. Take it to the dear lady, and my son.

"*All* of it, George?"

"Come on, Nellie."

"But, *all* of it? *All* of it? You didn't keep *any*?"

"Oh Nellie. What was the point. I would just have drunk it."

Nellie had run to the harbour, hoping to find the man and beg at least some of the money back, to pay the most aggressive of their debtors. But the ship had gone. It had sailed, within the hour.

They were always gone: they had always sailed.

"...that profession which is, if possible, more distinguished in its domestic virtues than in its national importance."

"But what happened to the little boy?" demanded Anne.

"And to the– to his mother?" seconded Elizabeth.

Mr Elliot spread his hands expressively; shook his head.

"Dead, as well?" Elizabeth guessed.

Who knows?

"Or living on, in that foreign port; the flaxen-haired, blue-eyed boy never learning to lisp his mother-tongue— his *father's* tongue, I should say", Anne corrected herself.

"Perhaps never knowing his true place in society!" This from Sir Walter. "Never knowing himself the son of an English officer."

"Abused, no doubt, as just another mongrel guttersnipe; another by-blow of war." Mr Elliot sighed and, musing, turning the glittering lock this way and that before the candle-light:–

"...The saddest thing, of course, is that thewife of our bold truant— our errant officer!— herself an Englishwoman— his wife in the eyes of the *world* — never once acknowledged the existence of this child: never attempted to alleviate the child's condition."

There was a short silence at this.

Mr Elliot glanced up at them all. Seemed to register their reaction with a little start. And laughed self-consciously; "But of course— why should she?

"And yet..." He seemed drawn back to the lock of hair, and the play of light upon it... "and yet...

"There were no other children, you know. None at home.

"More: there is reason to think— I am *told* there *was* reason to think— that the wife, the legitimate– the legally-*sanctioned*– wife— was aware..."

Mr Elliot sighed.

"There had been an illness, apparently. A girlhood illness. Of the kind which... well. You understand me. And kept secret. It was felt, by some, that the bride-groom should have been warned."

He let the lock of hair drop into his lap, and sighed again, this time to the fire. "How might a man feel, under such circumstances?"

The pause that followed was long enough all to reflect that Mr Elliot was, himself, without an heir.

"...and how— forgive me, ladies, but– how might a wife feel? I am a man, merely!– and cannot therefore be expected to truly understand! But— child-less *herself*, you know. One feels– that is, a man cannot help but feel– that in relation to this helpless infant, quite innocent, as it was, of its parents' sin... Did the womanly instinct never stir in her? The maternal instinct?" He frowned: distress. "The son, after all, of her husband! Of the man that she had sworn to honour, and to obey."

"Assuming she was true to those vows: that she ever spoke them in good earnest!" put in Miss Anne tartly.

Mr Elliot nodded; thoughtful.

"Yes. Miss Anne is right of course: yes. To so deceive him, at the very out-set of their life together, as to the likelihood of God's blessing them with chil-dren of their own— Can it ever be allowable?" He cast himself back in his chair. "Can it ever be *forgiven?*"

Sir Walter answered: once, and for all.

"Never!"

"*Never*, Sir—" repeated the younger man, with a deferential inclination of his head.

"Never! Such deception— *Such* a deception— is beyond the bounds of comprehension, evil! To deprive a man, *knowingly* to deprive a man, of any legitimate son and heir! To lure a man into a sterile marriage, a dead-end, a– a– And, to leave him there, perhaps, his whole life! No!– it is beyond the bounds of all proper, of—" but Sir Walter was now lost for words; could only splutter, "—Appalling! Appalling!"

— but she had *not* known! How could she *possibly* have known? She was *pure.* She was *nineteen!*— *What* childhood illness? Nellie cast wildly through her memory for something, that she might have mentioned to someone— measles?– but that was boys— Oh God, is *this* what everyone had been saying about her?

(But how had he got hold of the hair? Nellie– *Nellie!* How had he got hold of the hair?)

Nonsense this wasn't even necessarily the same hair!

Yes it was.

Nellie hadn't exactly looked, when she disposed of George's effects, for the hair. But she'd noticed that it wasn't there.

So.

He'd given it to some friend, no doubt. She certainly didn't want it around.

She'd have burnt it.

Yes. That is the kind of wife she'd been, in the end.

Chapter 15

This was by no means the end of the lock of hair. It was a talking point, in and about Camden Place, for many days to come.

There were the serious discussions: duty versus love; the law of God versus Nature's imperatives; Civilised Man versus Man in his pure, raw, Primordial state— when I say 'serious', obviously I don't mean 'bland'.

Then there were the more light-hearted ones. Swinging her hips along the Gravel Walk, with Mr Z on one arm and Mr Elliot on the other, Elizabeth could be overheard speculating on the contributions that may have been made, in the Tale of the Little Cast-Away, by a 'sailors' disease'. It was a delicate topic between a lady and two gentlemen, and hence was provoking much clever circumlocution and laughter.

Red-faced and dull-headed, Mrs Clay stumbled along behind them.

Mr Elliot was concerned for her isolation. More than once she had glimpsed his face, troubled, turned back towards her; his own laugher was often uneasy. Yet the linked arms towed him on.

Now he was protesting: she could hear him protesting. "Well but it simply strikes me as a matter of logic: I am puzzled at the *logic* of your case! You seem required the sailor's wife er— 'under the weather', as you put it, Z— and yet the husband, not."

"A sound point: a logical point! What have you to say to my cousin's logic, Mr Z?"

"Oh well I can't pretend to know all the *ins and outs* of the matter you know", demurred Mr Z, to giggles from Elizabeth. "*–but.* I *understand*—and this does seem logical, so it will appeal to you, Elliot— that a man, and a sailor especially of course, may laugh off *inclement weather,* which would have the fairer sex cowering for shelter. Laid, quite low." Elizabeth trilled, a cascade of pretty giggles that turned heads all around them... Oh Elizabeth.

Oh you poor, blind girl.

Don't you know that this is is not the way to Mr Elliot's heart? These old-fashioned sophistications; they cannot capture him. Mrs Clay, trailing behind them, stumbled again— almost fell.

"Or perhaps", Mr Z continued, more gaily still, "this wife of his caught it from some lover."

A shocked guffaw from Mr Elliot!

Elizabeth, however, was sophisticated still. "O come Mr Elliot. Don't round your eyes like that. You tell us yourself:– the lady concerned was by no means regarded as *incapable*..." — she let her voice trail off— arch.

Then resumed. "That much, at least, is clear: deception on her part; that much, we know, *all* agree upon. As to quite how far that deception extended — I am not sure that I, for one, wish to know more!" She dropped their arms and turned sharp about: it was time to walk the other way.

Mr Z sighed.

But Elizabeth had put an end to it, for now. It is important for a lady who enjoys a good session of this kind to be, also, the one who brings it to an end — and, just a fraction before others have quite tired of it. This makes it clear that there is a great deal that the lady simply cannot stomach; even if others can.

You see, Nellie? Elizabeth isn't so silly.

Mrs Clay stepped aside to let the trio pass.

Of course; there must have been speculations about her. Everyone she knew.

The very Barratts must have talked about her. Alice and Richard. They would have had conversations about their dear friend Nellie.

The *Comte et Comtesse* wouldn't have *said* anything to each other, surely? She couldn't imagine it.

They must have thought things, though.

After all, she'd wondered herself. She'd began to doubt— as the had years passed, and still no baby— if perhaps George had not brought her, from all those foreign parts he visited, a more lasting gift than usual.

"Nothing obviously amiss. No sign of the common issues, either: sound as a nut, in that respect, my girl, so don't you worry about that."

George had rather inclined towards consulting a doctor—Plymouth had more than one— but by that stage Nellie's pretensions could not reach to being in debt to a doctor. So it was the apothecary who spoke, as he washed his hands; you will know that, back then, the medical profession was not much given to washing its hands, but there are some things that call down all time for hot water and a towel. "In most cases, there *is* no obvious cause. It simply pleases Providence, perhaps, that some women do not bear children."

Well yes. It's not as if they could afford even one child; one hot, perplexingly heavy little bundle. One set of tiny mottled fists and feet, one pair of dark, astonished eyes — what life, for it? What future?

But George.

George had been insistent. All his friends were siring children. Siring sons, capturing prizes, making names for themselves. Something must be wrong. *She* must be something wrong.

"It might be helpful if Mr— ah— your husband could see me. Or, see someone. Of his choice. The problem is not necessarily always on the, er, female side."

But George had put paid to that: George, and that lock of shining hair.

There's an upside to everything. At least, with that proof of his own virility in his pocket, George had laid off her, a bit.

(Oh heavens, she'd never thought, in that first year of marriage, she'd ever be grateful for that. Be one of those dry women.)

And if she'd had children?– had that son? What then, George?

It'd have been you and *your* father, George, all over again. *Your* son, despising *you*.

Why not? By now, where is the difference?

By now? Where?

Hm?

How was it going to be, that *your* boy grew up, in awe, and admiration, of *you*, his pisspot father!

She never said any of this of course. She said very little at all, in front of George. She wasn't stupid.

George was stupid. George was so stupid. Did he not think, did he not remember. He'd been glad, he said, to see his father lying dead. *'So glad he was dead.'*

You had very little compassion for him, didn't you, towards the end.

—But it wasn't even necessarily the same *hair*.

Oh come on. Of course it was.

Chapter 16

Now, WHY, in HEAVEN'S NAME, you will be asking yourself, is Nellie, in amongst all this, *not* trying to pin down the slippery Mr Elliot as to how he, Mr Elliot— of London, and suchlike— got his hands on this particular lock of hair, and this particular story, so very personal as they both are to a distant and obscure couple in Plymouth?

Also:– Why is she not wondering whether Mr Elliot could possibly have got hold of this particular lock of hair, tied with this particular ribbon, belonging to this particular little boy and to his unparticular mother, and have brought them right into Camden Place, right up to very other woman involved —... and yet, be completely innocent of all calculation in the matter?

Why is she not concluding: *No*. No, that is not possible. That is incredible!

Ah. So incredible Mr Elliot is, the things he can do.

Nevertheless— and without having for a moment fastened any blame, or assigned any malicious intent, to anyone— Mrs Clay did find herself wondering, in a wordless, vegetal kind of way, why an heir presumptive would do anything that might come between Sir Walter and a woman whom he knew would guarantee no heir apparent. An heir presumptive should be on her side — but that was to judge him by her standards, because the heir she knew would speak out— but he wasn't. Which suggested he *was* on her side— but then he wouldn't draw attention to the infertility question like this— but he was. Which suggested that he wasn't on her side— but then if he wasn't on her side, he would have to be on her side— because

at this point her train of thought, such as it was, would shoot off the rails and into a bright, white space, where there was only a humming noise.

*

Her gratitude to Mr Elliot, when he at last relieved her anguish, was proportional to that anguish. That is to say, it was abject.

She entered the drawing-room one day to find him standing alone over the fire, twisting something small and white between his fingers.

She didn't look.

After a bit, though, Mr Elliot sighed, communicatively. Caught her eye. With a short, almost humourless laugh, he tossed the white shining worm into the fire— where it frizzled, spat out a small stench, and died.

"There! Let there be no more talk of sailors and– and sad little tales. I cannot approve of what this thing has become amongst us.

"A point of speculation. Even, of gross speculation. A lowering thing.

"It is surprising— isn't it?— to what uses the most innocent little relic can be turned.

"So– there!" and he stirred an unburnt log with the toe of his boot. "You see? It is gone."

Chapter 17

She had misjudged him!

How grossly she had misjudged him!

Mrs Clay felt tearful, when she thought of how dreadfully she had mis-judged him. She hadn't judged him *at all* of course, yet she felt tearful when she thought of it. She felt tearful, even when she was thinking of quite other things. She was strangely weepy these days. Sensations of relief, gratitude — revulsion— though at what, she could not have said; Mr Elliot was a good man, a wonderful man; loyal to his friends, even where they failed in loyalty to him; trusting, while others paid him out in cold mistrust. Mrs Clay dwelled, every free moment, on the goodness of Mr Elliot.

The thought of that goodness of his tended to induce a swooning weak-ness **now**; which, once yielded to, became not unpleasant. And much easier to do than anything else— even the most everyday task. She could scarcely sew a straight line these days, for example, and her fingers had began to look like pincushions, particularly about the thinnest and most sensitive skin, that cov-ers the nail-beds.

So it was with eagerness (and also, a sort of fumbling confusion) that Mrs Clay set out, at Mr Elliot's direction, to meet him at the Milsom Street library on a dark February morning. As she hurried down the steep descent, anxious not to keep her friend waiting, she allowed herself– in tiny snatches– to won-der again what need he had for this meeting, and why he had insisted, when giving the details of the *rendezvous*, that her friends at Camden Place should know nothing of the matter. "Not— one— word!" he had murmured, with a comical play of earnestness. "We must pull the wool over our friends' eyes, just this once!"

*

As one should have expected, it was 'to do good deeds in secret' that he aimed.

It was an unhappy story: a saddening story. A couple– once wealthy, once intimate with some part of the family of Elliot; now fallen, through their joint extravagance, into hardship; thence, to dissimulation, imposture, vice. Efforts on their behalf, unavailing: recidivism the constant theme. Thrown off, years hence, by the better part of their friends— and, one must hope, by them almost forgotten, "since the memory of such a descent, such decay, on the part of those who were once sharers in youth, that sweetest season of life — mmm. The pain, for those left behind by the giddy career of the guilty pair, must be acute."

Mr Elliot paused at this point; shook his head, and gazed at her with some earnestness.

Placed the tips of his gloved hand upon her arm.

"It is not to be spoken of. One could not wish to touch such painful memories. One should not, *must* not, awaken, in an affectionate and ageing heart, afresh the agonies belonging to youth. You understand me?"

Mrs Clay nodded, with an earnestness to equal his own. What was he talking about?

"This is why *I* choose to intervene, and fend off these impostors. To draw their fangs, Mrs Clay, *before* they can use the trusting missives of a long-ago youth, to besmirch the name to which we both feel such attachment."

So, there were letters? Some youthful indiscretion of Sir Walter's?... It was hard to imagine.

"...now living, in such a low way, here in Bath..."

...hang on, no it wasn't...

"...unpleasant to witness, and unpleasant in its implications. As you see; my suspicions are sadly vindicated. The duplicity and cunning natural to poverty, united with abilities and understanding retained from their days in more respectable circles —" Mr Elliot looked at her again, and shook his head regretfully. "Yet– shorn of principle; coarsened, too, by contact with the lowest elements of society..." he hesitated. Turned to the shelves.

Trailed his fingers across the volumes. A trace of consciousness had intruded upon his air.

"... One can imagine... Their sojourn in such quarters, you know; '*touch pitch and*'..."

Be defiled.

He gave a tiny nod.

"We all know, do we not, Mrs Clay, how much we need to be on our guard against the– well1– sadly the *rapacity* of such types–"

Mr Elliot cleared his throat, and endeavoured to start again:–

"...*however* poignantly associated they may be, with happy memories, of a more innocent time, a more innocent *friendship*, in the days when they— er— moved in more respectable circles."

To express the intensity of her fellow feeling, Mrs Clay pressed both hands to her chest. The hands felt icy, and damp, even through the winter shawl that interposed between her gesture and her own skin. It was imperative that she should speak. She spoke with fervour.

"How can I help, Mr Elliot?"

It was exactly the right thing to say.

Thank God.

For Mr Elliot abandoned his embarrassed toying with the books, and turned to her at once with a countenance that spoke frankly of relief.

"Oh, my dear Mrs Clay! How glad I am to hear those words! I did not know— that is, I could not be sure— could not, rather, *expect*—

"But how grateful I am, to your sensitive affection, and your active spirit! So many would rather enjoy only the *sweets* of friendship; would rather shrink, from facing the difficulties, ay and the dangers, even, that may threaten our friends. Shrink from facing, and defeating them— to protect those we love, and to whom so much is owed!

"Yet, when I thought of what needs must be done, I began to see that only you, Mrs Clay, could achieve it— that to you, only, could I turn. On your resolute spirit, I was almost sure I could rely! And I see that I am, indeed, vindicated in my trust!"

It was a joy to Mrs Clay, to do for Mr Elliot, everything— a privilege too — anything— to help dear Sir Walter, and dear, dear Miss Elliot. Her voice sounded strange. They were in a silent corner of the almost empty library, and her words seemed to come back to her, or perhaps, run ahead of her, leaving her unsure, afterwards, of who had said what...

In the end Mrs Clay left the twilit rooms sure only that these Smiths, though they were of course to be pitied, like all the poor, were nevertheless also to be thoroughly taken down– and that she, Mrs Clay, would be instrumental in this, just as soon as Mr Elliot had determined how best they were to act.

"*And,* that it is all to be done without concerning Sir Walter or Miss Elliot in any way. To speak of it, would be to alarm them inexpressibly: to involve them actively would be to heap distress upon distress. No, let us move in this independently, decisively, and discreetly." Mr Elliot tapped the third finger of his left hand to emphasise this final point.

If she could not see her way further than these three points (what was the first one again?) it was nevertheless enough. She could rest in the assurance that Mr Elliot had taken charge.

And she did so rest— and, in spite of everything, with a sense of relief. Muzzy as her head had grown, these last weeks, Nellie found it hard to determine her own direction in even the smallest things. Or to determine, in the first place, what *were* the smallest things, what the important ones; she could spend an entire morning trying to form a decision about how to make over Miss Elliot's latest cast-off... alternatives, that could once have been passed in orderly review, scampering in and out of consciousness as she turned the cloth over and over, each half-formed plan trailing such tangles of consequences and of so many different sorts, practical, social... There was relief in submitting to his leadership.

*

Mere days later, walking home with Mr Elliot by lucky chance (it had been a busy morning, and Miss Elliot had been spared this long tramp, having been found a place in Lady Dalrymple's carriage, then passing— entirely due to Mr

Elliot's quick eye and quicker feelings, which made him ever sensitive to opportunities for her advantage— for everyone's advantage, one might say —)... walking home, Nellie's arm drawn firmly within Mr Elliot's own— pressed, on occasion, against his breast— or at least the breast of his coat, which was a thick, winter one, but one could easily imagine the nature of the breast beneath it, and Nellie, wobbling along Gay Street, did— "...so you see, Mrs Clay, how fortunate I feel myself to be, to have such a *confidante*; such a *comrade*" (with a little pressure of the arm) "as yourself, in all this. I feel like Bonaparte, turning to find at his side General Ney— or perhaps these days Davoust might be a better choice, eh?"

(As choices go, what is wrong with Nelson, and Hardy? They were not quite as topical, but at least they were British. *And* they had won.)

Mrs Clay did not think this— thinking it would have been harder than trying to manhandle great, heavy blankets, of which she could not find the corners, or even an edge. She was attending only to the flow of his voice... which was now murmuring "simply a matter of examining the rooms, as I say — the landlady is expecting you— and finding that box of papers. Here–" and, drawing her after him into the quiet doorway of a shop, he handed her a paper; "our stratagem– our *blueprints!*"

It was a drawing of a box, with a pattern of inlaid wood.

"I am told that it looks something like this; and you see the dimensions, here." And he gestured: Oh!– He took her own hands, and placed them before her! showing her how her hands would be filled by the box...!

"... regards the weight."

She nodded quickly and drew in a sharp breath to steady herself.

"Do you think you can remember that pattern?"

Mrs Clay nodded again, in what she hoped was a business-like fashion.

"Though I doubt, from what I understand, that there will be more than one such box in the rooms in any case."

Mrs Clay inclined her head and pulled her mouth sideways, deploring the circumstances with which they were forced to engage.

"*Not* very big, you see. Any large reticule should hold it: that blue one of yours, I'm sure, will be just the thing. Be sure to take that with you. Be sure to take your large, blue reticule."

Mrs Clay nodded again.

"The name will be Hubble. Mrs Hubble, is the name the landlady is expecting. It is written on the paper. Here, you see; so that you may remember it. I'm sorry about the little untruth just on that point! but it *is* only the one, and we must remember that we play for high stakes here. That the well-being of our shared and closest friends is at issue." He had handed her the paper, she held it vaguely.

Mr Elliot looked sharp into her face. He reached to take it from her — hesitated; then pushed it back towards her. "Look at this again tonight, and tomorrow morning before you leave. Then you may as well dispose of it in the– No: perhaps... Bring this paper back to me, tomorrow, with the other things. Yes."

He looked at her again, acutely. Fumbling a little, Nellie folded the paper, and tucked it in her pocket.

"So."

He drew her arm back, within his; gave it another, longer pressure. He even placed his free hand upon her enclosed one, to emphasise his next point.

"This action of ours, Mrs Clay. It is all that is needed to clear the way– to free the law, to swoop down upon these parasites, and sweep them from Bath. From our sight; from our presence." They walked on for some time in silence.

(And then? Would he have her marry Sir Walter? The thought strayed, of its own, across her blank mind. She viewed it blankly. It seemed both familiar, and utterly foreign; a sort of French *émigré* of a thought.)

"And who knows, Mrs Clay. Perhaps our little circle will be drawn even closer, in the coming months. Closer ties are things I welcome now, Mrs Clay; now that I am grown old enough to judge the value of family. Family, and friends."

This broke through the muffling confusion like a shepherd's whistle through a fog-bound hillside. She lifted her face to smile at him, seeking eagerly for a further glimpse into Mr Elliot's inner heart (his *inner* inner heart)... But he remained thoughtful, gazing yet about the street along which they walked.

So Nellie too was silent; respecting his reverie. She would share his burdens where she could: where she could not, at least she must not add to those burdens with her importunity!

Firmly, she turned her mind, and addressed it to the task he had trusted to her; to run, in review, her part in the adventure that lay before them... how awful if she failed... perhaps if she... And again it began, each of her imagined actions, as she projected and considered it, sprouting a half-dozen possibilities, and each possibility, when she tried to follow it to its conclusion, forked into yet more eventualities, until her mind wandered, mazed... And one image intruded– and again— and again. It cut off all attempts to think through other lines of action. Until eventually, and tentatively— "...and– Mr Elliot— supposing..."

But his thoughts were far away.

She tried again.

"Supposing— this Mrs Smith—"

"Mmm?" Mr Elliot was drawn back, as from great distance.

"I do feel a little concerned–...What should I do?– in that case?"

"What case would that be, Mrs Clay?"

"Well"– she hesitated. "...because... if this Mrs Smith — if she returned —"

"Hm?"

"...and... found— were to find me in her rooms —"

She trailed off. Mr Elliot's face had hardened.

Now he stopped.

With one quick movement he shook her arm off his. "Oh for God's sake. Use some sense." He glared up Gay Street, as if the sight of her were more than he could tolerate. "It'd be the landlady's problem not yours. The greedy woman thinks to let the rooms out to a higher bidder well let *her* try to explain it. Just keep your mouth shut and get out of there. What's so hard about that?

"Hm?

"Where is your difficulty?"

Where indeed? Where— Mrs Clay was unable to answer him.

'*I* have done everything. Arranged everything. Taken all the difficulties and the danger of the business upon myself as far as is humanly possible. If you yet cavil, at doing this one small thing for me, to preserve and protect the safety of Elizabeth and Anne— of *Miss Elliot*, and *Miss Anne*— If you quail at doing even one deed, for the honour and peace of mind of Sir Walter– what am I to think of you? What am I to think of your place amongst us? Mrs Clay?"

Her hands flew to his arm — but he jammed it rigidly into his own ribs. A flood of half-formed words began to rush from her but Mr Elliot turned his face away. Then he said—

"I am so disappointed in you."

*   *   *

For three days he could not endure her presence: for two nights and three days she had no chance to apologise, explain, make amends.

These were days of agony for Nellie. Not by word or deed did Mr Elliot offer a single remonstrance. After that one, dreadful, heartfelt outburst in Gay Street, he had recalled what was due– if not to Mrs Clay– then to himself, as a gentleman; and his courtesy was henceforth inflexible, his *politesse* relentless. Oh, Mrs Clay had only to think of a need, and Mr Elliot would step forward punctiliously to meet it!– more promptly even than before. The good breeding he opposed to her pusillanimity was the worst of all: flawless, hard, and cold as marble.

And desperate though she was to atone, to retract all that she had said– or — done— there came not a single opportunity.

Providence had so often favoured them, recently, with little opportunities to speak apart. Often, there had been a precious moment when, private amongst the crowd, they had been able to exchange a thought or a reaction; a look, or a smile.

What had happened to the world, and time? For all the contact between them now, Nellie might been watching him from the moon; or from the other side of Stall Street, where lingered, always, a shabbily-dressed idler or two, watching the ladies and the gentlemen walking in and out of the Pump Room.

Oh but he did avoid her, he did, he did! It was Miss Anne, now, chosen to walk home with him from Mollands, when there was not room in Lady Dalrymple's coach for all of the ladies; Miss Anne who could be glimpsed from those misty coach windows, joy radiating from her dazed face, as the two clung together under the shelter of a single umbrella: she'd got it bad, poor girl.

And got it, so very obviously, at Mrs Clay's expense. In these, the days of Nellie's eclipse, she never met Anne's face but there was a smile lurking the corners of that woman's mouth! Smiles– and laughter, too.

Nellie'd had no idea that Miss Anne had hated her so much.

Indeed, there seemed more laughter amongst them all, now that Mrs Clay was excluded from their circle.

Lingering outside it, like this, she could see that among them, the tone had relaxed. It was now the easy exchange of equals, the bantering good humour, the jesting and nonsense, of those who are allies in spirit as well as in blood.

Perhaps, after all, they did better without her.

Perhaps, all this time, it had been *she* who was responsible for the daily estrangement she had witnessed between the sisters. She, at any rate, who had intensified it; fostered it, somehow, for her own purposes; played upon it to serve her own ends.

She, too, who had somehow widened the distance between a warmhearted (given the opportunity), bumbling sort of father, not overly-bright, and his intense, clever, difficult daughter. Look at–

— But this was a line of thought which Mr Elliot did not wish her to pursue just now. Desperate at her exclusion, yes. Approaching, however distantly, the idea of life apart from them all: no. On the close of the third day, the resignation that was stealing over Nellie's spirit was blasted once more into tumult; on shaking hands with Mr Elliot at the evening's end she felt her limp fingers, *not* permitted to slip from his grasp, but retained— and on looking up, she found his eye bent on hers with a look in which sorrow, and hurt, and just a little puzzlement, were blended to a nicety.

Hope surged so suddenly that her breast was near to burst. Her own hand convulsed on his. She gasped, to speak—

but Mr Elliot, concern and amazement clearly displayed, was holding a gloved finger towards his lips. He gestured minutely towards the others— And he was gone.

But he would speak to her, he would let her speak! He *must*—

No.

She must.

Mr Elliot didn't have to do a thing.

... She must speak to him. Or she would die.

Chapter   18

Followed a day of inexpressible agitation, through which it was almost impossible to perform her duties at Camden Place with a tolerable appearance of composure. The evening would bring a private party with Dalrymple friends, noble and mutual: Mr Elliot was certain to be present. If she could but be alone with him for half a moment, in some one or other of all the multitude of interconnected rooms offered by their destination! —

— and Mr Elliot laid down the bow with which he had been playing her.

He laid it down with some reluctance; for what artist wants to cut short the melody which he is, with such genius, calling, singing, from his instrument? but Mrs Smith went into the warm bath on Monday. It was now Friday, much still to be done. Mr Elliot took Mrs Clay quietly by the elbow as she passed the library on her way back from a trip (yet another trip; even Mrs Clay's bladder was weak, these days) to the necessary offices— took her, and drew her into dark, warm privacy. "Mrs Clay..." *"Oh Mr Elliot!"* Mrs Clay clutched his arm with both hands and burst into tears.

It was more than Mr Elliot had bargained for.

Perhaps he had played her a bit too long, a bit to intensely — from sheer joy, as I say, of the art. Nevertheless one felt the pressure of time. Nobody had used this library for fifteen years; but still. "My dear Mrs Clay! What does this mean?" — But now she clung to him! actually laid herself against him oh my *God,* wept onto his shirtfront– would it show? "Mrs Clay– Mrs Clay <u>compose yourself.</u>"

He injected into his tone all the vituperation which he abruptly felt. Jesus! This fucking woman! "Oh Mr Elliot, please —" "Get *off* me!" – and he extracted his arm from hers with a vicious jerk. "Mr Elliot *please*–" Nellie was still some way from being able to say more— *"Mrs Clay!"*

Mr Elliot gathered himself up, and spoke with all that he could, of command, and contempt.

"Compose yourself. Mrs Clay. Or will I be forced, at last, to concur– with those, here, who so often exclaim, that your name is a perfect match with your nature."

The blow, aimed with savage exactness on the worst-macerated part of her psyche, rendered her numb and quiet. At last.

"Mrs Clay.

"You have something to say to me?"

But no, she could say nothing. Only look at him dumbly, and smear the tears on her face, with shaking hands.

How disappointing! He became sharply aware of how much he had been looking forward to the song of her submission; to hear its overture whispered, here in the dark of the library; to pick out, from Mrs Clay's unforced confessions, the themes that would be developed, at length, between them, in later meetings. Instead they were going to have to cut the whole thing short. Such a pity. After getting her to such a pitch; such a pity. And capitulation is never as complete as when the accused willingly formulate the accusations against themselves.

But more than one set of feet had passed the library door already, and Mrs Clay's disarray was such as, once glimpsed, and in his company, could never be entirely explained away. (Death of a child?) "Mrs Clay.

"Am I to take it, by this *distasteful* imposition of— of—" Mrs Clay lowered her head; helpless, of course. "That you– what?"

No. Still incapable.

"That you regret your— well your *Plymouth* style of behaviour, of recent days? That you– what? That you feel you still have something to offer me?

"Something to offer the Elliots?

"Some justification, for your continued presence amongst us?

"Because it pains me to say it, Mrs Clay; but when your behaviour falls so far short of what I expect, and am accustomed to encountering, in the circles in which I and my friends have moved all our lives— well. What am I to think, Mrs Clay?" He gazed at her, more in sorrow than in disgust (but only a teeny tiny bit more).

"No.

"No: it has always been clear to me. Even though you are permitted to move in terms of equality amongst us, it is daily clear to me that you are not entirely *of* us. Manners, education; speech, and thought; even it becomes evident morality, self-sacrifice, *courage*... — I was surprised at your presence in Camden Place. From the first. Excuse me but I must speak plainly."

Her head had drooped so low he could not be sure if she were crying. Christ, she'd better not start up again.

"Well perhaps I have been mistaken. Mm? Perhaps there is more within you than appears on the surface.

"You do after all come, originally, of reasonably good family. Perhaps I should not have expected your long, unfortunate, fifteen years, to be swept away, by a mere few months spent at last in better company.

"But now— I ask myself— *can* you rise above those fifteen years? *Can* you rise above the degrading influence of your marriage?

"Can you show yourself, at heart, a true daughter of the old stock. The old flower of Europe.

"Mm?"

At last she spoke.

"I will do anything you wish."

"Anything?"

She nodded. Seemed to have exhausted her speech capacity again.

A burst of distant laughter from the drawing-room down the hall– cut off by the boom of a closing door.

"I fear it may be weakness in me, Mrs Clay, to even think of reposing confidence in you once more. I, who have so often looked at you and thought, with pleasure, that one can yet trace, faintly, in your face, the lineaments of the old nobility of France, of Italy... And even now— shaken though I am... yet, *still*, I cannot but fancy that I see, in you, the features of those scions of a kingly Europe. A nobler past, that once was yours. And that may be yours again.

"Prove me right, I beg you, Mrs Clay. Prove me right, O exiled daughter of France." He had moved a step closer. His right hand closed— oh, so lightly— on hers, where they were pressed in a livid knot beneath her chin.

Almost, as his hand softly withdrew, it seemed that a finger traced her cheek!

Nellie raised her eyes—

And found his own bent upon her with a thrilling glow. His voice, though soft now, rang deeply.

"I think I see in you, Mrs Clay, the whole of France, degraded by that monster, who now lies himself in chains. Break free of those chains, I implore you, and rise with me–" damn! someone had brushed against the very door! – Quick lint-clad feet rushed onward down the corridor. "Tomorrow morning at ten in the Bond Street jewellers."

*

And in the end he consented to her continued participation. In Bond Street, leaning, at a little distance from him, over the trays of cameos, Nellie sensed, radiating from him still, his doubt— perplexity— disappointment.

But; to whom else could he turn?

She was the reed to which he was forced to trust his strength.

*

There was no leisure now for discussing things, and explaining the ins and outs of it. Her recalcitrance had placed the affair at such risk– everything now was required to be done in such haste– that they must henceforth adopt the formality of a general and his troops in the press of war. Immanently the battle must be joined: immanently Mrs Clay must go behind enemy lines, beard the lion in its den (oh! hopefully not!), steal the Promethean fire. Orders must be issued and executed. The task was too pressing to allow of anything more.

He did not also say, that he no longer felt her to be one with whom he might share all the minutiae of the business; a friend, to whom he could unburden his anxious heart. No. Of that, he said nothing.

Well, what could he have said?– Nellie asked herself in quiet misery. There was nothing to say.

Oh, admitted: the irrepressible disgust she'd at last elicited from Mr Elliot *had* created a humiliating sort of intimacy between them; a puling, glabrous thing, like that between child in nappies and its nurse.

But the intimacy of equals — the intimacy which had seemed theirs, in that blissful walk up through town, when her hand had been pressed beneath his arm, and they had talked so eagerly of their plans, and he turned, and placed his hand, on hers — That was gone. And Nellie felt a sick, settled hopelessness of it ever returning.

*

What of us, though? Can we, likewise, repose upon Mr Elliot's excellence, even more completely, more abjectly, than heretofore? For one cannot but remark that he has spoken hastily to Mrs Clay, and most unkindly; even quite roughly (though not, as the event shows, unwisely):— can anything be said in his defence?

More might be said, at any rate, than a reader of Austen would suspect. Mr Elliot would tell you himself that he has just been through a thoroughly wearing few weeks. While everyone else in *Persuasion* has been busily about their leisure— dinners, concerts, parties, renewing old acquaintance, making new ones, and generally enjoying life— Mr Elliot, alone, has been hard at work.

The unwelcome discovery that the widow of his old acquaintance, Charles Smith, is not only right here in Bath, but actually and furthermore reunited with an old gossip of her own, and *that* old gossip none other than *his cousin Anne*— it was an absolute cat's cradle of unaccountable connections, a tangle of all things vexatious! Why he had allowed the woman, after the close of business with her husband, to simply wander off willy-nilly into the sunset, Mr Elliot could not for the life of him recall.

Well no. He could: and in fairness to himself, he had seen her so wander, not only wan and hideous in black, but also without friends or family or a penny to her name, and severely ill to boot. Rather than fussing around her it had seemed, at the time, more fitting to withdraw; let Nature take its course.

And this was the result! In more than one hurried and inconvenient trip he had been forced, these weeks past, to track down and gain access to various of the strongboxes still held, in Charles Smith's name, in diverse dusty nooks about London and Kent. There had been interesting stuff in some of them — he wouldn't call his time, in that respect, totally wasted — but costly and wearisome it had most certainly been; nor had he received anything like the reward he'd looked for in terms, specifically, of letters from himself. Charles seemed to have kept very few.

Which was a little sad. Mr Elliot had always kept every one of Charles'.

So by now it looked as though, if there *were* any documents left with which Mrs Smith could conceivably make herself a nuisance, they must be in those rooms of hers. Probably in that inlaid box of her mother's: that was where she'd always kept the interesting stuff.

And then, *that* conclusion had necessitated, most recently, the distasteful business of investigating the relict's routine: servants, presences, absences and so on... and from *this,* it had emerged that the damned woman was nearly always at home! It was scarcely to be endured.

Yet endure it, perforce, he must. And had.

So if Mr Elliot had not the patience left, just at this point, to humour Mrs Clay's feelings, and jolly her along– well: one can only shrug one's shoulders. If she didn't like the heat, she should have stayed in the kitchen: she should have stayed in Somerset. She should have stayed in her father's house.

Chapter 19

Mrs Smith went into the hot bath every Monday at noon. She was carried from her rooms some twenty minutes before that. Mr Elliot therefore specified a quarter to twelve at Westgate Buildings.

It was nicely-judged. Nellie would have just time enough to introduce herself at the door, view the rooms, locate and extract the box, and bring it straight to Mr Elliot who, on the stroke of noon, would be waiting two minutes away at the colonnade by the Pump Room. He did not expect it to take her any longer than these fifteen minutes. He did not *wish* it to take any longer. Mrs Clay was not unpromising– not at all as unpromising as he had judged it expedient for her to think– but as an applied instrument she was still untested. There was no sense in allowing her possession of the box for any longer than it took her to hurry inconspicuously down Bath Street, and deliver it into his waiting hands.

*

But Mrs Clay was so very anxious to oblige Mr Elliot, really very very anxious. Through heavy fog, her wandering mind calculated, and re- and recalculated, and then, calculated again, the periods needed for each step of the way, and everything that might happen at each step... and she tried to allow time— plenty of time— there must really be lots and lots of time at each point, for who knows what might go awry— there seemed so much that could... getting out of Camden Place, walking to the bottom of town, going into the Cross Baths, and there changing out of her Elliot gown and into something more suiting the kind of person who might be interested in outbidding a cripple on two dank cells in Westgate Buildings. Or perhaps — yes! she should leave *so* early, that she could pop out in that garment already, without being seen even by a servant! Oh, that was a huge simplification!

The result is that here she is, in a dress of the material known as 'stuff', scuttling back and forth in front of Westgate Buildings— no, no, better to stick to Westgate Road— oh Lord!— half the world was walking straight at her along the crowded street!... and she was more than an hour, near *two* hours (was it?) before the necessary time— oh God help me. Best turn down here— not even a servant of anyone she knew would need to go down here...

That change of clothes; it was Mrs Clay's very own contribution to the scheme. When Mr Elliot called on her to rise up and march with him, she had soon seen, firstly, that she couldn't possibly do it dressed as she was, and secondly she felt, with anxious pride, that she, Mrs Clay, alone among them all, did know exactly what kind of garb was called for. Less than half a year ago, in another life, she had folded up just such a garment for the last time, and put it aside to make into trousers and a stout pinafore for the children. It had come with her to Bath for that purpose— for the spare moments, above stairs, when the Elliots did not need her— and had lain in the bottom of her trunk ever since.

It unfolded a little stiffly, that Plymouth dress, after its months in the dark. And there it was.

Was it? Had she really worn *this?*

The background so be-greyed, the little sprigs of flowers on it so faded, as to be scarcely visible. Darker discolouration, about the neck and cuffs, that no amount of lye could shift.

She looked closer, in disbelief.

It really was the same dress. She had worn this— this dress— for years.

Now she was putting it on again.

Only for a few hours.

And only for Mr Elliot.

So ducking down Parsonage Lane into the warrenlets that back the thoroughfares of Bath, Mrs Clay felt out of place for only a moment, a surprised moment. Shade and cloud passed off her together, and the cool, unexpected brilliance dazzled her so completely that she halted— squinting, bewildered; unsure even of what was this strange all-transforming whiteness.

Sunshine.

Oh.

"'Way, lady!"

It was a man with a barrow. Oh.

Nellie stepped aside— then stepped aside again, to get out of the way of a small eddy of foot traffic; wandered on a short way, into the path of two women with a massive basket between them– Then she pulled herself together, and took refuge in front of the stalls that lined the building frontages and narrowed the passageway to a jostling stream.

Browsing. That was what she was doing.

She hitched the reticule higher onto her arm, and set about it.

Some time later the town clocks rang out, fresh in the sustained sunshine. Ten o'clock. Goodness, still heaps of time! She browsed some more.

Food prices here were far higher than at home.

Bread was fearfully expensive! Safe in Camden Place, she'd had no idea.

But the tableware! What bargains! Heavens— did they need anything at home—? (No. Because their house was full of Hardcastles. Her heart, which had expanded in the sunlight and the quiet, familiar pleasure of walking about alone, twitched)— she drew sharp breath and it hissed through her teeth.

The stall holder didn't even glance up. Twitches and grimaces and little ticks were common enough among the clientele, here in the back streets of Bath. Nellie let the breath out... She had forgotten what it was like, to be nobody.

It was— she had never appreciated this before— to a very great extent, to be free.

Free to creep along in the last stages of inanition, of course; to wander the street gibbering to herself, like the sadder beggars did.

But— No servant shadowing her. No friend arm-in-arm, with their two maids behind, and a man too, ideally– all to protect her from the indignities that might be offered to a woman alone. Nellie had smacked aside more than one wandering hand already this morning, the old gesture as automatic as an Antipodean shooing flies.

At least, when you were poor, it was only one level of insult. A lady should be above approach: in bearing so elevated, in air so imposing, that pinching fingers grew weak, leering eyes faltered before her; faltered, and fell. That's if you were the real thing.

No wonder they felt themselves so delicate.

The clocks were calling the hour again. She was in... "Trim Street, this is". She walked on quickly—here, no woman should loiter if she didn't want to be misunderstood— and soon, the surroundings grew pleasant again. Second-hand-clothing stalls are nearly always fun... this dress, for example, was not at all bad! Lovely pattern, on quality material; plenty of wear left in it.

Cuffs almost new.

But a little too small... "Beautiful colour for you that would be. Go with your hair lovely."

"Aye but not much in the seams."

"You could piece it, though—" An expert toss, and the dress opened out before her like a flower in the winter sunshine. "Take it off the width in the skirt— see? Look at that width!"

It was excellent, of its kind. And such a reasonable price! It's not like she was going to be in Bath forever... Would this material work for Josephine?

There was time, too, for a cup of tea— Goodness! so much cheaper than Mollands!

(In her Plymouth days, she would have considered it an expensive treat.)

And still the sun shone, on the street outside, and on the people, amongst whom not a single soul turned to look at her.

A little later, another corner, and she found herself gazing once more down the shabby length of Westgate Buildings. The morning brightness had opened half the windows along its stained front.

Her stomach contracted.

But the clocks had not struck even eleven, so she didn't need to think about it, she could wander on in happy independence... Nellie turned to retreat, when from the shadows in the other side of the street, a child darted. It was a pale, ragged creature, its face angular from cold and inanition...

No, bugger that— Nellie found herself accosted by a neatly-dressed, well-fed boy, in thick warm working boots, well wrapped up against the fresh winter air. A lad whose eyes, almost uniquely in period literature, held neither the gleam of precocious intelligence, nor the brutish dullness of degradation. From a countenance that beamed cheerfully upon Mrs Clay, bespeaking a sunny, trusting disposition (yet without any approach to imbecility), the lad enquired as to whether she were not the lady with the duck-egg-blue reticule, as to say, Mrs Hubble– after a moment's blankness, she recalled that she was– and then, requested her to follow him. For his mother had sent him out to look up and down and about for her, in the shops and the streets, just on the off-chance. For the lady who rented the rooms was gone into the warm bath early today. So she might look at the rooms as soon as convenient— this very minute, if she wished it.

Oh God help me.

She's across the threshold— in the hall— good location, yes I see— just the two rooms— And, how many...? Oh I'll step out to check on that for you, mum, if you don't mind to just wait alone here—

Now!

Mrs Smith has so little. Sorting through her belongings takes only a frantic minute, the breath roaring in Nellie's ears, the bumps of the landlady clumping up the narrow stairs on the other side of the deal wall and— there, on the highest shelf of the closet, right at the back, just where Mrs Clay would have put it herself– a small inlaid box.

Did it hold the papers?

A key drooped loosely in the lock. Her hands fumbled to turn it— 'God just take the whole—' and lurched to stuff it straight into her bag– no— snatched again at the lock, she *had* get the right box— and papers exploded out onto the floor. From somewhere came the gasp of someone drowning. She swept down, hopping about the floor on her haunches, stuffing papers frantically into her reticule, one after another slipping and dodging between her shaking fingers. Crushing them hopelessly crumpled in handfuls into the bag, and two shitty *shitty* things flick up out again like living fish but she *has* them and the bag *closed* and springs upright smoothing her skirt "be it ever so long or find yourself another such nice spacious set; not this close to 'em!" The landlady nodded confidently. "She that lives here now gets herself carried across, ha'pence, and she's poor enough, for a lady, so you can see what I say is true." Mrs Clay agreed to it all, agreed to she knew not what—

—in the street walking rapidly away with her reticule bulging under her arm and her own ragged breath shaking her.

Around the corner... and out of sight.

Chapter   20

She had done it! Done it! *Done it!* Oh!—She could have danced across Kingsmead Square.

And it was scarcely gone– eleven?... She searched the skyline for a clock... Yes! Nearly an hour before Mr Elliot even began his strolls about the Pump Room!

(Actually, Mr Elliot was still in bed. I will not attempt to excuse him.)

Breath still shuddering, she began to hurry back– But, don't hurry! Don't rush– walk calmly— Walk normally... Nellie was walking, walking normally, back to the working class Mollands in which she had drunk that tea. There were others along the way, each throwing out the temptation of a rabbit-hole to dive down, but she sought the familiar— and when she had gained it, it steadied her further. There was her own very same table, from before; it was still empty.

Oh the relief.

She sat down, and ordered a halfpint of porter, and a small something. Waited until it came. Smiled, and thanked the boy.

There.

She even drank. Not the sips of Camden Place, but a good long Plymouth pull.

And another.

She was extraordinarily calm. Extraordinarily clear-headed. And efficient.

With neat, sensible movements, she arranged upon the table a natural-looking barrier of her reticule and her shawl.

Flanked by this cover, she then simply took out the box, opened it, and began to sort briskly through the contents. A distasteful task— but a necessary one, and one that she, Mrs Clay, competent and clever, could just sit down and do, thus sparing Mr Elliot an odious fifteen minutes. ('O! Mrs Clay!– Your foresight! And, your tender care...')

They were all addressed to Charles Smith, Esquire: ah, no, here was one to Mrs Charles Smith. And here was a copy of a letter *from* Mrs Charles Smith— and signed, 'Carolina'; pah!– a poor pseudonym! But mostly Charles Smith.

Much of it Nellie could make neither head nor tail of really. Bills. Bills paid. Bills (mostly) unpaid.

Lawyers...

More bills unpaid.

Phew. That one was a corker.

Ah: a *will*. That was unexpected. And– yes: with it, documents regarding probate— and dated over two years old. So, Mr Charles Smith was dead?... it seemed...?

No hang on surely not! Mr Elliot had said a couple. Husband and wife; with the husband in London.

But maybe it wasn't him anyway. A brother or something.

Some lists of properties. No *billets-doux* so far...

Oh so the properties had been sold? — All of them?

...Shares...

Cashed in, though.

And then, the rest was... lists... memoranda... Letters yes; not that many. Odd rubbish.

Just ordinary personal correspondence.

Not a single note, in Sir Walter's thoroughly familiar sprawling hand... no... No...

No.

Oh dear. (...Mr Elliot wouldn't like this...)

She triple-checked, more slowly still, scanning content as well as form...

Yours truly,

Wm. Elliot.

What?

I wish I [something] *but Elliot. I am sick ...*

What???

But even held right beneath the light of the dirty windowpane beside her, the words looked the same.... Elliot. Wm.

It must be to someone else.

It must have been to someone *else*, and the Smiths had got it, acquired it stolen it, and they were– it was Mr Elliot that they were blackmailing!

Mr Elliot! Mr Elliot bared, and vulnerable!– Naked to the world. And, *she– she*... Nellie almost moaned.

It was a moment before she could turn to the top of the letter.

Dear Smith, —

Oh. Smith.

Dear Smith, —

I have received yours. Your kindness almost overpowers me. I wish nature had make such hearts as yours more common, but I have lived three-and-twenty years in the world, and have seen none like it. At present, believe me, I have no need of your services, being in cash again. Give me joy: I have got rid of —

"*...Sir Walter*, and *Miss!*"

They are gone back to Kellynch

Yes— clear as day!It said 'Kellynch'!

— and almost made me swear to visit them this summer: but my first visit to Kellynch will be with a surveyor, to tell me how to bring it with best advantage to the hammer. The baronet, nevertheless, is not unlikely to marry again: this year he had a shot at Mrs Bradley! Yes, Charles, I hear you laugh. But she is known for her broad mind, and if she did not choose to abandon London and half a million in order to close with his offer of love in an antiquated West-Country pile with £10 pin-money a year borrowed from her dressmaker, one still would have expected her to put him to the usual use. It seems, though, that there are men whom even her strong stomach

cannot accommodate. If he does put his head in some noose or hole or dark moist place, however, they will leave me in peace, which may be a decent equivalent for the reversion. He is worse than last year.

I wish I had any name but Elliot. I am sick of it. The name of Walter I can drop, thank God! and I desire you will never insult me with my second W. again, meaning, for the rest of my life, to be only

> *Yours truly,*
>
> *Wm. Elliot.*

Good God.

The cover—?

...Yes. It was addressed to the same man: the very same. *Charles Smith, Esq.* At Tunbridge Wells.

It was dated...

—here!—

> *July, 1803.*

Nearly twelve *years* ago!

Nellie flung her hands into her hair and clawed vigorously. Stopped; frowning.

The correspondence.

She shuffled hastily through the pile.

Yes. Here were more letters, in that same confident neat hand. The same signature. 'Wm. Elliot'.

Nellie's breath grew short. But hot.

— and some of them were very recent. This one– only — only November last. Only *three months old.*

*

At first her reading was scrambled, unsystematic, so rapid that she took in little of what she read.

But that was enough.

—and she caught herself: stopped. She should sort things.

Get them all.

Letters addressed to or from Mr Elliot went into one pile: the rest, into a second.

But– hang on–

—that second pile was then scanned for mentions of Mr Elliot's name... Mrs Smith's distinctive curling capital Es or Ws were all she need seek in the copies of outgoing letters; and only Mrs Smith had kept copies of outgoing letters, it soon emerged... Such mentions rate transfer of the letter back to pile one.

The husks, pile two, went back into the box.

Now: pile one.

*

She read each letter several times over. First quickly, and then, more slowly.

Then she sorted the pile again, putting them all in chronological order.

Then she read through them once more. Turned back, often, and sorted through, to re-read one that she had set down; cross-checking.

*   *   *

And when she had done, at last— when she had taken in each letter, fully — and deliberately, now— she set these letters, too, one upon the other— one by one... smoothing out, and smoothing out, the creases each had incurred in the course of their theft. Carefully, she placed that leafy bundle, too, into the box, and the box into her reticule; and then she sat back, staring at the table before her...

She remained thus, staring, unseeing, utterly still, for so long that a small boy at the table opposite, staring at the strange lady, insensibly became entranced in his turn— and had to be shaken back into awareness, when his mother rose to leave... and stumbled out still dazed, hanging from the mother's arm— yet still Nellie sat.

*   *   *

At last she blinked. Ouch.

Ouch.

Her eyes burned.

She rubbed them— Cupped her palms over them for a while, until the pain eased.

Now, she lifted the mug beside her; sipped, slowly; placed the mug back upon the table.

So.

Mr Elliot.

(No. *It could not be.* There *must* be some mistake. Some explanation—)

Certainly. The explanation was that he had led her by the nose.

No no *unthinkable!* I mean— This Mrs Smith! What does one know of her? Beyond these letters?

What is her real character her real history?

How much is understood between them, of past crimes and perfidy, to which Mr Elliot need not, would not, refer?

She probably deserved it!

She didn't sound like she deserved it.

The letters— she sounded, mostly, surprised. Terribly surprised.

Somebody was horrible, though. That much was clear.

Really really horrible.

An arsehole.

A shit.

*

She sipped again.

Then, with a blank mind— an open mind— she turned again to the letters.

*

Yes. They were blackmail quality.

*

There was no sign, though, that it had even occurred to Mrs Smith to use the letters as such.

The occasional copy of her own spoke only, with increasing disbelief, bewilderment, and finally with near-despair of chaos and bailiffs, of staying with a friend– with the family of her maid– I write from an inn, help me, please, Mr Elliot, foremost friend of my husband, first and oldest friend of my married life. The very last letter speaks also of pain, in her hands and feet, knees, hips, heart. It is an intense pain, a burning, as of live coals pressed, relentlessly, down and through into the bone.

Mr Elliot's replies, too, show no fear as of a threatened man, no caution even. They were clear and open to the last. Fuck off, Mrs Smith. Fuck off and die.

(Nellie sipped again at the porter; once, twice; three tiny sips. Set the tankard down with gentle care.)

(... Moved it a little to the right.)

Granted, the lady might have gone through enough, by now, to have started exploring other avenues.

And if she had, Mrs Smith would be the last person to make a careful copy of the letter. Or even to write a letter — blackmailers, of any sense at all, probably didn't.

The date of her arrival in Bath...?

— The first letter addressed to her here was a year old.

So: no premeditation, then. It was quite by chance; her presence here, in the same town.

And the poverty of her rooms declared her as poor as a lady could be, before dying or going on the game. Not even the comfort of a servant-girl: draped by the tepid hearth, where she had washed and hung them herself, had been her monthly clouts. If she had turned to blackmail, it could only be very recently, and she had had no returns so far.

Needed to lift her game, poor creature.

So that was Mrs Smith. Successless entry-level blackmailer, at best. At worst, honourable near-destitute sap.

Now: the other party.

Mr Elliot....

Nellie bowed her head over the boards of the table. Her body — her abdomen — wrung with a pain so exquisite... she closed her eyes.

Mr Elliot, unmanned.

We must allow Nellie a long moment.

No come on I mean a long moment. Don't just skip the gap bit.

Seriously. She needs some privacy. Here; stare at these subtly-irregular asterisks.

*

*   *   *

*

Alright?

There.

So: Mr Elliot.

'Wm.'

What were his precise intentions in all this?

— Oh who knows??! How could she, Mrs Clay, possibly know? Mr Elliot— who knows what this Mrs Smith has done? What her deserts might be? Her real deserts.

That aside, though. His aims.

Most immediately— Well yes. Clearly. To discredit Mrs Smith.

To take, from the widow of a trusting, affectionate, and open-handed friend— for such the letters, with super-abundance, demonstrated her Charles Smith to have been, to a near-penniless young Mr Elliot— to take, from the woman who had lost such a man; lost, in him, a husband warmhearted and much loved; a woman who had subsequently lost, also, nearly everything else– wealth, and health, home, and friends, and position– To take, from this comprehensively bereft woman, the fragments that remained to her.

Viz., her good name: if Mr Elliot was serious about 'the law'; and why not. He could make trouble anyway. That would be enough; it wouldn't take much.

Mrs Smith had so little, it wouldn't take much.

With reputation would go her few remaining friends; shortly after that, her life. Anyone of Mrs Clay's experience could recognise a precarious hold on that commodity– when faced, for example, with a once-magnificent green silk pelisse, lying on the tiny table by the hearth, its old-fashioned short skirt being cut into fresh oblongs to join those pegged drying on the line. Silk is near-useless for the job, and the jacket was wearable, and hence saleable— Mrs Smith wasn't thinking straight. She was just doing whatever.

There's a critical point, you see; beyond it, you no longer make plans. Little scenarios may run through your head, maybe; little fantasies, little dreams, where– something happens— and then everything is alright again!– everything is back how it was!— They're nothing like what other people would recognise as actual plans. But you are placid; you are detached.

You may appear almost cheerful.

And you just do whatever falls to hand.

Mrs Smith was at that point. No; it would not take much.

Then, moving on and looking further afield, as Mr Elliot himself was no doubt doing— Well, suppose he did marry one of the sisters.

If he did it was clear, as clear to Nellie as her knife and spoon resting together there on her empty pewter plate, that he would quickly tire of Anne Elliot. Even Elizabeth. But especially Anne; it wasn't a sustainable proposition. When they came to the end of what Anne could offer Mr Elliot, he would– what– Take off, I suppose. Resume a life more sophisticated than Miss Anne could endure to witness, in London or wherever; leave his boring wife to it, in the country.

In possession of Kellynch Hall, mind you.

And of countless new justifications for feeling unappreciated: Mrs Clay snorted. A most suitable connection, everybody must consider it; but who knows, it might also be a very happy one.

Yet.

What intruded was a recent image of Anne– it was in Mollands the other

day; Anne, with a flushed, youthful smile, an air of happy shyness, as she chatted to some acquaintance encountered by the door... She had been looking up
at him, as any young girl looks at a man who could be, might be, *him*— you
know— *The One*. Nellie had looked at men that way when she was seventeen.

Anne Elliot was twenty-seven! It was laughable.

Though it happened all the time, late marriages.

And the man had definitely been looking back. After all, Anne did have ten
thousand pounds. Or would, some day; probably.

I mean *heavens above!*— A burst of exasperated stewardship intruded on
Nellie's thoughts, familiar and (under the circumstances) comfortable— *Ten
thousand pounds!* It was a whacking great amount! Any respectable man in England, almost, would be delighted! Why was there all this unspoken wailing and
gnashing of teeth over the girls only having ten thousand apiece?—because
how many times had she tried to hint to Elizabeth, just stop this pretence that
your peers are the men with twenty times that amount– Oh! and Mr Yates —
oh so *unspeakably* vexing! The little ninny had needed only to reach out her
hand and she could be preparing, right now, for a spring wedding!

And Anne, that sad sack; just the same. Marriage wasn't impossible, or
even the slightest bit unlikely, if they would just pull their dainty fingers out.

Nellie was a fool to worry about them. No, the real question, the *only* question was; what of her own family? What of Ariosto (they really must do something about that name, it wouldn't do, not in England) and Josephine (Lord,
and that one too). What about papa? What did all this— all this bundle of letters— what did it mean, for the three souls most dear to Nellie?

Well they would just have to make themselves useful to Mr Elliot.

They would have to be useful to Mr Elliot, non-stop. All of them.

Because, look. Look here, in these letters; what happens, when you are no
longer useful to Mr Elliot. It isn't pretty.

*

Nellie thought about nothing for half a minute. Such a relief.

*

There used to be a future without the Elliots— hadn't there? She frowned
as she tried, here among the voices and bustle of the eating house, to reconstruct it. How had it gone?...

Its starting point, the point from which all dependants started:– On Mr
Shepherd's death, the children would have one thousand pounds each.

The reader will recognise this sum, no doubt: it is the classic inadequate
dowry of so many novels, the unworthy portion of so many brilliant and beautiful heroines.

It was solid wealth, my God, to the throng in this shop. While she lived,
add her own twenty per annum, the lieutenant's widow's mite, and they had

between them one hundred and twenty a year! *Unearned!*— you could call yourself genteel then; so yes, there was even that!

Or sod it, she could work again and they'd have even more. No George, this time, spilling it all into a gutter somewhere between the pub and their dreary lodgings. Thirty shillings a week to keep house, *and* put a bit by— oh! it is a glorious, soul-expanding vision of comfort and security, to nearly every-one upon these islands! And then, a leg-up for Ariosto, a junior clerkship, and he'd make it. Josephine the wife of some tradesman, competently managing his household and accounts; what's so bad about that?

Just this: working people need, not so much *good* luck, as, not too much bad luck.

'*A run of bad luck*—' That's the phrase. Everyone knows it. Everyone knows the story that follows, the commonplace tragedy; ever new, ever old.

Or, there was Sir Walter and £3,600 a year— The leap of imagination required to move between the two futures is so violent that her head, above its greyed collar, jerks on her shoulders: and now she is sitting in the Elliot's car-riage, her carriage, as it sweeps up to stone steps of Kellynch Hall. Mr Elliot— this Mr Elliot, here in the letters— appears on their height, to welcome her. He has been expecting her.

Mrs Clay's mind, just here and now, rejects the formulation of words about Mr Elliot. It is too perilous. She might start to jabber obscenities. She might leap up and fling the table over and beat her hands at nothing and scream. Also, Mr Elliot might send a bolt of lightening through the ceiling to strike her dead. Oh Jesus.

How could she be sitting in this eating-place? dressed again in this old dress?... An hour or two of a Bath morning, and suddenly it's like this...

Mrs Clay has been thinking very clearly up until now— brilliantly clearly— quite unlike the fog of recent weeks— but at this point it all breaks down again. Her jaw slackens in bewilderment. The corners of her mouth droop unattractively. Hot liquid surges into her face, and after only a second of prickly pressure, gushes from her eyes and— when she jerks forward to hide it — her nose.

Press your hand over your mouth, Nellie. Rub your eyes; pretend to yawn. Well done.

This brings her to her last problem: What, finally, of herself?

Well, she would have loved to have been Lady Elliot.

— *Would have loved, to have been*... conditional past perfect... is that right? and an embedded clause... There was a whorl just there, in the thick wood of the table. She reached forward to trace it with her finger. Perhaps I could teach grammar, she thought after a while. French– people said there was a new demand for it.

... singing, of course.

If she was too old, and tired and scared, to face juggling private pupils, then a school somewhere. (Oh God, after all this: a schoolmistress.) (Could she even get references?) Once papa died...

That's if it didn't work out first, going back to Dashe and trying to marry the grocer.

He was a nice man. It was a good business.

John Magee.

He'd probably think about it, at least. Look her over.

She, who could have been Lady Elliot.

Could *be* Lady Elliot! Gently born as she was, to a line of wealth and undoubted gentility; even semi-demi-nobility, sort of. Quite as good as the Elliots, anyway. Reared in surroundings that let's be straight put the Elliot's efforts at culture and sophistication to the laugh! And then, she had lost it all yes, but under really dramatic circumstances; yes, and romantic, too.

And she had a voice. Her voice could bring tears to people's eyes when they were in the right sort of mood. That's how beautiful it was.

So if anyone is indisputably formed, by all that Nature and Fate can do, to be a Heroine, thought Nellie– Penelope– Mrs Clay... Mrs George Clay, *née* Shepherd— Madame Clef— it's me.

Thinking carefully of nothing at all, she opened the little inlaid box and tucked the papers back in. Mr Elliot's letters she tucked, most securely, at the bottom.

Then she took them all out again. She sorted briefly through them, and extracted anything that looked like it could perhaps be useful to Mr Elliot, in– well, any way... or, the loss of which could be a blow to this Mrs Smith. It was impossible to know, of course, exactly what else Mr Elliot might find handy... and time was getting—

—Oh goodness no! Was *that* the time?

Those letters should come out yes yes, anything to or from Mr Elliot, and anything financial should come out yes. The will– It was quite a bundle.

She stuffed it into the bottom of her own reticule. The rest she restored once more– closed the box– secured the hasp.

Oh.

Opened her reticule again, and searched through to extract a milder letter or two from Mr Elliot; something just a little caustic, just a little incriminating.

Just enough to persuade him that he could now tick this box; could cross this poor creature off his list of things to do. She shoved them into the inlaid box bound for Mr Elliot. Secured the hasp.

Shook the box.

Opened the box again. Shuffled the papers about until they really did approximate the mess in which she'd found them. Closed the box and secured the hasp– there.

That was everything?

Yes.

*

Thus, when she encountered Mr Elliot in Bath Street exactly as the clocks chimed noon— "Ah, Mrs Clay! Such exactitude!"— and passed to him that pretty old inlaid box; when she met him fifteen minutes later, at the same corner, and took it back again— "Thank you Mrs Clay, you are quite the Mercury of Bath!"— when she paused in the doorway of an abandoned shop, to re-insert the separated stash of incendiary papers back into that box (and then opened the box again, and extracted just one of Mr Elliot's; just as a keepsake; just for luck); when she walked, once more, to the narrow door of Mrs Smith's lodging house, and knocked— through all of it, her mind was clear as an empty glass, her heartbeat only slightly faster than is necessary for a brisk walk on a sunny-showery late-winter day.

"If the lady is still out...? Ah! Then— the dimensions of the rooms, and in particular the closet– I must take them somehow, get some estimate, for we have furniture, you know... boxes..." and that was done, too. Done, while the landlady stood in the very room with her, nothing but the closet door swinging between them; done, while Nell agreed that Bath was lovely when the sun *did* gleam through– she placed the inlaid box back in its corner and closed the closet– "thank you Mrs Reed, I'll speak to my husband... it all looks most satisf– it all looks vastly comfortable and nice"— and she walks out into the sunshine.

The streets are thronged. Everyone who can be out is out, lively under the miraculous blue of this February sky.

In its brilliance, Nellie, poised on the doorstep, pushes a wisp of hair back under her bonnet; tucks the near-empty reticule under her arm.

Then she steps down into the living river, and is borne away— tacking easily through the crowd. Comfortable as a leaf on the flood. In her ordinary gown, her ordinary bonnet framing (it nearly always happens, as soon as you stop trying) an ordinary, middle-aged face... perhaps Austen could have picked out the vulgar schemer of *Persuasion,* but I'm sure that I could not.

Chapter 21

It must be something in the air, because today Mr Elliot's own kaleidoscope of conceptions, options, desires, and whims have also collapsed to a single understanding. All he seeks is domestic seclusion: the Somerset countryside, himself and his lovely wife, and their old family seat of Kellynch Hall.

A little place in town for the season, the occasional refreshment abroad, and what more does a private gentleman require?– a private English gentleman, of the kind that is going to command taste for the next century or more.

The only obstacle left is the Baronet and his egregious eldest daughter.

*

Praise, warm, just, and discriminating, of Mrs Clay, hooked Sir Walter in no time. Mr Elliot always opened with some observation on the devastation of social order in France, but this was soon an established signal between them to turn to their local case in point: Penelope Clay, and the lofty expectations which had rightly been hers, in the splendid house of her Parisian childhood. (Mr Elliot had seen the house, as it happened, and was able to assure Sir Walter that it was very splendid indeed.)

Together, the heir and the Baronet would then deprecate the ravaging of those expectations in a savage and unjust war. A war in which even a King had perished, Mr Elliot would remind them. Sir Walter would nod, his eyes swimming: a King– and a Queen.

They spoke next of the fineness of her mind — Penelope Clay's mind. Sir Walter had noticed that already: he had noticed Mrs Clay's fine mind himself, simply ages ago. But Mr Elliot pointed out the corresponding fineness of her soul... which really was awfully good of him.... Without having allowed any thoughts, incompatible with the strictest co-equalities of rank, from troubling his own consciousness, the Baronet was nevertheless guiltily delighted to find his future son-in-law so impressed by Mrs Clay. Indeed, once they'd reflected on her soul for the third time in five days, Sir Walter was feeling so very chipper that Mr Elliot felt they should stop at once. One doesn't want things moving along too fast. Ideally, he himself should be installed first at Kellynch Hall.

Next, Elizabeth... Mm. For as long as Mr Elliot remains single, Elizabeth probably cannot be disposed of completely.

After the wedding, it would be a different thing. Then, he judged, she would become savagely determined to marry. But first, and before that, she was going to do all she could to be troublesome and disagreeable.

The need of the moment, then, is to render her opinions powerless, which is to say, to isolate her by destroying her friendships and her family ties.

It shouldn't take long.

Anne's disapprobation of Elizabeth is a given thing. Mrs Clay's repudiation of her friend is Elliot's to command. Lady Russell need only be taught to see it as a duty, for her to shrug Elizabeth off, as thankfully as one shrugs off a hot, clammy coat that one has been forced to wear through a long journey in summer rain.

Then, the Laura-Place connection had never been personally fond of Miss Elliot as such. Happy to see her, of course– but happy enough, no doubt, to see her no longer. Sir Walter's alliance with his eldest daughter was all that remained to break.

To this end— and sitting, still, over Sir Walter's brandy after dinner– in Mr Elliot's company, Sir Walter has taken to drinking brandy after dinner— Mr Elliot begins to offer Sir Walter sympathy, sometimes, for all that Sir Walter has had to do for Elizabeth.

"Ah, she certainly repays the expense. You must admit that— eh, Elliot?" And Sir Walter, smirking, and repeated something that Colonel Wallis had retailed to him, about Elizabeth being called the most eye-catching woman in Bath.

Mr Elliot inclined his head with a polite smile: fuck Colonel Wallis. Did he really think he was being helpful with stuff like that? And fuck Sir Walter: Mr Elliot had tossed out the hint three– four– five times already this evening, yet it continued to bounce straight off that powdery head. He decided to move on to Point Two anyway:– the baronet could catch up on Point One at some later date.

Still; she remains unmarried.

A twist of pain screwed in the corner of Sir Walter's left eye, distorting his regular, vacuous features. Mr Elliot followed up his advantage...

... yet by the end of an evening of featherlight touches which would usually have cut, by now, halfway through three-inch plate steel, Mr Elliot had gained only the certainty that Sir Walter was more fond of his eldest daughter than one might have counted on, and that getting him to turn his back on her would be correspondingly onerous.

A deep and resilient affection can pop up in the most unlikely places; but as it isn't necessarily reciprocated, the wisest strategy is to turn promptly to the other person. Elizabeth's filial affection should be an easier nut to crack...

Thus reflected Mr Elliot, rattling home after the profitless evening. (A jolt — an unavoidable dead dog, wedged between two cobbles— flung him against the side cushions. He hammered angrily on the roof with his cane, and outside the coachman grimaced to himself.) So— Elizabeth...

Well!– but when her father announced his intentions with Mrs Clay, Elizabeth would turn on Sir Walter like a wildcat!

It wasn't so poetic, or so prompt as was ideal; but with so many demands on his time right now, it would do; yes. He would leave this event to take care of itself.

And after that— after there had been time enough to fully appreciate the weakness of Miss Elliot's new position, what with Mrs Clay the titular dame of Kellynch, and Anne the actual one— it was of all things probable that some wealthy bachelor, of more appetite than sense, would drift by; and when he drifted off again, so too would Elizabeth.

So it was settled! First, himself and Anne; then Sir Walter and Mrs Clay; then, Elizabeth and somebody. 'Three Elliot weddings in as many months!' people would exclaim. About time, too.

Then they would all have to go. Sir Walter and wife, especially, can't be taking precedence at Kellynch forever.

...They would live on the Continent, Mr Elliot felt; they would need to live somewhere cheap. Rome?...One would enjoy visiting Italy now and again... In short— and Mr Elliot stretched, as his carriage pulled up at a nameless house in an unknown location[†] — it was time to bag Miss Anne.

Exciting times!

Chapter 22

Camden Place soon has another evening of Mr Elliot, suave, talkative, eyes everywhere; "you really are a remarkable woman, Mrs Clay." You really are a remarkable woman Miss Elliot, Miss Anne. O you are *such* a remarkable woman Lady Russell, Lady Dalrymple, Lady Kiss-My-Arse. What a creep. What a—

We will draw aside here, while Nellie expels a few more gouts of poison from her system. The magnificent calm with which she had walked away from Westgate Buildings had carried her precisely to twelve o'clock that night. Then she had jerked bolt upright out of her sleep, incandescent with rage, spewing bile.

Ever since, her mind has been a sort of 'maar' or 'stratovolcano': periods of frozen calm explode unpredictably (but frequently) into a molten earth-boil roiling with hatred— vicious, incompetent, powerless hatred— of Mr Elliot. Her inner tirades at such times are monotonous in the extreme, consisting merely of the reiteration of the words 'arse', 'shit', and 'arsehole': not an imaginative curser, our little Nell, never has been. The ventings also issue, when in her own chamber, in bursts of scalding tears— though these are becoming less frequent, now; which suggests she really is making progress. Just–

"— total arsehole shit of a—"

No. Still going.

They are to have another such Mr-Elliot-infested evening tomorrow, at a

---

[†] Have you noticed (Parker, 2001) that you don't know where Mr Elliot lives? Neither do I.

concert for one of Lady Dalrymple's poorest hangers-on. The morning of the concert— waking, in her dim bedchamber, to quiet susurrations and cracklings, as the little undermaid sweeps out the grate and draws up the first flames of the day— there are more hints of progress: Nellie could contemplate the situation, and the day, without having to twist Elizabeth's fine linen sheets until the roll of cloth creaked under the strain.

She twisted them just a bit. It would be good to get out this evening anyway; avoid another family night with Mr E. The concert, too, is really expected to be a good one, good musicians, a few interesting pieces at least; and there was to be a singer, a mezzo, of whom great things were expected... Nellie had had many opportunities, since the arrival of the relatively musical Dalrymples, to compare her own voice with those pronounced to be the best in England. Bath was not London, but most were of London; taught and performed there. She had been reassured, and deep down not a little surprised, by what she heard. There were better voices than hers, of course, but hers was really good enough that its inferiorities could be passed off, in fashionable circles, as matters of subjective opinion.

Beyond that, half of it was appearance and air. She could do all that now. Polish up a bit of *coloratura* stuff. The rest was patronage...

... London was not impossible perhaps. Given the right kind of support. Maybe she could persuade Lady Dalrymple to patronise her. The Elliots? Elizabeth even?

Terribly awkward.

She kneaded the sheets.

And she would have to give up all pretensions to rise, then. Well, to rise with the Elliots.

— Oh God! Starting all over again! Leaving the children behind, leaving papa! And London: oh– *so* much more difficult! A thousand other women around her. Ten thousand; oh Lord. Couldn't she maybe get the Elliots to London?

London! That'd be the end of Sir Walter.

But– she twisted herself in the twisted sheets– she had to do something, or marry someone, or in coming years she'd be a burden on the children herself. Papa couldn't live forever. (Half a dozen years? Ten?) She had to do *something*.

*   *   *

"Ah, Sir Walter! Miss Elliot! ... and Miss Anne."

This last, with hint of insinuating softness. Nellie was once more easily detecting inflexions that others felt only when Mr Elliot leant in to share their breath... "Mrs Clay."

"Mr Elliot."

She was conscious, too, of not saying his name quite as before.

The lingering pressure on her hand was not released: the intense gaze lengthened.

As the Elliots spoke ringingly to their noble cousins, voices dominating the Octagon Room, Mr Elliot, by the simple expedient of rotating his body and retaining his sticky grasp of her hand, drew her slightly apart from her friends. "Dear Mrs Clay... Our angel in all our little difficulties...

"I have another little difficulty; or rather, my friend Colonel *Wallis* was hoping to profit from your advice. Do you think– dear Mrs Clay– that you might be kind enough to sit, *with* my lovely cousin Miss Elliot, and between the two of you, explain to Colonel Wallis... oh dear!– it is purely a woman's affair and– Mrs Wallis is to reappear amongst us all very soon, as you know —" (the beautiful Mrs Wallis had been delivered, a few weeks ago, of a fine healthy boy), "and Colonel Wallis was hoping for some advice, foolish old soldier that he is— Jewels, dress— something to launch her upon. Fashion, you know, changing so fast just now; something truly of the moment, truly *à la mode*. Of course, I assured him– *your* impeccable taste, and Miss Elliot's name: between the two of you, I am sure you can offer some direction. In words that even our dear Colonel Wallis can understand!"

It was not how Mrs Clay had hoped to spend the first half of the concert; but it seemed a harmless request. On such topics, Elizabeth would in any case talk enough for both of them.

Accordingly, she manoeuvred Miss Elliot onto a bench between Colonel Wallis and Lady Dalrymple, and saw them all happy. Alone and refreshingly neglected on the end of the same bench, she found herself free to listen to her heart's content.

There was a fair bit of listening going on at that concert, that evening: more than most readers of Austen have probably imagined. What follows is Mrs Clay's bit.

*

Mr Elliot had installed himself on the bench immediately in front of them all, beside Miss Anne. It was in the pause that followed the Scarlatti aria, delivered quite creditably by the London mezzo (Mrs Clay could have run rings around her) that Nellie first distinguished Anne's words. She was stumbling through a translation of the lyrics printed on the programme.

"'*O cease to plague me*— *O let me die*—'... Er... '*Lights... lights* ungrateful... — I think—... '*merciless...*'" — Miss Anne could read Italian, it seemed! After a fashion. The English fashion. She must have taught herself: Elizabeth, who had had the best of everything in that family, didn't even recognise the opening bars of *O sole mio*.

(... Teach languages. Teach French, and Italian and German. Like a million other stranded *émigrés!*— Nellie shook her head–)

"For shame, for shame! This is too much of flattery!"

It was Miss Anne again, flirting with Mr Elliot on the bench just in front of her.

He was murmuring something to her now, so low that Anne had to incline her whole body in to him, and tilt her ear, delicately, towards his mouth — And now she was swaying back to gaze into his face with glowing albeit mature lineaments, bright eyes– "Indeed! How so?" — and now leaning in again, eager and inquisitive: her hand on the bench was a bare inch from Mr Elliot's knee.

"But– no! You can have been acquainted with my name only since I came to Bath!— excepting as you might hear me previously spoken of in my own family...?"

Mr Elliot had slung one arm over the back of the bench, the better to turn his whole body towards Anne. With his other arm on his hip, he made the very picture of the dominating lover. "Ah!– but you see, I knew you by report, long before you came to Bath!"

Anne was exclaiming and blushing again: Mr Elliot retained his poise, and only smiled more deeply. "I had heard you described, by those who knew you intimately", and he raised his eyebrows still higher, to give the word its full, Regency, bodice-ripping emphasis: "Intimately. Oh yes; I have been acquainted with you, Miss Anne— by character— for many years."

"No!– no!"

"But yes yes, cousin Anne." Provoked, seemingly, to the brink of laughter, Mr Elliot was nevertheless making show of endeavouring to twist his mouth into an imitation of solemnity. "Your person, your disposition, accomplishments, manner— they were all described; they were all present to me."

And now Anne really did laugh, expanding before of Mr Elliot's regard, like a flower, or like any Elliot basking in warm attention. "It is– but surely— but who else but my family can have known *me*, and known *you*... I cannot conceive..." Another blush, and a glimpse of her teeth as they creased what was just now, in the warmth of the Concert room and the conversation, a rosy lower lip. "*Do* tell me, *dear* Mr Elliot!"

"*Dear* Miss Anne; can you not imagine?" She shook her head, still with that lower lip caught between her teeth.

"Do we *really* have no mutual acquaintance?"

Another shake, and a tilt of her head, her hair catching the light; yes, even her hair was looking nice. "Come!– search your mind, cousin Anne!"

But Anne, though clearly searching it, doesn't seem to be finding anything.

Ah.

But our Mrs Clay: *she* finds something.

She finds— she has found— Mrs Smith.

It was Mrs Smith!

That fight, last month, when they had been summoned unexpectedly to Laura Place and Anne had refused to go: she had a prior engagement. With an old school-fellow. A Mrs Smith.

A *widow,* Mrs Smith.

"...a widow Mrs Smith, lodging in—"

Heavens! Westgate Buildings!

"A poor widow! Barely able to live! Between thirty and forty!"— That was Sir Walter, frothing at the mere thought of insufficiency, marginality; he always did, it always threw him into a frenzy of repudiation, denegation. "Mrs *Smith!* Of all the people and all the names in the world, to be the chosen friend of Miss Anne Elliot, and to be preferred, by her, to her own family connexions among the nobility of England and Ireland!" Naturally, Anne had here started darting meaningful looks at Nellie and Elizabeth– "Mrs Smith! Such a name!..." Mrs Clay had heard no more, for she had felt it advisable to slip out of the room at that point.

And certainly not impolitic. Miss Anne might behold many parallels between her own poor friend and her sister's, but– Nellie was far more struck by the fact that Sir Walter obviously did not! Could his appropriation of her into his mental household really be, now, so complete, as to utterly confound his ruling passion of snobbery? Incredible!— and yet it seemed so clearly attested, by Sir Walter's tactless speech, that Mrs Clay feared to betray her own gratification and amusement!... Lingering the upper corridor for it to all be over, she could hear only the echo of elegantly raised voices: Sir Walter's steady boom; Miss Anne's low clear tone, infrequent, but cutting.

... But– Mrs Smith!

Jesus wept!

An old, impoverished, sick, widowed, childhood friend in Westgate buildings, that Anne visited— *Of course!*

Mr Elliot continued to tease his pretty cousin, Anne to exclaim and to doubt, but it was clear by now:– Anne knew nothing of the many years' connection between this man, and Charles Smith, and Charles Smith's wife. Anne's old schoolfriend. Mrs Smith.

*

The first act was over. Nellie went out, in quest of tea and continued freedom from scrutiny— but even lingering with the Durands and their *trois enfants bien élevés,* she was aware of Mr Elliot's eyes intermittently boring into her back. He always seemed to eavesdrop when Nellie chatted in the language. In certain necessary experiments (and how contrite she had felt, only days ago, at the memory those experiments!) in certain necessary but rather amusing experiments, Nellie had long ago determined exactly how much French each of her little circle understood... Yet here, as ever, hovered the monolingual Mr Elliot; making every show of listening attentively to— what?

After his dereliction in the first half, though, Mr Elliot had a lot of ground to make up with Anne's older sister, and as they all resettled themselves, Nellie had the satisfaction of seeing him suddenly pinioned between Miss Elliot and Miss Carteret. Beyond them she could see Sir Walter and Lady Russell, listening politely to Lady Dalrymple's description of what they had all heard in the first half, and what they were to hear next. At the far end of the bench– yes; Miss Anne had drifted, once more, to the edge of the group. And Colonel Wallis had ducked out the back for a smoke.

Mrs Clay, alone on the foremost bench, was securely forgotten.

So!—

If *Mr Elliot's* Mrs Smith was also *Anne's* Mrs Smith– but Anne didn't know it!– but Mrs Smith *must* know it, for who could describe even an hour in 10 Camden Place without mentioning Mr Elliot's name?— Well!....

....*What then?*

For the remainder of the concert, Mrs Clay's powers of calculation plunged into a workout so extreme it would have left a top-flight British football team begging for a chance to stagger to the touchline and throw up. By the time the last performers were taking their bows, Nellie, hands clammy and pale forehead bedewed, had sketched out three broad scenarios.

There was the nice one:– Mrs Smith was not only a naturally honourable woman, but had remained, in spite of all her trials, honourable. She would not allow herself to interfere between family members, simply because she herself had fallen foul of one party.

Mrs Clay felt tempted to exclaim "Oh, but nobody's *that* good!', but she fought the temptation. Her father had often pointed out to her that in such declarations, 'nobody' means 'I', and that the emphasis with which they are asserted is fuelled largely by indignation that anyone dare set the bar so high. Some people can. Some people really are much, much nobler than you or I.

(On the other hand, Nellie found it pretty implausible. I mean nobody really *is* that good, are they.)

Then there was a less nice scenario:–Mrs Smith calculated she could make more from the letters with Anne ignorant, than she could with Anne informed.

Anne— delicate, high-minded Anne — *informed*, would turn from Mr Elliot with loathing. Unless and until Mr Elliot actually married her, then, he very much needed Mrs Smith to keep quiet. *After* he'd married her, Anne would soon be in possession of all the information anyone could possibly want, poor thing– and it wouldn't make a jot of difference.

So, in this second scenario, Mr Elliot would be wanting to push along with the wedding as fast as he could.

Assuming he *did* choose to marry Anne... oh dear...

Then, there was a middle way, which could stand alone, or be included with either of the two possibilities above:–

Whatever Mrs Smith was or felt; whether honourable or degraded, whether cherishing her old school-mate, or whether she had never particularly liked prissy little Miss Anne; still: she— anyone— might well calculate that, in the long run, Anne would be far better off, married to Mr Elliot.

She'd have her disappointments, of course: she'd find out she was married to a thoroughgoing nasty piece of work; but, lots of women do. She'd adapt.

There was the money, you see. Money would blunt this pain, as money eases, or removes, so many sublunar pains. One day— sitting, perhaps, in her own drawing-room, in the halls of her own dear Kellynch, after the last guests have bowed out— 'Lady Elliot'— and soundless footmen have whisked away all disorder, and invisible hands have placed the late-night snackeroonies and withdrawn, and a midsummer moon gilds the leafy tops of the woods and parklands that stretch to the sighing silvery-dark horizon, she would turn to her old friend and say— oh, Miss Sharp!

I mean Mrs Smith.

— oh Mrs Smith! Regrettable as it is that my husband and I must live apart like this; he at the house in London, Paris— Milan— Vladivostok– I myself all alone here save for you, dear friend, and my beloved children, and those other few souls truly close to my heart, selected from the crowd of attentive and well-disposed acquaintance I have about me now that I'm the rich Lady Elliot; yes, execrable though the situation is, nevertheless, how superior to the only future I saw for myself, when I was twenty-seven! When we met again, all those years ago– do you remember? In Bath?—You, so pressingly in need of a wealthy patron: I, a withering spinster, neglected by society when not actively mocked by it; the lowest of dependents, in the cash-strapped establishment of a hostile, antipathetic parent.

Nellie sighed.

"Are you trying to *souffler* the orchestra to Bristol, Mrs Clay?"

It was Catherine, wriggling forward on her bench to insert her face next to that of her friend.

Nell smiled. "No no— They are quite good, of their sort." She spoke in French: Lady Dalrymple had begged her to do all she could to improve Fiona's really disgraceful French, and Fiona– Catherine– was supposed to do the same.

Catherine, however, took towards French the attitude of Voltaire towards Charles XII: one may admire, but one need not imitate. "Ah! then it must be from getting up *so* most horrid early the other day. Out at *nine*, my goodness! Mamma isn't even getting up at *nine*."

Mrs Clay twisted on the bench, to gain a clearer view of Miss Carteret's countenance. It was smug. The rear windows of No. 2, Laura Place, look clear across the valley to the facades of Camden Place, and Miss Carteret, with the sharp eyes of youth, enjoyed surprising Mrs Clay from time to time with her knowledge of the family's movements. "You spend more time in the back offices of Laura Place than is appropriate to your station, young lady."

"Oh indeed and indeed. Your clothing at nine of the morning did not look entirely appropriate to *your* station, so drab as it was. I should not have believed it were you, but for your blue reticule."

"A blue reticule means nothing. Many people carry one. Don't you know that Colonel Wallis also carries a blue reticule? Privately, and early in the morning?"

"Colonel Wallis is *stchooopid*."

"He is too old to be clever to you, it is true. Come! —" and she made an effort to shake all this off: "Among all the men here, which do you think looks to be the most agreeable– the best company– if you were — ... ah..."

"—trapped in a cave in Italy by a snowstorm!" suggested Miss Carteret.

"Very well. Do we have food in this cave?– and for how long will we be cut off from such civilisation as Italy affords?"

"Why do you ask, my dear Mrs Clay?"

"Do you see that fat gentleman in the green coat? If we have food, I might expect no quarter in the competition for it, whereas if we have *none,* and are locked fast for *weeks*..."

— she finished the sentence in a whisper.

Miss Carteret squealed with laughter. "Mrs Clay, that is wicked!"

"What can you do?" Nellie lifted her eyebrows and shrugged, deploring the necessity. "You may nominate three."

'Nominate three' had formed one of their private entertainments in public places since the earliest days of their acquaintance. Miss Carteret entered into it with gusto, and they pointed out their first, second and third choices to each other, exclaimed in horror at each other's taste, and generally cheered each other up... Miss Carteret's Number Three, given with slightly ostentatious carelessness, was familiar, by sight. He had come a careless third in Catherine's nominations already; once as a neighbour in a painfully crowded public coach to London, another time as a sewing companion on a rainy Sunday, and now today, starving in an icebound Italian cave.

A *very* young man; but an eldest son. Of good family and character, and pleasant, if youthful, address.

Not without style, either: tonight he was costumed so quietly, in the height of coming fashion, that he stood out even beside the subfusc Mr Elliot. Nelliehad once considered short-listing him for Miss Carteret herself.

But he was borderline, as regards fortune. And unlike Mr Yates, he'd only ever be a Mister; Mrs Clay had gently gathered that this was quite a drawback, to the vague-seeming Lady D. All things considered, Mr Brownlow hadn't made the cut.

"What about *him*?"

It was Mr Yates himself, some distance away among friends. Miss Carteret looked; shrugged. "He's alright I suppose."

Mrs Clay studied him. He was laughing, as usual.

"How is his nose these days?"

"Empty!"

"Really?"

"Empty, and— *huge*. Like a cavern. Like *twin* caverns! On a bare Italian hillside."

Mrs Clay sighed. Then she reverted to English.

"Catherine."

She spoke softly, turned quite away from the couples around them. "Catherine— look at me."

The girl's eyes promptly lowered. She was pleating the edge of her fichu: concentration.

"Catherine:– you do need to be sensible."

A moment or two; and the small, rather watery blue eyes rose — apologetically— to meet her own. Nellie smiled: compassionate; serious. "You don't want to end up like Miss Anne."

Voices. Scrapes, and the squeak of chair legs on parquet.

Now the violins begin tuning up.

"—Although—" Miss Carteret suddenly dropped the fichu and was hissing eagerly; "she does look *better* these days, doesn't she?"

Mrs Clay glanced around; tilted her head; equivocal. At the moment Miss Anne wasn't looking good at all. She was perched at the bare end of the bench, turned away from them: Mr Elliot, it appeared, had grown tired of her.

"*I* think she's in love!"

"Really."

"Come, Mrs Clay— don't you think Miss Anne is in love? I do! Mama and I often laugh about it. I wonder who with!"

"'I wonder, with *whom*.' You don't know?"

"Well it's not him!" She indicated, with a minute jerk of her chin, the man to her left.

Mr Elliot was engrossed with Elizabeth, his back as much to them as Anne's to all her company.

"Everyone says it's him— but I'm quite-quite sure it's not!"

"Really."

"No *but* really!" Catherine became even more confidential, her whisper more breathy. "*I* was in love, once. I remember."

Mr Yates was wandered off.

Young Mr Brownlow, though, was hovering.

"Your number three. He's a little thin for our purposes, surely?"

"Mmm— but he looks as though he could hunt for food."

"Why yes. He does. He has a quietly resolute air."

He did too. Terribly long in the chin as well; ah, like calls to like. George's freckles had enchanted her, when first they met.

"I do think he looks lovely, but I understand that the family doesn't have much money."

More silence. More plaiting, again, of the fichu.

"The thing is, Catherine; I was in love once, too."

Catherine's eyes did not rise. The girl bent lower, even, over her mangled scarf, and mangled harder.

You don't want to end up like Mrs Clay.

Chapter   23

On Wednesday night, though, reviewing the day, the unenviable Mrs Clay calculates that she has more than one good card, now, in her hand.

She knows some interesting things about Mr Elliot's past; his behaviour to Mrs Smith, his declared opinion of the Elliots. She has hard evidence, too: she has a letter of Mr Elliot's (hidden at the bottom of her box, which is hidden in turn under her bed) in which Mr Elliot refers to Sir Walter repeatedly as Mrs Bucket, a reference obscure but clearly insulting. As of this evening she knows, too, about Mrs Smith and Anne Elliot. That is three counts to her.

Four!— She has these cards, but Mr Elliot fancies her hand is empty.

*

Across town— or perhaps, alternatively, much closer than you think— Mr Elliot is subjecting life to more mixed reviews. In truth, he is feeling some of the ennui that not infrequently came over him with the assurance of success.

Very well, those old letters to Smith were secured at last, that was a plus. (Did he have them all, though? He seemed to remember a couple... certain phrases, that had made him laugh as he wrote them— *that* one (hilarious. Pity to waste it on her)— and... *that* expression... surely he'd first come up with *that*, when writing to Charles' wife?)

Anyway. The old girl didn't have them now.

And without them she was nothing.

Which was exactly what he'd valued Carolina at, two years ago; otherwise he'd hardly have indulged himself, to quite such an extent, in their final correspondence.

So all that was good. And then today Anne, at the concert, had proven herself innocent of all knowledge, as regards Carolina. No narrowing of the eyes, at talk of past mutual acquaintance, no conscious turning-away; just that charming wide-eyed wonder. Too, she had been looking gorgeous again this evening: she had been a credit to herself.

But— Anne Elliot was moody. That was the worst of her.

Inconsistent, and erratic.

Look at her reaction to his lovely words, for example; words over which he had really taken some trouble:–

"The name of Anne Elliot has long had an interesting sound to me... mmm. Very long has it possessed a charm over my fancy. And — if I dared! — I would breath my wishes... Anne?– that the name– might *never* change."

Beautiful!

Beautiful lines! Lines for a young lady to write with trembling fingers in her journal: he looked forward to seeing them there. Words to whisper, too, in strictest confidence, to a few close friends. After which it would inevitably get around. Mr Elliot would be playfully understanding about that.

... Though, perhaps the Anne-type really wouldn't whisper?

Maybe, this type would guard the words as forever a precious secret between them?

Yes, that would be alright. Then, he would sometimes hint at them, to raise a gentle glow, a gentle shrinking, at which others could but stare and wonder. After all *'full many a flower is born to blush unseen, and waste its fragrance on the desert air.'*

The thing is, though: she hadn't seemed to appreciate the words at the time.

In fact— Mr Elliot had to confess it— he was not at all pleased with Anne Elliot's behaviour, just at that very point. Right up to it, she'd been blushing, laughing, sparkling up at him– really looking gorgeous and very distinctive. People had been looking at her, and then, smiling knowingly at Mr Elliot — and he'd come out with his beautiful words, and– she had frozen! Her head drawn down suddenly, between her shoulders; such an unbecoming pose. Like a fucking heron.

And then she'd just stayed like that. Gaze fixed and glassy. No response to his gentle "Anne?"

When animation returned, it was worse! She was... well!– she'd literally been unable to look him in the face! Writhing about like a girl at her first party; twisting, and staring, and craning her neck, like a duck that's heard a dog in the reeds. Anything, rather than catch her lover's eye!

Mr Elliot had been unable to suppress a trace of distaste.

(So often, this happened, when a scheme was coming to fruition. Distaste. Loss of interest in the game.) Honestly now, did he really want this odd, jerky creature to go about in society beside him?

On the other hand.

It *does* illustrate, quite beautifully, how very out of the world she has lived.

'Her whole world, bounded by the walls of her father's park.'

Chaste as a nun.

— Yes but to be so grotesquely overset by one little *hint!* It's not like she was sixteen for God's sake! Blushes, certainly: obviously. Face crimsoned over with modestly by all means. Even a tear or two. Damn it, a burst of joyful tears that drew the whole concert to a standstill and required her to be sent home in Lady Dalrymple's carriage, that would have been perfectly the thing.

But this jerky tic — these eccentric evasions —! It was hardly gratifying.

Modesty, and purity, and all that, were all very well, but if Miss Anne hoped to keep her place in his heart, she would have to start putting out a bit.

Chapter 24

In a very quiet way, the next morning marks a turning point in the lives of several of our characters.

The weather gave no sign. Dim and drizzly as ever, it was well past noon before Miss Anne was able to leave Camden Place for another of her philanthropic visits to Westgate Buildings. "Can I fetch anything for you in town, Elizabeth?"

"Oh— no— no thank you Anne."

"Mrs Clay?"

"You are very kind, Miss Anne, but there is nothing worth your trouble."

"It is no trouble, I assure you", replied Anne; and she had waited, with remorseless courtesy, until Mrs Clay was forced to admit that she was not, in fact, in need of anything at all.

"Are you quite sure?"

"Quite, Miss Anne, I thank you."

Anne Elliot inclined her head. (What did that mean?) "Very well. I shall return by four o'clock, walking via Gay Street." She walked quietly and neatly out of the room: after a neat, quiet interval, they heard the front door shut.

"Well thank Heavens for *that*."

"Miss Anne will have a wet walk of it, I'm afraid."

There was something of a blank.

"So– Penelope— did you enjoy the concert last night? I don't know how it was, but we barely spoke to each other the whole of the evening!"

"How could I speak to you, monopolised as you were, first by Colonel Wallis, and then by Mr Elliot? Anyone would have thought they were competing over you!"

"Mm."

Another blank.

"It did strike me, Miss Elliot, that the final aria of the first half would be very suitable for your voice. It's very easy to transpose, too— I think I even have it myself, scored for soprano. Did it please you, particularly?"

"Oh– it was pretty, I suppose... I'm afraid Colonel Wallis was at the height of some nonsense just then, so I wasn't able to attend to the music as I wished. He can be so tiresome, and he seems to get worse and worse. *How* pleased I will be, when his wife reappears among us! She will be at our evening party on Saturday, you know Penelope. I do hope she can pull him back into line. I really found him quite– quite importunating."

"Ah Miss Elliot", responded Mrs Clay automatically, "men being importunate is something that you will have to become accustomed to, I'm afraid."

"I *am* accustomed to it. It's just that Colonel Wallis was particularly vexing. I was particularly wanting to listen to Mr Elliot at that point. He seemed to be saying to Anne that he had met her before somewhere! Well I can't imagine where. Anne's never even been to London. She just wants to stay stuck at Kellynch all her life."

"They met at Lyme, I believe—"

"Oh yes everybody knows about Lyme. But he was talking about something else— something more. Or– I don't know. But Anne didn't seem to know what he was talking about, either. Why he kept on and on about it I can't imagine."

So that was the problem. Mrs Clay hesitated.

But the opportunity seemed to good to miss.

"He certainly carried his point rather *too far,* I thought."

"So you heard it too?"

"I happened to be sitting closer to them than you were..."

"–but it was Anne's fault really. She kept on giggling, and wriggling at him– and we all know how men fall for that kind of thing. Even Mr Elliot, it seems, lacks the discrimination to see through it. She is so *naïve,* so *jejune;* she has no idea how to comport herself with men. At her age!– it's ridiculous."

"I wonder– it seemed to me– Well, they happened to be right in front of me, you know, and... Lately, Mr Elliot's behaviour in relation to Miss Anne has not always entirely pleased me, I must confess."

—but, Nellie is being hopelessly direct! Though longing to inveigle her way to wealth and security; though all of her keen intellect is consciously bent to the task; though her spine has been formed, by a decade of ever-increasing burdens, into a slight cringing curve, perfect for her needs here— it is apparent that she *still* has, as a default setting, frankness!

Lordy me.

You can see why, at this stage, she doesn't even dream of going head-to-head with the serpentine Mr Elliot.

Naturally then, when Nellie thus owned that Mr Elliot's behaviour had 'not entirely pleased her', Elizabeth, who was even less pleased with it– who was reaching the outer fringes of dread, as to what it might signify for her own future— immediately knew whom to blame.

"I did not realise it was *Mr Elliot's* behaviour which was in question. I'm sorry that my cousin's conduct hasn't pleased you, Penelope. I can't say that it strikes me as in any way inappropriate. But no doubt you are the best judge."

Mrs Clay backpedalled furiously. "I wasn't setting myself up to criticise–"

"Of course you weren't, Penelope."

Another silence.

Then Nellie tucked her needle into the fabric, put the whole down, clasped her hands together, took a very deep breath, and frankly and directly began:

"Miss Elliot–"

—but someone is knocking at the door!

No, not a knock: someone is positively beating a tattoo; light and lively, bouncy and blithe, an airy, breezy, sunny little rhythm.

Elizabeth starts from her chair–

"Mr Elliot!"

*

He doesn't look like a man against whom Nellie holds four cards.

Odder still, to an Austen reader, he doesn't look in the least like a man who is wildly off-course about Anne Elliot: I find I can project onto him none of the faint foolishness of ill-founded complacency.

On the contrary, he is radiant this morning. He is Helios himself. His countenance sets the room a-dance; every gesture scatters a fusillade of light; while outside the rain is surely vanquished, the clouds dispersing and–

"*Do* you realise, Miss Elliot, Mrs Clay, that by the new, meteorological calculations, it will be Spring, *within a week*? Today, right here, as we speak, but five days stand between us, and Spring!"

"Good Heavens!" the women exclaim.

"How shall we celebrate?" demands Mr Elliot.

He sat down with the abruptness of a jack-in-the-box. Stick between his knees, he beamed, his ebullience floating them up... Nellie finds herself smiling!

As for Elizabeth, she has already flung herself into the game. "Let me see! If it becomes *fine*, we shall— oh, *what* shall we do?"

"Climb up Beechen Cliff!" is the prompt reply. "Then, let us drive as fast as *six* horses can take us, to Bristol, and bathe in the sea!"

Elizabeth peals with rich, upper-class laughter. She leans back in her chair to do it, yielding him an advantageous view of her reclining, quivering figure. "Heavens! And– but– this *rain*. O, this endless rain is the ruin of everything! What if it continues to rain, Mr Elliot?" †

"We will climb Beechen Cliff all the same, and at the top, draw lots, as to who is to be flung off as a sacrifice for the return of the sun."

"O, that will be me!– I am always the loser when I draw lots. It was the bane of my childhood, I banned the drawing of lots in the end, it was *too* unfair, I am sure to lose!"

"But that is excellent news, Miss Elliot! The Gods of Spring cannot fail to smile upon the sacrifice of your body to their clutches, to do with as they will."

Miss Elliot's laugh was a little less practised this time.

"We will have the fairest summer that England has seen since the Druids walked the land— sacrificing a beauteous virgin every spring to propitiate the Dark One! Don't you think that is a good idea, Mrs Clay? Don't you feel, that the offering of ravishingly fair virgins to the old gods is a tradition worth reviving? I know I do. Not enough trembling maidens, faint with fear– not enough graceful forms, and white necks, and rounded limbs, are consecrated as playthings for the gods to sport with, these days. That is my feeling, at least!"

He was flushed, expansive, uninhibited. Was he drunk?– so early in the morning? Yet his eyes were quick, his movements, for all their vigour, were if anything more precise. Elizabeth was giggling rather wildly now, her fluttering fingers tracing her neck. Mrs Clay could feel her own smile becoming strained. "– And *your* opinion Mrs Clay? About resuming the spring sacrifice of fair virgins?"

"It certainly was a colourful practice, indeed; but I can't help but think it more cheerful to see the maidens of Bath dancing at a ball, or playing cards, or walking in the Crescent. I prefer modern ways."

"Oh but they would still dance. They would dance first— wouldn't they, Miss Elliot? They would dance, in a line, while the priests watched; and assessed them, and selected. The fairest among them. She of the longest, whitest neck. Graceful as a gazelle. And then— they would seize her! Drag her from the dance! Lay her upon the altar, the music of horns and tambours

---

† It *was* to be infamously wet, that spring of 1815. Just by the way. Not only in England, but all across Europe; and as you read this, Mr Shepherd is sheltering under a cafe awning somewhere on the Continent, squeezing the water out of his stockings.

rising above her shrieks, and while the drums reached a frenzy, *then*, the shining blade would enter her body— seeking the tender quick."

Surely this was all in rather poor taste?

"But no: no Miss Eliot, of Kellynch Hall: we offend Mrs Clay, Mrs Clay, of–... Ah Miss Elliot, a classical training– it is the bane of a gentleman's life. It stocks a man's mind with words and images of a savage splendour, too vibrant for drawing-room sensibilities. Mrs Clay is quite in the right. Let us talk of *modern* things!"

There was something of an hiatus at this.

Elizabeth continued to stare at him with shining eyes.

"For example: what, Miss Elliot, did you think of the concert last night?"

Miss Elliot snapped back into action. She chattered eagerly of the programme, expressed a swooning admiration for the aria that she had not been able to hear, averred that she longed of all things to essay it herself, dragged a copy of it (for of course Nellie had a copy of it, everyone had a copy of it, Scarlatti) from the piano, and demanded of Mr Elliot a translation of the whole, "for I understand that *Anne* accorded you the English version of it!"

Mr Elliot cocked his head, like a manic robin that detects the faint gurgle of a worm's insides.

"Indeed she did!– indeed she did! Imagine my gratification, Mrs Clay, on finding yet another talent in the Elliot household; an Italian speaker, no less! But *as* your sister, Miss Elliot, I must suppose Miss Anne, too, to possess positively scores of astonishing talents, that will continue to emerge to astound me on a regular basis. Speaking of which; Colonel Wallis was delighted with your advice to him last night. He has acted on it already!– to the raptures of his wife, and I found her quite overcome, this morning, with pleasure at Colonel Wallis's gifts! Bought, he assured me, in *scrupulous* accord with your recommendations. I have just left the happy couple— the happy *family*, I should say— at Marlborough Buildings!"

He writhed gleefully.

But Miss Elliot barrelled ahead, still firmly on her own scent; "I am glad you found *something* to talk about with Anne, she *can* be a little heavy going at times and I felt such *concern* when I saw you seat yourself by her side— but you seemed to have a great deal to say to each other didn't they, Mrs Clay! We were just speaking of it— which is *such* a coincidence– Mrs Clay felt that you had rarely enjoyed a concert more!"

"Did she indeed. Well well well."

Nellie's heart dropped all the way to her flimsy Regency flats.

"Well well. Is that how it appeared to you, Mrs Clay."

"No!— not in– I simply mentioned–"

But Elizabeth was speaking again. "We were agreeing that, on the whole these days, there are few people whose company you seem to enjoy more than Anne's!"

"Oh I'm *delighted* to hear this, Miss Elliot!– delighted that my attentions to Miss Anne can convince, that I find her an enjoyable and sophisticated concert companion. I only hope that your dear sister is similarly reassured. For it was within days of Miss Anne's arrival here that I remember saying, to myself"— and Mr Elliot cocked a leg over his knee and eyed the ceiling, brightly reminiscent— *'I must endeavour to cheer Miss Anne!'* Perhaps it was presumptuous of me but– well she seemed at something of a *loss* here in Bath! While the rest of her family illuminate with such graceful assurance the most elevated circles, Miss Anne in contrast seemed so little accustomed to– that is– her pining for the *country*; for her cousins; for the old familiar *retirement* on which she dotes— The contrast between my two cousins certainly struck me forcibly! So I said to myself–" (and he briskly tipped himself upright again) "I just said, 'I really must try to *cheer Miss Anne,* that she may not feel quite so much at a loss when she appears, in company, beside her intimidatingly beautiful sister!'"— with a lively, whimsical smile and bow to Elizabeth.

It did the trick. Elizabeth looked more than mollified, and opened her mouth to reply—

—but Mr Elliot had already cast himself upon one elbow, hand to cheek, and resumed the *view halloa* after his own line of thought. "And I really do flatter myself that I *have* managed to instil, in her, some degree of confidence. That she may *begin* to feel less out of place– here– immersed in this more *cosmopolitan* society, that is her *family's* natural milieu, but not until now perhaps, her *own*. Do you feel that? Do you really feel, then, that Miss Anne grows a little more cheerful, here in Bath?— begins to enjoy our social occasions, somewhat more? Please say that you do, my dear Miss Elliot; please, say that you do, Mrs Clay"– turning eagerly from one to the other— "I would *hate* to have laboured so long, and so hard, in so many conversations with Miss Anne, to hear that it has all been quite in vain!"

"But not at all, Mr Elliot! People are always telling me that Anne seems so much more cheerful these days! And it is very kind of you to try to brighten her up like this. It's just that I'm only afraid it comes at great cost to your own comfort, to spend so much time on her! I hate to see you casting your pearls before swine."

"Oh Miss *Elliot!*" Her cousin almost shouted with laughter. "Oh my–... *Oh!*" He clapped his hands to his cheeks and gazed at her with hilarity all over his countenance. "Only *you* are allowed to say things like that, Miss Elizabeth Elliot!"

At which the dashing Miss Elliot–

No. It is the footboy, interrupting.

To say that the dressmaker has arrived. Miss Elliot's new gown, ready for trying on. "Tell her to leave, Jeremy. Tell her to come back– *when* shall she come back, Mr Elliot? What are your movements today?"

"But no, Miss Elliot, on no account! Are we not to see this new gown? Are we not to give our opinion? Is my expertise in ladies' apparel" — and he tilted his eyebrows with comic sorrow — "all my studies, all my keen attention — is it all worth nothing in your eyes?" Elizabeth tittered, almost helpless. "*Do*, Miss Elliot, try on your new gown and 'model' it for us, as they say in Paris."

When he put it like that, she was incapable of disappointing him: she rose readily, and moved to the door with a smile on her face. "I shan't be long — I leave Penelope to entertain you!"

"Oh but we wish to see hair, and shoes, and jewels, *all, complete!*" called Mr Elliot at the closing door. The answer was another titter, and the sound of Elizabeth's hasty slippers fading down the hall.

Mr Elliot turned, and stared steadily at Mrs Clay.

Nellie cleared her throat.

"What a pl—"

"So you feel that I paid rather a lot of attention to Miss Anne last night? Hm?

"Oh– no I–"

"And you mentioned this to Miss Elliot?"

"Oh I– well I— Miss Elliot actually–"

"You were sitting directly behind me so I imagine you heard the whole conversation and have passed it on to your dear friend?" He frowned faintly. "This is how you spend your evenings here, amongst us?"

"No I— not at all I–"

"– because I could certainly hear the whole of your conversation with Miss Carteret; though it would not normally occur to me to mention this to others."

"Well I–"

"The two of you appear to be good friends."

"Oh I hope we are."

"Mm. Charming."

Mrs Clay had intended, after certain glances of Mr Elliot's at the concert last night, to guard her revolt of feeling from him more carefully. The rapid series of questions had already thrown her, however — and that insane, impotent anger had began to stir.

She bit it down.

"Nine o'clock", was observing Mr Elliot, to his cane head, "is very early to leave for an appointment near noon, even in Westgate Buildings."

"Oh but I wanted to be quite sure of getting there in time Mr Elliot. I was so very concerned that I should not disapp–"

"Yes and you certainly would have been. Quite sure." Mr Elliot cocked his head at the cane. "I should hate to think of you wandering the lower streets of Bath for so long; all alone. And in that dreadful dress."

"Oh I felt that I should *look* the part. I thought about it ever so carefully! I was *so* worried I must say! Well not to say worried but I must confess there *was* a *little* suspense."

"And you certainly did look the part. You did remarkably; you are a remarkable woman Mrs Clay."

Almost the Mr Elliot of old— and yet— sped up. "I scarcely recognised you. Had it not been for the blue reticule, I should not have known you myself. And yet, you know— you looked perfectly natural! You blended in!– so to speak. Not many ladies could do that. None, really."

Nellie twisted out a smile of feigned gratification.

"So Mrs Clay how *did* you while away all that long tedious stretch of time yesterday morning, if I might enquire?"

"Oh!– I walked about the streets– well no I tell a lie first I went to the Buildings and made *quite* sure that I could be *certain* of which door I should knock upon– and *then*, I walked about the streets, staying very close to Westgate Buildings of course as you may imagine, and just popping up this street and that street until the clocks told the hour."

"Hm! That must have been a lot of popping."

Mrs Clay looked at him blankly. His countenance was the picture of sympathy. "Quite a lot of walking", he explained. "Up, you know, and down— So did nothing catch your eye? Did nothing entertain you, in all that pacing of the streets?"

"Oh well I did spend a little time browsing the stalls– the market stalls, you know— they are set out on both sides —"

"Yes I know about market stalls Mrs Clay."

"Oh yes how silly of me. Well and so I just wandered up and down, browsing in the stalls— I do think I looked very natural! There was a lovely sort of flame-coloured dress at one stall, I recall, that would have suited Josephine to perfection, but she is still a little young for such a colour and the *cut*, you know, there was perhaps not enough material to reshape the neckline and so I hesitated—"

"You went to second-hand clothes stalls? And looked at second-hand clothes? For your— forgive me but I've never been quite clear on this— your daughter? But she's not your daughter, is she? Your... why!– Your *second-hand* daughter."

Her eyes must have rolled back in her head: time and light flickered.

"Oo. That touched a nerve."

"Yours or mine?"

"Yours of course. I have no nerves."

"No. I can believe that."

And there he has her.

Yet Mr Elliot continued to sit, crossed legs, steepled fingers, scintillating at her, with the exhilarated air that possessed him this morning.

From somewhere a scuffling– He tosses his cigar into the fire and advances swiftly, smiling like an Etruscan mask, light-footed as a Pierrot– to greet Elizabeth bursting flushed and glowing through the door. She bounces before him wordlessly in her new dress.

"No words will express how you appear to us now, Miss Elliot!"

Chapter 25

And what did she have, after all? Three cards, forsooth; who would believe her? Elizabeth? *Anne?* And the letter, one pissy little letter! She had thought she was so clever, so very very craftily self-preserving and foresightful, when she had thought, at the last moment, to extract that one single sheet, and take it away and hide it under her summer gowns. Why had she not taken the lot?– the whole story? Could she make *anything* of just the one that she had?

Well of course she could.

Well of course *not*. She would be branded a thief too, as well as a liar.

Would she?

Wouldn't she?

Since that was unanswerable Nellie leapt from her bed— it was that same evening, it was night— and jerked the curtains open, and strode back to bed.

What was he up to anyway, with Anne and Elizabeth both? He meant Anne to think he meant her. He meant Lady Russell to think that too. Maybe it was more about Lady Russell?

But why would he care about Lady Russell? Only if he meant something in relation to Anne.

Was he in cahoots with Anne?

Certainly, she'd tell him anything he asked. If he asked it cleverly enough. And Mr Elliot could ask cleverly, alright.

One thing seemed pretty clear: he meant nothing in relation to Elizabeth, and it was more than her place here was worth to try to prepare the girl for that. After this morning's bare few minutes' approach to honesty, Mrs Clay had been forced to spend the rest of the day in damage control. It was Miss Elliot's job, and hers alone, to deride the idea of Mr Elliot's devotion: it was Mrs Clay's, to insist upon it, with admiration.

Nellie turned her pillow over and pounded it.

But *did* he mean to marry Elizabeth nevertheless?

After all, he had been very attentive when he returned, later that same evening. The first five minutes with Miss Anne, yes; but she had given him the brush-off. Little fool. It had probably worked for her at nineteen, increasing a man's interest by rejection: she needed a long hard look in the mirror, before she tried it now. Mr Elliot had promptly taken himself off, and he'd spent the rest of the evening with Elizabeth, giggling together at a distant table; looking over one of those volumes with curious plates. It was still many months before the protective crape came off his hat and sleeve. Not until... Lord– late June. It seemed an aeon away. Meanwhile, a mourning widower, he could lead any woman any dance he chose.

But what did it matter which he married?

Or even if he didn't marry either— did it make any *difference*? for Nellie? Now?

The next three hours of the night, Mrs Clay spent trying to calculate a plan of action under a range of possible eventualities.

At about four o'clock she gave up. There were just too many unknowns. The greatest unknown of all was Mr Elliot. What on earth was he driving at?

Mr Elliot.

Mr Elliot. Should she not try to attack the problem here, at its root?

Attack Mr Elliot. Oh certainly. Yes indeed– and– The question kept interrupting her: *Why was Mr Elliot a problem at all?*

How had they ended up, apparently, on opposite sides?

She and he should be like peas in a pod. Like ham and eggs; like crime and punishment. Just because she read some letters and now she didn't like him.

Wasn't it all in her own head?

No. It wasn't.

And if she and Mr Elliot were ever to be ham and eggs, she'd have to get the ground between them more level.

On that appalling mix of metaphors, she fell asleep.

*

Nellie awoke to certainty.

The house still slept. Not even a maid stirred.

The downstairs clock chimed five.

Her skin prickled all over. She would play her three cards. She would go there, and try it. And then— take the consequences as they came.

I mean there was always papa's home in Dashe. Or teaching.

Or the goddamned grocer.

Chapter 26

Mrs Clay set off immediately after breakfast. Tomorrow's evening party demanded plants, for the drawing-room, and surely it was wisest to inspect and select the specimens in person, rather than trusting it again to the nursery: remember what happened with that lily last time! (But what had happened?– Oh Miss Elliot so you didn't notice; I'm so glad. I did my best to conceal it.) Better that someone should supervise directly, and dear obliging Mrs Clay — whose feet, and hands too, were without pretence as cold as ice — felt the need for just such a long hard walk, to get her blood flowing.

*

The nursery was on the other side of town. Nellie discharged her unnecessary duty, to the civil resentment of the head nurseryman, and headed back into the grubby heart of town. Directly behind the baths: Westgate Buildings.

Not calm at all. Heart, battering at her ribs, like an animal trying to climb the walls of the slaughter chute. Don't think. Just walk up to that door.

Just knock.

"She's gone to the warm bath. Be another hour or more. Be ages."

Mrs Clay's face puckered; "... I thought Mrs Smith went into the baths on Monday?"

"Mondays and Fridays."

Nellie and all her resolve stood confounded on the doorstep.

It began to rain. To add to the confusion. "Like to wait for her inside too Mrs Hubble?"

"Oh. Well... Yes. That would be... Be best, yes."

The boy— it was the same boy— held the front door wider for her, and in another movement opened the door to Mrs Smith's parlour, huddled as it was cheek-by-jowl with the main entrance. "Made you a real nice fire." She stepped through, and the boy closed the door smartly behind her and whistled off down the hall. She was alone, once more, in Mrs Smith's apartment.

This time, though, it looked positively cosy. The rusted grate had been grey when Mrs Clay last saw it, and almost cold. Now it held a bright fire on a lavish bed of coals. The blaze warmed and lit the small room delightfully, and its soft pleasant rustle counteracted, most comfortably, the hiss of the burgeoning rain on the other side of the small, smeared glass. Outside, through that glass, was cold, and disorder, and wet creeping up your gown and down your neck, as you squeezed by towering carts thundering, and splashing, and hurrying feet. Here, was repose: here, security. Here, no matter how humble, was home. There ought to be a song about it.

Also, the back of Mr Elliot's head.

He was seated in an easy chair, facing the fire, legs stretched out before him. A sheet of paper in one hand; in the other, a cigar.

On a tiny table beside him was the inlaid box. It was open.

Papers lay scattered about.

He spoke without turning.

"Forgive me if I do not rise, my dear. It's not a necessary formality, is it, between husband and wife."

On the floor as well. More papers.

"But sit down yourself, do, my dear Mrs Hubble."

There was nothing to sit on.

"I believe there is another chair in the bedroom."

Nellie walked numbly into the airless windowless cave that was Mrs Smith's bedroom… picked up the wooden chair that stood beside the bed head. Carried it back into the parlour.

Stood, vacant.

Mr Elliot gestured, widely and slowly, towards a worn patch of carpet on his left.

Nellie set the chair down— stood beside it a blank moment; sat.

"Now we are comfortable, are not we?"

"Yes, Mr Elliot."

"Good; good." He studied her.

She made no move to speak, but sat with a nerveless stillness that, in the end, seemed satisfactory to Mr Elliot: he finished his inspection with a small nod:–

"Well Mrs Hubble, since we have at least an hour before this room will be crowded by other occupants, why don't I go on with my business here, while you just sit there quietly like a good wife and think of what line of shit you're going to spout when I speak to you again." He turned back to the letters.

He was sorting them. As Nellie had herself, only three days ago… He was taking a paper from the box, running his eye over it, and tossing it briskly either onto the table, or into the flames.

One or two of the condemned, whose flight had reached only to the brick hearth, were there beginning to buckle in the heat, and the smell of scorched paper mingled with that of tobacco.

Rain; the whisper of the fire; the slight rustle of paper.

Now a slight grunt from Mr Elliot: surprise, or recognition, Nellie could not have said. He had paused over a paper— examined both sides— grunted again and sat back, as to read it through.

More snorts; and as he sank into engrossment, the raised paper came between his face and hers.

There was one letter that might be within reach of Nellie's foot. She dared not turn her eyes towards it even now, but as it had skimmed the hearth, she had recognised the charming little sketch, with which the young Mr Elliot had illustrated it, all those years ago — a sparrow, picking crumbs on the sill of his law-student garret-window. It was a good letter, that one.

She slid her left foot towards it.

More...

It was almost out of reach but not *quite* and with leg extended now like a crippled dancer...

froze, at a sudden chuckle from Mr Elliot—

but he was writhing in relish at whatever he was reading.Her foot, quivering over the edge of the paper, descended... she breathed out, breathed in again... and with paper pinned now beneath it her foot recommenced its stealthy glide back this time towards her.

The minute susurration of paper on carpet seemed to pierce through the hiss of the rain, the fire... but she could not risk a lighter pressure, she might lose it... Slowly as a snake in the weak sunshine of April her foot still grasping its prey slid at last under her skirt.

Released her breath. A shaking, careful exhalation. Had to fight, quick and hard, with the urge to gasp for air. Slowly *in... in... in....out* out out out oh thank God and *in... in... in...* and out. She was breathing again. Mr Elliot gave a last appreciative guffaw, snapped aside the paper he had been reading, and pinned her with a bright smile.

"Hilarious."

He dragged himself upright in the chair, crushed the letter he had been reading, and flicked it into the flames.

Two or three more went the same way, and half a dozen perhaps joined those on the table before Mr Elliot, losing interest, dropped a last one onto the desk, stretched extravagantly, and stood. "How tiresome business can be."

He tugged down his coat where it had ridden up, shot his cuffs, picked up the box with its remaining store of unexamined papers and emptied it whole-sale into the fire. Then he walked over to Mrs Clay and taking her chair by its arms flung chair and sitter back against the wall.

Percussion of her head against the brick rendered her, for a moment, quite helpless.

It was a half minute, at least, before she was able to–... she struggled, onto her side, and then, pushed the fallen chair free from her legs, and entangling skirt.

Mr Elliot was standing arms akimbo on the hearth, watching as the sparrow joined its brethren in a whirl of black fragments fleeing up the chimney.

He turned to her.

"Oh my dear Mrs Clay. What are you doing there? How on earth did that happen? Here; let me assist you, I beg." Assiduous, he stepped around the fallen chair and helped her to her feet; "dear me– dear me Mrs Clay what a case you are in— dear *dear* how vexatious your hair seems to have fallen over sort of sideways and— oh my goodness look!— a titty has come adrift."

It was true. One of Mrs Clay's unfashionably large breasts had escaped the confines of her bodice, and was making its presence known through the transparent muslin fichu that was supposed to protect chest and throat.

"Well and how glad we must feel that this has happened only amongst ourselves. We would not want Sir Walter to see you now, would we Mrs Clay? — let's tuck it back in, that's better— Sir Walter, or Miss Elliot." Having placed her politely on the newly-upright chair, he perched on the seat opposite, steepling his fingers with a solicitous air.

"Feeling better?"

In the end she answered him.

"Yes, thank you, Mr Elliot."

And it was true. She was swinging, and floating, like a jellyfish, in a swell; and she knew that the pain would eventually begin; but she was more functional than most of us would be, bare minutes after such a blow to the head. Boxers tell us— and those who have been married to George Clays know it to be true— that you do just get used to being hit. "Good, good!" Mr Elliot did seem pleased. "Very good—

"So:– dear Mrs Clay. Dear dear Mrs Clay.

"What a silly girl you have been. Mmm? What were you thinking, Mrs Clay?

"Mmm?

"I do want an answer, Mrs Clay. I feel that I *deserve* an answer."

Nellie could think of nothing.

"An answer?"

She shook her head and the room swooped. "Mrs Clay– understand me. This goes beyond disappointment. This is an act of the greatest dishonesty on your part. Now, isn't it?

"Mmm?

"Dishonesty, and ingratitude.

"A task I hoped to find done, and expected to find done— it is undone.

"A task that you undertook: you have left— well— in shambles.

"A complete mess, Mrs Clay.

"Mmm ?"

With a soundless boom, her head began to throb. Each beat of her heart drove a fist of pain up her spine into her skull.

"Mmm?

"A complete mess. That is what I see, when I look about me.

"And I do look about me, Mrs Clay. You really have been terribly foolish. We have always got on together so well. And now; look what you have done."

Tears began to leak from Nellie's eyes.

"Mmm?

"You have very nearly ruined everything.

"Mrs Clay, I have so many acquaintance who are eager to help me. At every turn, I find people *anxious* to help me: they trust me, and confide in me. Sir Walter; Anne; Miss Elliot. Lady Russell: Margaret. Do you know her first name is Margaret."

The tears were flowing faster.

"Do you.

"Do you know that."

Nellie shook her head a fraction, and the pain burst out in yellow blossoms.

Mr Elliot stared at her; shook his own. "Not to mention Lady Dalrymple— Fiona— she is a Fiona too, such a beautiful name isn't it.

"All these people; they are so fond of me. You alone don't seem to want to work with me.

"It's very disappointing, Mrs Clay. And so foolish. You have been so very, very foolish."

A sob escaped her.

"So.

"So it seems we have a problem here, Mrs Clay. My inclination is to send you back to your family. Yet we have a month or two until your father's return, don't we?"

He retrieved his cigar from the table at his elbow, and examined it critically. "I mean, what are we going to do with you, Mrs Clay?

"Where are you going to stay?

"Are we going to just drop you out on the streets?"

— and the sobs shook her at will.

"Mrs Clay. You think you are so useful to the Elliots. You fancy yourself indispensable perhaps.

"And I have to laugh. When I see this in you, Mrs Clay, I have to laugh. So much is going on, of which you have no idea.

"No idea at all.

"Did you know, that Sir Walter owes more, in London, than he ever acknowledged to your father."

"Mm?

"*Mmm?*"

The question was not rhetorical?

"No..."

"Ah: well there you go. He does."

Mr Elliot studied the end of his cigar again, and adjusted the ash.

"... So, you didn't know that."

"No."

"No. There is a lot that you don't know, Mrs Clay. And yet— it seems that I do!

"Know, I mean." He drew on the cigar, "In detail", and blew out the smoke. "Things just come to me: people just tell me things. Not like your father, who had to pay for it. Detailed knowledge was his specialty, I understand."

(She stopped crying.)

"Did you know that it was your father's specialty? Hmm?"

He leant forward, suddenly animated.

"Did you know that your father was a spy, Mrs Clay?"

(She had almost stopped breathing.)

"He spied on the French, he claimed. My information points to a more flexible arrangement. Your father was given to flexible arrangements, Mrs Clay: there are a lot of people who would be shocked to know, how flexible."

"That is not true." (This came out quickly.)

Mr Elliot rounded his eyes and mouth: for a moment he was a huge, cigar-smoking, bewhiskered little boy. "You mean he wasn't flexible? But that's very bad, Mrs Clay! A spy must be flexible— must bend and flex with the turn of events." He moved his left hand sinuously, to demonstrate. "An inflexible spy is of no use to anyone, Mrs Clay. Are you sure your father was inflexible? — yet he got out of the *Conciergerie!* Alive!

"Doesn't that indicate a *remarkable* degree of flexibility?"

"It is not true–"

Mrs Clay stopped; uncertain as to what her words were denying, and whether they should.

It was this— this very conversation— that she had become truly afraid of, at some unspecifiable point after the appearance, in Bath, of Mr Elliot.

To be accused of vulgarity; of being poorly educated (in English); of having picked up all sorts of coarse expressions, and habits of mind: this is what had filled the fore- and middle ground in the landscape of her anxieties for many a dreary year. But in the background, looming over all other concerns, was this huge ice-capped mountain range of fear, for papa.

George used to say– when Mr Shepherd was alive again, and suddenly free, and back in England, and Nellie spoke of visiting him— perhaps for some time— George used to say, of her father: *His past will catch up with him.*

Your father's past will catch up with him, and then he will be for it.

In the navy, we knew how to deal with men of that stamp.

After all, they couldn't execute you for vulgarity.

For treason there was, in law, the gallows, followed by disembowelling, and then the slicing of the body into four. It doesn't seem to go with white muslin high-waisters and little silk parasols: but thus it was. (I must stress, though— in practice, they hadn't gone the whole hog like that for years. Now, with this peace, it was even less probable. Nellie is catastrophising: she is such a worrier. Simple hanging, without the frills, was the probability; at her father's age too, even just prison, transportation.)

... but loss of character would be enough. Loss of his place.

A little gossip, in fact, would do it.

And then: Papa, old and ill and homeless. "Mrs Clay? Mrs Clay? *What* is not true?

"Mrs Clay?"

Another cigar-smoking silence. Then again–

"What is not true?"

Mrs Clay searched her mind for a weapon, or a shield, a card, but her head, her head, and the fire so hot. "Hmm? What is not true? I would like very much to hear what is not true; since you are so emphatic about it. Something must be very much on your mind.

"What is it, on your mind, Mrs Clay?

"I would very much like an answer. Mrs Clay."

"My father is loyal to England."

"Oh my *goodness* Mrs Clay! What an announcement to make! What an odd statement to come out with. Why would you feel the need to say a thing like that?

"Hmm?

"Why would anyone say a thing like that?"

"You were trying to insinuate that he wasn't."

"Oh Mrs Clay! How you mistake me!" Mr Elliot was genuinely amused, though at what Mrs Clay could not determine. Perhaps he was simply in a good mood. He seemed to be in a good mood: expansive; relaxed. Mrs Clay realised that she had never before seen Mr Elliot looking utterly relaxed. She was seeing it now. "You quite mistake me! You are an anxious daughter, aren't you?

"I shall tell Sir Walter that, perhaps.

"'Mrs Clay is very quick to defend Mr Shepherd', I shall say. 'There I was, talking about I cannot recall what, and she flew out in defence of him! "My father is loyal to England!" she cried!– Well, even if he did make France his home all those years, I cannot see why she felt it necessary to fly out like that. Why did she feel it necessary, do you think, Sir Walter?' I shall ask him, son to father, you know; seeking his insight. 'What, in Mr Shepherd's behaviour, could give you a clue?'"

Nellie shrugged minutely. "Why don't you just tell him some lie yourself?"

— But at this Mr Elliot moved his cigar aside sharply, and frowned at her with distaste.

"Lie?"

He spat something into his handkerchief; a fragment of tobacco.

"Lying— I don't know how often you indulge yourself, Mrs Clay— lying is common among the lower orders, isn't it? Most of my class set it aside when they set aside childish things." The tobacco, if tobacco it was, required another two wipes of the handkerchief across his tongue tip. "I cannot recall the last time I lied; but I know I was still a mere child, struggling to make headway in the world..."

And now Mr Elliot seemed genuinely lost in reverie.

 No doubt he was thinking of the letters.

"Hasn't your father taught you that?" He was back already. "Hasn't your father taught you that lying is anathema? I'm sorry to hear you were so poorly brought up, Mrs Clay. Perhaps I shall have to mention that to Sir Walter too; and Miss Elliot. 'Mrs Clay asked me, the other day, why I didn't *lie* about something. I really cannot recall what. But there I was, agonising about how to frame a little unpleasant something; she suggested it would be more conveniently solved by simply *lying*. Perhaps I misunderstood her. Her father, I'm sure, could not have failed to instil the strictest principles— such a position of trust as he is in— no; I'm quite sure I must have somehow misunderstood her. Please forget that I mentioned it.' Shall I say that, Mrs Clay?" He looked directly at her.

The silence drew out.

"Shall I say that, Mrs Clay?"

The fire was dying down a little. Outside, the streets of Bath were lashed with the soft swish of rain. Here was warmth, and stillness, and Mr Elliot, waiting for his answer.

"I said: '*Shall I say that, Mrs Clay.*'"

"No."

"No?" The fire sighed. "No, it could be so unpleasant."

Thrown by a sudden gust, rain dashed against the windows.

"So— what shall I say, Mrs Clay? Please. Tell me what I shall say. I only wish to help, you know.

"Do tell me.

"What shall I say to Sir Walter about you; what shall I say to Miss Elliot?"

"Whatever you wish. Mr Elliot."

"Oh, no!– do please, advise me!"

"I should like to be of service to you, my dear Mrs Clay— in any way I can.

"For example— and you do seem a little pale still, a little shaken by your fall— I would be delighted to assist you into the bed in there. If you feel it would be at all helpful to you, I would be willing to join you, and attempt the resuscitation of your body with my own; I understand from your acquaintance in Plymouth that you found that sort of thing most refreshing."

It was a suggestion that Mr Elliot often used, with gently-reared ladies who had somehow found themselves, with him, in broadly similar circumstances, and similarly without recourse. But where it reduced said ladies to speechless mortification, it was an offer only too familiar to Mrs Clay– as for example on any of the many occasions on which she had struggled to drag her husband, three parts insensible, from some crowded drinking house, and then, half-carry him home. She shook her head wearily.

"No, Mr Elliot. I am sure you could not really wish to expose yourself to my 'sailor's disease'."

Mr Elliot laughed delightedly.

"Very clever Mrs Clay!— very clever indeed I must admit I see the *logic of the case!* Though— We are not being so thoughtful towards Sir Walter are we?

Mrs Clay had no reply.

"Hmm?

"I said, you are not being so solicitous towards Sir Walter. When you flap your boobies at *him;* you don't seem so concerned for his future with the clap."

Nellie considered trying to muster the energy for a shrug.

But it seemed all too hard.

"ANSWER ME!" Mr Elliot slammed his fist onto the table. The box jumped. So did Mrs Clay. "Yes Mr Elliot."

He subsided, mollified; pulled on his cigar. For some time there was only the sound of the rain, and the puffs and smacks of his lips and lungs at work. In spite of the overwhelming vulnerability of her position, Mrs Clay found that her next words suddenly uttered themselves.

"So you still intend me to marry Sir Walter?"

Mr Elliot held the cigar one way, his head the other.

"I don't *know*", he replied, with every sign of genuine intrigue. "Sometimes I think *one* thing, sometimes I think an*other.*

"And sometimes", he ashed onto the carpet, "I think something else com-pletely! It's all quite up in the air, it seems, at this stage. But– surely, Mrs Clay–" rearranging his crossed legs— "surely there is no need for us to rush into anything with Sir Walter, or with anyone, in *haste*. Marriage is an irretriev-able step, after all, and– so well-situated as you are just now– would it add to your felicity, to abandon your single state once more? You need to be quite sure of your future happiness with the love object, you know; as sure as one can be, of anything in this imperfect world: and sometimes I wonder if Sir Walter is really the man for you. I mean look what happened last time. You don't want to end up back at Mill Bay or — what was that place near Stone-house Pool? Or any of those other places do you? Mm?

"And it could so easily happen, if you married Sir Walter. At least, that is what a friend of mine assures me: he has bought up most of Sir Walter's bills of hand, you know. So we would want to go about it very carefully, wouldn't we?– if we married Sir Walter."

So that was it. (All of it?)

"...want to talk things through, with people. Come to—" he waved a smoking hand— "a *lasting* arrangement. Satisfactory to *all* parties. Mm?...

"In the meantime, though–" Mr Elliot lay back in his chair and thrust a fist into his trouser pocket, "and to remind you of times past — and times future perhaps..." he drew out a small limp twist of something. "You, of all people, really should have this. It means the most to you."

He twirled the thing between his fingers, so that its pale surface flickered in the light of the fire. Then he held it out to her.

Nellie did not move.

"Come Mrs Clay. Hm?

"Do take it."

No.

Eventually Mr Elliot tossed the shining hair and its rag of ribbon onto her lap. "There. Don't feel that it creates the slightest obligation. I can get plenty more."

The fire hissed; the rain hushed; Mr Elliot slobbered softly over his cigar.

And now, through the wind and rain, bells struck the three-quarter hour.

Mr Elliot sighed, and ground the burning end of his cigar into the varnish of Mrs Smith's little table. "Ah well. All good things come to an end. It is time for us to venture out of our haven, and into the streets of Bath!" A bright smile. "It has been good to have this little chat, Mrs Clay. I feel it has cleared the air between us. Needless to say it would be superfluous in you — a work of supererogation— to pester Mrs Smith any further. If you have any curios-ity, in regard to this sadly fallen woman, why not bring your questions straight to me: save yourself a long walk.

"But—", he added, standing, "do let me know if she bothers *you*. She is the kind of woman, you know, who sends people anonymous notes. I would hate for you, or any of your family, to be exposed to that kind of thing; most dis-tressed, to hear that she had involved them in any way. Children take that kind of nonsense so seriously. Or if they don't, their teachers do." He was helping her to her feet, retrieving and arranging her shawl, which had caught on some-thing, and torn. Opening the door, he ushered her politely through.

Outside, rain had vanished. In the erratic manner of Bath, a sun was attempting to shine.

They walked, arm in arm, along Bath Street.

At the end, under the colonnade, Mr Elliot drew her smoothly to a halt. "Here we must part, I'm desolated to say Mrs Clay. You will no doubt be wishing to rejoin our friends in Camden Place, and I'm afraid duty calls me another way."

He took her hand in an easy goodbye.

"Until tomorrow, then!"

And he turned and walked off down Stall Street towards the river, his hat at a jaunty angle, his back irreproachably upright.

When a cold, weak Nellie at last reached Camden Place, the principal rooms were vacant.

Miss Elliot, Sir Walter, Miss Anne too: everyone was out. Only her feet, shuffling, quietly, over the marble.

Upstairs, step by step, to her chamber.

Kneeling, with difficulty, on the floor; sliding her box out from beneath her bed; lifting the lid. The letter was gone.

Chapter 27

A day that went on forever, head pounding, a huge bruise blooming black on her elbow. Elizabeth endlessly talking about modifications and extensions to Saturday's evening party, Mrs Clay smiled and nodded through it all, yes, yes; all could be comprised in a short sentence to the housekeeper: there will be six more in the party tomorrow— the Musgroves, the country cousins, were in Bath. It would have been very important to learn all their names, and all about them, before they arrived. Papa would...

Head clear, but empty. Moonlight, lying in gelid calm on her bed, her dressing table, her wardrobe.

Across a chair, the latest dress that she had inherited from Elizabeth, awaiting its turn to attend, in newly furbished form, Elizabeth's party. Today's party now— the clock below was striking the small hours. These things were cut from the darkness by the moon, waning, yet still fully able to glare on all she surveyed. Beyond her ghastly light, the corollary of that icy brilliance; a dark so utter, a vacuum so complete, that in it one must suffocate.

Her next memory placed her in the middle of that party. She must have gone through most of it on autopilot, because here the card tables have already broken up. People are sitting about the room. Chatting. It must have been a successful evening, because no-one seems in a hurry to leave, save the

Wallises, who are at this moment stepping into their carriage outside; yes, she could remember; the Wallis baby had, with the spontaneity typical of babies, died a couple of days ago, and although no-one was expected to go into mourning over six-week-old infant, the old Colonel's attempt to cheer his wife up with an outing had evidently misfired. Nellie consulted her memory for an image of her, sharp enough to enable some observation to Sir Walter; pretty woman, a bit pale at the moment, what had she been wearing?...

Everything else was going swimmingly.

The two fine rooms, folding doors secured flat against the walls, stretched in one gracious, airy space, and though they were but a small party the arch above them was filled by the hum of chatter and laughter. One of the visitors, one of the clutch of country cousins, had just spread her arms, and was twirling with slow grace in the opening between the card tables, and a gentleman in a naval coat turned to bow and give her his hand— would they dance?

For a moment the idea hung in the air—

— but ah, first it would be music!– and the piano was open and the usual tussle ensuing over who should be persuaded to go first, and now Miss Carteret was sitting down, laughing– "Very well then we shall start at the *bottom*, with *me*, and work *up*, to Miss Anne!" — and was playing; and someone was singing too, really very creditably; by the fires, and through the room, others stood or sat and the murmur of voices lapped gently. Every face smiling, every countenance, relaxed; a spirit of candour and generosity seemed to pervade and unite the room.

No coldness, no formality. It was nothing like the usual Elliot effort.

What on earth had happened?

Look!– there sit Lady Russell and Lady D., together and positively chuckling! Lady Russell usually had trouble reconciling her respect for a Viscountess with her disappointment at how little effort Lady Dalrymple made to be one; yet here they were, talking over each other, the plumes on their head-dresses wobbling and waving, as if the birds that had grown them lived and danced again. Ah!— And *there*, no doubt, was the cause of Lady Russell's liberal mood: her eyes, straying to her young protégé, now beamed with fond pride. Anne stood between Elizabeth and Catherine at the piano, and—

Goodness!

If Anne had been in looks on Wednesday, she was positively radiant this evening! A flood of life visibly filled her limbs, flushed her face, and glowed in her eyes.

More: the transmutation was one of spirit; of feeling. She radiated happiness with a brilliance to outshine the fire in the hearth.

Like the fire too, her warmth was extended without any discrimination: right now she was chattering convivially to Catherine— and smiling at her, what's more– and Catherine, even after two months of distant hauteur from

Miss Anne, was unable to keep a puzzled, good-humoured smile from lighting her own face in turn... Where was the self-pitying spinster, sour, and souring, that they had left behind them at Kellynch? Nellie was looking at the sudden rich blossoming of all the change that had been growing in Anne here in Bath.

An engagement. Anne *must* be engaged! Nothing less could make a spinster of twenty-seven so agreeable.

Mrs Clay's eyes turned to Mr Elliot, fully in time to catch the last half of a conspiratorial smile he was sharing with– yes, Lady Russell— back on the sofa, whose bosom now actually swelled, swelled, and subsided, with a deep, irresistible sigh of happiness

So: that was that.

No getting rid of Mr Elliot now.

At her thought, the man turned and looked her full in the face.

Lifted his hand to the back of his own head, and cocked an enquiring eyebrow. That bump on the head— all better now?

He smiled, and turned away.

Right then and there, Mrs Clay should have commenced rapidly calculating the effect that this rearrangement of their social network was going to have on her own position within that web. Elizabeth; sobbing in fond dependence on the neck of her one remaining friend?— begging Mrs Clay never to leave her, now that sister and cousin both have conspired to humble her? Or lashing out with humiliation at all who had glimpsed her now-dead hopes? And Sir Walter: inspired to matrimonial emulation?– or, on the contrary, alive afresh to the dignity of his place, as he posed in the company of his rich, new-fashioned heir and son-in-law? Above all, Mr Elliot. Mr Elliot: what— or—

... or what?

Yes, there was a lot for Mrs Clay to think about. But did she?

No.

Instead, there in the Camden Place drawing-rooms, surrounded by pot-plants and visitors, she drifted, off, back into that fugue state in which she has been hanging, now, for most of two days. Pull yourself together, woman! What kind of an intriguer are you?

No— she's not listening.

All this while, Anne has been going through the music on the piano, select-ing something, seating herself, settling in: now, she begins to play.

She plays, as you would expect, like a woman in love. That is to say, she fudges a few notes– almost unprecedented, for Anne Elliot— but then, one of the cousins' party had cast his large naval shadow across the score as he quietly slid in beside her... and the piece evolves into a four-hander— a spir-ited, an almost inspired improvisation, that has the company laughing, applauding, smiling and nodding to one another their appreciation.

Mrs Clay, the Camden Place authority on music, misses it all.

And still Mrs Clay attends not, while Elizabeth pushes forward into the rippling close of the sketch and thrusts another piece into her sister's hands. Oh dear! —

It is the score of the aria that they have been working on for a bare three days!

Simple enough, if she *keeps* it simple; but, it requires Elizabeth to sing in Italian, which prior to last Thursday she had never done in her life; and here she is, stepping up, to attempt it in public! – But is this advisable? Nellie?

Nellie?

Anne takes the sheets, and studies them intently. Still with face averted from the company, she fingers a few chords — isolates a not-terribly-tricky passage, and practises it a few times — quite a few times — The room is growing expectant, Miss Elliot impatient, she is drumming her fingers on the piano top, for Elizabeth of course is flooded with apprehension and right now wishes of all things to sit down again, though she would drive a chisel into her own bare white arm sooner than have anyone suspect it, and the delay, which she should be gratefully using to surreptitiously warm up her voice, is dreadful to her feelings. And her throat is closing tight.

Anne plays the opening bars at last. Elizabeth turns with a brittle smile towards the room. She sucks air into her upper chest like any total amateur, and begins–

But Miss Elliot does not lack this kind of courage. First, and quite soon, she remembers to breathe. Then, at the end of the first verse, she gets the register change so relatively neatly that her frozen face thaws a bit. On the second verse, she remembers to add the dynamics — gets the swell-and-fade bits very nicely, the slow steady crescendo very nicely indeed— chucks in the optional grace notes as if she meant to do them all along— completely forgets to pathetically fade through the last phrase and lands instead on the final note bang!- forte, and triumphant! — with exactly the full, round sound that Nellie has been coaching her towards since the dawn of their days in Bath.

"Lovely!"

... "Superb!"

"Glorious...!"

"Italian!"

Elizabeth beams at her audience.

"... and how proud your sister must make you Miss Anne!– have you ever thought to emulate her singing?", and Mr Elliot; "Ah, Sir Walter; if Mr Z were among us tonight, hmmm?" In the roomful of faces turned admiringly on Miss Elliot, Mrs Clay's, alone, is absent.

She is staring blankly at nothing in the corner.

Elizabeth declines to sing again.

Declines, perhaps, rather curtly. "Oh dear me no— it is my teacher that you should hear. Mrs Clay's voice is quite wonderful; isn't it, Penelope?"

"Do let us hear it, then! If Miss Elliot cruelly refuses to pour balm on our thirsting ears..." (what an image—! but Mr Elliot spots an opportunity here– such an opportunity)– "then let us hear from her instructress!"

"Yes! Yes, do let us hear from Mrs Clay", Lady Dalrymple seconded happily. "She has done wonders with Fiona's voice, just from giving her advice, you know, and I hear Fiona singing so nicely, now..."

"Then let us hear from Miss Carteret!" was Sir Walter's cry— because Nellie is still staring into the corner, in spite of a dozen pairs of curious eyes and the repeated mention of her own name, and it is getting a bit awkward.

"There then, Fiona my dear, what do think of that?"

"Oh no mamma! Please no, I couldn't bear it I should die of embarrassment entirely! Don't make me, there's a darling. Mrs Clay!–" and, childlike still, she ran over and shook her friend's arm– "Mrs Clay, wake up do, and sing for us now!"

Nellie emerged from her daze; to find the entire room staring at her, and smiling.

"...you *must* indeed you must, or they will make *me* sing, and you know that will be uncomfortable for all of us. Especially you", Miss Carteret assured her, growing solemn. "You will be in *agonies*."

"Sing?... Miss Elliot is the performer in our household."

"Oh come on Penelope. Don't be so coy. Modesty is only charming up to a certain point, you know."

"After the extravagant claims Miss Elliot has not scrupled to make for you", said Mr Elliot, with mock mock-seriousness, "your spirit, Mrs Clay, may well quail at the task. But do not give her the lie, Mrs Clay– do not prove your dear–"

The word 'patroness' hung in the air.

"– *dear* friend, mistaken in her estimate of your voice! Give of your best, Mrs Clay; and we will promise to be generous in our judgement."

Elizabeth was turned away already, talking brightly to one of the Musgroves.

Everyone was waiting, in the murmury, talk-amongst-yourselves way that a polite audience does.

Oh well.

Nellie glided to the piano. She had no sensation of her feet touching the ground, only of the room swimming around her. Music was scattered on its broad rich surface, gleaming in candlelight.

Something simple. Something Miss Anne, still seated at it, could play by sight. This, right here at the top; yes. It would do.

"Can you transpose this for mezzo? Down a third would be ideal."

A startled look from Miss Anne, and an "Oh... but surely..."

"Never mind. I'll sing unaccompanied." Still Anne hesitated on the brink of speech— Mrs Clay sighed. "It's no matter at all. I'm used to it." With no further formalities she turned to the room and began.

O cessate di piagarmi— O lasciatemi morir!

Chatter hushed.

Luci ingrate, dispietate,

All through the room, heads had turned.

Più del gelo e più de' marmi

fredde e sorde a' miei martir.

Beyond the bright stage of the drawing-room, along the poorly-lit corridors, across the cold, marble-clad hall, in the red-tinged cave of the kitchen, the servants' ceaseless motion slows, stills...

Più d'un angue, più d'un aspe

Crudi e sordi a' miei sospir—

...and on the back stairs that hearth-sweeping undermaid, nameless to us, wraps sinewy arms about herself and weeps, vanquished by all the beauty that is out of her reach.

Occhi alteri,

Ciechi e fieri,

Voi potete risanarmi,

E godete al mio languir.

Total silence.

Stunned faces.

Actual slack jaws, in one or two cases.

Except for Anne, who, in company with the piano-playing gentleman, was composedly admiring a fine display of greenhouse plants at the far end of the room.

Sir Walter— so tone deaf as to be unable to distinguish *God Save the King* from the *Marseillaise* without the aid of text— is gazing at Nellie as at an angel.

Now Mr Elliot begins to clap: slowly, smiling; deeply, deeply amused.

Others, awakened by the regular, leisurely whip-cracks of his salute, begin to add their tentative patters of applause, their murmurs. Some look shocked, some, as if suppressing laughter, others— Miss Carteret for one— troubled.

People are talking of the lateness of the hour. Now they are standing up. Someone is looking for a misplaced scarf.

Someone is ringing to order their carriage.

Mrs Clay turns towards her pupil and patroness— but Elizabeth has risen and is engaged in the business of farewelling her guests. Very engaged; every time Mrs Clay approaches, to take her accustomed role in that business— finding gloves, calling servants, helping on with shawls— Miss Elliot's snowy shoulder, or ice-white back, or glacial jawline interposes. And when the last guest has been inserted into her chair and clattered off, and Nellie has returned to the drawing-room fire, and been bowed goodnight by Sir Walter, with his usual salutation— "I shall leave you ladies to pick all of us to pieces! Do not stay up too late, to the damage of your complexions, I beg you; and have mercy, in your sallies, upon my poor self!", to be remunerated with the usual "Oh Sir Walter, how could you fancy such a thing! Do you not know that you are the standard against which we measure all others?"... when Nellie, as I say, has seated herself by the low-glowing drawing-room fire, in the expectation of the usual happy past-party coze with Elizabeth— she hears, instead, the swish of Miss Elliot's skirts along the hall outside, and then, the rapid tap of feet on the stairs as that lady ascended, with vigorous resolution, to the bedroom floor.

Had something come adrift, in Miss Elliot's *habiliments*? That sense of creeping slippage, which all women are familiar; that slow, but inexorable movement, of cloth across flesh— It would certainly account for Miss Elliot's manner over the last half hour. Or perhaps her period had started?

But if it were something like that, Nellie would expect Elizabeth to come running down the stairs again just as soon as the matter was set to rights, to plump herself down beside her friend and describe, luridly, and choking with laughter, her evening's Sword of Damocles experience.

But she didn't.

Nellie waited.

Then she waited some more.

Then she thought that perhaps she would go and tap at the door of Elizabeth's chamber— ask if anything was amiss.

But Miss Elliot could not be seen. Miss Elliot had a headache. Miss Elliot was already in bed.

"Can I not be of assistance— bring her anything? or read to her?"

No. Mrs Clay could be of no further assistance to Miss Elliot.

INTERMEZZO

While Mrs Clay is wandering off to bed, her mind in some suspense (and rightly so, because the ghastly shocks of recent days are but an overture to the massed chorus of thunderbolts that are now jostling for their chance to strike at her throughout the coming months), we must ourselves take another direction, and head back through the events of the last few chapters.

For in spite of appearances, smacked heads and so forth, for the last week our heroine has been wandering, blindly and unbeknownst to anyone, along the very brink of spectacular success. Nellie's stars, had they been consulted only last Wednesday morning, would have announced the imminent eruption of the most tremendous fireworks, followed by a glamorous wedding in Bath Abbey, and a happily ever after for anyone at all deserving of one.

Since then, however, the planets have rearranged themselves in a way that no-one could possibly have foretold and suddenly, tonight, they form a new constellation, thus:–

*

*   *   * *

* * *O Mrs Clay, you are SO screwed!* * *

* *

*

It predicts, more specifically, that poor Nellie is about to be ejected from the cultivated landscape of Austen, and forced once more to pick her own way across a jumbled desolation, a sort of bomb-scape, of genres. Volumes 1 and 2, after all, ran parallel to the two volumes of *Persuasion*. If not actually *in* Austen, we were at least Austen-adjacent. In entering Volume 3, though, we leave that civilised world, and from now on anything could happen, even True Crime; even Western. Even Paranormal Romance. Well maybe not Paranormal Romance. But anything else can be found, drifting about in Nellie's stars right now, if you go deep enough— absolutely anything. The stars are often pretty useless that way.

Consequently— and before we fictioneer into the wilds of Volume 3— it will be of some interest to locate the precise point at which Mrs Clay's fate suddenly jumped the rails of Destiny, crashed through the safety barriers that line the suspension bridge of Hope, and tumbled into the chaotic waters of Literary Mash-Up.

'Ah', you'll be thinking. 'It was that instant where Mrs Clay chose to hide the letter in her room, rather than keeping it on her person'. Or 'the point, at the concert, when Catherine said "you were out at nine o'clock", and Mr Elliot overheard it', or even (if you think her relationship with Elizabeth is the real key to her position– which could certainly be argued) 'the bit where she knocked the house sideways by belting out the very aria that Elizabeth had just essayed— and by the way, absolutely nailing it to the wall'.

But no: it is none of these things.

It is an event that took place offstage, so to speak.

Or rather— a nonevent.

Gather 'round, dear readers (unless you haven't re-read *Persuasion* recently, in which case, duck off *right* now and do so— we won't go on until you get back, I promise)...

*

Very well. Draw closer, now, and hear how Nellie's father's brilliant masterplan for Sir Walter, and Sir Walter's family, and Sir Walter's estate, and all the estate's dependents not forgetting the steward and all the *steward's* dependents– plans which would have brought such happiness, to so many— had a spanner chucked in to their fine-tuned works by none other than...

Anne Elliot.

That famously lovely person.

*

So!—

You know (at least, you ought to know) that on the Thursday morning after Wednesday's concert— while in Camden Place Mr Elliot was entertaining the ladies with images of ritual sacrifice, remember?— Miss Anne was taking her fluttering, Frederick-filled heart down to Westgate Buildings, *just* failing to spread perfume and purification all the way, to discharge a visit that she sort of owed to Mrs Smith.

You know, too, that during that visit, Mrs Smith finally spilled the beans to Anne about Mr Elliot, and his nasty ways. You know that as proof, they went through certain letters, which Mrs Smith kept in a small inlaid box — the very letters which, only days before, had been so thoughtfully sequestered, and then returned to that box, by Nellie.

You realise that on the subsequent Friday morning, while Nellie was preparing to march forth and beard Mrs Smith and– who knows?– attempt an alliance with her, perhaps?— Miss Anne had been shifting from foot to foot wishing the dreadful Clay woman *gone,* because that very morning Anne herself wanted to trot, quite solitary, and private— i*d est,* with no superfluous Mrs Clay hanging off her arm— over to Lady Russell's apartments in Rivers Street; there to consult the dowager as to what she, Anne, should do, about all these terrible things she'd discovered about Mr Elliot.

The subsequent scene was only fifteen minutes from reality. A short hurried walk; a "*Dear* Anne", "*Dear* Lady Russell"; a few preliminary hints– a puzzled look of enquiry— a tremulous, breath-baiting pause!— and the whole story would have exploded among Lady Russell's teacups.

And it never happened.

As you know.

Because, instead, Anne had been hanging around, and *hanging* around, until Nellie had finally left the house.

The result was that, thirty seconds later– just as our heroine was beginning the descent of Belmont– there, panting triumphantly to its top, were a middle-aged lady and gentleman of rural hue. Nellie's hurrying half-boots passed theirs in mutual non-recognition (save for an admiring glance, from the gentleman, at her neat yellow nankeen ancle); but–

Yes.

You, dear reader, realise at once:– here are Mr Charles Musgrove and his wife Mary (Mary Elliot as was), about to surprise their snooty relatives with the news of their own family's arrival in Bath.

Another minute, and the rustic pair are knocking at the door of Number 10— and just, *just* catching Miss Anne, before she could leave for Rivers Street!

Not only that, of course: this crowd of cousins, and all their hangers-on, are subsequently to distract Anne for two crucial days. Each morning will find Anne meaning to visit Lady Russell, and appal her with Mr Elliot's perfidy: each evening will see Anne yet more *distrait* with love and hope, and Lady Russell and everybody else as ignorant as ever, and Mr Elliot's reputation living on, "like the Sultaness Scheherazade's head"— only of course an odious, two-faced version of it— for another day.

And oh, that Anne had spoken! Oh, that Lady Russell had heard! It was all so close! On Friday, if *only* Mrs Clay had delayed announcing her going out, even just half an hour! Twenty-seven minutes' delay on Nellie's part, in fact, and it would have been *Anne* who scuttled out after breakfast; to speak to Lady Russell, exactly as planned.

Or, had those Musgrove cousins been hampered, on the road, a little longer than they were, by the sore shoulder of the offside lead horse.

Or had Mary, Mrs Charles Musgrove, actually decided, as she nearly *did* decide, as she had almost half a mind to decide, to pop up, before leaving their hotel, for a quick precautionary pee.

Or— even with Anne waiting, as she did, for Mrs Clay to depart first, and getting caught up, yes, by the Musgroves in consequence — well even *then*, had the Musgroves only *not* been so very fond of Anne! Had not Anne's recent offices, in snatching young Louisa Musgrove from death, quite possible death (a clear mind and a besetting urge to set people to rights bursting spectacularly into its own in what was, for once in Miss Anne's fettered life, a real emergency)— had this not lent such urgency to the Musgroves' affection that they promptly claimed all of Anne's company for all of Friday morning, and then, all of Saturday too... Oh! *surely*, in that case, Anne would still have found time to visit Rivers Street— and come April, she would have had a new step-mother.

But she didn't; she didn't.

And Mrs Clay's rosy future is laid waste.

Tiny, innocuous, deadly choices: forks, in the great road of life. Paths we choose so lightly, so blithely, all unknowing, and yet the left hand leads to Heaven, and the right, to Hell... or the other way around... How often is it, that on such trivial choices, our destinies do turn? It's almost enough to make one abandon Romantic Fiction and start writing companion volumes to Thomas Hardy instead.

*

By the by, though: it is as well, for Miss Anne, that she did not speak.

I do not demand that my readers care overmuch for Anne Elliot– I do not care for Anne Elliot myself, much– I'm afraid you may have noticed that— but I realise that, in spite of everything, there may be readers who do: who care for Anne Elliot, strongly. Those latter may be interested to know that, *had* Anne succeeded in disclosing to Lady Russell the duplicity of Mr Elliot, *before engaging herself to Captain Wentworth*— Well!

It would have been Anne herself, who ended up in the soup. Anne, and Captain Wentworth.

It would have gone like this:–

First: what would Lady Russell quite obviously have done, in response to Anne's terrible tale?

Naturally enough, she would immediately have commenced arguing Mr Elliot's character with dearest Anne; arguing it, non-stop, through all of Friday, and much of Saturday morning too, to the complete exclusion of any chances for romantic *éclaircissement* between Anne and Captain Wentworth.

And even then, she would still have required the proof of her own eyes. "Let me see those letters."

Could any responsible mother-figure do otherwise? All of Mr Elliot's devastating eligibility must not be condemned on hearsay alone! And who knows how a letter– or two– oh very well then, a handful of old letters— may be mis-read, misunderstood? (Especially within the gloom-ridden (and, one has no doubt of it, sinister) parlour of one so socially and financially unsubstantiated as this Mrs Smith!) With what intensity would Lady Russell have felt the pointedness of the application!– But. Still. She would have demanded a good old gander at those letters herself.

And *they would have been gone!*

Clever Mr Elliot.

And then: what must, inevitably, have happened?

Clearly, to start with, that Saturday evening party would have gone quite differently.

It would have been the usual Elliot flop, because Miss Anne wouldn't have been in such an extraordinarily magnanimous mood. She wouldn't have been engaged yet, remember?— so true contentment could not yet be hers, and so it couldn't be anyone else's either; not if Miss Anne could help it...

.... and as the evening's good-byes spilled out, rather early, as usual, into the hall, the drawing-room grows silent, and sad, and empty... save for Anne, and an abandoned pair of naval gloves.

And Mr Elliot.

Who, popping his head back in to spy Anne lingering alone and misunderstood among the hothouse plants, would have– pausing only to claw his hair such that it tumbled with Romantic disorder across his brow– run lightly the length of that shining floor and flung himself before her on his knees.

He'd thought it through, you see, since the damp squibs of the concert, and her constraint the next day. No: she really was perfect. Her very coldness was proof of it.

I mean, only weeks past, Byron had actually married what's-her-name, who was famously well-read, and earnest, *and* pure! It just goes to show how the tide was turning, if even Byron did it— Only, Byron's new wife was also an heiress, twice as much as Anne, ready money down, and firm prospects of further inheritances. And everyone knew Byron was up to his ivory brow in the red, so come on!— How artless could the Childe claim to be?— in spite of all that poetry.

With Anne in tow, Mr Elliot was pretty sure he could knock the frightful little cockerel off his perch.

Mr Elliot's calculations, as you see, were complex, and thorough; and completely wrong. When he hurled himself gracefully at Anne's feet, all amidst the Saturday-evening-party greenery of that parallel world, he found himself rebuffed.

Yes. Brusquely, and unequivocally: rebuffed.

He clasps his brow!

He springs to his feet!

— He is swept away, pell-mell, by a sudden resurgence of his so-recently-shed character of Byronic impetuosity— a recidivism triggered by finding himself once more kneeling by the chair of a beautiful woman, attempting to overcome her scruples— in those heady days he used to quickly wear a sheen on the knees of each new pair of trousers— *Overcome* (as I say) by a brief burst of his old *persona,* O! how Mr Elliot would have stormed about the room! Imploring explanations, from Anne, from the Heavens, intercession! yes intercession from her father, from Lady Russell (both at this point tumbling, astonished, into the room), from her sist– no maybe not. But, *anything* rather that this divine creature should spurn him!

Dear God–

–he felt–

—He felt he should run mad!

Tremendously romantic.

And *then,* it would suddenly all have come out: Anne's dark tale, about Mrs Smith and those poisonous, incriminating and– it would now appear– invisible letters.

!!

But— Sir Walter (who has been trying to get a word in edge-wise for quite some time)– Sir Walter would have *spurned* to listen to all that letter-y folderol! *Spurned* the very idea! On the contrary, on the absolute contrary. He *required* of Anne that she accept Mr Elliot and his NINETY-TWO *THOUSAND* POUNDS, O Dear *GOD, at once.* Here and now. In this very room.

And Anne, after feeling and thinking all that was gentle and refined about it, would have found herself unable to oblige her father on just this one point.

Could the situation be more fraught?

Yes! (!!!)

Because just then, Captain Wentworth would have appeared at the door and– halted upon its threshold, shocked at the scene before him! Captain Wentworth had returned to Camden Place for his gloves.

(Anne was clutching them. To her bosom. Anne had received, in the course of the evening, a hastily-scribbled note along the lines of *I must speak to you or my heart will burst. Meet me after the party behind the Gymnospermae. S.W.A.L.K., F.W.)* Anne gasped, and dropped the gloves, and flew towards him—

— and Captain Wentworth knelt.

Before them all, he offered Anne his hand, and heart, and fortune.

!!!!

— But! —

Sir Walter would have found Captain Wentworth's risible little twenty-five thousand utterly *de trop* just at this point thank you very much!– and in the next moment, perceiving, from Anne's impassioned countenance as she gazed upon her lover, that *here–* in *this man–* lay the obstacle to the almost *unbearably* desirable connection of Sir Walter's family with more of Sir Walter's family, together with all that this would entail– .... Sir Walter would have turned savagely upon Captain Wentworth, and expressed himself with a vigour that no man of spirit could endure.

And a terrible silence would have fallen.

And Captain Wentworth would have picked up his gloves, and broken that silence with the classic words:

"My feelings for your daughter, Sir, and my respect for your age, forbid me from demanding, from you, the satisfaction which I would not hesitate to extract from any other man."

! ! !

And after piercing Sir Walter with a killingly-contemptuous glance, Captain Wentworth would have swivelled about and glared, with blood-shot eyes, full at Mr Elliot.

Who glared back. Both of them, quite white about the lips. Two young rivals. Anne's impassioned suitors. All silhouetted against the crimson drawing-room curtains.

.... Which Miss Elliot had chosen. Chosen with – ah!... what hopes!...

And at this point Miss Elliot, cowering by those curtains, and for the first time in nearly fourteen years overlooked by everyone in the whole room, and overlooked *in favour of her lovely sister Anne*, must tear the silence apart with an hysterical shriek. And run, shrieking still, from the room.

*   *   *

Do you need a break? Are those asterisks enough of a break? Because we still have heaps to go.

*   *   *

In haste and confusion the whole Elliot family would immediately have decamped to London. Anne too would be carried off with them, forbidden by her own sense of personal respect to her father (as regards which she was scrupulous: she tells us so herself) from defying his direct order that she enter the carriage– .

.. and after all, what else could she do?

Because, where, o *where* was Captain Wentworth??? (Pacing a channel in the carpet at the White Hart. He had no idea they were all leaving.)

And, given what her father had said to him— it is too awful to retail word-for-word in these pages; too awful for any gentleman to forgive, surely?— well! Could she even hope to see Frederick, ever, ever again?

!   !   !

Sorting out the resulting mess would have required a further one hundred closely-written pages.

Just to start with, Sir Walter's creditors, seeing their golden goose waddling post-haste towards the Shambles of London, conclude that all is up with him and close in with the rapacity of harpies, determined each to snatch a mouth-ful of flesh before the writhing bones were stripped pink-bare.[†] Her family's resulting disgrace and poverty would have added real piquancy to the complic-ated soup of conflicting desires, obligations, and principles that were to beset *Persuasion's* heroine, and its hero– ... and... I could go on for some time. Not unexpectedly, though, it still ends up that Captain Frederick Wentworth, R.N., once more and finally throws aside all that has kept him proud and aloof for eight years— all his *amour-propre*, all his achievements— all, except his feelings for Anne; his dearest Anne.

Upon which Anne, in her turn, would have discovered within herself a moral principle by which she was obliged to elope with him to Gretna Green.

*

There! You've always wondered about that missing third volume of *Persua-sion*, haven't you? Nice to know at last– isn't it?– how it would have gone.

Nice, too, to see Austen branching out like that.

Quite a departure, in many respects, from her usual style.

*

The remaining tale of Mrs Clay, on the other hand, could have been told in one short paragraph. Halted on their flight to London by the need to change horses, and feeling the need of a leg-stretch themselves, Nellie and Sir Walter would have wandered off into a charming old chapel nearby; where, light-headed from lack of sleep, they would have confessed their affections, altered (with pen and ink borrowed from the vicar) the lady's name on a special mar-riage license that Sir Walter happened to have about him, and married.

The sudden acquisition of an impoverished Frog as a step-mother would have added its own spice to all the new obstacles of pride and propriety then

---

† Austen would have been thinking of her brother here; of Henry, so recently and humiliatingly plucked.

besetting Anne and Captain Wentworth; while as for Elizabeth— when her father and her companion strolled back again, arm in arm and smiling foolishly— her feelings on the occasion would have been so intense that she would have had to make the rest of the journey to London strapped to the imperial. Mrs Clay's own story, however, would have reached—

Not its end: no. But certainly, the point at which a biographer could release the heroine to her own devices, happy in the assurance that a short final chapter summarising the prosperity of the marriage, the fates of Anne and Elizabeth, and the ultimate discomfiture of Mr Elliot, would discharge the whole of the writer's remaining obligation to her characters.

Would that my task were so easy, or so agreeable.

*   *   *

As everybody knows, in reality— that is, in *Persuasion*— Anne did *not* speak to Lady Russell. Yes, she kept on meaning to: but she never did.

In consequence, at noon that Saturday, Anne wasn't arguing with Lady Russell in Rivers Street. Instead, she was off down town, getting engaged to Captain Wentworth.

The ensuing evening party, which Nellie spent in such dangerous abstraction, was passed by Miss Anne in a haze of bliss, liberal-mindedness, and candour, such as she had not experienced for eight long years. It was hardly the frame of mind in which you broach your cousin's crimes with your oldest advisor, so she didn't. And at the end of the night, after her lover had stolen a goodbye kiss in the hall, Miss Anne, pink as a girl of nineteen, had shot straight up to her room, there to conceal, and to indulge, her agitation and her joy.

*

It was Monday, therefore, before Anne finally did tell Lady Russell about the Mr Elliot stuff— that, and that she was engaged.

And once it had been made quite clear to Lady Russell, irrevocably clear, that her dear Anne was quite definitely going to marry that cocky, pretentious, egotistical vainglorious *arriviste* of a Wentworth after all, with his bulging calves and– Adam's apple— to be candid, for some time it really didn't seem to matter very much, to Lady Russell, what shenanigans Mr Elliot might have been up to. Yes it all sounded most distasteful, from what Anne had said; it would eventually, be beholden upon Lady Russell to determine exactly how matters stood; but before all that, and for a few days at least, she simply wanted to lie in a darkened room with a cool compress to her head.

"Are you quite sure, my dear, that you explicitly said 'yes' to Captain Wentworth?

"Quite sure, Lady Russell."

"Ah. Because even if you said— as you quite easily might— that you were, perhaps, *overwhelmed* by his offer; or that you... you 'did not know what to say'... that it was *most unexpected*—...Well, then! No gentleman could be surprised if, on thinking it over, you later came to realise... *Did* you mention to him that you were overwhelmed? By his kind offer?"

"No, Lady Russell."

"Quite sure? In the agitation of such a moment, a lady may say things which— er— which she can only reconstruct, later, after considerable reflection. I'm almost certain, Anne, that your first reaction would have been to say, that his proposals had taken you *by surprise*; taken you, quite *unawares*. That you were in shock."

"But I wasn't, Lady Russell. I have been waiting eight desolate years for him to renew his proposals. And then, first he wrote me that lovely letter, and *then,* he spoke to me; I could not honestly describe myself as anything but palpitatingly ready."

Her friend winced.

"Dazed, perhaps", Anne added, scrupulous, "and I feel somewhat dazed still: but only with the extremity of joy."

A low moan escaped Lady Russell's soul. It mounted to her lips, there to be blocked by her incisors: gripped. Crushed.

"If that is the case, my dear, then I can only wish you every happiness."

Anne pressed her old friend's hand with warmth, reached for the bell, and, leaving a pale Lady Russell in the hands of her maid, walked– skipped— danced!— back down to the White Hart, and Captain Wentworth: Wentworth the handsome; Wentworth the dashing; Wentworth the successful, and solvent, and sober.

Austen's heroine is home and hosed.

Instead, it is Mrs Clay who is in the poo, and there silently swiftly sinking. And it will take all that a third Volume of any kind can do, to rescue her from its clammy, mephitic clasp.

VOLUME III

undress of Bum-be-seen ___ The Year (1840) a Lady's full dress of Bombazeen ___ The Year (170

THE FASHIONS OF THE DAY or Time Past and Time Present.

Chapter 1

It is recorded, in *Persuasion,* that Mr Elliot 'soon' left Bath; and that Mrs Clay left 'soon afterwards'. The tale is told largely through the perceptions of Anne, and since Anne at this juncture was confessedly dazed and inattentive, the source of this sequencing error probably lies in her scattered recollection of events at home.

One would hate to think, alternatively, that Miss Austen herself had lost track of the two.

Still, she had a lot on her plate at that point: a wedding to arrange, the family's reactions to handle, a plausible reconciliation between Captain Wentworth and Lady Russell to pull off, Mrs Smith to rescue, Anne's own sensations to delineate, a quick happily-ever-after to imply; and all this in less than half a dozen duodecimo pages. Remember, too, that throughout *Persuasion* (which is to say, in Anne's presence), Mrs Clay displayed considerable skill at fading into the background— while Mr Elliot, at all times and places, is a very slippery character indeed.

Whatever the origin of the error may be, however, the facts of the matter are these:–

*   *   *

Tuesday morning was the time chosen, by Anne, for the revelation to her family of Saturday's engagement to Captain Wentworth. Sunday must be set aside for prayer and reflection, Monday, as we know, for a confession of her situation to her first of friends, Lady Russell, and a discussion of practicalities with her beloved. So Tuesday. Tuesday morning, when the egregious Mrs Clay would be out changing books at the library; that seemed as good a time as any to break it to her father and sister. The evening that followed, Anne was to be out herself, with the Musgroves at the theatre. If there were anything to blow over, it could blow over then.

*

In the end, though, there wasn't that much to endure. After the restrained histrionics of Lady Russell, the appearance of indifference in Anne's family was a relief.

Sir Walter's main sensation was mild astonishment. It took him aback, for some ten minutes, to hear that Anne had found anyone to marry: and then, that anyone had found it worth their while marrying Anne. A naval captain. A brother of Sir Walter's tenant, Admiral Croft; the Croft who rents Kellynch.

Not an ill-looking man.

Complexion somewhat damaged, naturally... but, really, not an ill-looking man at all, at this stage. He held his left arm a little oddly. A splinter wound, Anne said. What he would be like at fifty-four, of course, was anyone's guess.

Elizabeth's emotions were more complex. Surprise was quickly subsumed in resentment: it seemed an underhand sort of way of doing things, to get engaged without anyone knowing; to arrange the whole thing, quite by herself. And then, to break it like this, in the middle of a dull morning at home — so that one would have to know that Anne had eaten breakfast with them, and then, sat a good half-hour with them in the drawing-room, sewing away at the air-balloon, thinking about being engaged, but not telling them. Not until it suited Anne to mention it.

Though he was only a Captain, after all.

Though, Anne had mentioned prize-money. More than once.

But really, how much could he have got? They simply didn't get much of a cut unless they were Admirals or something. As far as Elizabeth could ascertain, it didn't seem that they would have even thirteen hundred a year. Which was just... I mean where would they even live?

Who would be their friends?

                                        *

When Nellie returned from the library, it was to a strangely quiet house. She felt the difference as she walked upstairs; a sort of breathing silence. Now she sits on the edge of her chair— she is still in her pelisse, has still her reticule in her lap— and studies her friend. Elizabeth is huddled over the fire.

Elizabeth never huddles: she knows what is owed to Miss Elliot, and she delivers. So she must be feeling pretty bad.

"Wentworth— that was one of the naval gentlemen whom you included in our evening party last Saturday, was it not?"

Elizabeth nodded.

"The rather gangly one with the strongly marked features and the crippled leg, in the threadbare coat?"

"No, the shorter one."

"Ah— with that injury to the arm."

Elizabeth nodded again.

This was tricky indeed. The man in question had been arresting, and this no less in handsome regularity of features than by virtue of the air he possessed. It was the air typical of naval success, a manner at once decided and open, accommodating yet commanding. Well-off, too: excellent clothes, tailored with London skill. Over a figure that distracted even– while she had been mentioning to Mrs Clay that at a party of this nature, ices were an unnecessary– Lady Russell— while Lady D. had been in a continual course of smiles, chatting with Captain Wentworth at every opportunity; never had the Dowager Viscountess enjoyed an evening at Camden Place more!

So yes. Tricky.

"Rather her than me!"

Thus began Mrs Clay; artless, tactless, comfortable Mrs Clay.

She continued— casual, careful, exploratory Mrs Clay— "I thought that both the naval gentlemen seemed rather out of it, here in Camden Place...?– though they certainly supplied a very agreeable *variation* to the company..."

... a microscopic nod...

"... so, *yes*, they were very *well-selected*, as *company*, from *that* point of view of course. But... Well! I suppose, once married, Miss Anne will mix with other people of the navy, where her husband will be moving at his own level— *We* will see very little of them."

Miss Elliot nodded again; seemed to take some comfort from the idea.

Mrs Clay sighed, and became confidential.

"You know, I have seen many a naval marriage in my time, Miss Elliot– and, with the war behind us now, Captain Wentworth will be lucky to spend any time afloat. It is not just the loss of income that will press them (though of course naval officers, unless they have a private fortune, must perforce be very attentive to *that*)— but it's also the case that, without the action that they are used to, without *something to do,* I am sorry to say that men of the navy are not always so good-tempered as the popular story gives them credit. And they are nearly all–"

Now, how to put this? 'Fools with money' might strike a bit close to home.

"...well... *gullible*, shall I say; I have seen so many of them, once ashore, pour out their money into the pockets of charlatans, and gain nothing for it!"

Miss Elliot perked up a little more.

"It is fortunate, then, that they start off with *some* money between them."

Mrs Clay smiled: "Miss Anne is a careful enough manager, I dare say! — and she has the character to bear with any little ill-humour, that might emerge, once the wedding is fairly over."

"Oh, it is a good enough match in its way. Anne has done nothing that can embarrass us, at least."

"Oh yes, that. Certainly."

Nellie twitched to ask when the ceremony was to be; but it was wiser to conceal the little fizz of feminine inquisitiveness she felt even now at this, the life-defining event: a wedding. Miss Elliot's needs must take priority, however. And right now those needs were for as much conversation as possible, on topics as remote as may be from marriage, and sisters, and the passage of time.

Only later, in her room and dressing for dinner, could Nellie indulge and examine her own feelings.

In which she was ruefully amused to detect— a twinge of envy.

Ten days ago, such a self-discovery would have been food for days of self-excoriation. Now Nellie— lifting the day dress off over her head and shaking her hair free— felt only a detached regret at noting her reaction; her only-too-commonplace reaction. It's better not to indulge envy; that's all, really, she thought. Not to feed and water the little... gremlin, should she call it?...

But yes: just now; a little envy, alas alas. For one thing, that Anne Elliot, for whom Nellie had so long enjoyed a dislike (!— oh dear...), should be marrying at all. For another, that she should be marrying such a very well-set-up man. Quite the dashing hero, Anne's Captain had been, as he moved with graceful strength about the drawing-rooms of Camden Place, laughing that rich baritone laugh.

But Nellie had married her own real-life story-book hero, and look how that had turned out. No; life would bring Mrs Wentworth disappointments enough.

So, personal envy apart: on the whole, it was good news, wasn't it?

For a bit, Elizabeth would have her nose put out of joint by Anne's success. Would be sick at times with fear, in other words. For a bit, Miss Elliot must lie awake at night contemplating her own profound and primary failure, which her sister's coup here would throw into horrid relief.

But goodness, at least it was only to a Captain Wentworth! It had so nearly been Mr Elliot. In such case, Elizabeth would have been truly to be pitied.

There were positives, too, for self, sweet self. Nellie had always suspected Anne of being especially useful to Mr Elliot, as regards that awful Mrs Clay. More than once, she had come into a room to catch them close together on the sopha, their faces aglow with the gossip's zeal— and from the way their eyes then swivelled towards her, and their murmuring stopped dead, it was evident that they had not been discussing the lives of the Popes.

Heavens!– all of Camden Place would profit from Anne's departure! No longer need any of them brace themselves against that sharp little sniff from the far corner of the drawing-room at some careless, carefree remark; no longer encounter the quirking of that supercilious brow, each time one of them moved, or dressed, or exclaimed a little too loudly for Miss Anne's refined taste. Yes... Yes, from that point of view, it really was marvellous news!

Quite marvellous!–

– and as the advantages mounted in Nellie's mind, and her mood accordingly mellowed, she even found, in her heart, a little charitable pleasure for- Anne herself.

An old maid, after all. Ever since her first hopeful 'coming out', she has been yielding her place again, and again, to yet another triumphant bride: sitting each year yet lower at the dinner-table; standing yet further back, in the progression in or out of a room. Those who pass— young or old, high or low — may amuse themselves openly at the sight of intelligent, refined Miss Anne, losing her place yet again in the queue. It is everyday chatter, to remark the fading prettinesses of her person, to mock her sterile interests, and to triumph, at the sight of a strong mind locked into an eternal social cadetship.

It would be hard, wouldn't it, to keep your mind a pleasant place to be. You'd have to really struggle, in fact, to keep your mind a pleasant place.

For example, it would be hard not to long, as you aged, for Death. Her father's death; her dear friend Lady Russell. Only after one of those deaths could Anne ever hope to inherit a little independence.

She would still be a spinster of course; still "the proper sport of boys and girls", the object of public smirks, and private ridicule. But, Heavens! — how relatively delightful her position would feel to her!

Thus thought Mrs Clay.

*

And I suppose she has a point.

Well of course she has a point I know she has a *point*, I admit I–... anyone would have to share that point of view if they really thought about things.

Actually, in spite of my civility in assigning them to Nellie, most of the last paragraphs have been mine. Mrs Clay, smug safe widow, only thought part of the way through the earlier ones.

(Though– it's hard to tell... She is changing. This whole Elliot thing; she's come out the other side, feeling pretty different. It seems that, ripping that Evangelical poultice off her mind along with Mr Elliot, more has come away with it than enslavement to him and those ideas. So yes, she's...)

I guess, when you frame it like that– when you put it in the context of just how awful it really was, back then, to be a spinster; just how shameful; just how socially helpless you truly were, almost inconceivable to us now, you have to imagine yourself in the nastiest American high school in film, being mocked by the Queen Bee and all her hive, only everybody outside high school also thinks QB is quite in the right; it truly was that way— What really annoys me, about Anne, is not her suppressed bitterness at the chiselled beaks stabbing gleefully at her; at this floundering flock-mate, a failure in spite of all her gifts. No, what upsets no no, annoys me, *annoys* me, is the way that she willingly takes the knife to herself! She's forever dutifully topiarising away at her own spirit, snip snip snip, o my emotions, are they subdued, am I yet fully sub-missive to circumstances, are my thoughts appropriately shaped.

And, she wants it both ways. She's right because she struggles heroically not to despise everyone, *and* she's right because, really, gosh— aren't they despicable!

But anyway.

To get back to our story. To get back to our own heroine's thoughts tonight...

....as she slips tonight's dress over her head, and stands while the maid deals with buttons, and then, looks for the sash:– Nellie had yet the energy for a little amusement, too.

After all– she thought– what a turn-up for the books! Anne Elliot, of all people, to turn out to have a friend in the corner!

Well well.

What a sly old thing she was.

Chapter 2

Dinner that day was a silent meal. Anne was absent (those theatre tickets, with the cousins), and it would have been most natural to talk over her engagement, but even Sir Walter intuited that the topic might not be a welcome one to his favourite daughter.

... Nevertheless one had to say *something*, surely?

Eventually, then, he greeted the cheese with the words, "So he got her at last, it seems."

Elizabeth very nearly screwed up her mouth and snorted. She caught it in time, and flicked up a light eyebrow instead. "Or she got *him* at last."

Mrs Clay looked her query, and Elizabeth explained: "Anne had wanted to marry Captain Wentworth years ago. Before he made his– any money."

Ah, so it was *he*– the very man! The hero of Anne Elliot's notorious romance!

"Oh. What a nice story it makes, then; the two reunited at last."

It seemed an innocuous observation, but one could see that Miss Elliot was not pleased. "And with enough to live on this time!" added Mrs Clay. "I understand there were difficulties, priorly, when it came to fortune...?"

"Oh yes. Desperate, the man was!" Sir Walter, too, suppresses a snort. "Cast ashore without a ship– years ago, this is — and just barely made commander. Half pay of course. No prospect of a commission. No connections at all beyond his brother-in-law, Croft; the Croft who rents Kellynch; and *he*– Croft, you know– a mere post-captain at the time. He declares all this to me, without disguise; yet he proposes to marry Anne. Anne Elliot!"

Daughter, he could have added, of Sir Walter Elliot, Bart., of Kellynch Hall.

"Favoured me with the usual naval display— actions, captures, prize money. For all that, he had not a penny to show for it when he tried for Anne. *Not – a – penny"*, repeated Sir Walter indignantly. "He'd blown the lot! You should have heard him, when we came to talk marriage articles."

Nellie nodded thoughtfully.

Sir Walter hadn't finished, though. "So: looked about, spotted Anne; thought instead to make his fortune with a little land piracy instead."

"You discouraged the match, then?"

"I certainly did. Though Anne..." Sir Walter hesitated. "Oh — I don't mind saying it to *you,* you've seen it all for yourself anyway; Anne never listens to me, you know. To us. Well!– Not much point in coming the heavy father over it then. 'Forbidding the banns' and all that. Just make myself look silly when she went ahead on her majority. So I bowed out— thought it an hopeless business. End up some drudge of a wife, married to a drunken knocked-about half-p–"

Sir Walter reached abruptly for his wine, swilled a rapid mouthful, choked — choked for some time. At a gesture from his master, the butler stepped respectfully forward and thumped him on the back.

"Thank you– Cubbins– That will..."

(Cubbins snuck in a last hearty thump.)

"– that will *do.*"

The butler bowed, and withdrew.

"So yes—" Sir Walter drew in breath, and with his napkin mopped— *dabbed-* his mouth, dabbed his streaming eyes... "Yes. Lady Russell certainly did us all a favour, there. She pulled Anne out of the soup. And now, you see, it's all turned out perfectly well in the end."

Elizabeth's countenance disagreed. Yet all she said was—

"*He's* made his fortune; and *she's* certainly had a more pleasant eight years while he was about it. All this time. Instead of scraping soup bones for him in Portsmouth she's been living comfortably at Kellynch with us."

And that was quite enough, Elizabeth felt, on the topic of Anne's engagement.

∗

It had to be broached again, though, when Mr Elliot dropped in after dinner. You couldn't afford not to be the first to tell your cousin about something like that. It would look odd.

"*Well*, Mr Elliot! We have had some news since we saw you last" said Elizabeth, a little breathily; this is once the greetings had been got through, the enquiries as to health, and the sitting down around the fire, all accomplished.

"Good news, I hope?" enquired Mr Elliot smoothly.

"Oh, the best sort of news! A wedding, you know."

"An *engagement*", inserted Mrs Clay, deprecatingly.

"An engagement", agreed Miss Elliot.

"—but given their characters", continued Mrs Clay, "I shouldn't wonder if the wedding was not to take place rather soon. Just a quiet one, you know. It's not exactly a fresh romance, and Miss Anne— but excuse me Miss Elliot..."

"Oh no you are quite in the right, Penelope."

"I *mean* to say just Miss Anne is... her bearing– and *manner* I should say— rather staider in *manner,* than her years might seem to justify the expectation of. Some people are like that; and I'm sure it's very admirable in them."

"Miss Anne?" Mr Elliot's voice was still smooth, but his air was all attention.

"Yes my sister Anne. An old flame from her school days, a Captain Wentworth. You met him here at our evening party last Saturday, I believe." Mr Elliot bowed acknowledgement. "It came to nothing at the time, but now she tells us that she has patched it up, so it is on again, and they are to marry. It has come as quite a surprise. But Anne always was rather cagey about her personal affairs."

"But what delightful news. Miss Anne and Captain Wentworth. Yes a most gentleman-like looking man. But do please tell me all about it."

"Well there is not a great deal to tell, is there, Penelope?"

"Oh it is all news to *me*, as you can imagine, Mr Elliot. If her own dear sister and father were surprised, you can conceive *my* astonishment; I had no idea at all! He seems a pleasant enough man, as you say– and I am sure we should all be very happy for her. Miss Anne, you know, does not seem to enjoy the gaieties of Bath; the contrast to the country life, which Miss Anne so much enjoys, I remember you mentioning it yourself Mr Elliot; and a quiet retirement, in some naval port, will probably suit her down to the ground. A very happy solution, for the two of them."

"Yes. Absolutely. And— So it is all settled?"

'Quite settled, it seems, Mr Elliot. We understand that Captain Wentworth has a little money put away, so they should be comfortable enough– Miss Anne's tastes being so very moderate. It is all quite fortunate!"

"Then— they have nothing to wait for, it would appear."

"Nothing at all."

Mr Elliot tapped his teeth with the head of his cane. "Have they set a date?"

"I'm afraid I really couldn't say, Mr Elliot."

"Mm." And he made no further comment, but continued to tap his teeth and stare into space. He betrayed the air of a man who was rapidly reviewing a series of fairly complex plans.

Of a man who had forgotten where he was, and whom he was with.

Elizabeth stood.

"But Mr Elliot does not need to hear of our nonsense and small news. He is weighed by business concerns, we can see. Do not let us keep you, Mr Elliot. Please."

He looked up at her, a little blankly. He was still seated.

"Please. Do not stand on ceremony with us." And Elizabeth actually rang the bell. "Mr Elliot is leaving", she announced to the footboy. "See him out."

Nellie had risen when Miss Elliot rose. There was nothing for it: Mr Elliot had to spring to his feet– with startled eyes — He bowed his adieus in silence. Pressed Miss Elliot's hand (a little too expertly). "Perhaps I can hope to see you at the Upper Rooms tomorrow, Miss Elliot?"

"Perhaps."

"Mrs Clay."

"Mr Elliot."

The front door boomed.

Delighted, and incredulous, Nellie turned to Elizabeth — but to her elated "*Well—!*" Miss Elliot gave back an impassive, full-face, unreadable stare.

Chapter 3

Miss Elliot was *not* at the Upper Rooms the next day, though Mr Elliot had made sure to be, and when they did chance next to meet, he got but a cold reception from Miss Elliot. Look: she is passing him in Belmont; she has walked out alone, without Mrs Clay. (In the last few days, Nellie has more than once run downstairs to find the lower rooms empty of all but the embarrassed footboy: "Miss Elliot has walked out alone.") Now Mr Elliot is bowing to Miss Elliot with all the spirit he commands; yet in return, Elizabeth barely inclines her head.

Unabashed, he turns to walk with her—

... and he soon has her laughing again. He has a fresh-acquired stock of information about Captain Wentworth, and he is retailing it to her. I don't know exactly what he is saying, and if I did, I could not be sure it is true, but look; it is cheering up Elizabeth enormously.

How quickly he turns her!

On the other hand, she has loved him for at least twelve years. After such a huge investment she may feel, with some panic, that she cannot afford to find herself mistaken in him.

Mr Elliot also entertains Miss Elliot, on other fortuitously private encounters in Milsom Street, Union Street, the library, with gossip about Mrs Clay: about Penelope. Nellie, when she detects the signs of it (in the small smiles, and glances, that slide between them, after any of her more typical utterances) is surprised as well as hurt.

And she thirty years old! How resistant we are to the logic, and to all the evidence, that those who delight to tattle with us about others, will tattle delightedly with others about us. The Spanish even have a saying for it. Yet still, there is surprise, when we find that our own dear gossips have convened a venomous symposium about us.

So yes: Nellie is hurt.

*

There were other sorrows, too.

Miss Carteret, following petitions to and negotiations with her mother, as largely mediated by Mrs Clay, is now spending carefully-supervised time with young Mr Brownlow– he of the short rent-roll and the long, long face. Number Three was a well-brought-up boy; Nellie had thought him so from the first.

Consequently it transpired that he could not approve of Mrs Clay, and Miss Carteret's intimacy with the woman made him uneasy. (This after all that she had argued on his behalf! Nellie began to think that she would never again trust a man in a loose cravat and simple, unpretentious black trousers.) Catherine was too affectionate, and open-hearted, to withdraw from her older friend upon the first creased brow of a new acquaintance — but given time, she would. Heavens, she was only fifteen; and under the influence of Mr Brownlow's youthful solemnity, his earnest piety, it seemed to Mrs Clay that sometimes Lady D.— Lady Dalrymple— also began, these days, to look at Mrs Clay a little uncertainly.

*

On the plus side, Nellie reminds herself, Miss Anne is scarcely ever at home now.

The mood in Camden Place, however, benefits but little from the change. Elizabeth's inexplicable revulsion of feeling towards her companion continues — and when Mrs Clay finally asks her if she has– perhaps– in any way, offended...?– the response is only a bright, hard assurance:-

"Why no. Of course not, Penelope. In what way could you conceivably have discommoded me?"

Yet Elizabeth's manner continues to spike cold disregard with gushes of brittle, patronising civility— until Nellie more than half expects her to announce a pressing need for the second-best spare bedroom.

*

As for Mr Elliot: he ignores Mrs Clay, in private and in public, with expansive and ostentatious relish.

His effrontery is astonishing, and completely successful. With Anne no longer an object, Lady Russell rarely even an observer, Mr Elliot has switched off the flow of higher sentiment as easily as one switches off a tap.

In its stead, these days, he deploys that line which toys with scandal by

deprecating it, at length, and in detail. Sincerity is now performed only in special, quiet moments with Lady Russell; or with Elizabeth, on the sopha. At
such times Nellie finds him at his most repulsive; she can hardly bear the sight
of his smiles and mildness, or the sound of his artificial good sentiments.

*

But this is nothing, my dear girl. Far worse lies ahead.

*

They are visiting Mrs Craven, that proud mother of seven. It is the first
spring-like day of the year, and though the fires are lit the windows are ajar,
because the room is full– full with all of their usual set, and more. Every chair
holds a muslin-clad body, every second sopha-end has a man perched on it.
By one fireplace, Colonel Wallis and Sir Walter have poised their near-military
figures. By another, Miss Elliot is talking to old Mr Craven: he is marvellously
youthful for his age, the dear old millionaire; he is dabbling his watery eyes in
her cleavage. Mrs Craven, like a good wife, sees none of it — she and Lady
Dalrymple are admiring the current baby, and Miss Carteret is on her knees
playing with the toddler. A silent Mrs Wallis looks on. Meanwhile, half of
fashionable Bath is standing, or sitting or walking about the rest of the space,
which is a-roar with voices in spite of being large enough to swallow both the
drawing-rooms of Camden Place, and inhale the rest of the upper floors with
it.

Mr Elliot has charmed all these adults long ago. Today, he has withdrawn
to a quiet window seat, there to charm the rising generation. With the four
little Craven girls he forms a pretty group, their fair heads and his dark one
clustered around a wax doll that is stretched on a cushion: they are discussing
its health.

— But where is Mrs Clay?

Nellie has slipped away to an open casement. Her head feels light, and odd,
and... she is wedged limply, here, in the corner of the next window seat along–
slumped between the sash and the wall, the curtain concealing her weakness
from remark. She inhales gratefully the cool street air, spiralling in almost
impalpable gusts against her face... a last swoop of nausea... and the spinning
subsides. Oh, thank God...

Nellie breathed smoothly and deeply and her head suddenly cleared.

The Craven children have fallen very silent, she notes. Hidden by the
swags of the curtain between them, they are almost within touching distance.
But there is only Mr Elliot's voice, hushed and serious:

"And this, you must never do. Do you see? Like this."

Silence, while something was demonstrated.

"There. Just three minutes. Less, with a little one like this. What do you
think would happen— mmm? If I did this... Mmmm.

"You must press down gently and firmly."

... And again, the silence.

Nellie leant out a fraction, forward... sideways...

A loop of curtain framed five still faces. No, six. The eldest boy, thirteen and teetering between the mamma's angel and the lout, hovers on the edge the group. He is watching too, with an air of suppressed intrigue.

And now Nellie sees a seventh face. Inside the ring of living ones, the wax doll stares up, with fixed eyes.

And again there are six.

"Mmmm? What do you think would happen?"

The littlest girl suddenly pressed close to Mr Elliot. Winding her arms with pleading dependance around his leg, she gazed up at him imploringly— but Mr Elliot's countenance remains still, rapt; bent over the little doll, and the cushion covering its face.

Nellie turned just in time to vomit out of the window.

They had come in the carriage. It was growing musty with relative disuse, but overpowering its fug of fungus and damp leather, all the close, jolting journey back to Camden Place, no-one could ignore the smell that lingered on Nellie's breath, despite the best ministrations of the Craven's housekeeper.

Sir Walter, who of all things found the smell of vomitus the most noxious, faced rigidly towards the windows— which he adjusted, as they travelled, further and further ajar, and breathed very shallowly— until he could scrabble out of the fumey confines and stride jerkily up the steps into his house.

*

A recent letter from her father forms her only comfort. He is in Paris still, and all is going well– quite well. Every bit as well as could be expected. They would have to see; but his return might, possibly, be brought forward.

Let's hope so. In that case, if and when Elizabeth threw her out, Nellie would at least have somewhere to go.

Chapter 4

Life wasn't meant to be easy, of course. Nellie knows that, better than most in Camden Place. It may be that, in scarcely a fortnight, she has managed to fall foul of most of Bath; but what she needs to remember, in the rough patches, is that here, still, is Sir Walter. Her father has set her this task, for the sake of them all: it is her duty.

And she has come to see, furthermore, that it is achievable.

Alright, so his manner just now seems perhaps a little strained. (Often, when she draws near, she thinks she detects him surreptitiously snuff the air.) And? What of it? How often, in the tightrope-walk of her dependent's life, has she steadied things back up from far wilder wobbles than this? A few smiles, a few compliments to the Baronetcy, a peppermint drop or two, and things would be as before.

Very well, so she needs must face the inevitability of Mr Elliot. She must accept the fact that he'll marry Elizabeth. She must recognise that he will then take over at Kellynch Hall.

What use, then, to cry over spilt milk? She and Sir Walter can take themselves off to some discreet corner of Bath. Being Lady Elliot in a nice little terrace house, sharing the retirement of a baronet of good estate; it was not exactly hardship. Papa would live near them. (Unless he had other plans.) The children would definitely live with them; and for Josie, for Ariosto, what prospects must then open! Yes: even from a Bath terrace, a Lady Elliot could achieve miracles, relative miracles, for the children, for her father— for them all.

And to Mr Elliot, she would always be that most precious of things, the stopper on Sir Walter's fertility. If a commoner, a naval widow for Heaven's sake, with exactly £20 a year to call her own, could nevertheless near-seduce the man– in a few short months, and right under Elizabeth's nose– Well! Could Mr Elliot, of Kellynch Hall, ever risk easing his father-in-law out from under his feet?

Answer: no. Not unless married to a Mrs Clay.

Accustomed as she is, though, to running multiple comparative calculations, Nellie has begun to notice that, while he might need *her,* Mr Elliot did not need her father.

Or the children.

Or even, really, Sir Walter... And by this stage, in the flames of every fire, Nellie starts to see a dancing Indian god. Each time it flares up again it has grown more heads, more arms; but one hand, always, waves high a lock of infant hair. Another, low, slips long fingers through a wound in Elizabeth's ribs. Beneath one light foot, Nellie glimpses her own face. And now, another hoof presses upon the false battlements of Kellynch– and a heel sinks through its roof, beams cracking... and it is her father's parlour beneath; prehensile toes curling and sifting through its wreckage, while a peacock tail of arms has sprung from his back and then a hand tweaks the scholar's cap from Ariosto's head, another caresses Josephine's shoulder...and she turns at the touch, her face melts with a worshipping smile, something slides under the hem of Nellie's own skirt, an elephant's trunk, thick and wrinkled and grey... and looking down she sees also now Sir Walter, cowering beneath the drawing-room table, sheltering from falling chunks of ceiling. He has his arms wrapped around the Baronetage, and he is crying. The comic touch.

And there, sailing up, and down, and up, is a doll on a cake plate, sealed under a bell jar, while a thousandth elegant white hand now lifts the glass, now settles it, over the waxen figurine. Just three minutes. Less, with a little one like this.

She had thought she was doing so well. But no. This is what expertise really looks like.

*

And then suddenly the fire is just a fire and it all seems incredible– come on! People are always dying. Mothers die, children die, babies die all the time for God's sake, it's 1815, what do you expect?

*

Mrs Clay was interrupted in the absorbing business of batting the topic back and forth fruitlessly while staring blindly into the drawing-room fire, by the interposition between herself and the uncertain flames of a salver... A salver that phosphoresced with the soft, powdery light of well-polished silver. Beautiful, really.

Grubbily, in its centre, lay a square of cheapest notepaper.

Supporting the salver was the butler, looking discomfited. Like most of the staff he had, after an exhilarating period of convivial jeering, developed a grudging respect for Mrs Clay. Last quarter, the respect had become less grudging: they had all got paid. Even, there were indications of some back-pay, this Lady Day, and they all knew who they owed it to. But Cubbins could never feel comfortable about presenting her with these greyed letters, which still came, every now and then, from Plymouth.

This time it looked particularly bad. The edges of the paper, coarse and frangible, were already disintegrating under a drenching in watery ink: it seemed that an attempt had been made to convert it to black-bordered stationary, by the economical resort of drawing the border in by hand. "Thank you Cubbins." Cubbins bowed, and withdrew.

It was from the *Comtesse*.

Nellie sat for some time with the letter in her lap, still staring at the fire — but now her mind was silent, and her heart, sick and cold. (Sicker, and colder.) It could only be the Count.

She had been expecting it, hadn't she. Ever since she had left Plymouth, she had been expecting this letter.

Suddenly it struck her that it might nevertheless announce the death of one of the Barratts. In an instant she had torn it open.

No— it was the Count.

... sur la deuxième de ce mois ...

...la mort d'un chrétien ...

Nellie walked, slowly, upstairs, to her bedroom.

*   *   *

When she came down again, an hour later— there had been no enquiry, in all that time, from Miss Elliot— every cloud has a silver lining, thought Nellie, absently— it was to find Sir Walter, hovering, in the hall below. At her step on the stair above, his face cleared. "Ah!— Mrs Clay! Mrs Clay. I was becoming a little concerned."

Nellie smiled gratefully at him; continued her slow descent.

"All well I hope?" His enquiries had revealed, from Cubbins, that all was not.

Nellie took breath to speak, but this of its own volition carried on instead into a massive sigh, which concluded in the leakage of a tear down the inner corner of her eye.

"Oh my dear Mrs Clay..."

She shook her head, and wiped the tear away, inelegantly, with the inside of her wrist. It was an odd-looking process, a habit from her married days, when crying mostly had to be done while simultaneously engaged with bare hands in dirty household tasks.

"Your father—? Er the children—...?"

"Thank you Sir Walter, my father and the children are all well, so far as I know. No, I have been distressed by some sad news which I have just received from Plymouth." Mrs Clay usually avoided mentioning her ongoing connection there. Now, however... well. "An old friend; a very old friend. From our Paris days, in fact. Whom I met ('Goodness', her mind noted, from some remote distance; 'The objective form of the relative pronoun has become natural to me.') ... met again, with his dear wife, in Plymouth—"

She drew a heavy breath. "Who shared our exile and our– struggles. Our poverty, Sir Walter. He and his dear wife were even worse off than ourselves... but they were always so courteous. So generous with–"

'their time and attention' is the usual second half of this phrase: but all was lost in tears.

"Oh my dear Mrs Clay. Oh how terribly sorry I am."

He dithered in front of her, hands lifted to her shoulder height but wavering in the air, manners quite forgotten. At this point the drawing-room door opened and Elizabeth stuck her head out.

"Mrs Clay! What seems to be the matter?"

And Nellie was drawn into the room, and seated by the fire, and brandy was rung for, and lavender drops supplied in a low, gentle tone. Elizabeth's manners were superb in such a crisis: all was smoothness, softness, measured and conventional, all sharp edges were smoothed, fresh wounds anaesthetised, emotions, obtunded. Under her stabilising influence, Sir Walter's compassion too was soon quietly controlled. Everything is alright. It's alright.

It's alright.

Nellie breathed in deeply, and found that her breath was smooth. "A little better, my dear, Mrs Clay?"

"Thank you, Sir Walter, yes; much better."

"That's good, that's good."

Nellie took another breath. It didn't require such a deep one this time.

"Sir Walter— Miss Elliot— I'm afraid that this sad news means that I must wish, of all things, to be with my friends in their time of trouble. There must be many arrangements to be made, and a removal— the Countess I am sure— almost sure— will wish to leave their old apartments, and she is quite without assistance. At least— the Barratts..." She shrugged. "They have the shop to watch, you see. And although I am sure Alice is with the poor Countess at this moment, it cannot be easy for them, and will straiten them as to many things. I could be of most material assistance to them all."

"Of course, Penelope, nothing could be more natural."

"But—"

"Papa you must see that her friends need her."

"But *we* need her!"

"*Papa!*"

Sir Walter got a grip. "Do excuse me Mrs Clay, that was most — most— ah... of me, of course, you *must* do, just as you think best."

Nellie took another smoothed breath; said something nice about her regret at leaving them, her obligation for their kindness, reluctance to diminish any pleasure of theirs by deserting them at the beginning of all our spring plans: but she had to go.

"Soon?"

"As soon as possible. I hope to join the coach tomorrow morning. I shall pack now."

"But who will accompany you? Elizabeth, my dear, which servant can most easily be spared—"

"Oh Sir Walter. I have travelled, quite alone, since the age of fifteen. And I have never been inconvenienced; nothing worth speaking of."

Sir Walter was about to protest, to insist on a footman, to create all sorts of difficulties from his utter inability to comprehend that even a maid was a luxury, however basic, that Mrs Clay would rather not engage (she would be paying her own way now for everything, and who knows how long her money might have to last?) — but at this point Mr Elliot was ushered into the room. They had not even heard his knock.

   Oh God.

So Nellie had to go through it all again: old acquaintance, sad death, friends in need, Mr Elliot meanwhile the picture of concern; "But who are these old friends? Are we not to know their names? — and you to go among them, dear me, so far from your friends in Bath, Mrs Clay."

Nellie heaved her sluggish lungs for another effort. *'Le Comte et Comtesse du Richelin de Beaufleuri.'* There was a pause at this; as well there might be. "And the Barratts are brother and sister. They own — they used to own a ship's chandlery in Gun Lane. I will probably lodge with them in the first instance." She turned to Sir Walter, and Elizabeth: "But I understand that their business, which for so long flourished, has this last year been doing but poorly. They have had to sell up." Explanation began to seem hopelessly difficult, the relevant and the irrelevant, Plymouth and Dashe and Camden Place, jostled, cheek by jowl. "Peace, you know, strikes at the prosperity of naval towns. They— they have taken a loss on the stock." Stylistic incoherence; it often happens, when one speaks from the heart. "However. A letter addressed to the old shop will always find me out." She wondered whether to repeat it for them: 'Barratt, Gun Lane'... No.

   "And; these — the er — your noble French friends. You— assisted them — in some capacity?"

   "You mean, Mr Elliot, did I work for them? Oh Heavens. None of us afford to pay anyone anything, even to scrub our clothes. But I was the perfect age, I think. To help. Old enough to feel the same sensations of humiliation, young enough to face the need to wash our clothes, and to..." what was the word? Nellie cast about... began to patch in some translation from French, "to devise the means, and then, to... er to roll up my sleeves..." (she gestured)– "and commence. But the poor Countess. And the Count. For them, it was so much harder; they never ceased to feel the degradation. Me, I soon got used to it. The young ones mostly did. One adapts."

   "So you did their laundry?" Mr Elliot's eyes gleamed at her: momentarily, he had forgotten that they had a larger audience.

   "No. The Countess did not permit it. She knelt down beside me at the tub."

   Nellie looked at Elizabeth's face. Inscrutable.

   At Sir Walter's: an open book, albeit with a few wildly contradictory things jostling for page room.

   At Mr Elliot's — and an expression of disgust gripped her mouth. She made no effort to hide it.

   "But yes. I fetched the water every wash day. The Countess tried, but her arms were not strong enough. She was kind to me, however. They were both so kind, after our mother died."

Into the lengthening silence, Mr Elliot at last laid some delicate enquiries as to exactly what the *Comte de*— the Count had fallen victim to...?

How to answer. Mrs Clay didn't know, didn't want to think.

...Ultimately, probably, of aristocratic integrity; contributory cause, love; intermediate cause, inanition: he ate less, so that his wife might have more.

But most immediately a pleurisy, which, sensing the weakness of his long-starved system, had scaled his barrier of immunity with ease, wormed its way into his lungs and, in that house of ceremonious want, had feasted.

Nellie murmured an excuse, pushed herself wearily to her feet, and left the room.

Chapter 5

In 1919, in one of the first triumphs of the newly-formed Government Code and Cipher School, the following letter was decrypted. Something of the lay-out is retained.

> *You can see dearest papa ,*
> *From the postmark*
> *where I am, which tells you enough. Well and safe, children ditto, but abandoned the Lady E venture a week past— now we hear of Corsican Usurper's escape and progress towards the capital— so vexatious.*
> *Nevertheless the future baronet proves too dangerous a foe, or friend, for me. Safest for all if I retire. Your own position with Sir may be under threat. The younger one does not baulk at murder.*

(No: she removed this last. Papa would perhaps fancy that she was being irrational, unreliable. It was imperative that he rely on her information.)

> *Feel strongly that my failure, and its possible consequences, make your success the more important. If you are delayed, will manage things at this end as per instructions. £20 draft requested from your man of business. Please reply telling me your position and confirming receipt of this;*
> *Details will,*
> *Then Follow.*

*

But he never did.

And the request to Mr Bletchley, of Chancery Lane, for an advance of £20

— submitted by Nellie in all confidence, in accordance with her father's directions for just such an eventuality— was refused. Only three days ago, the
account had been emptied.

Buonaparte Escapes from Elba

Chapter 6

Nellie crouched at the low window. Through its cramped, rain-smeared panes, she was watching the latest disembarkation from Brest spill out over the Plymouth quay; the latest gout in the disgorgement of *les Anglais* from France. Two weeks, Bonaparte had given them, to be out. Then he would hunt down the stragglers and imprison them.

English tourists were floundering, now, in their thousands, along Continental roads, awash with undrainable quantities of storm-water, streaming, lemming-like, to wind-tossed Channel. What slowed them all down, apart from the disgusting weather, and the scrambling masses of each other, and the consequent incredible price of horses, transport, lodgings, meals, were their pyramids of Parisian purchases. Ten thousand monkeys with their fists in ten thousand gourds, screaming in fear for their lives– and yet unable to let go of what pinned them down. Even now, boxes upon boxes were creaking out of the hold, lurching across the water, swaying, on the bent backs of porters, across the storm-slicked quay. Here and there a pale face, strained and exhausted, floated briefly in the subfusc turmoil, like a bubble in a pot, looking up at the buildings that circled the quay. Next they must find hotels, rooms, shelter from the drenching rain.

Amiens, indeed. 'The Peace of Amiens', all over again.

And now? Another ten years of battle, of slaughter?

After which the *Empereur de la Canaille* would entertain them again, maybe, by swearing off war a third time.

Upon which another generation would flood across the Channel: "But, this lace!... And so *cheap*—"

A step made Nellie half-turn her head. The Comtesse took a place beside her in the window-seat. She was holding a plate.

Buttered bread.

She held it out companionably to Nellie, then took a slice herself. Munching together, they turned their attention back to the struggling crowd in the wet streets.

After a while the Comtesse said (in French of course), "In an hour, less, most of them will be inside somewhere, warming themselves."

"Let us hope so."

They chewed over the wet external scene a bit longer, enjoying the caress of the small fire that burned close at their backs. Small, low rooms are smoky, but ah, so quick to warm. Rich people overlook that.

"And they are here, at least", added Nellie. "So many don't return."

The Comtesse glanced at her: Nellie must be thinking of her father. He was still somewhere (one must guess) on that foreign plain that stretched away from Brest and the channel, across Europe, to the Alps. And beyond: he could be anywhere between here and Rome. Prussia, even– perhaps he had been over towards the east when the news had reached him, perhaps he had fled east across the border into Swisserland. "He is such a clever man, such an able man. *He* will take his needle from the game. And then he will find his way back, my dear."

Nellie turned a puzzled face to her companion– Smiled vaguely– the Countess must be thinking of Mr Shepherd.

Actually Nellie had been thinking most immediately of her long-ago brothers. John, and Charles.

She was trying not to think of her father these days, trying to push him to the back of her mind, and the bottom. But that remote cellar was where the boys crouched; side by side, knees drawn up; arms wrapped around the hideous wounds that had killed them. Motionless. Unprotesting. They'd given up, she'd thought, trying to break back out into daylight.

Only now, each time she stuffed papa in with them and tried to slam to door, they were scrambling up and slipping through.

After all this time, they looked quite as ghastly as ever. Smiling tanned faces that turned pale as the blood was torn from them, eyes that closed and sank away from her; shining child's curls that grew lank, then stiff, with dirt and— matter. Little Charles, dancing with glee in their dark garret room: she had just told him that she had found a place for him as a volunteer in the *Blenheim*. "A million thanks dear sister! I will be grateful to you for the entire rest of my life!"

Yes: when they do force themselves into your sight, they look quite as awful as ever; the dead. No matter how many years have passed. Successful grief resolution is almost entirely a matter of learning not to think, with any clarity, about the person who has died.

And Nellie had lost the knack, it seemed. Or when she turned, sharp-about, from one of them, it was to find the other before her, radiant with admiring gratitude: "Tell me again about the *Blenheim, ma sœur si sage...*" She'd been almost as full of glee, that morning, as little Charles himself. As she swung him about her, she had felt so pleased with her success. The little mother, taking care of everything— *prenant tout les dispositions nécessaires; tout en charge;* both of them! Fed, and clothed, and sorted! Now she could turn her attention just to herself.

"They will all grow warm again, poor wanderers. The blood will flow back into their faces, and the hands and the fingers; they will know they are safe. *'On home soil.'*" The Countess enunciated the English phrase carefully, with a trace of pride. *"Home soil."*

Never so mindlessly, so wickedly careless with Ariosto, with Josephine.

So Nellie thought– watching the crowds slowly thin from the quay. Somehow she must keep them ashore. Me for the drowning. Me for the cannonball and the fatal splinter-wounds. Me, at any rate, first.

*   *   *

"Still a bit wider with the gap. You are still a little flat on the *Soh*— the top note. Imagine it is filled with alligators, the gap, and your voice must *jump* across it to the high note, and then *jump* straight back again to low one, and back and forth and back and forth and never put a *toe* in the gap between, or the alligator will snap you up!" She demonstrated with her fingers, hopping back and forth across an imaginary alligator.

"What's an alligator?"

"Er— leeches then."

The child scowled some more. Its mother had expressed the belief that it could sing like a little bird.

"Come! Try it!" Nellie demonstrated, lilting encouragingly.

*

"I'm sorry Mrs Clay. I don't mind for myself. You sing like a bird, you do indeed! But Mr Newsome is complaining about the others. He doesn't like the noise."

"Can I perhaps change rooms with another lodger? Someone who would prefer to be on the upper floor?"

The landlady looked doubtful, and said nothing.

*

"I want to go *home*."

"Just a few more minutes, and your mamma will be back for you. Won't she be pleased, if you can sing this song nicely for her?"

"I want to go home *now*."

*

Sitting with the Barratts and the Countess over their little fire after hours. Mr Barratt has plodded in, late as usual. Business is booming, is frantic even, under the agitated chaotic direction of its new owner: there is much call on the experience, and the steady head, of the man whose shop it was for so long.

That man sits, with a long sigh.

He sees the look on Nellie's face, and smiles; wry, but unapologetic. Mr Barratt cannot afford debilitating emotions, and what Mr Barratt cannot afford, he does not indulge. These days he gives briefly his analysis of problems, and then moves to solutions, and then, to tired silence. These days, he speaks to Nellie less and less.

So Alice speaks for him. "Don't pull that face, Nell. Look at us! A roof over our heads, a fire in the grate. Good food on the table— take this toast,

Richard, it's nice and hot. Old friends about us—" she smiled at Nellie and the Countess, "and Jessie has a..." she couldn't really say 'a young man', as the person in question was older than herself; "a suitor calling on her, that any lady in this town would be proud to welcome! It's all we dared to hope for, just weeks ago; and better than we feared. Than we had good reason to fear."

Richard nodded. "I give thanks to Fortune." He waved his bread, in salute to that feckless goddess, and took a massive bite.

"Jessie? But—" But she's fourteen.

"We've told Mr Threadgold he must wait a year", said Richard indistinctly.

"Or two", added Alice.

"Or two", agreed Richard.

Then more likely those skinny hips of hers will be up to it.

And then it would be— America? Canada? Alice had been telling Nellie of her brother's ideas last night. They would not like to talk of it now, before the Countess; arrangements would have to be made for that lady's hips as well. The Barratts could not possibly leave England any time soon. It was just talk.

And here was tall baby Jessie herself, the last left of all the throng, sidling into the room, looking abashed.

"So you have the men calling already, Miss Jessie?" Nellie enquired cheerfully.

Jessie smiled, and squeezed onto the sofa beside the Countess and slipped both arms about her waist in a single smooth movement. Known about Plymouth with eighteenth century robustness as 'the one that killed her mother', Jessie had always been a silent child. Albeit sweet-faced and obliging. Many had wondered if she was a little lacking— the girl's mother was not the only one, after all, who might have found the birth taxing— but no: the truth was that Jessie, unlike any of her siblings, had always suspected she was surplus to requirements.

Only the Countess had always had time for her. Jessie rubbed her cheek against the tiny lady's sleeve. She had to bend her neck, these days, to do it.

The Countess smiled fondly up at her. "That Mr Threadgold will not be taking my Jessie from me!"

The words and accent were Plymouth: the delivery was Versailles. It sounded odd to Nellie, now.

But she would get used to it again.

*

"She says she won't; she says she'll have harp lessons next. She's took against it so violent. Well you did try, I know."

"Naturally, Mrs Collins, singing is not for everyone, but—"

"And it's no use. I never can get her to do anything she doesn't want."

*

"Just the Old Count left then."

They studied him: he stared impassively at the wall beyond them. Calm oval face, luminous skin, silver-blue hair swept up in a cloud above the immaculate slope of forehead, that dropped to eyes as dark as pools beneath a castle keep. The frame was massive.

Nellie stared, in fascination, at the thought that one could sell it.

Cut the portrait out, of course. That goes without saying. But then, sell the frame, along with all the other furniture.

Well she had been doing a number of unexpected things, the Countess. Her daily trips to the bakery, for example; each took a good hour, now. She had been chatting, she would say, with Mrs Thomason, and she always came back with her grey-worn shopping-bag distended. The other day, as a break from their labours — sorting, deciding, washing windows; clearing the decades of dirt revealed by the removal of massive closets, opulent chests, all of which had stood empty for twenty-three years — the Countess had summoned Nellie and Alice to the salon, and there shared with them, scrupulously three ways, a large cream bun.

The Old Count didn't seem worried. He gazed over their dusty head-scarves with the detachment of the Crown on its way to the tumbril. Here, in the echoing apartment, his son had maintained a spacious public room, with good coffee and wax candles for guests. (You can see why they couldn't afford them: guests; acquaintances; friends.) If his son's relict chose now to abandon these ways... and for bakers' goods! — The Old Count hadn't eaten a crumb for fifty-five years, and was all the better for it.

"Do you think we could carry him between us?"

The Countess frowned up at him. "The frame alone is very heavy. I cannot feel that it would be secure in our hands."

"Perhaps Mr Barratt can help us, after the shop closes."

Perhaps you could sell it.

*

"So now their father says, as he *bought* the piano, too bad, she *must* learn the piano... So then Mary, and Lizzie too, they'll all do the piano this quarter, I'm sorry but the master coming cheaper for three, you see."

"Yes quite– but, do *remind* your husband, that there is *no better accompaniment–*"

"And maybe little Janey too, start her off young. You like to play on the spinet, don't you Janey? Finger out of your nose, my pet."

Janey, who showed every sign of singing exactly like the vanishingly-rare little birds of which everyone in Plymouth was emulous, wiped a tiny wet finger on her pinafore front and nodded obediently.

*

A letter from Elizabeth, in tardy response to her own. Short: formal. It tells of little more than the Frazers, who are visiting in Camden Place. The house is full of Frazers: this is made very clear. This, and Elizabeth's delight in Mrs Frazer; the two of them go everywhere together.

*

Nellie, tired and preoccupied, is sitting once more in the small cheerful parlour of the Barratts. It is just the three of them. Richard, Alice and Nellie. The Countess is pattering about her miniature room upstairs, 'arranging things'. She is a mouse in a wainscot, joyfully secure of her tiny niche — and now, just a bit of straw, and a scrap of wool– and some feathers!... Old age, misfortune, hunger, the cat; they stalk about outside. In here, right now, you are safe.

The Old Count is nowhere to be seen.

*

"But where is Mr Clay? We was expecting him. He must sign it."

"I am a widow, ma'am. I am renting on my own account."

"Oh."

The woman poked at her lower lip with an index finger that bore abundant traces of household labour.

"Oh well..."

She dug the finger into her chin; made a third attempt; managed to blurt it out:–

"Oh well I'm sorry but we don't rent to ladies unaccompanied."

"Surely—"

"No I'm sorry but it's a very strict rule."

*

She needs to decide about the children. By the time she has paid the fares, from their schools to Plymouth, there will be left, of her father's money, five shillings and eightpence.

Alice is darting her tiny glances, between helping everyone to muffin.

Nellie shakes her inward self, and sits up a little straighter. Leans forward, to pick up her weak tea and sip (secondhand tea-leaves, from the cook at the White Hart; at this time nearly everyone in England knew the taste of second- and third-hand tea.)

Because it is anyway lovely to be here, at the end of the day, with the Barratts. Here is contentment: here is comfort! The Countess's mite is coming in most handy, and the Countess herself, flush with the proceeds of the furniture sale, is still spending up big on life's simpler luxuries; the muffin is accompanied by honey and jam. "Regale yourselves!" she had commanded, before trotting back up to her room.

"...Australia then", Richard is saying. "They're practically giving away land there, to free settlers."

This is the only fly in the ointment, the balm, of Nellie's evening treat: when Richard talks, these days, it is so often about emigration.

He somehow calculates that they can afford it. After child five left the nest (child eight through six having died), it became successively more possible to save a mite each year. It is getting repetitive:–

"Imagine, Alice! A farm of our own!"

"And what do we know about farming?"

"As much as many that go, and more than most."

The Barratts' savings will cover either two passages out and very little more, or one passage, plus one decent fit-out for the new world. It is not enough. Nellie is sure it is impracticable.

Still, Richard says. Even now, with care, they may save; they may save.

"The children hate the idea, Richard. They are all against it", Alice would then reply. 'The children', some of them in their thirties, and most with children of their own, have been crowding anxiously about their parents *manqués* with offers of corners of rooms, thirds-of-beds, ingle-nooks. "What real need is there, for us to take such a risk?" That is what Alice always says next; and Richard always responds with–

'Hundreds of acres! Sheep— I'm sure that would be the way to start. Then there's no clearing, no ploughing, not to start with. I would go out ahead, you see, and you would stay here, just until the time is right." This was the version Richard favoured. Starvation, or slaughter by indignant natives, was something to which he would rather not expose a woman. "Mary thinks it a wonderful idea. She says, if the news is good, she and Tom will follow us."

And then Alice would sniff: "Mary! She always was the romantic!"

But Nellie, watching Richard Barratt's profile as he bent over the fire, reflected that Mary was not the only one. At open the threshold of life, Richard and his sister had had prudence thrust in upon them: now it appeared that in Mr Barratt's bosom there had survived, somehow, a secret germ of romance. Strange that such a practical man had never seen fit to pinch the life out of it.

He had been looking ahead, perhaps, and waiting. Richard Barratt played the long game.

In a distant tower a clock was chiming ten. Nellie grimaced, and reached for her pelisse.

"Will you not stay, Nellie dear? Will you not come in with Jessie and me? You know you should come in with us entirely. Paying rent on rooms when there's room for you here: how is that practical?"

"Foolishness", Richard agreed.

"Or Jessie could go in with the Countess. Jessie would like that of all things!"

And then, thought Nellie resignedly, they'd tell the Countess to pay less on the rent. "No no; I have my own room to go to!" My own living to earn, my own dependants to support. (The schools were paid up until a month from Lady Day. What would she do after that?) Richard offered to walk her home as always, and as always Nellie refused. "It's kind of you, Mr Barratt, but you need your rest more than I."

He remembered the days when she would have said "Don't be silly! I can find my way across the street, I should think!" And he might have pulled her ear gently, for giving him sauce.

Well no he wouldn't. He never had. Pulling that ear would have meant what— three, five, ten more children. He and Alice had their own thirteen already. A life of most anxious, wearing, youth-killing labour: that was all he could ever have offered. No. He had kept quiet, and hoped, for her sake, that she would do better.

And then she had married George Clay.

— And then, she had never had a child anyway. In spite of George Clay's shining locks.

Meanwhile, Nellie felt her way across cobbles by the thin light of a thin moon. And oh to have stayed in the warm room that she had left, among those undaunted faces.

She was keeping it to herself so far, about her finances. Nellie was not so proud as to choose to starve rather than impose her worries and expenses on her friends, but she would do what she could. For as long as she could.

Heavens, it was always like this, with the teaching! One day someone's husband's duty took half her pupils off to Bristol; the next, a family of six girls would come sailing in from Portsmouth, all keen as mustard to learn singing, and the mother as well. She reached the top of the stairs and felt for the lock.

The door opened with a little susurration.

There was a note beneath it, cancelling the Melville's lessons "for the forseeible futur."

*

Another night— it is every night— waking with a jolt, prickling with sweat, disembowelled by fear. She clutches her pillow to the wound, pressing it tight against her abdomen. Still, her breath is ragged. Still, her heart thumps, so hard that the sheet beneath her ear creaks minutely in time with its desperate kicking.

*

A tradesman's wife, thirty-five and looks every long day of it, taking her first singing lesson. In the old days she'd have had no trouble in being kind, encouraging, to the elderly *primagravida*. "Everyone can improve! Everyone can sing nicely, according to their voice type. We simply cannot all sing the *same* way."

Now she looks at this anxious, fading woman, hiding, behind that fixed middle-aged-lady smile, the realisation that she has attempted more than she is now entitled to hope for, and sees herself.

*

If he knew, if she told him. Then Richard might ask her to marry him.

Though there was no denying that he would be better off without her.

They would all, over there, in those warm rooms, be better off without her.

So he might not.

*

Another day– the last day on which Nellie will have the cash pay the children's fares.

"*How* much?"

The coachman chooses to treat her question as rhetorical. He has answered it so many times today, from so many angry people — and this hollow-eyed woman looks like a gin-drinker anyway, in spite of her respectable dress.

"But... only last week, they told me half that price!"

He looks beyond her at the crowd of jostling travellers — desperate to get out of Plymouth, desperate to get into it and join their ships. "There is a war on, lady, if you may have noticed."

*

Another dreary winter morning. Nellie sits in her room, waiting quietly for it to be the day after tomorrow at three, which is when she next teaches. Although she now sleeps, at night, scarcely at all, she finds that she dozes as she sits — as she walks — as she teaches.

Steps on the stair; soft, deliberate steps.

They stop at her landing...

A knock!

A new parent? A new pupil? Nellie leaps to her feet and flings open the door.

On the landing stands Mr Elliot.

Chapter 7

Mr Elliot smiled— of course— and lifted his hat.

"My dear Mrs Clay! I trust I do not discommode you, calling at this unexpected hour?"

She could only gaze at him, speechless.

He smiled again. And replaced the hat. "Does this not call to mind the exciting days of our early acquaintance in Bath? Those unexpected morning calls, those late night visits, with the dear Elliots? In and out at all hours!— How happy we all were together."

Below in the narrow stairwell a door crashed open, releasing a surge of noise– children's cries, the hoarse voice of their father, cursing them– followed by a billow of steam which, rising past them in a visible cloud, refreshed the pervasive smell of boiling cabbage. Mr Elliot smiled again, and gestured slightly with his cane and eyebrows...

So habitual is courtesy to those schooled in it that Mrs Clay stepped back and made the movements of inviting someone in.

It was three steps from her door to the middle of her tiny parlour, and one more step to the fireplace, where two rickety chairs did duty for half the furniture. She gestured again; again automatically, using the graceful wave-form motion that she had been schooled to in her Paris childhood. Mr Elliot, inclining his head graciously, sat down with a flip of spreading coat tails, on one side of the fire.

She resumed her chair on the other.

Mr Elliot laid aside his cane, and positively beamed at her.

"Well, how pleasant this is, Mrs Clay. What a charming set of rooms you appear to have here. Sir Walter and Miss Elliot must be delighted to have you so well situated. I hope they are in good health?"

Mrs Clay stared blankly. "I have not seen them these several weeks, Mr Elliot. I left you with them, in Bath. Should I not be asking you, of news of them?"

"Ah! So you should, Mrs Clay." He paused, and gazed at her brightly.

He looked very... smooth.

He looked full, and sleek, and bright. Success expands the face, especially the male face: failure collapses it, like a withered balloon. After weeks of creased, grey working cheeks, Mr Elliot's countenance glowed before her like a waxing moon. He even smelt nice.

Mrs Clay wondered what she must smell like, by now.

"The Elliots – Sir Walter, Miss Elliot – did you leave them well?"

"I did indeed, Mrs Clay, very well indeed. Bath continues to agree with them." Mr Elliot shut his lips ostentatiously, and twinkled at her again.

Again, Mrs Clay made the effort of recalling, and performing, some strangely disjointed duty: "And Miss– Mrs Wentworth— how does her marriage to Captain Wentworth proceed?"

"Delightfully, Mrs Clay. They seem the happiest of couples." Again the closed lips, and the eager gaze, as of a committed teacher putting a dim child through a lesson. Nellie stumbled through enquiries after Lady Russell, Colonel and Mrs Wallis, Admiral Croft, Mrs Croft, Mr and Mrs Musgrove, Louisa and Henrietta, both their new husbands, and was enquiring after the health of Cubbins when Mr Elliot interrupted her. "That will do, Mrs Clay. I suppose the butler is well but I really have no idea. We are not here to talk about the butler."

"What are we— What were you wishing to discuss, Mr Elliot?"

"We are here to talk about *you*. Come, come, Mrs Clay!"

She stared, frankly bewildered.

Mr Elliot wriggled to the front of his chair, and slung his cane back and forth between his hands. "Dear Mrs Clay!

"You are like a heroine in a book, you know— dashing off like this, to set up, quite independent, in these remote and dangerous surroundings! Your friends are so concerned for you! Sir Walter sits alone, late at night, over his port – do you know that? Just staring into the fire. He misses you terribly."

It was a surprisingly affecting picture, even though Mrs Clay knew Sir Walter never touched port. It enlarges the veins of the nose.

"And here you are, all alone— amongst the barbarians!– mm?— depriving Elizabeth of a friendly bosom in which to pour her confidences. At this, such a delicate time of her life."

"Delicate?" managed Mrs Clay.

"Indeed! Delicate indeed! In only a few months, she will be thirty! Unmarried, and thirty!— What is to become of her, if her friends do not rally around her?"

So— what?— he wanted her back in Bath?

Still he sat there, brightly, neatly; the very picture of a gentleman making a morning call. By now she should be offering him tea.

Mrs Clay looked away from him. It was an effort.

"I am sad to leave my good friends in Camden Place."

"Good, Mrs Clay— that is good!" interposed Mr Elliot.

"But we both well know that they would have been my friends no longer, as soon as I ceased to submit to your demands. You would have seen to that."

"Oh, Mrs Clay!–" began Mr Elliot–

— but for the first time he was not allowed to interrupt. "I have given up my ambitions to rise, Mr Elliot. I will be content in the lot— any lot—

wherever Providence and my own exertions place me. You cannot tempt me, or threaten me, with the Elliots. Or anyone. I am no longer in your power."

It was a fine statement. It cost her a lot to utter it, and she might as well have saved her breath.

"So your children mean nothing to you? Your aged father– oh by the way you forgot to ask after your father."

"I have been in regular correspondence with my family since the events of September, Mr Elliot. I am informed of their well-being."

Mr Elliot tilted his head and stared musingly at her knees, shaking his head slowly. "Ah now... Do you delude yourself willingly, Mrs Clay? That is not what I should have thought of your heart."

Her eyes, of course, had strayed back to him. "What do you mean?"

"Ah, Mrs Clay. Resting on the assurances of your best, your most unselfish of fathers. 'My health is improving every day, Penelope dear, so do not trouble yourself with it.' Mm? That's what a loving father would write, of course. 'The winter air agrees with me. Do not worry, Penelope dear. Pursue your own schemes.' Meanwhile, his cough every day was tearing further and further into his lungs. By Christmas he was spitting up great quantities of phlegm, the apothecary tells me. Tinged, just before he left England, with blood."

"Blood? When do you speak to our apothecary? When– what is the name of our apothecary, Mr Elliot?"

"Blood, Mrs Clay. And you leave him–"

"What is the *name* of our apothecary?"

"–alone, Mrs Clay. Alone, to raise your two children, as his health fades and his life fades, and the one person who might nurse him and brighten his sad days, even bring about a reversal!– a new spring of health and of hope–"

"What is the *name* of our apothecary. His *name*."

"— denies him the comfort and duty of a daughter *how the fuck* would I know the name of your pissy little apothecary Mrs Clay." Mr Elliot stared at her with such savagery that, though undaunted, she was silent. "He's a new man. The old man went to Lyme for his health. He got in a locum."

And somehow, she could not quite disbelieve him. Blood.

One had always feared.

She leant forward and put a hand over her eyes: "What is the point of all this, Mr Elliot?"

"A morning call, Mrs Clay! Does one need a point, for a morning call between such friends as we have been?"

She straightened up. "Well yes."

He could not resist a small, arch smile.

"To business, then, Mrs Clay:— What a business-woman you have become, I see!"

She said nothing: only waited.

Mr Elliot wriggled forward in his chair. Clasping his hands over the top of his cane, and setting his chin upon them, he furrowed his brows in an exhibition of most earnest supplication. "All I ask of you, Mrs Clay, is that you quit this scene of public triumph, and consent to move your establishment to London." The breath escaped from Nellie in a noisy gasp. "There, I will be able to recompense you for the loss of your bevy of Plymouth pupils, by introducing you to a most select circle, who I am confident will be delighted by your abilities."

"Dear *God!*"

Mr Elliot smiled, and raised a responsive eyebrow...?

Nellie spat out another breath.

"You want me to live in sin with you!"

"Good Heavens. Mrs Clay. What shocking ideas you do have." Mr Elliot shook his head in disbelief.

"'*Sin*', indeed. No no. Sin will be quite unnecessary. No no no; you overestimate your charms if you imagine that they could tempt me to expose myself to your '*sailor's disease*'."

"I do not–" She stopped; and Mr Elliot laughed at her most heartily.

"'You don't'— 'you do'—'you don't'... Make up your mind, Mrs Clay!"

But she folded her lips — and after having his laugh out, Mr Elliot resumed his main purpose. "Well: perhaps, yes, you would not exactly teach *singing*, as you do here. But I feel, that you will give evening concerts instead; mm? Private concerts. With select musicians— you would select them, you would do all that bit– and then you would close the concert, by singing. I imagine people will beg you to sing, as your voice becomes known, so splendid as it is!– and you will oblige. Apartments, gowns, an instrument— a companion, of course, to accompany you, a highly respectable woman — all, in the finest taste. Now, my dear Mrs Clay, could anything be more reasonable, more convenient, more agreeable to all parties, than this?"

Why?

"Why?"

"Mmm?"

"Why?"

No answer.

She extended her arms in a gesture of hopeless incomprehension.

"*Why?* Mr Elliot?"

He sat smiling; smacking his cane with idle emphasis against his booted leg. Eventually—

"Well– let us just say... I feel the need for a change. A refreshing change."

He smacked the cane some more.

"Bath has become a bit same-ish for me. A bit...

"I find it..."

"Well perhaps you know, Mrs Clay: I was not always the model gentleman you see before you now. I was— I *am*— at heart, something of a Radical... yes."

"Yes. I have always been, at bottom, a man of Radical sympathies."

"A *visionary*."

"A visionary, yes. And now that hope springs again amongst us– amongst men of my stamp, 'why not'— I feel— 'why not seize the moment, and reach forward'—

"Mrs Clay?

"Mrs Clay? Are you quite well? Shall I ring for your *femme de chambre*?"

"No Mr Elliot I am not well. I am afraid I must ask you to let me retire. Perhaps it would be convenient to continue our conversation tomorrow."

"Ah but tomorrow–"

"Mr Elliot, unless you wish me to vomit here and now on your waistcoat, I suggest you let me retire." Mrs Clay was highly familiar with vomiting, of course, unusually so: every cloud has a silver lining, and she could– leaning forward and staring fixedly at Mr Elliot's mustard-coloured waistcoat– imitate the early stages of it with gag-inducing vividness.

Mr Elliot stared; sprang up; bowed himself out of the room.

Nellie almost fell against the door behind him and with trembling fingers locked it. She could sense his presence still pressing back on the other side of the thin planks. Fortunately for the verisimilitude of her excuse, she was at this point able to empty her stomach noisily onto the floor.

Silence.

Then, Mr Elliot's fine soft shoes stepped, delicately, to the head of the stairs, and descended.

In the coldness of the room, the halitus of softly-steaming vomit rose to enfold her face. She closed her eyes.

Really, what was the point.

What did she have to lose.

She should be grateful, quite honestly, that someone still judged her suffi-ciently attractive to make the offer.

*   *   *

"Twelve thousand pounds."

"Twe– !" Mr Elliot, who had tipped himself back in his chair, dropped his jaw so low that Mrs Clay might have counted his missing molars.

She continued silent, though; so Mr Elliot restated his incredulity, by means of the sound written *'hunh?'* Mrs Clay did not respond.

Elliot slammed the front legs of the chair down again.

(Not a good move, with rented furniture.)

"*What?!*"

She studied him a moment. Then enunciated, with exaggerated clarity: "Twelve– thousand– pounds." Again, Mr Elliot gave a disbelieving and contemptuous gasp.

Again Mrs Clay remained silent.

Again Mr Elliot was forced to speak.

"You must be kidding!"

"No I am not Mr Elliot. Are you unable to afford twelve thousand pounds?"

"I can afford to buy you lock stock and barrel Mrs Clay. But it would not cost me twelve thousand pounds."

"Yes it will, Mr Elliot, or you will not buy me. That is my price."

Silence. Then another explosive *'pah!'* "Think you're made of gold, Mrs Clay?"

She gazed at him, unmoved.

"I can pick up dross like you anywhere."

"Oh I think not, Mr Elliot. But, be that as it may..."

More silence.

Gracefully, Mrs Clay– or possibly it was Madame Clef– rose from her chair, glided elegantly to the door, and opened it. "I am sorry we are unable to come to an arrangement, Mr Elliot."

Mr Elliot, still seated, stared at her from his chair.

Stretched out his legs, deliberately. Crossed them, and folded his arms.

Mrs Clay left the door open and glided smoothly back to stand over him– perhaps rather close– it was a very small room. "So you wish to negotiate further?"

"*Negotiate!*"

"Well no. Bad choice of words. I should have said: 'I can only infer from your continued presence in my rooms that you have accepted my offer, and are thinking of ways to secure the cash, which must be paid to Mr Bletchley of Chancery Lane before my engagement with you commences.'"

Mr Elliot tilted back the chair, to look her up and down. It was just a little hard to do with Mrs Clay looming over him like this, but Mr Elliot did not choose to stand up. (It struck her that the slightest push, right now, would send him over backwards.)

"Or perhaps, Mrs Clay, you'll do it *gratis*, to avoid– certain... inconveniences. I can arrange inconveniences, Mrs Clay."

"Yes I know you can. The first Mrs Elliot was greatly inconvenienced, wasn't she. And little Wallis–... *what* did they call him? I do hope he was christened, before being so badly inconvenienced. And Colonel Wallis, yes, I suppose you could say you inconvenienced him too, along with Mrs Wallis.

And of course Mrs Smith, whose letters you may or may not possess in full. And you know, according to papa, your capacity for inconveniencing others stretches back much longer than that. Papa is very flexible: we spoke of it once, remember? and he works through all sorts of nooks and crannies in the course of his researches. He has an enquiring mind. Lots of contacts. He's always making contacts."

She gazed at him impassively for a moment.

"So it could be fatally inconvenient to more than just myself, if I — or anyone I know— say took an overdose of laudanum, and died: with bloodshot eyes. It could well turn out, really, very inconvenient to you, Mr Elliot."

He did not reply. With an air of explaining further, she added: "Mortally inconvenient."

There was a long period of stillness.

Mr Elliot was accustomed to using such, not only to review his plans, but also to undermine the nerves of his interlocutor. However by now Mrs Clay had, as we know, both feet planted firmly on rock bottom. She continued to regard him steadily.

The room echoed with his scream—

"That is EXTORTION, MRS CLAY."

Beyond the open door, up and down the stairwell, the building stilled. Clattering pots suspended; voices hushed; the breathing silence of attentive neighbours; cocked ears.... Next door, Mrs Clay was, attempting to– what?

Blackmail her dapper visitor?

Blackmail!...

Mr Elliot stood, took a deep breath, and resumed his broadcast— stressing key words with a force that made his eyes pop, a little, on each one. *"After what you did to that* POOR MAN*, Mrs Clay,* NO DECENT WIFE *will let you near her* FAMILY AGAIN.*"* Mrs Clay had flinched back, her animal body recoiling from the performance of enraged alpha male and his storm of accompanying spittle. But her omega soul stood firm. "Go ahead", she hissed over (or rather, under) his tirade— "See what comes out— Up and down the length of England. There will be so many holes burning in your reputation you won't know where to look next. My father wasn't a spy for nothing."

Mr Elliot folded himself calmly back into her inadequate chair and resumed a conversational tone. "So: you confess to me now that your father was a spy, Mrs Clay."

"Assert and deny what you please, Mr Elliot. I will assert, deny, *nothing*. Because we both know how pointless that would be, oh no, when someone in my position points a finger at someone in your position."

"I'm glad you appreciate that, Mrs Clay."

"It's other people who will be talking."

Mr Elliot's countenance showed no reaction. His breathing, after the exertion of performance, had already returned to its normal, remarkably slow rate.

And now the chair clattered to the floor as he stood up and walked out of the room.

*

Austen *aficionados* of purer taste may wish to skip the following section, for after a few days of silence, Mr Elliot tried line of persuasion more appropriate to the later 'Sensation' and 'Newgate' novels which were to mark the decline of taste and morality in the late nineteenth century (just as the Gothic novel had for the eighteenth). It involved a stalking, and a stealthy attack, by a large man in a heavy overcoat, while Mrs Clay was walking home in the scanty evening light across Stonehouse Bridge. Such engagements almost always end badly for the slighter member of the pair: hence the naturalness of female inferiority.

Mrs Clay, however, seems to have some of Anne Elliot's grim luck with heights and falls and seaside adventures. For her, indeed, even more was done by the action of the rising tide: the body was not found for days. On hearing of the shocking discovery, Mrs Clay was calm; as calm as any twenty-first century heroine should be. Inwardly, chilled and nauseous, as is usual now; but outwardly quite calm.

Mr Elliot, however, was furious. Every time one ventures into this sort of thing, one places oneself forever at a disadvantage in relation to some of the most brutish and unprincipled types; and so Kevin[†] had been a real find, a jewel among thugs; mute, illiterate, and interested only in getting paid and getting drunk. Mr Elliot felt his loss deeply. It was two days before he was prepared to even broach the subject.

*

"Mrs Clay; Mrs Clay."

They sit facing each other, bracketing the tiny hearth: they make a formal, eighteenth-century composition. "Mrs Clay.

"What an unusual woman you are."

Mrs Clay inclined her head graciously.

"A man is dead, Mrs Clay." She inclined her head the other way. "A man last seen in your company."

"Really? What man is that, Mr Elliot?"

"A gentleman– an employee— who had a message for you, Mrs Clay. Now he is dead. How would that go down with the authorities?"

"A message? From whom? Who sent him?"

"— that poor dead man– poor Kevin, cut off–"

"Who sent him Mr Elliot? Of whose employee do we speak?"

---

† *Kevin???*

"To– to pay you— to–"

"You'll have to think of something better than that." Mrs Clay sighed. "Alas, Kevin never arrived."

" I have a witness who saw him enter your door."

"And I another, who spent the evening with me."

"Who would that be? Some old drunk?"

Yes: Mrs Williams, with whom Nellie had spent a pleasant couple of mornings recently, talking in detail over the fun they'd had on Wednesday, when Mrs Williams had visited Nellie— and who, for all Mrs Williams knew, had actually done so. "Heavens Mr Elliot who is *your* witness?"

Mr Elliot narrowed his eyes and froze intimidatingly in his chair– but she allowed him only a second or two of it before interrupting.

"Come. It's not like you to waste time on trivialities."

She nearly added, when you hold your breath like that, your eyes get all bloodshot; but prudence forbade. Instead:

"I think that we are, at bottom, two of a kind, Mr Elliot. Two wild creatures, each battling the world. *'Europe and Afric on each other gaze!'"* A bit of Byron often soothed the savage breast of Mr Elliot; Nellie had noticed that. "Don't you feel this, Mr Elliot? Don't you feel, that this poem expresses our situation, quite beautifully?"

Now Mr Elliot was a practical man. He could not but see that he had been making no useful headway with Nellie, and this in spite of having gone to considerable– well– inconvenience. One would not say he was ready to *give up*– Mr Elliot didn't *give up* on his points: but like the lady in the song, he was ready to change his mind.

Nellie was appreciative: Byron again—

> *"The lone chieftain, who majestic stalks,*
> *Silent and feared by all...*
> *Though friendless now, will dream it had a friend."*

— but he must fork out the twelve thousand pounds.

"Twelve!—"

This time, though, he said it in the way anyone might say it as when, for example, they've spent a year chasing a particularly sought-after landscape gardener, and then they finally open the quote.

They were getting somewhere.

Chapter 8

In the end they agreed on four thousand eight hundred down and instalments of three hundred per quarter, plus upkeep of house, wages of servants, and dress allowance.

Nellie was satisfied. Four and a half years. If she could last four and a half years (which in cooler moments she really very much doubted, but– whatever), she would have her ten thousand. The twelve, let us confess, had been an ambit claim: ten was what Nellie really wanted. From quite early in her acquaintance with the Elliots, there had grown to be something about the phrase, *'ten thousand pounds',* that spoke to her.

It was an absolutely extraordinary price. As Mr Elliot could not forbear often remarking.

Mrs Clay– already beginning to earn it– replied, with a soft pressure of the hand upon his arm, that Mr Elliot was an extraordinary man.

*

And there was no avoiding the fact that his situation was critical; his need, imperative. Only weeks past, the whole of Europe had been scrapping fleets, and dispersing armies, and turning sailors back into regular folk by the simple expedient of tossing them ashore. Now sixteen countries were mobilising for war. Bonaparte alone was whipping up an army of a quarter million — and who knew what lay ahead? What defeats?– what reversals? By the end of the year, England could be a Republic.

No: really.

Faced with Napoleon, monarchies had fallen year after year after year. Kingdoms that had withstood centuries of war were converted into republics, by that brisk little man, typically in a month or two apiece. Britain was annoying, yes; but only because of the Channel.

Now the Corsican Midget[†] was on the loose again. The width of Europe, and Britain too, lapsed Revolutionaries leapt to get their irons back in the fire. For Mr Elliot, Bath was suddenly stifling– Camden Place, intolerable! In London there were pots that were calling out to be stirred, geese shrieking to be cooked, wheels and palms to grease and oil and all right quickly— and as in his own Radical past he'd always had these domestic tasks performed for him by an attractive woman with a strong stomach, he sought to recreate the old set-up with all speed. Nellie was to hand; Nellie was more or less familiar with his ways; Nellie it would have to be.

And yes it was unpleasant, and irritating, to be constrained to come out with so much money down. But on one hand it guaranteed Mrs Clay's interest in the success of his affairs; and on the other, Mr Elliot felt tolerably sure that sooner or later an opportunity to redress the inequity would arise.

Meanwhile, though, Mrs Clay is ahead by a small fortune.

*   *   *

---

† I *KNOW*. French inches, English inches, I *know*. I'm just quoting *them*.

"I am going away to London."

Alice nods. The situation is clear.

After a moment, they reach out across the gap between them and embrace.

"May I write to you, Alice?"

"Of course."

She pulls a smile. "And will you *answer* me, dear?"

Alice nods.

Then the Countess steps forward and embraces her too. Her cold, twiggy arms hold Nellie as tight as they can. "*Bon courage, ma petite.*"

Nellie wants to cling to her and cry and cry, but it's neither the time nor the place.

*   *   *

They are heading up to London in Mr Elliot's carriage. Outside, on the other side of the tightly-closed glasses, it is sleeting, and the coachman's greatcoat is black and heavy, with ice and rain, the horses splashed to their bellies in mud; one of them is coughing, steadily and harshly.

Inside, the carriage is lined with sheepskin. Wrapped in fur, and then, packed about with hot bricks (each of which is also wrapped in sheepskin), the inmates slouch, one on each long, sofa-like seat. Nellie plaits her fingers inside her new ermine muff.

Then she unplaits them, and wriggles them through the fur again. She cannot stop stroking its intoxicating softness.

She hasn't been so warm since last she stepped out the door of Camden Place, and heard it close behind her.

Chapter 9

So there it is: Nellie has done what Jane Austen refused to do. She has traded her sovereignty, and her services, for the means of living in ease.

Oh dear. I don't know what to say.

In *Persuasion,* I would argue, the underlying, unifying rule is something like 'strive to be principled; if you can, be intelligent; and whenever it would not be *too* impolite, speak the truth from your heart'. Don't you think? That those are the criteria by which the worth of each of its characters can be ranked?

And I agree with it all myself. I still do. I expected that this set of rules — this one thing, at least — would carry forward, unchanged, into the story of Mrs Clay. Yet after two and a bit volumes in the frightening uncertainty of Regency life, I honestly find myself feeling *so* relieved that Nellie is pretty much ditching the lot, in order to survive in some relative degree of security. I know it's wrong, but I'm just so glad to see her in that carriage.

Maybe I've matured.

Do you think I can say that?— say 'oh, I've matured'?

It's what people usually say, when they're forced to see that they've started making compromises on really key principles.

... but, I mean; it's not like *Nellie* has any timeless novels to write.

It's not like *she* has a hoard of precious manuscript in that trunk of hers; no three unpublished novels. No; nor three more ahead of her.

Though anyone of moral fibre would promptly see the nonsense of that. 'Quite irrelevant!' they'd exclaim. 'It's not the outcome that matters: it's the sticking to your principles, come what may.' That's what principles *are*...

... and *then*— and this is the point of writing a Regency novel as far as I'm concerned, a proper historical romance!— within the genre, *as* it happens, your virtue *will be* rewarded. I like that. I do enjoy that bit so much, when it finally arrives.

I just don't know, though, how much longer I can suspend disbelief.

For example: it's customary to be grateful, as well as awed, that just days off Austen's twenty-seventh birthday, she rejected Bigg Wither— his lovely estate of Manydown, the chance to make his very nice sisters her own (Jane Austen didn't like many people— who can?— but she liked *them*); to marvel at her integrity when, rather than marry a man she did not love, she chose to continue enduring the humiliations and confinements of spinsterhood. To be Jane Austen, rather than Mrs Bigg Wither.

I also exclaim at Austen's courage. Her integrity. I too am— and I use the word correctly, of course— awed.

But... grateful?

Because nowadays I can't help remarking: it didn't seem to change things much, for her writing.

Yes there is a burst of effort: she sends off *Susan*, she starts *The Watsons*— but it soon peters out. She publishes nothing, writes almost nothing, for— how long?

For exactly this long:- As long as she remained one more scrimping-and-saving, making-and-mending social nonentity, in the dreary anonymity of serial cramped rentals, in serial dreary towns, being peddled, by her mother, about their lower-middle-class drawing-rooms and parlours; offered by mamma— obliquely, hopefully; hopelessly— to the men.

For exactly as long as it took, until that little trio of left-over females were restored to security, and dignity, at Chawton.

*

The mother and sisters of Steventon's squire!

*

Apart from the squire himself (the *brother*, you know), there is, in all the rural peace about them, no family higher. All the district knows your name already and to all your intrinsic worth is obvious, all you meet are eager to wish you good day, "Good day to you, Miss Austen; good day to you ma'am! And how do your sister and your mother do?"...

Oh, how respectable and happy she must have felt! Two re-writes, three new books, four publications in the next six years.

*

So where is the bit that proves being principled gave us Austen? To me, a long, unflinching look at the evidence proves we owe the books to social and financial security.

It's horrible to admit this. It's not at all where I expected to end up, well into Volume III.

But — *look*. We even have what is called, medically, a 're-challenge':– A court case starts to threaten their hold on Chawton cottage, Austen's publisher pockets all the lovely profits from *Emma* (to offset an unsuccessful reprint of *Mansfield Park*, and by the way I *bet* her brother Henry persuaded her to insist on that reprint), Henry Austen's bank breaks and takes his brothers' money with it— and Jane Austen gets ill.

And then the rich uncle expires, at long last, leaving them... nothing.

And Austen takes a turn for the worse and dies.

*

"Single women have a dreadful propensity for being poor."

*

So, just suppose.

Suppose that, next morning, instead of fleeing dramatically in carriage, she'd smiled at Mr Bigg, and pressed his hand; suppose she'd married him next spring.

You could argue— you probably do— that if she'd betrayed her sense of self to that degree, she could never have written again. And yes, it seems certain that she could not have written the books she did. *Persuasion, Mansfield Park;* even *Emma* could not have turned out quite the same.

Maybe, though, she would have written other books.

Many, many books. Right up until she died. At eighty-eight; like her blasted mother.

Even better books.

Because (and this is even worse morality, but–) I can't help thinking (oh, God help me....), maybe, the consciousness of having made, in her marriage, a wee bit of a compromise with her principles... a little— these things sound nicer in French– a little *accommodation*... (And, too, with such agreeable results!) — Well, then!

One can easily imagine it inducing, in her, a certain...

– a certain detachment?

A certain maturity.

Which, in its turn, would have enabled her to observe the nineteenth century's coming tide of moral tyranny with cynicism. *Insouciance*. Whatever. Lift her eyebrows at it and float, light, over its spreading floodwaters. As plenty of quietly intelligent people, in the fifty, sixty, seventy years to come, quietly floated.

As many of us, perhaps, will find it wisest, some day soon (perhaps today? Perhaps today, you decided, 'wiser not to post that remark', hit that upvote, leave that e-trail...)... wisest to cultivate detachment. To quietly float.

Rather than to risk going under.

As I think she did.

Oh, who knows. Who knows. I don't want to press the argument; I don't relish it. Its tendencies are demoralising. I mean I'm just speaking my thoughts to you as they arise. The author can damned well edit this out. It's about time she pulled her weight it seems to me– did something more than typing and proof-reading. Why doesn't she help me out, ever? Who wants to be rudely confronted, in the middle of a nice Austen spin-off, with a reminder that, after a lifetime of sculling easy towards the rising sun, suddenly you are being hurled backwards by a riptide of social change and it starts to look like you will be flotsam on that riptide for the rest of your life. Hm? Who wants to stare too long at the idea that your only choices, now, probably, are to flounder clumsily on—red-faced, and stupid-looking, and going astern all the time anyway— or— to turn your canoe around.

To paddle westward, with the tide... ah!... smoothly... elegant once more, and smiling (don't forget that bit) like it's all your own idea. I mean who wants to think about it?

What good does it do?

The point, thereal point right here, is just this:– In the case of our Mrs Clay, come on; it's not like the world is going to miss out on much.

...and as the miserable countryside reels past beyond those snug-fitted, water-tight carriage glasses, Nellie, on the right side of them once more, stretches out her warm feet– shining, rosy, in new satin slippers– eases them onto the foot-warmer, and wriggles her toes.

Mr Elliot, jolting on the seat opposite, looks on with stony face. The first downpayment is already out of his account and into Bletchley's; his purchase is irrevocable; and although he does not customarily doubt the wisdom of his actions, just now he is experiencing a nasty attack of buyer's remorse.

"So, Mrs Clay. After my–... *extraordinary* generosity–... What guarantees have I that you will deliver on your part of the bargain?"

She smiles her best Parisian smile. After so long in disuse, it feels fantastic.

"Il faut que vous me fassiez confiance."

But Mr Elliot can only narrow his eyes to slits, and twist his upper lip.

So she translates:

"You will have to trust me."

Chapter   10

London in 1815 was a maelstrom of historical mystery and romance, and Mr Elliot plunged back into it like a salmon into the spawning stream.

It was a dizzying few months, those One Hundred Days: dizzying times, dizzying evenings; the punch powerful, and the news every day more thrilling, and the company brilliant in at least one sense of the word. His life in Bath, if something brought it fleetingly to mind, he recalled wonderingly, as a dream; all those long, polite evenings, talking music with the frumpy Viscountess, or sitting on the sopha with Anne Elliot, discussing the role of the clergy in an emerging Britain... It struck him that if he'd been confined much longer to Camden Place, he'd soon have suffered agonies of genre dysphoria.

Mrs Clay gave Mr Elliot no reason to regret his outlay. On the contrary, Madame Penelope proved all that he had fantasised, and more. Even her speaking voice was charming. Such a titillating French accent!– though there were debates as to how thoroughly she understood the English tongue. Some claimed that she could follow the language almost as well as a native, and that her moments of incomprehension were all a calculated performance: others disagreed, and as proof, hinted at long conversations that they had had before her, or beside her, of the most intimate nature, without eliciting any recognition or reaction. Mm. There are always people like that.

Indisputably, though, her singing voice is glorious! Everyone agrees about this; everyone *raves* about Madame Penelope's voice. A tremendous diversity of people, previously thought to be united only by their irrepressible gabbiness about politics, flock to hear Madame sing— and under the influence of that smooth, satiny mezzo, they found themselves more passionate, more eloquent, handsomer and more beautiful than ever before.

And the private Mrs Clay was a revelation. Mr Elliot found that he had secured for himself that oxymoron, a reasonable woman! No sudden eruptions of sensibility; no attempts to impose, out of the blue, liens upon his time, energy, or imagination. On those occasions when the pace was particularly demanding one never need fear, from Madame, any plaintive resumption of the tale of her arcadian childhood, girlish hopes now lost la la la— or alternatively, that sudden, peculiarly feminine compulsion to make minute enquiry into Mr Elliot's feelings, and to explain her own, in repetitive detail, well into the night and then taking it up again next morning the minute you walk in to breakfast.

Nor, should Mr Elliot betray his indifference as a listener, did his new acquisition have that nasty trick of going out over the next few days and running up a score of shopping bills. Mr Elliot appreciated that difference in particular. Mrs-Elliot-as-was had developed that habit, you see, towards the end, and it had been very annoying; another reason why Elliot had been glad to see the back of her. Or as it turned out, the horizontal front of her, laid out with hands folded on breast: so sad.

But from Mrs... Penelope?... No. None of this nonsense.

Just, at the fag-end of each day, a business-like review, presented with admirable clarity, and a request for instructions going forward; instructions which Madame then followed to the letter. Could his wife have done the same! How different his married life might have been.

All this didn't stop Mr Elliot trying, as a matter of course, to screw Nellie out of her three hundred a quarter. But when the first advance remained unpaid a fifteenth day, Madame Penelope was that very night not to be found at her customary station, and for thirty-six tense hours the inconvenience to Mr Elliot was considerable. Finally, he essayed the strategy of sending some part of the money to old Bletchley in Chancery Lane— and when he added the rest of it next day, Nellie re-appeared within hours.

Albeit with a new footman in tow. A man large, even for a footman, and to all appearances devoted to her, and whom she addressed— to his evident confusion— as 'Kevin'. (Could his wife have done the same?)

Beyond that, I would like to draw a veil over most of these few months; they are so very indelicate.

No— not particularly in *that* way.

Not that Nellie even conceived herself in a position to make it another non-negotiable. Outwardly, at least, all here was perfectly conventional: Madame Penelope operated from a charming apartment, in fashionable Belgrave Square, where she lived with an elderly companion, a Mrs Smith or something, beige and negligible— you know how it's done— and Mr Elliot called at all hours, and was always admitted, just as all the neighbours had anticipated.

Perhaps, too, there may have been, for Nellie, initially, some little *désagré-*

ment; a few dreary tasks. *Eh bien,* what woman has not, at some time, performed them?— and very rarely for such good returns as a Regency four thousand eight hundred down, plus three hundred a quarter, clear. But Mr Elliot, like any other gentleman of means and sense, had long-established arrangements by which his needs in this respect were regularly and, he believed, hygienically met; so in the end he did not put Mrs Clay through more than is demanded here by any man's *amour-propre.*[†]

Events were going swimmingly for our heroine, in short, and it was only briefly each morning that Nellie, opening her eyes in the pretty, sunny bedroom, to the chink of the tray as Hortense brought in her tea, would have a half-minute of... well. Not regrets.

Would find that overnight her heart had, like the liver of Prometheus, regrown; only, as a river-smooth, river-cold boulder, weighed with dreads — the girl, the boy, the future— that she would thank any passing eagle to pluck out.

So she would drink her tea... and then the rest of the time she was too busy to think about it much. In the evenings, especially, she often felt even a pleasure in her powers.

*

By May, Mr Elliot was having, quite literally, the time of his life!

I have hinted that their little set-up was not strictly pre-eminent within the Radical faction. What of it? There are strategic advantages, Mr Elliot held, in moving a little below the exposed social peaks. For if the most bruited of the Radical set were not appearing at his little gatherings, well!– his own *soirées* were all the more useful, Mr Elliot liked to think, to those engaged in the real business of Revolution!

It was, above all, with this set of grimly-smiling men that Mr Elliot wished to see himself; yet, in all his years with Eugenia, none of them had ever dropped in. So the evening, in late May, when he turned to find one standing silently by his elbow... it was the greatest moment of his life.

An exchange of glances, on each side keen, and searching. A silent, mutual recognition. A half-bow. "We hear of your work Mr Elliot. And I see, about me, that Rumour speaks, this time, no more than the truth."

Then the man suggested that he and Mr Elliot might have a quiet brandy in a more private room.

So he and Mr Elliot did that; and the next day the man came back, bringing a friend, and the next day the friend brought a friend, and so on, until by June, it was a semi-regular thing: they would appear quietly at the door, and that would be the signal for Mr Elliot to turn his back on the chattering flock and withdraw quietly with his new associates to the library.

[†] He might have done so... he usually *would* have done so... but that, deep down, he was no longer
    sure that he had been inventing it all. About Mrs Clay. The whole 'sailors disease' thing.

And in that room— in near silence, among cowled eyes, drably gleaming plumage, bare, wattled necks— Mr Elliot felt himself to be breathing in, as a numinous presence, at last, real power.

*

All in all, then, it was a couple of chapters straight out of Georgette Heyer: and in the middle of it, during an evening especially lively, at which several *bona fide* auxiliary members of the French postal service were mingling and schmoozing and hoovering up the drinks in Madame Penelope's hot, over-crowded apartments, Sir Walter turned up.

How ordinary the Baronet looked.

How provincial, in the latest Bath clothes. How homespun was his best-Bath-drawing-room countenance, when one saw it here, in this ocean of cosmopolitan faces all aglitter with relative cleverness and scintillating with life.

He was peeking about him, though, in uneasy delight. On every side his gaze bounced off hard, confident faces, breastplates of what looked exactly like diamonds, breasts scarcely less firm than the corsets that, beneath the gauze, encased them— he is tossing in a turbulent sea of utterly splendid creatures! A tiny part of him suspects that he might be out of his depth. All of him feels, breathless, that he has finally stumbled into that secret inner circle; the crucible, where fashion itself is forged.

The poor old thing.

No— the idiot! What did he think he was doing here!

Now his bobbing head turns her way, and he stares avidly at her too. After some moments, she saw recognition dawn, in the slackening of his face, the retreat of his jaw.

Oh well. Better get it over with—

She sailed through the room toward him, the crowd parting before her as the waters are cleaved by a fine-built, swift-moving frigate in full, magnificent sail. (That's not me; that's the Baronet again.) "Sir Walter. How delightful! And what an unexpected pleasure. Shall we retire to a quieter room? This way, if you please." Sir Walter was tottering through his eighteenth-century forms as she turned to lead the way— casting back, over her shoulder, an all-encompassing, all-indemnifying Gioconda smile, which had become rather well-known— was emulated, in certain circles. The door of the private salon closed behind them.

"Sir Walter."

And he was bowing: he was kissing her hand. A little shower of hair powder, freshly applied, fell onto her sleeve. How quaint.

"My *dear*–... my *dear* Mrs Clay!"

He wasn't aware of the powder, of course, his eyes being what they were. She tried to pat it off discreetly as he delivered the opening sentences of his inevitable speech. It was a new dress, a favourite dress. Silk is never quite the same after rencontres with hair powder... he was talking still: "brilliant" and "glittering", and "venturing to leave a card" (he had left a card?) "toast of London"–

"But this is most remiss of me, Sir Walter! I had no idea that you were in town. I'm afraid my companion— a dear old friend, but not the most sophist-icated of ladies— sometimes fails to identify just those cards which I would most wish to see. How very kind of you to call on us, in spite of my shameful negligence." She enquired after his household with smooth rapidity and replied to his enquires with the same fluidity... "But Sir Walter, I a m so *delighted* to see you, conversation, with a dear friend like you, demands far more than these few formal minutes snatched from an evening party, why do you not call again tomorrow?– any time after four will find me at home, and able to do the justice to you which now is impossible among the *demands"*— (with just the slightest suggestion of casting up the eyes) "of guests! How I look forward to it; how pleasant it will be, after the meaningless babble of London, to talk at leisure with you. Shall we say tomorrow then?" All this delivered with the air of intimacy that Nellie now automatically assumed while getting rid of people.

Sir Walter was touched. Mrs Clay had never stroked his arm like this; had never stood so close; never leant her body, thus, in towards his, nor lifted her face with such confiding candour towards his own.

"I will count the hours, madam— the–... count the very minutes!" And he pressed her hand again– bowed over it– kissed it. Mrs Clay smiled sweetly at him, easing him over to the footman who with equal suavity conveyed Sir Walter onwards and the old gentleman found himself outside.

He stood for some minutes, on the pavement, in the darkness, still dazzled by the illumination in which he had swum. Drawn back to it, too. The front doors opened to admit another guest, and a gush of heat and light rolled out, a surge of music, voices swelling, competing with the violins, laughter, to vanish in the vague cold air of the London night... Almost, he could have thought of lingering, until the evening's entertainment were over; and then, when the last guest had gone, quietly stepping up to the door, and knocking...

But– his knees. Even two minutes, on cold flagstones, is a long time when you are subject to rheumatic twinges. His own fireside seemed suddenly very far away.

Perhaps he could hail a chair.

Chapter 11

The next day, Sir Walter did *not* call, thank Heavens. A regular morning visit: Miss Elliot would never have allowed it. Mrs Clay would never have allowed Miss Elliot, if it had been either necessary or possible to influence the girl. To find her even that one night, Sir Walter must have escaped, in secret, from whatever place they had taken— had he mentioned where they were staying? — crept away, and hurried to Belgrave Square like a lover through the night. It was a touching, an amusing image.

The image of Miss Elliot's face twisted with rage and disgust was less amusing, yet it would persist in forcing itself on Mrs Clay's inner eye from time to time through the following morning.

In this she was prescient. That was exactly how Elizabeth's face had looked after she had ascertained, by the medium of the footman and her maid, just where Sir Walter had gone the previous evening. "I have been humiliated enough, I should have thought. I have been punished quite sufficiently for my candour in taking her up. An adulteress. Who seduced the– the man we took into our circle, and debased and degraded him along with her. Who perverted our cousin. It is always thus, I believe, with those souls who are too generous, too trusting. But now you join with them in exposing me still further to the disdain of the world. Neither of you can keep away from her it seems. In spite of those hideous blotches on her face. Pah! She has charms enough, I suppose, for *that* kind of liaison..." and so on. Because what else can one expect. Nellie knew things like this would happen, so why should she flinch and whine when the event arrives? She does not.

Heavens, she does not. Elizabeth— well. They were friends, once. But Nellie had had to be friends with her.

Not that Elizabeth was too bad, poor creature, there are worse natures than hers, it's just that she has very little to say for herself and no interests beyond her position in life and her dress. Far worse opinions are held about Nellie, she is aware, by people whose company and good opinion she would have valued, once, a great deal more than Elizabeth's. One of the season's little blips, then; no more distressing than any others.

And less troublesome than most. There was, for example, the something-or-other from one of Mr Elliot's more thrusting parrots, and a week later by one of his more saturnine vultures. (Twice in ten days, Heavens. What was she doing wrong?) Both were inconsiderable, as something-or-other goes– being cut short by the mere appearance of the massive, silent Kevin, cloth over arm, champagne glass on tray: they also serve who only stand and wait. Then there were the missives delivered to her door by some Evangelical Society, and the morning the servants found writing daubed all over that same door, fortunately only in whitewash. The pace was varied by the arrival of a small box containing a bloody fingernail— far too thick, too horny— labelled '*M. Shepherd, petit ongle, gauche*', and a suggestion that she should sent money by return address; Nellie ignored it of course. It could have been anyone's nail.

(That was the trouble with most body parts, as Mr Shepherd had explained to his children one long-ago evening, cuddled together about the nursery fire. "Either it belongs to them, or it doesn't, mm? Isn't that so? *Mes enfants?*" Like most French parents, he was concerned that his children should have logical minds. "*Alors*; if it *isn't* theirs, you get all worked up about nothing. Which is silly! And if it *does* belong to the person concerned—" Mr Shepherd checked himself, "used to, that is—" for possession is, indeed, many tenths of the law– "well then! They are– or were very recently– still alive; mm? *Enfin!* You should never be anything but pleased to receive a fingernail! I know I always am.")

Oh papa.

Once, too, Nellie caught a glimpse of Elizabeth stepping into her carriage in Grosvenor Street.

She looked very much the same: being disappointed yet again in her dearest hopes hadn't damaged her appearance a bit. Though, Elizabeth had been disappointed of her dearest hopes since about seventeen, so perhaps new lines of sorrow were not to be looked for. Grosvenor Street did not come cheap, and the horses did not look post. Had they gone and bought new ones? Nellie wondered how much they...

—Oh for goodness' sake! It is her own finances that need all her nurturing; all her maternal care.

*

Only three months in, and those finances are looking good.

Nellie has just over five thousand pounds, invested (as safely as one can, these chaotic days) through her father's man of business in Chancery Lane. She has quite a lot of jewellery, loaned her for evening use, which she has no intention of returning at any point. She has, also, a few expressions of admiration from various guests, mostly gold-set; she prefers gold. The best are from a quiet, watchful gentlemen of Tory leanings, who has indicated that he would happily step into Mr Elliot's shoes, should Mr Elliot ever feel the need to shed them– perhaps for something lighter, and easier to run in.

Not that anyone has any idea of the kind right now. Far from it; the news from the Continent was such as to encourage the most reckless expressions of Republican fervour.

"Reckless? You call me reckless, Mrs Clay?"

"I just think it makes more sense to wait and see which way the dice fall, in the first few battles, before committing oneself so publicly to a position that, *however* widely held yes by many well-connected people, is after all officially treacherous. It seems unnecessary. Not that I do not enjoy our work here. *Je suis bien amusé."*

"I can see quite well which way the dice are falling already, Madame; can you not? Do you, in spite of *our work here,* share the blindness, the self-regarding delusion, of so many of these English?" ('These English'? So he was, what, French now?) "It is mere weeks since Bonaparte escapes Elba with the connivance of his British guard– the *connivance*, Madame", he insisted over her protest; "He simply sets off strolling towards Paris– quite openly, quite alone–" "Personally I think over a thousand–" "*—armies* are sent to meet him;" "—men is quite a crowd." "—when they *do* meet him, what does he do?... He..."

Mr Elliot's voice slowed. His eyes drifted, to gaze on a scene, far away, in which a man who looked an awful lot like him... "steps forward... stands alone. Throws open his coat... *He who will kill his Emperor, let him now work his pleasure!"*

"Yes; that was brilliant. That was inspired. But world domination doesn't automatically follow, and it's the *whole* of Europe this time against him, not a divided–"

Mr Elliot waved aside the whole of Europe, intent on the intoxicating recital. "And this opposing army– to a man!– what do they do they shout— *'Vive l'Empereur!'* Yes! *'Vive l'Empereur!'* they shout! Ah! What a scene!" (Madame Penelope rolled her eyes just a little. Men.) "They fall in behind him! He marches on to Paris— His army grows with each mile— The King threatens; still he marches, still his army grows — the King flees, Paris flings open its gates, the French flock to the Emperor-King—"

"Just 'Emperor'" murmured Nellie.

"— oh by all means call him that for now– Yet again the tottering monarchies of Europe mass their armies against him, yet again our hero *flings* these armies aside—"

But this was new. "He has?"

"You have not seen today's newspapers, then?"

There it was, buried in the usual lines of close type:– "**...an action ... glorious and bloody**" Yes: that meant our team had taken a thrashing. "**... falling back... repair their losses...**" Applying the usual mathematics to newspaper reportage of the war, it looked like an indecisive outcome for the British troops in one tussle, and in another, a convincing score for Bonaparte over the Prussians.

And these had taken place– when?— Four days ago. The embargo on Calais had slowed news to a trickle.

"Can you be sure of this?"

One never could be sure, really. Only, something more like the truth might begin to creep out, a week or so after the first blustering reports.

"My dear Madame Penelope, such caution. Such *Gallic* suspicion. Do you imagine me to be relying on the *Morning Post* for my information?"

Of course not.

"Of course not, my dear Mr Elliot. So what do your pigeons say?"

"– Pigeons?"

"Never mind— what do your little men from Colchester report?"

"That Bonaparte is snapping them up, snap snap!"

The thought projected him out of his seat, where he had been lounging with an abandon that would have shocked Lady Russell. Mr Elliot was prancing about the room now, he was positively dancing with glee. "He has snapped up the Prussians. Next he will snap up the little British boys, snip snap snip! Then it will be the Russians. Then the Germans, gobble gobble gobble. And then he will come up the Channel– sail up the Thames — and snap up London!" Elliot danced up to her chair. "Snap snap!" He demonstrated— crocodile-jaw hands, inches from her face. "*Snap!*"

"Your confidence in your leader is delightful."

As usual, calling Bonaparte *his leader* steadied Mr Elliot.

What kind of leader he would turn out to be seemed clear in broad outline: the baronetcy was safe, as were the investments of anyone who hadn't been too terribly Tory—but when it came to running the country, it would be a whole new thing.

This was the exciting part. When Bonaparte found out just how supportive of him Mr Elliot had been, all sorts of delightful things were almost sure to happen. Just as long as other people didn't shoulder ahead of him in the queue... And how to ensure—

"—Getting past the British navy?"

"Hm?"

"You've skipped that step, *mon ange.*" Nellie knew she was skating close to the edge here, so she did it in French: when he wasn't enraged with her Gallic insouciance, he was delighted with it. *"Tous ces petits matelots Anglais."*

Mr Elliot's foot lashed out and connected with the leg of her chair. Oops: yes, she'd overdone it.

Mr Elliot detested the navy. It had been the bugbear of Radical hopes for over fifteen years; but it was more than that, too. Ever since the Captain Wentworth thing, his sensitivity to a blue coat had become painfully acute. Mr Elliot had swung away from her, but now he swung back. Mrs Clay steadied herself.

The day he kicked Madame Penelope and not the chair leg was the day she would have to move on. Until then, think. Three hundred a quarter.

"Remember yourself, Mrs Clay."

Once he had left the room, she took up the newspaper and read it through– trying to detect, beneath the words, the tone of the reporters.

Nervous? Defiant? The loss at Ligny— how severe had it been?... Oh, how familiar this state was! Guessing; speculating; never sure just how alarmed you should be. Nellie had few memories that were not set within war. The recent remission had held for less than a year, and whatever the outcome of the battles that lay ahead, there was hardly a precedent by which to imagine that any would be decisive. How old was Bonaparte?... Another fifteen years of *his* wars, maybe; fifteen, twenty.

Then, someone else would take over.

Nellie could not imagine, really, a world at peace.

But in his own apartments, Mr Elliot danced on his frenetic dance.

One in four.

This little spat on Friday, that the British papers had only just got wind of — It was old news. It was nothing. Sunday had seen an *enormous* battle! A glorious battle!

A decisive battle.

One in four!

That was how many British troops had fallen— wounded, or dead.

*

"And Bonaparte has hardly got started!"

"As you say, Mr Elliot. As yet, it is only June, the twentieth of June; our leader has been at liberty scarce more than one hundred days."

That had been a certain Mr Smith, dropping in this morning with the amazing news. "I felt that you should be the first to know, Elliot, as you've been such a supporter of our cause."

"A magnificent cause. I am proud to support it."

"That's good; that's delightful to hear, Mr Elliot."

"And now you want me to support it some more?"

Mr Smith grimaced, in a manner radically French: humour, regret, cynicism, and just a tinge of the man of action– of hazard. "What would you?Our plans, Mr Elliot, must now push forward with all speed. Others will soon be scrambling to seize the same opportunities, and we must be sure to keep our lead over them." He shrugged. "So yes, you are quite in the right Elliot; we must indeed deal with that little matter now. It is a wrench, I know, I feel I myself; but needs must when the Devil drives."

"That would be the Corsican Devil, would it not?" riposted Mr Elliot; smooth, swift.

Mr Smith bowed acknowledgement, and took a half step towards the library.

Mr Elliot—sporting a wry smile, significant of cynical amusement and regret— lightly sighed, and followed: Ah!– Revolution does not come cheap.

A HIGH WIND in the Park!

Chapter 12

THE MORNING CHRONICLE

LONDON

THURSDAY, JUNE 22, 1815

TOTAL DEFEAT OF BONAPARTE

*

— No.

No.

*

THE MORNING POST

SECOND EDITION

LONDON

THURSDAY, JUNE 22

GREAT AND GLORIOUS NEWS

ANNIHILATION OF BONAPARTE'S WHOLE ARMY

AND HIS OWN NARROW PERSONAL ESCAPE

*

"No. No no no— bah!— these English make a victory of every stalemate! *One in four!* Do you know? Do they tell you? British casualties? No! *One in four!* And they try to tell us it's a victory!"

"But *mon cher*, look how enormous is the font. I think it suggests a significant setback for the man."

"No. They have repeatedly underestimated Bonaparte." (They had?) "He will astound them yet. 'Narrow personal escape' forsooth!— He's given them the slip again. He's outwitted them. That's all."

That was Mr Elliot's line, that evening, when the rooms at Belgrave Square were packed to capacity and beyond. Every Radical that had ever drunk there, it seemed, had flown back to share his alarm with the flock. It's not just that no-one knew what would happen. No-one even knew entirely what *had* happened. Announcements of victories, whispers of defeat, reversals from one week to the next— it had gone on, for them, all their adult lives.

Though— rarely in such large typeface.

∗

LONDON

MONDAY, JUNE 26

BONAPARTE'S ACKNOWLEDGEMENT OF HIS COMPLETE DEFEAT, AND HIS REPORTED ARRIVAL IN PARIS

The noise of the flock, if you had been listening from the street, would have sounded harsh now. Over them all wheeled the immense shadow: Treason. Anyone could be forgiven for having liked Bonaparte *once*— every-one had liked him, once. He'd been awfully good-looking, too, at one stage.

But, to have declared for him *twice*...

∗

LONDON

TUESDAY, JUNE 27

MOST IMPORTANT NEWS FROM FRANCE

BONAPARTE'S ABDICATION —
ARREST OF HIS PERSON...
ADVANCE OF THE ALLIED FORCES TOWARDS PARIS...

... and the latest additions to the lists of dead and wounded, which were extended with each new issue, until it seemed they would never end: over one hundred thousand people, maimed or killed, in less than a week.

Up like a rocket, down like the stick.

∗

But Mr Elliot— after ten minutes stock-still over the newspaper— taking a calculated risk—

"They thought he was finished in April last year. Finished! He abdicated, for Christ's sake! And it was all a ploy.

"He is testing us."

Chapter 13

As you see, then: Mr Elliot, this time, showed less celerity in shedding his Republican feathers; more loyalty to the cause, and to the man. After all, he'd been completely flatfooted last time.

They'd *all* been caught out last time— that's what he kept returning to. Except for men like Hazlitt, who was a freak anyway. This time, Mr Elliot's name would not be among those fazed by the brilliant feint from he who was at once *Petit Caporal* and Emperor; no, Mr Elliot would distinguish himself. "And then, by July, there was but one man left in London who still spoke your name boldly, openly, with hope, and pride! Your Imperial Majesty, allow me to present— *Mr Elliot*."

Or "Sir William Elliot." That was even better.

Lord Kellynch?

The Marquis of Kellynch?...

— but August dripped in, and eventually there came to seem so little chance that Napoleon would ever get to hear of his loyalty that Mr Elliot found it best dispensed with. Madame Penelope came home from a visit to the jewellers to find the front door wide open, and the hall within laid with matting, along which a series of silent men were carrying cabinets, vases, tables, trunks. No-one came to take her wrap or her bonnet; she entered the drawing-room untying its strings herself. A group of sweaty men were gathered in low-voiced confabulation around the grand piano.

"Where is Mr Elliot?"

They turned to look at her.

"Don't know, ma'am", replied the best-dressed of them, eventually. "We're just here to empty the rooms. That's the orders. Empty the rooms."

Madame Penelope nodded. "Very well. Carry on."

With elegant celerity she skimmed upstairs and into her chamber but— no. It was too late.

"They started here, madam."

And Hortense was finishing it, from the look of it. Madame scudded over to the maid where she crouched by the bed— shot a hand into her pocket. So: her pearls. Well, the pearls she had been wearing the past few months. The maid was muttering something, apology, excuse. Nellie strode to the alcove in which the girl slept and tipped the contents of her box onto the floor... amongst it were two shawls of her own.

"You are paid up until the end of Michaelmas, are you not?"

"Yes'm."

"Go now. Take your things and go." With head shrunk between shoulders and a whisk of skirts she was gone. The chiffoniere and the dressing table were already gone too, with all their contents: a square of dust on the wallpaper marked where each had been. But the wardrobe —! She darted over, flung it open.

Empty.

Nellie was unable to stop herself, all the same, from running her hand over the upper shelf, the completely empty upper shelf. And then, standing back — there was no chair to stand on — and jumping; trying to catch sight of the second packet, where she'd left it on top, out of sight, centre back. In the end she ran to find a chair– smacked it down beside the wardrobe– scrambled onto it. Bare. Something between a groan and a whimper made its way out of her chest.

No. Keep going.

Slipping now from room to room, snatching up things light enough to be carried— the trunks must be in the attic. The attic!

— Which held only a few of those classic broken packing cases.

In the end she tumbled all she'd gathered onto a small carpet still lying in the housekeeper's room and rolled it all up and secured it with the housekeeper's dressing-gown cord. There.

A man, standing in the open doorway.

He shifted awkwardly.

"Our orders is to take everything, ma'am."

"Even the housekeeper's old clothes?— Come. Carry this for me."

And he did; down the stairs and out into the street.

"A hackney carriage."

And for once here is one just when you want it. The man swung her carpet roll inside; she groped in her reticule for a coin; "Thank you."

"Thank *you*, ma'am."

"Yes indeed; thank you." A hand had closed on her wrist, another on the reticule (and the workman rippled quietly back up the steps into the house). Mr Elliot helped himself to her purse; examined its contents with derision; took them all the same. "Your pocket, Madame Penelope."

The strength of his hand plunging against her belly made her recoil. He got the pearls though.

"And the other one." There, in the middle of the street, he parted her petticoats and extracted the profit of her morning's journey to the jewellers. Now Mr Elliot leant into the carriage. Looked about. Lifted a lip at her carpet roll: laughed. "Very well then. You may go, Madame. I would say it saddens me to part, but I'd be lying."

He tipped his hat, turned, and bounced briskly up the stairs. Stepped through the maw of the strangely gaping front door and vanished.

Nellie clambered into the cold, smelly vehicle. Her legs were shaking.

She pulled the carpet roll to her. Hugged it.
Sat back.

It was the coachman, at the window. He was grinning.

"Hope you've got your fare, lady."

Penelope pulled a silk pouch from her sleeve. It was small, but it chinked.

The man snorted: mocking; appreciative. "Well then!" And he settled his dripping hat.

"Where to, ma'am?'

Up like a rocket, down like the stick.

Chapter   14

Nevertheless.

She did have five thousand three hundred and odd pounds with her father's little man in Chancery Lane, and some very nice jewellery.

And while the adventure had left her, in terms of dress and personal items, with little more than those two shawls and the clothes upon her back, the clothes on her back were especially nice. The petticoat, for example, was sewn with seed pearls. Quite thickly, and at some cost to the maid in pricked fingers. ("Why, madam, when no-one ever sees it?" Why indeed, Hortense.) Yes, its dying moments had been nerve-racking, and ignominious; but one had always known they must be.

*

Thus thought Nellie Clay *née* Shepherd, once was Mme Clef, recently Madame Penelope, resting on her bed in a lodging house in Cheapside. There won't be much action this chapter: she's just lying there, taking stock...

(You may suspect, from your reading of Austen, that lying in bed during the day is not the heroic way to go about it. Even Marianne Dashwood only went to bed when she couldn't sit up, and it's not like *she* was a model of propriety; Anne Elliot never once lay down, the whole time we knew her. Clearly, Nellie is made of different stuff...

(But enough of this. She is thinking, and we need to listen.

(Anyway there isn't a sofa.)

*

... There is the Tory gentleman, for example.

A gentleman indeed; she has been in her current lodgings less than a day, and already she has in her hand– she unfolds the crumpled paper– a promissory note for £10 'to cover immediate expenses', and a courteously-worded offer to meet her as regards possible future arrangements. What a sweetie. Most men would have left her to sweat a bit: bring the price down.

He was also married, with a bevy of children, and a wife with hips like a carthorse, and a reputation for turning over his mistresses every five years.

Five years. She'd be nearly thirty six.

Old meat.

How much could she tuck away in five years?

And Josephine. She would be seventeen. Seventeen, eighteen nineteen, the prime years for getting married to advantage. Not a good age to have a superannuated mistress for a mother.

Well yes but the Tory gentleman would have contacts!...and Nellie' inner eye conjures an elderly man (elderly but continent, clean); wife dead, children in, say, Ireland– or no children, even better!– prostrating his shaky frame before the radiance of youth. Indifferent to questions of money, eager only to snatch at what pleasure he can before death takes him... Josephine could well end up a young widow with a fat jointure, able to give the whole of nineteenth century England the finger— you know: the one with the ring on it.

One can scarcely imagine a situation more enviable.

Though, with Nellie herself in the background, setting a bad example for everyone concerned, it's even easier to imagine Josephine launching out on her own account. And then— her young life sunk in sin... How much could *Josephine* tuck away in such a career?

Stacks, probably.

*

...But— Goodness me! Did you hear that thought? That last thought there?

What a thought!

What a thought for Nellie to have, about her own sort-of daughter.

So—but— then, do you think Nellie's going to Turn to Sin? *Permanently?* Catch the pox, and die in a Chelsea boarding house? Surely not! I mean, this is Romantic Fiction, yes? It's far too late to shoot for Literature.

Gosh.

I expected, when Nellie lay down at this point, to collect her mind and review her options, that she'd end up choosing this other option that I've got, all planned out for her. Since Chapter *One,* I've been looking forward to exactly this bit— where she is supposed to decide to give *them* all the finger— the Elliots, Lady Russell— Lady D. even, and little Catherine– screw 'em. Take her five thousand, and go off, and settle in happy independence in some 'dire-sounding place' like Bristol, or Birmingham.

I even have a house picked out for her. In Bristol, yes, as it happens.

Such a nice little place. A pleasant neighbourhood, with a sunny aspect and a ginger cat. Close enough to the docks that Ariosto can easily go on to find employment in the import/export business.

You see, she is meant to consciously choose autonomy, not simply over greater wealth, but even over *'caste',* as Charlotte Bronte so accurately terms it. Much harder. (As Bronte herself agrees; as all her heroines feel; Charlotte's romantic, but she's not crazy.)[†] Even now, caste is roughly as precious, to most of us, as life itself.

Nellie, though, was supposed to be up to it, by now. By now, her locus of identity was supposed to be internal.

But it's going on for lunch-time even, and she still hasn't swung her legs decisively off the bed and set about it.

I suppose– 'Bristol'. People like Anne think it's exactly where Nellie belongs.

—But, *I* don't mean it like that at all, Nellie! I mean it like, 'rich or poor, you're worthwhile *as you are*'.

Like the Harvilles, you know? In *Persuasion*?

*

No reaction.

*

And– Nellie I'm not suggesting it — Bristol, that is — I don't *mean* it Evangelically either. I don't mean *'submit to the situation in which it has pleased God to place you'*— like Fanny Price submits: like Anne Elliot chivvies herself, endlessly, to submit. Lordy! What a con that was! 'Submit abjectly enough', the story went, 'and ten to one, one day, someone of authority will be touched by your submission— stirred; softened; tenderised;— and will do a nice little something on your behalf'. And if they don't, you die and go to Heaven: it's a win-win.

Pah!

If my situation were as comfortable as Fanny's or Anne's, or any of those Tory moralists, I would gladly have submitted! What joy, to find yourself situated just even merely like Hannah More, for example: tucked up by her own fireside, snug as a bug in a rug on her two hundred a year annuity.

You know what that means, to a single woman? Two hundred per Regency year?

It means you don't work. In fact, you even have a couple of maids to do all the boring things! Being the new woman she is, Mrs More does set those girls of hers an example of industry herself, of course: she reads all the newest publications, has friends around to talk about the issues of the day and stuff, takes exercise (goes for walks), maybe does a little shopping... and in all this she finds time— *makes* time— to dash off her popular tracts for labouring folk.

Poor folk, with twenty pounds a year to provide for themselves and their God-given open set of children.

---

† Well... Borderline Personality Disorder, Charlotte and Emily; wouldn't you say? Oh and Type 1 diabetic! All those Brontes, that's what killed them, I'm sure: Type 1, just barely contained by a spare diet and all that walking around the dining-room table — and then Charlotte got rich, and they all started taking sugar in their tea and died.

Poor people, whose inadequate and uncertain submission to their situation — whose recently-revealed dexterity with paving stones and guillotines — was such a sad menace to their spiritual well-being.

Pah! *Double* pah! There are times, aren't there, when you just want to smack the whole of the nineteenth century over the head.

... It *would* be kind of fun, then– wouldn't it? — if Nellie were suddenly to jump up and do exactly that.

With — yes — a reticule weighted, cosh-like, with the wages of sin!

*

Though then: why should Nellie shape her life in opposition to their self-serving principles?– Any more than in conformity to them?

*

Also. There's a bigger problem.

I'm starting to realise–

When I first envisaged the Bristol escape, I really wasn't thinking so much of Nellie, was I?

I was thinking more of Anne. Or of Austen.

I mean; when I look at Nellie, now, I can't see that this massive descending pillow of nineteenth-century morality is a lethal threat to *her*. I can't see Nellie, now, lying down and submitting: not when it comes to essentials. Not now that she's been so thoroughly disillusioned. Not now she's acted so cleverly, and so often.

Not, above all, now that she is a widow, *with* five thousand pounds.

Unlike Anne, or Austen, a widow, *with* five thousand pounds, is master of her fate.

Once you have that, to be, in addition, the captain of your soul takes, not heroism, but merely a good serving of ordinary courage.

*

But that, in turn, saps the moral impact of the decision, the Bristol decision; doesn't it? Wouldn't it?

It's a philosophical change, yes; but that change in philosophy rests, really, on a change in real-world circumstances. Basically, Nellie's just been luckier than the other two: Anne, or Austen. She's acquired some cash of her own.

(Well. 'Luckier'...)

*

I hope you don't mind me filling in the silence, like this, by going on about my own concerns.

I realise I've been doing it a lot, lately.

*

For example:– When I began this book— and there's no harm in confessing this openly, because it all fell apart long ago– when I started, I really meant this book to illustrate that, when your decisions come from...

Even now, I don't quite know how to put this. Your heart?

No– your... your true self?

You know how Anne was persuaded to reject Captain Wentworth, yes? Let's call that the prototypical *not* true-to-self decision. 'Non TTS'– acronyms are such a blessing, aren't they; they make anything sound objective, well-reasoned.

And then, so, she regrets it; and, the *important point* is that it's just an endless, go-nowhere regret. It embitters Anne's life, and gnaws away at her soul, even though she *does* fight and fight against it poor lass, honestly I have to give her that, and by the opening of *Persuasion* it has made her a sad old sourpuss, a wilting wallflower in the herbaceous border of life. Gets her revenge, yes, by running a silent savage review of everything she sees.

Well so my deeper point, with Mrs Clay's life, was going to be:–

Contrariwise, *if* your initial decision *is actually* TTS, then, even when the outcome is in practical terms similarly a disaster, it's still a disaster *on a whole higher plane* than the disaster resulting from a *non*-TTS decision like Anne's.

It's even (the point would later develop) in some senses a *better* outcome, than a *success* which results from a *non*-TTS decision! —When we got to that bit, I hoped that you, reader, would get a lump in your throat. I certainly did. We'd all think about all the dreadful decisions we'd made in our own lives... and then we'd feel that really, yes: it's exactly those trials that have been the making of me.

So it was going to be, 'Certainly, Mrs Clay did the opposite of Anne, and it didn't work out for Mrs Clay, either— but *because her initial decision was TTS*, at a deep down *spiritual* level, it really still *did* work out for her.'

No seriously— Seriously. Because in such cases, you tend to accept responsibility for what is, after all, your own mistake.

And it's only when you accept your own responsibility for your own situation that you can face that situation. Work through it.

Grow, as a person.

Apart from being true, that's also quite lovely, isn't it? It would cheer you up to read a book like that. It fits beautifully with *Persuasion*— and it would be so easy to find a publisher.

*

Looking back, though; can anyone honestly suggest that Nellie *was* better off, soul-wise, from marrying George? I can't see it myself; not any more.

There are some disasters that really just are disasters.

*

Worse: now, also, when I look more closely... *Persuasion* doesn't harmonise totally with the TTS thing either. It seems to, in overall vibe; yes. But when you probe, maybe it doesn't.

To start with, don't you think Anne might have had at least a few well-suppressed incertitudes about Frederick Wentworth?

She tells us– she tells herself– Anne does — that she believed herself to be "prudent and self-denying principally for *his* advantage." So: what? She's telling us that she, a sheltered girl of nineteen, understood better than Captain Wentworth how much a battle-hardened naval officer could shrug off in the way of reversals?

This is either the bollocks it appears to be– which makes it a self-serving lie– or, it's true: Anne perceived, with her lauded clarity of understanding (all the critics laud it) that unless things continued to go reasonably smoothly for him, Captain Wentworth could go... well!

He could go— in his own, more civilised fashion— the way of George Clay. Don't tell me you haven't noticed their uncanny similarities.

If so, in holding back, Miss Anne showed a rational calculation which she, above all, would be anxious to disown.[2]

Yet even that is nothing, compared to *this*:–

At the start of the book Anne is perfectly clear: "under every disadvantage... and every anxiety... all their probable fears, delays and disappointments, she should yet have been a happier woman in maintaining the engagement, than she had been in the sacrifice of it". Unequivocal.

Then, at the very end, with Anne engaged again and everything sorted, she says this:–

"I was right in submitting to her" (to Lady Russell, that is— you'll notice that Anne is, still, right; *that* hasn't changed) "and... if I had done otherwise, I should have suffered more in continuing the engagement than I did even in giving it up, because I should have *suffered in my conscience.*" I mean— WHAT IS THAT?

OK, she's happy at that point; happy at long, long last. Delirious with happiness perhaps: "she had cheerful or forbearing feelings for every creature around her", which is so wildly uncharacteristic as to suggest that she's off her head. Maybe, then, when she says, 'she'd have suffered more in continuing the engagement', she's burbling?– maybe she's feverish?

Because, come on! Anne, who never wanted anything but her Captain Wentworth: we are being asked, now, to picture her, the beloved wife of that thriving husband, with her own house to manage, her own children to correct, her own servants to detect in dereliction— and even *more* morose? Impossible!

So no.

No; that last little bit of loveliness is either Anne, hanging on to the high moral ground— or, it's Jane Austen.

And it's more likely, I think, to be the latter.

Because where, within the events of the novel, does that spot of character development come from? Somebody, please tell me; where?

Yet there it is! Anne Elliot, after 87,000 words, has changed only in that she judges herself happier, in having submitted the direction of her life to a properly constituted authority, than she ever could have been if she had followed her own judgement— her own, demonstrably good judgement— through whatever life that judgement might have taken her.

To submit to that view is not just to submit to *doing* what is false to yourself: it's to submit to *being* what is false to your self. It is to draw your self to low divan; to encourage it, with soothing words, to lie down, close its eyes, relax; and there, to gently administer to it such a huge narcotic dose as to benumb its senses, sap its breath– stifle its sudden flailings–... until it lies passive (and you can't see, from the outside, that it's having a dream now where it still tries and tries and tries to get up but somehow keeps falling back, falling back again and again)— and then, with a firm and sustained hand, to press a pillow over what remains.

It makes an early death look perfectly natural.

— Though not by Addison's disease, surely. Rather by a cancer, one would think: a foreign growth. Or some auto-immune disorder. Or starving yourself to death, or plunging a knife straight up under your ribs into your heart. It certainly makes marrying yourself off to Bigg Withers look, to me, like a minor bit of self-harm.

*

but—

....

When a situation is unchangeable, the only sensible response *is* to accept it?

— isn't it?

History does have flood-tides more powerful than the isolated mind can withstand. It is fantasy to imagine otherwise. It is comfortable, early-twenty-first century fantasy.

And what are you going to do then? Keep on standing barefoot in the flood, like a self-deluded King Canute?— *'Back! naughty waves— You think to delude me, that this risible eccentric you reflect is ME? Faugh! I spit upon your vile seepage!'*

If Jane Austen had remained true to what I persist in thinking to be her self, in not such a very long time, she would have been an eighteenth century relic— and ludicrous on that count too, then, as well as for being a spinster. How long can you laugh and make jokes, when there is no-one laughing with you? How long can you write books, when there is no-one to read them?

Why bother, even, with a third volume.

I don't know.

*

I wonder what Nellie thinks?

It's hard to say. She's just lying there, as I said; staring at the ceiling.

If I press my ear up against her head, though, I can— OW! *OW*. Bloody *HELL!*— Did you see that?

Did you see what she just did?

She poked me in the eye!

Chapter   15

Shit!

That *really* hurt.

Chapter 16

After everything I've done!
— It feels like she scratched it even.

Shit.

Chapter 17

You think you know someone.

Chapter 18

What Nellie decided, that so-nearly-fateful day and night, will never be known. The very next morning, a letter arrived, hand-delivered by an office boy.

"Letter for Mrs Clay!" †

It was from a legal gentleman, the boy had insinuated; and the landlady was hoping for tears, an outburst— possibly even the whole juicy story from her well-dressed, under-luggaged lodger. Mrs Clay disappointed her in every sense, handing her only a copper 'for the lad' and closing the door in her face.‡

The squeal that broke out, from behind that closed door, consequently went unheard.*

The letter was from Mr Shepherd's man of business, with whom Nellie had maintained close contact as we know, and it was delighted to be able to inform Mrs Clay that her dear father, Mr Shepherd, was alive, and in Paris, and hurrying home to England, no doubt with all expedition, to rescue his daughter from her irregular position (as to say, her life of sin). It was dated... only yesterday morning!... and included, oh *Heavens* — Nellie tore apart the enclosure with trembling fingers— a hasty note from Mr Shepherd, from her father himself, from *papa!* which adopted a more liberal tone as regards the sin, running in part:–

> *English connections inform me that you have secured an excellent position, and have been doing extraordinarily well!— but that some change of circumstance might be feared in the near future.*

"I'll say!" muttered Nellie...

> *If I can be of assistance in any way, I should be delighted: if not, I shall keep a low profile, as you judge best for your situation. I do however hope to see you my dear, at least for a visit, and soon— we have so much to talk of, and I confess that, now it is all over (almost), I miss you and the children terribly.*

*   *   *

Physically, at least, Mr Shepherd looked absolutely awful; emaciated, and ragged in the last degree— though he had all his fingernails, as Nellie ascertained in almost the first minute of meeting. (A daughter in those days was very unlikely to see her father's toes.) And horribly, *horribly* suntanned!— Nel-

---

† It's OK; it's fine — it was just an accident.

‡ I just startled the poor girl. Looming up suddenly like that— she thought I was Mr Elliot!

* And she was so worried when she thought she'd hurt me! Clung to me, and stroked my arm even, quite distraught! I felt dreadful.

lie was so shocked, she was able for some time only to embrace him, and sob into his coat.[†]

Mr Shepherd was aware that he had looked a great deal worse only ten days ago; aware too that, missed meals and minor torture apart, he had had a rip-roaring good time of the old-fashioned romantic-hero sort he'd long thought to be far behind him; aware, above all, that the coat she was crying into on this fabulous morning smelt at last of nothing worse than a cleansing urea— so he also avoided meaningful conversation here. "Nellie my dear, Nellie my dear. This is not like you. This is not like the hostess of the most outrageously fashionable Radical nest in London. How clever you have been; and how brave. I am so proud of you, Nellie my dear..." So murmured Mr Shepherd, soothingly, while Nellie hiccoughed into the coat.

A young lady who gives way to tears must be recovered; questions must be answered, and surprises explained. Such scenes are very interesting, Austen declares, but the suspense of them (she adds) cannot last long, for which I share her evident relief. The mysterious horrid vanishment, last March, of father and family funds, all in one sinister *coup*, was shown to be accountable in the most natural manner in the world!—

— At the end of a long day spent hot on the trail of his strayed stock and bond, Mr Shepherd had stumbled straight into the lair of the very villains whom he had so long and doggedly pursued. Alas, in his debilitated state of health, the poor old gentleman had been quickly overpowered. Bound hand and foot, **he had been** dragged dizzyingly through the dust by a dozen coarse brutes and flung face-down at the feet of the debased scoundrel who led them — where, a gun pressed to his head, he heard those chilling words so rare in Austen novels:

"Your money or your life."

He had given his answer some thought.

— But after all, Nellie was doing so well! Her last letter, in particular, had been comprehensively encouraging; with respect to Sir Walter, and Elizabeth, and Mr Elliot, and Lady Dalrymple, and everything about her— So, in the end, he'd sent for the money. Alive, he could always expect to make more of it.

"And I, leaving Sir Walter, thought just the same! Your letters, so hopeful, the reports from France, all so moderate; why risk all that papa can and has secured, by duelling any longer with Mr Elliot?— that is what I calculated. Oh — curses! Oh foul foul *curses;* oh, what a chance I've let slip!"

"My dear, all's well that ends well. Listen: we are all alive. We all have our health. We have, thanks to you, over five thousand pounds amongst us, and there are still a few lines that I can follow up here in England which will secure us some further cash before we depart."

---

† I really should be more thoughtful.

"Depart?"

"Ah— yes..."

"Depart *England?*"

"Well yes."

A young lady who faints, must be revived...

No that's nonsense; of course she didn't faint. With Bath, and London, and Cheapside under her belt, and a nest-egg in the bank, our heroine is not so easily overcome. While the joyful tears of a daughter still stain her cheeks, the eye she directs at Mr Shepherd is expressive of a different relationship.

"Leave England. Why what an interesting suggestion. What do you have in mind?"

"*Well*— my dear. I'm sure you'll be delighted to hear— delighted, under the circumstances— delighted that is under *any* circumstances, but just at the moment it comes in most opportune:— young Ariosto has inherited."

Penelope gawped— she can still gawp. (She has not lost her old talents, merely added new ones.) Mr Shepherd smiled with greater confidence, and began. "You see:..."

*

What it boils down to, necessarily, is that all of the heirs above little Ariosto are dead.

They were many, you may recall; a melancholy abundance. The business of a young nobleman is war, however, and in those that swept Europe after Ophelia's exit from his Castle, old Count Ariosto's progeny had participated with fervour, and died, correspondingly, like flies. They had died in fighting against the Revolution, and then in fighting for it; they had died one by one or, in the livelier actions, three or four by five and more. Sons, grandsons— in the case of a few sad little drummer boys, great grandsons even— had fallen on the fields of Arlon, Bassano, Castiglione, and Diersheim; of Erbach, Froeschwiller, Genoa, Heliopolis and Jemmapes; in the sieges of Kehl, of Luxembourgh, of Mainz and Malta and Mannheim and Mantua (sieges one *and* two); at the battles of Neumarkt-Sankt Veit and of Orbaitzeta, of Pancorbo and Pla, Prenzlau and Platzburg and the Pyramids... oh, there are two dozen under P alone!– and you can easily make it all the way to Z. Except for the letter X. In the whole of the those wars, from 1789 to 1815, there's not a single battle of the X; not one.

Which feels incomplete. Doesn't it feel incomplete, to you?

By late 1812, then, only eighteen heirs remained ahead of our own Ariosto. Fully fife sixths of these— fifteen of them, that is— melted away like snow in the retreat from Moscow (froze slowly to death, actually; then thawed out again in the spring of 1813, and *then* deliquesced): this should help the younger reader to remember the proportion of Napoleon's 600,000-strong army that vanished in that action.

Then, after all those battles of the War of the French Invasion of Russia, which came after the War of the Fifth Coalition, there were the battles of the War of the Sixth Coalition; Großbeeren, Kulm, Katzbach and Dennewitz; Leipzig and Lützen, Bautzen and Dresden— like Santa's reindeer, isn't it? — which is counterproductive, because the point I'm anxious to emphasise is this: it doesn't strain narrative credulity in the least, that in all this slaughter, several dozen particular young Italians should have died. It's reality, rather, which strains credulity.

By the time our story commenced, then, back in Chapter 1— when Napoleon had abdicated for the first go around, and the Bourbons were restored, also for the first go around— there actually remained, ahead of our personal Ariosto, only the three older half-brothers. Only three!... Three heirs between yourself and the succession, however, are woeful odds in peacetime.

But then Napoleon escaped, and there was Ligny. And Quatrebras.

And then there was Waterloo.

Mr Elliot's information had been exact, by the way; astonishingly exact, considering how early he had received it. It was one in four of British troops that fell at Waterloo.

The trouble is, the poor old French lost one in three.

— And all of a sudden, little Harry Clay, as he was known in Dashe— that nice boy, at Shepherd's cottage, with the hoyden of a sister— *he* is the Count Ariosto! Ah, praise the Lord! We're back on track with Romantic Fiction.

"And while the castle is a ruinous pigsty and all its lands long alienated (oh that those Italians understood the value of an entail!) —"

"Ruinous?" interrupted Nellie. "Structurally? I mean we couldn't hope to paint it in warm neutrals and sell it?" [†]

"Goodness no. It's fit only for banditti." Indeed, Mr Shepherd had found a rabble of discharged soldiers dwelling at leisure within its remaining rooms— the crypts, the stables, the old kitchen with its solitary, sagging armchair— stirring themselves only to exact, with threats of violence, regular tithes from the neighbouring peasants.

"Good Lord, papa! How shocking! And how relieved the people must have been, to hear there was yet a legitimate Count living, to take over!"

"Um— yes."

"So you roused the local forces and cast those ruffians out?"

"Yes, I think we've managed that, for now." There had been some resistance, naturally: there had been language; quite strong language. There *had* been, even, a point at which, set upon suddenly by all the cowardly ruffians at

---

[†] ...though— now that I think about it— she did seem to be looking *straight at* me.

once, seized and bound and with a cutlass pressed to his throat, Mr Shepherd had heard those chilling words so rare (hitherto) in Austen novels —

"Papa you know there is a lovely retirement community in Lyme. Perhaps it's time we had a talk."

"A– what?— No!– Good Lord Nellie I'm perfectly— what on earth do you mean? Anyway we're going to Italy! It knocks the spots off Lyme."

"Are we papa. And on what, exactly? And with what, exactly, in mind? Because, call me a frail irrational woman, call me lady even —" and Nellie leant back in her chair— "but one ruinous castle with a banditti problem sounds, to me, like a crashing great romantic liability. Not an asset." [†]

"In itself *yes*. In itself I couldn't agree with you *more*— that is, those are my thoughts exactly: those *were* exactly *my* thoughts, from the first day of looking the place over. But!– Your grandfather Bouscogne— your mother's *father*, you know— has inadvertently left us with his own, *adjoining* properties, and *these*, with only a little care and capital... Ah! I thought that would interrupt your lolling about in that wingchair."

"Properties? How many? What size? What– what are they growing? Which ones? Can you describe them?"

"We have the lot, my dear, the whole of your mother's childhood estate. She being his only child, and hence *her* young Ariosto his only surviving grandson, and he in turn dying intestate it all comes, no-one can hope to successfully dispute, to *our* young Ariosto, who being a minor has to hand it over, *pro. tem.*, to me. Us. Well you I suppose. As his legal guardian."

"Intestate?"

"Yes: and I have your grandfather's will right here. It explicitly cuts out your mother— cuts out everyone except her first son, your half-brother you know. It's a model of clarity, tighter than a – than anything."

Nellie glanced at the curlicued lines, nodded briefly. "Alright: if you say so then excellent. But– my half-brother. To be relying on the *lack* of a will from him is —"

"I agree my dear; a sad extremity. If necessary, we can rectify it."

"Mm... And are there no other potential claimants at all? Relatives, natural offspring, no other... what about debt-holders for example, debts?" – Mr Shepherd held up a finger, and began to fumble in his satchel – "And the farms of the estate; what shape are they in? I mean– scarcely a man left to hold a plough I understand, in many regions — there will be much to be done to make it profitable I'm sure. More than we can afford perhaps. Do you have figures? Accounts for previous years? And the fields and orchards and buildings themselves (are there still those orchards?– that mama used to tell us of?) —do they still stand? Are they quite without occupants?"

---

† At the time, I mean. I seem to have an image of her looking at me *quite directly*. And then the finger coming up...

"The orchards yes are still there." ("But in need of replanting by now?" "Er... I'm afraid I couldn't say." "Mm.") "The accounts —" and Mr Shepherd emerged from his satchel with a stack of files — "what I could lay my hands on at the time is *here*; debts noted too you can see though no doubt more will come forward once we... and the farms, from what I could ascertain by a quick tour on donkey, do appear to have been neglected somewhat, and yet the mansion-house was not quite deserted — old servants you know — broken windows boarded up at least; the roof needs attention."

Nellie, seizing and opening with eager impatience the file labelled *Bouscogne: Accounts*, nevertheless managed to also make a head movement indicative of rolling eyes, as one who would say 'roofs!' "Papa, do you have maps?" He shook his head. She glanced up. "Can you sketch me some?"

The afternoon draws on, and the pair are still bent, heads together, over a table piled with papers.

Evening. Three candles provide the light to which they hold the documents each is severally examining. In the grate, the coal chinks, susurrates.

"Papa, what on earth is a *gredon*?"

"Er—" Mr Shepherd extricates his mind briefly from the history of the Bouscogne estate olive press. "It's the local word for a pencil."

"Oh."

Half a minute later– "How bizarre."

Deep night. Mr Shepherd has smothered the dying fire with fresh coals and is prodding the smoking heap irritably. Nellie eases the poker from his hands, stirs the flame, gently, to new exertions. Now they rest their eyes on its dance.

"... and with Bonaparte back in custody, too, we may still rake something back in France. While I think you'll agree now: Italy is a very strong thing indeed. And— as for *you*!... Well. My dear girl." Mr Shepherd's voice nearly trembles with emotion. "You have done us proud. Done us proud. You have kept us afloat, and more than afloat. And because of that, we can hope with some confidence to turn the six or seven thousand we will have" (Nellie raised her eyebrows at this: where would the other couple of thou come from?)[†] "into a thriving estate in Italy, and a happy life for us all. Let us gird up our loins, and march forward. It will be" — and his eyes gleamed with firelight, his skin prickled— "a great adventure!"

"Mm."

Mr Shepherd rubbed his hands gently. "You are not quite persuaded, then?..."

"I'm— ... Let's sleep on it, and go into it again in the coming days."

The coalfire whispers to itself.

---

† — Also... about that finger —

"I can't argue, Penelope, that it's not a risk. It is a huge gamble, specifically in the most perilous sense that if it doesn't come off, the costs are high.

"But Nellie you've seen those accounts. You see how well the place can do if we get it going again. And you've said yourself: the chances are that with this peace, European landholders may do better in the near future than Britain, for all her Corn Laws. So yes the stakes are high, but the *odds:*— I think that the odds are very much in our favour."

"Mmm." Nellie pushed herself, slowly, to her feet. "Let's look at it again tomorrow."

*

The following days the pace accelerated. Nellie was soon fully occupied with efforts to learn all that could be learnt, at this remove, of the grape industry, and with reckonings of their margins and reserves under various combinations of costs, profits, losses. Seven lean years; she soon felt they could count on that.

Meanwhile, her father was pursuing certain lines of his own. Various men called at various hours, not all of them looking entirely happy, and once Nellie stepped out into the little hall of their rented rooms just as her father came in through the front door arm-in-arm with none other than Mr Smith.

No, not Mrs Smith of Westgate Buildings' husband — he's dead, remember — the one from London. The last of Mr Elliot's vulturine visitors.

"Ah, Penelope my dear; allow me to present Mr Smith. Mr Smith– my daughter Mrs Clay." Mr Smith bowed: his air was indecipherable.

"Mr Smith and I have met."

"Have you indeed? Well that's nice; but I'm afraid we must talk business just now, so perhaps — tell Frith, coffee in the parlour, Penelope?"

"Certainly, papa."

"— So yes Smith– you are quite right; wisest to deal with that little matter at once. Ah!– needs must when a certain gentleman drives!"

"Certainly, Mr Shepherd." And Mr Smith, following her father into the front parlour, could not entirely suppress a small grimace, compounded of cynical amusement and regret. Not all that much amusement, though: it was mostly regret.

*

Which reminds me:— What of Mr Elliot? How has he been occupying himself since abdication, and where is he now?

Chapter 19

Mr Elliot has been having quite a nice time, as usual. Following the closure of the Belgrave Square house he did feel himself, for a while there, to be at something of a loose end, but he solved that by plunging into a vortex of dissipation. You may well object that Jane Austen advises against immersing one's characters in this way, but I confess that it seems beyond my powers, by this stage, to prevent Mr Elliot from doing whatever he pleases— and anyway the vortex, like all else that is morally denaturing, altered Mr Elliot not a whit. After a decent interval, he popped out the other end of it, looking pretty much as *soigné* as ever. He straightened his cuffs, and went off in search of his cousin Elizabeth; he had decided to marry her.

This accomplished, and the renters of Kellynch ejected, we find him today settled contentedly in Kellynch Hall with his wife at his side. She is smiling fixedly.

On the other side of him is his father-in-law. Sir Walter is smiling fixedly too: Mr Elliot has kindly paid off a great many of Sir Walter's outstanding debts— not all, no; but a great many— and the new son-in-law does tend to harp upon this, and upon the expenses of Kellynch, and upon the need for economy, and so on, with a civil persistence, which makes said father-in-law rather pine for the peace and retirement of Bath...

And of course Mr Elliot would have been landed with those bills anyway when the old man died, plus the extra interest, so his generosity made financial sense quite apart from creating, as indicated, an exquisitely humiliating sense of obligation in Sir Walter. As for Sir Walter's nostalgia for Bath, Mr Elliot is completely supportive of it and the sooner the better. The snag is this: one needs, first, to clinch a tight, conclusive ligature about the Baronet's ageing but still dangerous virility.

—So:– where *is* Mrs Clay, these days?

*

Here she is, in London still. She is arguing with her father about taking the children to Italy.

The children are urgent that they should come. Letter after splashily-inked letter is arriving at the London lodgings, begging in English, French, and Italian (that is Ariosto, proving his usefulness) and Byronic tetrameters that gesture at suicide (Josephine, obviously) that they should leave school and England and 'work on the estate', as the boy puts it.

('Partake of the Great Adventure': Josephine.)

Nellie was horrified.

'Adventure' is now most often synonymous with a guided experience constrained within limits attested to minimise successful law suits. In those days, though, something wasn't an 'adventure' at all if Death could appear in it only as an affronting and actionable surprise. In contrast, the children's schools were well-established institutions whose rational regimes, airy locations and good food were all reflected in their low mortality rates. "Surely, papa, they would be safer staying here? And their education! How much time will we have for that, engaged as we will be in all the business before us?"

"Safer— yes well. Italy is very healthy, my dear. It's like anywhere, outside of the cities and the towns and so on: you just have to separate the cesspit from the house. As for their education– if our future is in Italy, is it not wiser to give them an Italian education?"

Nellie lifted her eyebrows. "You mean there is such a thing?"

"Of course there is, don't be so British and insular. And then there is the self-education offered by a decent private library. Such as mine. How else do you think your mother could quote Sappho?– At such length? I can't say I always enjoyed it, but her knowledge of the literature could not be faulted. They won't learn that at some Academy for Young Whatsits, will they?"

Also— and although he did not confess this to his daughter— Mr Shepherd was by now calling in so many old debts, of such sensitive kinds, and involving exchanges of so delicate a nature, that England would subsequently be, for them, so to speak, a squeezed orange.

"A steady country society about us. Recognised wherever they ramble... and treated, you may be sure, with the consideration appropriate to their local status. I mean!– The chief landowners in the region!"

Nellie lifted her head.

"... Growing up as the first family in the county!" pursued her father promptly, "and– welcomed, yes, wherever they may ramble! For to them— to us— every house will be open; every dwelling a port, say, in an unexpected rainstorm. Imagine!– the local gentry hurrying our two little adventurers to the drawing-room fire— 'O _do_ take _your wet jacket off young Master Bouscogne, Miss Bouscogne, and allow me, too, to send for the carriage..."_ (Nellie swallowed–) _"...but first you simply must take a little something, and meet the all family, we do not see nearly enough of you, here at Keelinch Hall!"'_ Nellie had began to smile. "We should all take the name Bouscogne, don't you think, Nell?"

Bouscogne.

Mrs Bouscogne.

"_Senora_ Bouscogne— or Madame Bouscogne; they use both forms there. Which do you prefer, Nellie?"

Still, she could not quite allow herself to be persuaded.

"Though I suppose you could be exotic, and insist on everyone calling you _Mrs._"

Still, there was the other image.

"'Mrs Penelope Bouscogne'!" pursued her father. "It sounds good!"

A bewildered Josephine, clutching Ariosto by the hand, in some dreadful provincial Italian port. Penniless, and utterly alone.

"What if— well— Accidents, papa. Or ill-health. I mean right now they are unable even to speak the local dialect. If anything happened..."

Her father looked at her. She ducked her head.

"I suppose Josephine could always teach. English. Or singing or something. But if they were in England, at least there would be the Barratts... No—" for her father had opened his mouth to argue. "No— just... We'll see. Let's see."

Chapter 20

This is all very nice for Nellie, no doubt; her father safe, five thousand pounds in the bank. New plot lines opening up. Overseas travel looming, even.

And no doubt she deserves it: no doubt she's earned it.

We all know, however, that overseas travel never should happen in Austen.

And new plot lines emerging this late, that's poor structuring... Oh dear. I'm beginning to wonder if we're not heading for one of those rushed, scrambly sorts of endings, where the lovers' reconciliation has to be patched together as a sort of synopsis.

The really worrying thing, though, I've just realised, is the absence of lovers. Did you pick that? Have *you* been worrying about that? My God, half way through Vol. 3 and still no hero. I've only just noticed.

*

I mean, I always assumed that the lover question would sort itself out as we went along. I assumed— very naturally, I think— I mean, I think it was perfectly *reasonable* in me to assume it— that once I got her to Bath, going to all those concerts, all those parties– well! Nellie would eventually just attract someone. I suppose I proceeded on the assumption that, by Volume III, a competent woman would have someone in tow.

I mean, s*he's* so keen on getting the Elliot girls married off.

Seems to think it's a snip!

— Oh Lord.

The truth is, I'm starting to get that sick feeling you get when a major project is due, and you haven't done a thing on it, really; you've just had fun.

Fun!

Christ.

*

Still, there it is.

No good crying over spilt milk. We must soldier on.

If Penelope Clay, after all this time— and at this frighteningly late stage of the book— is not going to discharge even the most basic duties of a heroine, we must look elsewhere. And fast. *Some* yearning heart must find fulfilment in love. *Some* poignant outcast, reduced over the course of the story to the extremes of despair, and indigence too ideally, must be elevated by a last-minute reconciliation with the loved one to the bridal altar and bliss, God damn it.

I think we must leave aside the Tory gentleman. The depth of his feeling for Nellie is unknown, and in any case he can't marry her without his wife expiring absolutely *prontissimo,* so that he can get through a year's mourning in time to marry Mrs Clay by the last chapter, which would be simultaneously much too slow for our needs and yet, also, a bit lickety-split to be quite romantic.

What's left?

Chapter   21

There is— there always has been— Sir Walter.

Here he is, leaning on a gate in Kellynch park, a withered hazelnut forming the sketchiest of shelters between his complexion and a small, sharp-toothed winter wind. He spends more and more time outdoors, lately. In spite of the horrid weather.

You see, his favourite chair by the drawing-room fire tends, so often these days, to be occupied– and all the other chairs feel funny to sit in. His study, little used until now, has restless feet criss-crossing it– Mr Elliot often barges in, and then sees him and halts and says 'Oh—excuse me Sir Walter–" and goes out again, which is...

And when he *is* there— when he is anywhere— servants are constantly coming to bring him little messages, from his son-in-law; or his son-in-law's man, who has taken over the stewardship; niggly little queries, seeking detailed information about this, or that, which Sir Walter never has to hand, and never did. His own dressing-room is similarly haunted by his valet. Varens. He is no longer sure about Varens... the man is behaving oddly these days...

So here is Sir Walter, out of doors; leaning on the gnarled wood of the gate, which is blackened by rain, and damp, and slippery, and looking sadly at the grazing carriage-horses. He has a book in his hand.

No, not the Baronetage. It is a small book— a portable book.
A book of poetry.

> *John Anderson my Jo, John,*
> *When we were first acquent,*
> *Your locks were like the raven, Jo,*
> *Your bonie brow was brent...*

—what *did* brent mean? wondered Sir Walter, not for the first time. This
was his favourite poem; had been his favourite poem, from the day he had sat
upon this book where it lay abandoned on a seat in the library, into which he
had wandered quite often in the weeks after Elizabeth's marriage, in a vague
attempt to— what, exactly?... so 'brent' was preying on his mind a bit.

Still; it must be something good.

Unlike *'beld'*. Which sounded dreadful.

Sir Walter sighed quietly, and put a tentative hand up to his hair. His new
son-in-law had, courteously but firmly, put an end to Sir Walter's use of hair
powder. "Too old-fashioned for a man of your high style, Sir Walter!" was
what he had said. "Think, too, of the economies it represents."

In private, and afterwards, Elizabeth had tried to defend her father (it had
been only just after her marriage): Sir Walter, already outdoors, already haunt-
ing the terrace by the ground floor windows, had heard them at it. And in
reply, Mr Elliot had said— Sir Walter could hear him saying it, still— "It
makes him look like a footman, for heaven's sake. I'm sick of looking at it.
The man's embarrassment enough as it is."

So now Sir Walter's hair was fashionably short, and fashionably
unpowdered; and it must be this which was having such a sudden ageing
effect on his face.

> *But now your brow is beld, John;*
> *Your locks are like the snow...*

Now, well *that* wasn't right. It was more between iron grey and lifeless
brown. But, he was pretty sure his brow was beld. Whatever that was.

Perhaps, it was even very beld.

The next two lines, though, rewarded the courage of the resolute reader:
soothed the spirit, and elevated the eyes— the eyes of the heart— to heights it
- they- it— had never thought to glimpse, nor rest upon;

> *But blessings on your frosty pow*
> *John Anderson, my jo."*

Peculiar, the words these Scottish fellows used. And yet, one caught the
meaning of it, all the same. Caught it perfectly. Sir Walter, in his– well– as life

progressed— was beginning to understand why some people made such a fuss about poetry.

*

So that's Sir Walter.

Mm.

As a candidate, though, he does have powerful support in Mr Elliot, who is by now more than tired of having him hanging about the place. Even as Sir Walter sighs over the grazing carriage horses, indoors and upstairs Mr Elliot is remarking to his wife; "Your father does not seem perfectly happy, my dear".

He has sauntered into her dressing room, where she sits at her toilette, and has sent away her maid. "I begin to feel quite concerned for him. We will be in London ourselves in a matter of days; it seems sad, rather, to leave him all alone here. Such a pity he cannot afford to join us there. But he has economies to make. Ah, we can only discharge so much of his debt, my dear— only so much."

(You see? It can be useful, at times, to have Sir Walter committed to economies: and fun, too.)

Elizabeth looked carefully at her husband, but she did not venture a reply.

"How to keep him happy, then? In our absence. Happy, and safe. Mm?"

From Elizabeth, another careful look.

"Well? I am awaiting your suggestions, O wife of my bosom."

"Ah— Well... What would you suggest?"

"Now now. You don't sneak out of it that way."

Elizabeth turned her head away; bit her lip. Mr Elliot was still watching her, though, in the dressing-table mirror. She looked up into it.

He smiled broadly at her.

After a little more silence, in which Elizabeth held her lowered face over her fingernails, she hazarded the observation that Sir Walter had seemed very happy in Bath.

"Quite right! Quite right, my dear. I was thinking exactly that myself."

At this unexpected success, Miss-Elliot-that-was chanced raising her head and scrutinising him— briefly and circumspectly, and still in the mirror.

"Bath!" continued Mr Elliot. "He was so happy in Bath. I feel that we should get him back there."

Although in her new role as Mr Elliot's wife, Elizabeth had necessarily left her parental family and cleaved only unto Mr Elliot, still, the idea of losing her father's presence set scurrying a frantic panic in her heart.

However, there was nothing she could do to prevent it, beyond concealing as completely as possible how much it dismayed her. She kept silence still, therefore— and carefully averted her face, so that this time her countenance could not be seen either in the mirror, or in the flesh.

Mr Elliot, who could read her like a book, allowed his gaze to linger on her bent form for a minute... But there was more to be done.

"Ideally, I feel that he should marry again."

And now Elizabeth actually spun around. With widened eyes, and open mouth, hands spread and clutching at the dressing table, her chair-back, she stared at him.

"Mmm", resumed Mr Elliot, eventually. "Yes; I think he should marry again, and then, settle in Bath. Close your mouth, O wife of my bosom. You look like a frog."

... So where, and o where, *was* Mrs Clay now?

He sauntered out of his wife's *chichi* dressing-room and bounced down the luxuriously-carved main staircase, across the lofty hall which would impress any guest, to the tastefully-decorated study with its ancient, splendid linenfold panelling.

There, he rang the bell.

"Tell Cubbins that we will be leaving for the London house in three days. Pack for Sir Walter too. We will be taking him with us."

*

Nellie herself— as regards Sir Walter— sometimes talks of him in ways that show her not indifferent to his wellbeing.

Listen, for example, to this evening's conversation, as she sits with her father over the fire of their London lodgings...

"...safer and faster to travel by sea, Nell. By sea, we avoid as far as possible the whole post-war mess; and believe me my dear, it is a mess. No lack of sea-men and vessels at a loose end now, I should imagine. Surely sea travel should be *cheaper* than before?"

Nellie grimaced. "I suppose once things have settled down, it will be. In the old days I would have asked about, among my seafaring acquaintance; I'm sure I could have tracked down a cheaper passage than the shockers they quoted me today. If only we were leaving from Plymouth!"

"Well as to that..." Mr Shepherd looked up from his notebook; "...hm!— Why should we not? I must journey westward as it is, to wrap up some little matters about Kellynch."

"Ah. Easier to carry on to Plymouth after that."

"For the children, too; closer to Plymouth than it is to us here."

(They'll be getting to Sir Walter soon, don't worry...)

"Indeed Nellie, your intimacy with a naval port, its people its pursuits *et cet-era*— this could be invaluable. A mere eight and a half thousand pounds" — (eight? *And* a half? wondered Nellie)— "well; I would be happier with a more

reasonable sum for a family to begin such a venture upon. And every pound
we can save in the business of travel will be a pound more to spend at the
other end... Should we not all make our final arrangements from Plymouth,
then?"

A hum of anxious pleasure began to make itself felt, in and about the
region of Nellie's heart. "It would seem to make sense", she commenced; hes-
itant. "Usually, lodgings would be cheaper there, too. Though– just now– a
great many officers and men, no doubt, paid off and... shops out of business...
everything, perhaps, very different from before..." Her voice trailed away.

"Then the first thing to do is to write to your Barratts? Enquire. See what
they advise."

Nellie nodded... then nodded again, more emphatically.

"Hmm?"

"What?"

"You seem to have reservations, my dear."

"No yes I was just thinking— I could send them the cost of the postage
under the seal. So that would be alright..."

Her father continued to eye her enquiringly.

"Now– Papa you mentioned Kellynch."

(Ah! I told you, didn't I?)

"There is something I would wish Sir Walter to know before we depart.
Only I can't possibly write to him."

"Such delicacy! Heavens Nellie you're a widow, not a Miss on her promotion."

"No I mean— don't be silly papa. I mean, I'm quite sure Sir Walter's correspondence doesn't reach him before it's been read first by that man. Mine
never did. And I'd like to leave him— I'm sure you'll understand this point,
and support me on this, papa— leave him with a little information."

Mr Shepherd was attentive.

"Just a little supply of names, I was thinking: unless you have a better suggestion, papa?" ... but Mr Shepherd was suspending judgement... "Something
that he might be able to draw on, if things do ever get– well— bad for him.
The trouble is, I know; it's got to be very simple. I mean, he has to be able to
memorise it, and then, dispose of the note; so that it's only in his head."

Mr Shepherd was incredulous.

But Nellie pushed on: "There's that Mrs Smith I told you about, in Bath...
Though– I don't know— alright she's possibly not much use. But then there's
also a Dr Mills, here in London, that Mr Elliot *would* keep calling on, and he
took me along once too— poor man looked at him like a rabbit at a stoat, and
I really felt he would welcome an ally, it would take only the littlest push,
and... yes, there are a couple of others. From the Madame Penelope days."

"So you would like to write him a list? An annotated list, with explanations? My dear it is hopeless— the man is hopeless, believe me. He will never get his head around it, and even if he did, he would have no idea how to use the information or when to deploy it. He would simply moon about with this list in his hand until everyone got suspicious, and it would all come out, and then I'm quite sure your Mr Elliot would have much better ideas about what to do with your list of names– ideas of his own— and it would not do anyone any good at all. No", for Nellie began to speak; "No my dear: all we can do for Sir Walter, all anyone can do for Sir Walter, is to try to get him into a safe pair of hands."

"But exactly. Whose? He doesn't even have Hardcastle any more— Mr Elliot has put in his own man as steward."

"Yes I know; and I feel very upset about that. Hardcastle is a good man and a dear friend." Nellie glanced at her father suspiciously. "And that is why I will just pop down to Kellynch and see if I can't do something about that too, before we leave."

"They may not be at Kellynch. They may well be in town already; the Elliots."

"Yes they may. I'll write- no- I'll speak to his wine merchant. They always order through the same man when they're in London, so he's sure to know all about it."

"And another thing papa—"

(There! You see? Still, Sir Walter's needs fill Nellie's mind!)

"—the contents of the Belgrave Square house are coming up for auction. I think it's best if I buy back all of my clothes that I can."

(Oh.)

"They already fit me to perfection; no alterations, no work; but it means some immediate expenses..."

— and the back-and-forth of planning continues, far into the night.

Chapter 22

The wine merchant was as willing as ever to rabbit on about his customers. "Arrived only last night, yes, this very night past, very late, near on midnight and cranky enough so *I* hear, even though they came in *both* coaches. Oh no they're not at the old place; no no, you won't find them there! Took a quite a different sort of place, *this* time"— and he mentioned a street— "more to the taste, these days, of the young fashionable gentlemen, and the ladies. But then *you'll* be looking to catch Sir Walter, mm...?— ah I thought so!- yes, and he'll be hanging about the drawing-room this time of day, nothing more certain, you'll hear that from all who know! Mr Elliot and Mrs— you know, Miss

Elliot as was— everyone wants *them,* they'll be out to dinner again, every blessed night, just like last time. Leave the old codger to it, they do."

'Codger?' wondered Mr Shepherd. *Old* codger? He'd been 'the Baronet' to this man, when he and Mr Shepherd had last spoken. Even, after large orders, 'his lordship'.

The heir, however, was in the merchant's good books; in everybody's good books, he averred. Not only had the young gentleman, on his marriage, paid up many of the old codger's debts, he had also been so kind as to give people a hint, as he did so— just a hint, as to the worry Sir Walter's spending habits were to his family, and how grateful he, Mr Elliot, would be, if the establishments concerned did not yield again to any, as to say, requests for renewed credit. Much as it pained him to mention anything about it, oh, you could see how it pained him!

"Such a shame, Sir Walter letting the young people down like that— landing them with such expenses, at the very start of their married life. A happy day it will be, when we have a Sir William to deal with, you'll hear that from all who know."

*

A lifetime's experience of delicate negotiations had taught Mr Shepherd enormous self-control, but he still found it almost impossible, at first, to look away from Sir Walter's hair. God it was awful. And so ageing! He blessed the light at his rear— Mr Shepherd, wherever he was, and whoever he was with, nearly always managed to sit with the light at his rear— and dragged at least some fraction of his truant attention back to the intonation patterns of Sir Walter's speech. Sooner or later the man was bound to stop. Oh— he had.

"Ah, Sir Walter, indeed, yes yes indeed, no-one could put it better. And I need not say, Sir Walter, that the years I have spent serving you, and the ancient seat of Kellynch, have been among the most privileged and honoured of my life, while the memory of the paternal care afforded my daughter, when she had the extraordinary blessing and advantage of moving with you and Miss Elliot in your elevated circle in Bath, will remain with her all her days, and make of her a better woman, Sir Walter, a better woman." Sir Walter stared gloomily at his feet. "Ah, Sir Walter, what cares our children give us! And the humbler amongst us cannot hope to see such magnificent return for that care, as the beautiful Mrs Elliot, and her sister, have brought recently to the house of Elliot; such congratulations, Sir Walter, as must have flowed in upon you from all sides!"

So far was all on automatic pilot, but now there was a point or two he needed to make.

"It is, indeed, the continuance of my cares for your noble seat that presses upon my mind. For though I may soon be its steward no longer in law, Sir

Walter, in my heart I cannot set aside that honourable toil so lightly. I understand that Hardcastle has been let go, and an interim steward appointed? — a
certain Mr Townsend?"

Sir Walter bowed his head, in signification of dignified agreement. Gosh —
was that a glimpse of pale scalp, through the darker strands of unpowdered
hair? "Mr Elliot recommended him."

"Ah well then– well then. I am sure he must be excellent; excellent, for a
city man. Young Mr Elliot, *being* an Elliot, is sure to be a good judge of men!"

Sir Walter inclined his head again, a fraction less graciously this time, and–
yes, the old codger was definitely getting thin on top.

"But— *the young*, you know! Well, your heir is spoken of, about town, as
'the *young* Mr Elliot', is he not? Perhaps his choice of steward, at this point in
his *young* life, is not quite the choice that he himself would make, later, as an
experienced *man*; not the choice that an experienced *landholder*, such as yourself, would have made– that is– forgive me if I speak freely Sir Walter– an old
family retainer like myself— we do presume upon our richness of years sometimes!"

But Sir Walter was flashing his scalp again, with rather more sincere enthusiasm, so Mr Shepherd pressed on without further camouflage. "Mm– those
of us who have seen *more* of life, and life on a *landed* estate, you know, an *old*
estate— it is not the same, is it, in management, as the relatively straightfor-
ward affairs of a city man such as the youngster– the *young heir* do *please* excuse
me I meant to say– Mr Elliot, that is; concerned with nothing but stocks and
shares and so on?"

"Absolutely not!" Sir Walter had got his drift now; it was probably the first
time in his life that the idea of being rich in years had been of any support to
his mind. "Just what I have been thinking to myself!"

"Ah, Sir Walter. Of course you have. Everyone speaks of the kindliness
which you have shown to the youngs- the young *heir*– in this matter; accepting
his choice of man, when your own wide experience, the interests of your
inherited responsibilities, point so clearly another way! Everyone appreciates
the delicate position that the– that you have found yourself placed in."

And so on.

The upshot, after half an hour of smooth talking and three brandies (three!
It used to be one!), was the desired rearrangement of all the little points that
had been bothering Nellie, so that was good. Hardcastle would once more
take up the duties of steward, and this time the title too, reporting to Sir Walter again, just as he had in Mr Shepherd's absence; and the last of Mr Shepherd's duties towards Kellynch estate was to dictate a letter to Mr Elliot and
his Mr Townsend, congratulating them on the latter's release from an onerous
duty, and his full return, as Mr Elliot's man of business, to the care of his, Mr
Elliot's, more pressing affairs. Signed, Sir Walter Elliot.

Heaven knows if it will stick though, thought Mr Shepherd. He was glad to put this plum back into Hardcastle's basket; he and his son too: good men for the estate. As long as this young Mr Elliot did not again take a fancy to interfere. And as to that– lap of the Gods. He moved to take his leave.

But—

"And what takes you from England again so soon, Shepherd?"

"Family matters yet again, as I say, Sir Walter; family matters."

"I understood, from your letter of September— your Paris letter— that you have had some little success, with regaining your possessions there?... which must be most gratifying...?"

"Ah yes. Some little success. Just as you say, Sir Walter. Just enough for a cautious economical family to be going on with."

"And then– Madame Penelope... also leaves with you?"

A blank moment, while Mr Shepherd figured out who Sir Walter meant. "Yes my daughter yes; and the children too."

"... and... permanently?"

"Oh yes."

Sir Walter nodded; nodded some more; finished his brandy. Reached for another.

Better not mention that to Nellie.

"And..." Sir Walter was casting about..."you will be returning, I suppose, to that lovely dwelling of yours, that one hears of– in *Paris*— I understand? A pleasant part of the city? I have no doubt?"

Mr Shepherd hesitated; glanced towards the door; suppressed a sigh.

This would be a long conversation, if they were to have it.

And, why have it?

Long conversations with Sir Walter had been among his greatest amusements, in those years he had spent, post-prison, as steward of Kellynch. He used to feel, at times, that he could not give his employer too much of his attention; used to delight in seeing how massive a mockery he could get the old chap to swallow, as respectful praise given in good faith. Alone of an evening over his little parlour fire, wrapped to the eyes in his dressing-gown and with a glass in his hand— and looking and sounding rather like a skinny little ageing monkey, dear reader— he had spent hours giggling to himself as he sketched out absolute whoppers. And then, later, in Sir Walter's company, he would spend more hours anticipating just the perfect opportunity to dose him one— always striving, of course, to give them as unstudied an air as possible.

Well.

Well well.

That kind of thing happens, when a man hasn't enough to do.

He had more than enough to do now, goodness knows! It was a miracle his lungs were standing the pace.

Yet:–

"Come Shepherd! We have spoken thus far only of Kellynch affairs: we have spoken only of business! Sit back again, and let us have another brandy, and let me hear of your plans for France! My own family is out, as you know; you can make yourself quite comfortable."

"Ah Sir Walter, you are magnanimity itself..."

— And could he really be so indifferent? Because, in the old days, again; how many happy evenings would he have taken, to shape this news into the most disorienting imaginable series of explosions, trip-wires, man-traps, through which he, in high glee, would have led the reeling Sir Walter!

And now? Nothing more than:–

"It transpires that our young Ariosto– you know my grandson, my *wife's* grandson to be precise, my daughter's *nephew*, little Ariosto–" Sir Walter raised his head in signification of dignified recognition (though one could not but deprecate that name!)— "Well, the lad has inherited at last, in Italy and also yes in France; adjoining places, you see; his grandfather on each side well his grandfather on the *French* side and what is *left* of the Italian side, which is precious little, no more than a ruin alas!"

Sir Walter's nod commiserated: dago ruins.

"So we will be going out, all of us, as a family, to set the place to rights — the war, you know— and– well in short, our future is there."

"Then *congratulations* are clearly in order, Shepherd! Congratulations! A nice little property for you all, I hope?"

Mr Shepherd gave names and localities, and mentioned a total acreage. Sir Walter choked in a complicated way on his brandy. "And of course there is the title, too– for what it is worth. *Italian* titles, don't you know, Sir Walter, how often have we spoken of *them!*"— with a knowing chuckle; Sir Walter was goggling, and mopping his face, and murmuring vaguely. "Still; *as* a title, it *is* reasonably old: one must, at least, grant it that."

"Noblesse d'épée..." Sir Walter offered, at hazard, crumpling his handkerchief into a messy ball.

"Pretty much; pretty much", conceded his ex-steward. "Extant, at any rate, as far back as records *do* exist for the region, so we are looking at a minimum — and one *should* only mention minimums, you know— I'm a careful man, Sir Walter as I hope you will attest ha ha!– a careful man! — a minimum of seven hundred years. Dear me Sir Walter. Shall I ring for a servant?"

It was rather fun still. Call him a giddy goat; but yes it was rather fun.

...But not *that* much fun. It subsequently took twenty determined minutes to extricate himself merely from the drawing-room, and even then Sir Walter followed him out into the hall, and stood there, talking and talking still. "Mr Shepherd you must come to us again! In fact– you will stay to dinner? Can I not press you to stay, to dine with me; just a sup, you know; just 'pot-luck', as our people say! I do however have some fine old cognac; which I do not offer to most men; but I'm sure you, with your French-educated palate, will be capable of appreciating it!"

But Mr Shepherd regretted, it was fully three o'clock, things to do people to see. Perhaps some other time.

"Absolutely, absolutely! I will send a card. That is..."

Don't be foolish man. Your daughter would die of shame and vexation. After first killing you– Mr Shepherd arranged his scarf carefully about his throat.

"...Oh! And I believe I must mention— The young Mr Elliot– the *youngster* you know!" Sir Walter chuckled, "I believe he has been looking for you, Mr Shepherd! He, too, would like to see– that is, I forgot to mention... he has been looking high and low!"

Which is to say, he'd dispatched a three-liner to Shepherd, via Bletchley, that morning, appointing a meeting— Mr Shepherd was to find the note awaiting him when he arrived home.

"Ah, it is easier for the lesser to find out the great, than for the great to find us out!" The unction slipped easily from his lips as he shrugged himself, with business-like relief, in to his surtout— "(thank you, Cubbins)"— it being a phrase which he had invoked a thousand times to cover a quiet day spent, invisible, about his own affairs; puttering around Dashe, lolling in his garden. Sir Walter's chuckle faltered. There flew, between them, the tiniest of glances.

"So— perhaps, er Mr Shepherd, if your er daughter takes morning calls, I– we– I might venture...?" —and Sir Walter waved his glass vaguely. Social relations with one's daughter's ex-best-friend, one's son-in-law's ex-mistress, is capable of all sorts of malicious misconstruction. Nevertheless. Surely he, Sir Walter, a man of the world, could...

And besides— A Continental title! It opens up all sorts of vistas.

Vistas, quite unEnglish in many of their tendencies...

Mr Shepherd looked, not exactly *at* Sir Walter, but about him.

At his hair. At the glass, still in his hand.

At his new season's clothes; tailored, with painful sharpness over his subtly sagging figure: the slump of his belly was starting to make itself seen, at last, through the corset. He looked, too, at the empty drawing-room behind them, to which Sir Walter must return when Mr Shepherd had exited: there to sit, alone.

There was something different, too, about the way the Baronet stood. There was the suggestion of a hunch.

He even smelt different.

Only last September, when Mr Shepherd had packed the Elliots into their carriage and waved them all off to Bath, he would have given the old blighter twenty good years at least: a valuable husband, in spite of that entail.

Now: six to eight, tops. If the drinking continued to accelerate, three to five, or even less.

... And then there was Mr Elliot. And his Dr Mills, that Nellie had spoken of...

   No.

No: as Sir Walter was positioned now, an alliance of even the loosest sort must be not only dull, stale, and flat, but also most likely unprofitable. Complicated, and probably quite short.

"I am overwhelmed by your kindness, Sir Walter, I am quite overcome. But we are in the process of decamping to Plymouth, from which we will make our final arrangements; Nellie calculates on securing a much cheaper passage to Italy from Plymouth. She knows people."

"Plymouth? Madame Penelope mentioned– You will be staying, then, with the Countess of...?"

"No, we will take rooms. But we will be staying in the first instance with the Barratts. Above their shop. A ship chandlery; in Gun Lane; perhaps Nellie has mentioned them, too?"

Sir Walter's chin was sinking.

"Convenient, to live above one's shop, don't you think? I often wished I could."

The convivial smile was drooping, melting, into a mortified gape.

...Yet the savour of the business was gone.

"Sir Walter. We have so little for this venture that we need to husband every penny we have. It will take us the rest of our lives, perhaps, to get the estate back on its feet. Apart from anything else, it is sure to be carrying debts."

"And–"

Mr Shepherd glanced back, surprised.

Sir Walter was holding, yet, a tentative hand towards his turning guest.

"And so– perhaps then if I were to visit very quickly— tomorrow, perhaps, before you all..."

"My daughter has gone ahead of me, Sir Walter. She left this morning."

*

Mr Shepherd is thorough as always. He follows his self-imposed task through to the end; and next day, in that fashionable house in that newly-fashionable street, Mr Elliot breaks the seal on Shepherd's last letter, and holds it up the grey light of a city morning, to read...

> *... receipt of your generous note! I hurried around immediately of course, your letter still in my hand, and was most distressed to find you out... anticipate your wishes... found Sir Walter reluctant to lose his new-found command of your man Mr Townsend's time! His superior talents... cost to yourself...*

What??? The–

> *... simple rural affairs devolve to old Hardcastle. I am delighted to have persuaded Sir Walter on your behalf!*

Christ! Who is this busybody little shit!!! And then— look at this!—

> *And thus, alas, it will never be my fortune to see the house of Elliot's rising son*

Screw him.

> *if an old man may be permitted his flights of fancy!*

No *screw* him!

He'd actually been prepared to take on this man's daughter, with all her clod-hopping associations— *This*, then! This, was his return!

> *... boxes corded... distant lands, such regrets, Adieu* and so on, Your devoted servant, Mr S.

The letter trembled in his hand as there flowed, through Mr Elliot, that torrent of feeling which wives, servants, dogs, fled with all silence and all swiftness.

Then he flicked the letter onto the library desk. Fuck him.

Estate servant.

And his shop-soiled daughter– Heavens! What had he been thinking.

By the time he had pushed his chair out from the table his mood had finished its shift. I mean any old dame would do; as long as she was past child-bearing age. Some old girl. Some old widow, without children.

Some *other* widow without children!

By God!– He could think of– one, two— *three* even, (though *she* was...)... Lord!— There must be simply dozens of suitable women up for the season right now!

If Mrs Clay thought she had him over a barrel, how wrong she was. If Mrs Clay thought she was the only infertile woman he could lay his hands on, what a fool the woman must be!

The library was too small to contain him.

"Dear Elizabeth!" he exclaimed, breezing into the drawing-room. "We really must catch up with our charming cousin Lady Dalrymple! She's in town, *n'est-ce pas?*— visiting that daughter of hers, that little Mrs Whosit, that you were such great friends with."

Elizabeth, who had shied like a startled horse at her husband's sudden appearance, fixed her eyes on him now in bewilderment. "Yes of course Mr Elliot—"

"*Dear* Mr Elliot" interjected her husband.

"— my *dear* Mr Elliot—"

"No no; just 'dear'. I don't like the way some women say 'my'. It's vulgar, don't you think?"

"... dear Mr Elliot... I would like it of all things. To see our cousins again. But, are you sure—"

"Of course I'm sure or I wouldn't have said it. Send her a card and invite her to dinner. Just herself and the girl and her husband; that way we can put her next to Sir Walter."

Light dawned on Elizabeth's face.

Mr Elliot smirked into it. "You know you're not nearly as sharp as Anne. *She*, now, would have seen what I meant in an instant. So retiring, so high-minded and yet— so piercingly intelligent, your sister."

Elizabeth bit her lip, silently, until the blood came.

"Out of quite a different mould. People often remark on it." His wife muttered something. "What? Wipe your lip."

"I don't hear them say it."

"Well of course they wouldn't say it to *you*."

The woman had extracted her handkerchief and was dabbing her chin.

Yet still:

"Lady Dalrymple doesn't want to get married again."

"Really?"

"She said so."

"Really?"

"In Bath. She told papa: she has no thoughts of matrimony at present."

"Oh, I think you'll find she does."

Elizabeth lowered her head.

Eventually—

"Wouldn't she want to live at Kellynch?"

"Oh I think you'll find, she won't."

*

That evening, at the Waverley ball, they ran into her anyway; lumpy, dumpy Lady D., looking more homely than ever in these surroundings, and her little daughter, who in her turn was looking even peakier, probably pregnant by now. Elizabeth was thus able to deliver the invitations in person, and Mr Elliot, to follow them up with smiles and light banter, and two dances apiece.

And the Dowager Viscountess was of course delighted to accept the invitation. Absolutely delighted.

No but she was charmed, at the prospect!

By the end of the ball, she was *overjoyed,* even, and her elderly, dull cheeks quite flushed, her eyes sparkled, at the thought of the visitings that lay ahead, this season, with the dear young Elliots.

Mr Elliot coruscated more brightly than ever that evening. Everybody noticed: everybody remarked upon Mr Elliot and his regal, silent bride. What a difference it makes to a man; a suitable marriage.

Chapter   23

For Nellie today, London and all those within it are two hundred miles away. It is morning, and sunlight flashes from the stagecoach as it jolts and rocks down the final hill into Plymouth. Eager passengers — Nellie among them — are starting to peer, from its windows, towards their destination. From the imperial above her comes the first hullooing. The horses, too, are pulling on the drag, eager in spite of their weary legs; just ahead, right there, is the White Hart, and rest, and water and mash, and a good hard rub-down all over. And Mr Barratt!

How has he got away from the shop at this time of day?

Alice too; Alice is there, next to him!... Oh dear, she hopes he hasn't lost wages for her sake... And– that elderly lady, so upright on the other side of dear Mr Barratt, a hand on his arm, looking alert and brisk in a respectable brown stuff dress — it is the Countess! And the cheering and waving from the passengers, and the responding calls from the little crowd awaiting the coach, cannot drown out the boom of Mr Barratt's bass, calling out her name.

Nellie withdrew her head, which she had been craning in so very unsophisticated a fashion from the coach window — her place was instantly taken by someone else— and fussed about her in joyful, abashed distraction. Her reticule, where is her reticule? Her bandbox– oh dear oh dear the happiness of it, they are here to welcome her— in spite of— They are *all* here! The door swings open in a burst of light and noise, and everyone about her is in a scramble— someone knocks her elbow, and she drops her bandbox — and as she leans forward to rescue it (getting smacked on the head by a knee as she does so) tears spill from her eyes, making everything harder still.

She was the last, in consequence, to wobble up to the coach door, various ill-assorted bundles slipping from her hands and under her arms.

Strong brown hands corralled the errant bandbox, collared a hastily-rolled rug, and then relieved her of the reticule and passed these things on briskly out of sight. Then the same strong hands and their associated brawny arms pluck Nellie from where she dithers, on the lip of the coach step; swing her delightedly around, and place her— softly, delicately— here, back to earth, on the cobbles of Plymouth.

She gasps with laughter, and looks up into his face.

O, how open his countenance! After the closed, cultivated, indoor faces to which she has grown accustomed, how frank is Mr Barratt's, how honest, and glowing, and manly! Heavens!... After straying back, on her last visit, so close to the old territory of Misery Memoirs, the sensation is exquisite.

"Nellie, my *dearest* child!".. . "Darling Nellie!"... "Gracious, Nellie, what a lot of luggage you have!"

Nellie looked about her vaguely, tried to count; was it all here? It made a much bigger pile, she saw, than that with which she had gone away. "The rest is coming down by cart."

There is the shortest of silences.

In it, they note:– Nellie had always looked nice, of course; but now, she looks... Pale skin, that gleams like pearl. Picture-perfect clothes. And that hair! Has it grown?... A Pre-Raphaelite would wet himself. Save for a new aura of sophistication, they are looking at Nellie as she was when Alice first met her, fifteen years old and fresh from Paris; hovering before the baker's shop in Gun Lane, puzzling over the unfamiliar coins in her palm. The same, right down to, just at this moment, a stunned air.

"What a beautiful pelisse! I'm surprised you risked it in the public coach!"

"Oh— it's my travelling pelisse... the other ones are..."

Even her voice is different.

The Countess, like Nellie's mother before her, had always insisted that Nellie's tones should be low, yet clear— but who would have thought that losing your virtue would have this effect on your vowel qualities? A change in the way someone talks is the most disorienting of changes, the most disquieting. "But, Alice my dear– and Mr Barratt– " —yes, the way she utters 'my dear' has been changed somehow— "How did you get away from the shop?"

The shop— Mr Burley's shop— it has been shut up. Richard Barratt is out of work.

Most of Plymouth is out of work. (Most of the Navy is out of work.) Half of the Barratt's adult brood are out of work. Some have moved away.

Richard and Alice are eating into their tiny savings.

"And little Ariosto is a Count!...."

"My my!"

How things change.

*

When the rest of her luggage finally arrives at the coaching inn, Richard offers to go and fetch it for her with the handcart. After a moment's astonishment, Nellie murmurs no— no she will arrange for the carter to bring it to their door.

It takes half an hour for the men to get all the boxes up the stairs.

*

Not that Nellie has monopoly on discomfiting surprises.

"*Married?*"

Alice lowered her head over her work. Or more accurately a neighbour's work; these days Alice was taking in sewing.

Nellie wanted to continue, along the lines of, *but she's fourteen!* She held back.

"Jessie is nearly fifteen now, Nellie. A woman, almost."

Nellie bent over her own work.

"Mrs Clay, we were lucky that Mr Threadgold was still willing to take her."

"I thought you were asleep, Richard! You should sleep! Did we wake you?" Of an evening, Richard often fell asleep where he sat. He was picking up day labour along the waterfront, and talking, more and more, about emigration.

"How many men would stand by their word? No. We can be sure of the value of his affection."

"But *fourteen*, Mr Barratt!"

"Happy as a lark. Mistress of a far better house than we ever gave her. The wife of a respectable man. Safe."

It was unanswerable.

It was thin ice, even. Mrs Clay's reappearance among them last March, suddenly with so many nice new clothes; and then, sudden disappearance (leaving any number of loyal pupils in the lurch!)... and then, sudden *re*-reappearance, just now– and with so many more clothes, quite stunning clothes— it had been a matter of discussion, along Gun Lane; and beyond.

So Nellie shut up.

"And the Countess can stay with her, when I– after emigration."

The worst of it is that now, Richard is serious about Australia. What free time he has, he spends these days in reading accounts of the infant colony (and oh Lord, it does sound dreadful!) and writing lists of equipment, and in talking with old Bennett. Bennett is a find. He spent near twenty year in the southern colony, and returned only last summer, with just a nice bit of money and that unlucky scar about his ankle. Few can get him to talk. But the quiet Richard does.

"Yes", adds Alice; "Mr Threadgold says he is willing to welcome the *Countess*, too– which is, really, so very..."

No it's not! The Countess has her own little nest-egg! The interest on it, now, easily covers her own modest needs, while the whole must give, in the Threadgolds' house, a welcome grace to every fresh wrinkle on her face.

But alright. It is still very tolerant of Mr Threadgold. An old lady, no relation of his. And she will probably take up an entire bedroom.

"Besides which she will be a wonderful help with the baby."

"Baby?"

Richard Barratt glared at her.

Oh dear God.

"And- but-cannot— cannot Alice...?"

Nellie means, 'what of Alice?' Alice, who is peering at the cloth and sewing with a speed almost feverish.

He *can't* take her with him! To a country that has not, in all its huge wastes, a single brick building? Alice is over forty! She is tiny! How long before her eyes start to go, anyway?

My God, the Countess is the lucky one.

But Richard is glaring at her still. Nellie smooths her features and lowers her eyes.

Chapter 24

Once papa arrives, things go much better. Everything starts to move again. Everyone is busy, and there is money in the house.

The days when Mr Barratt could find no job on the waterfront, or was not talking to old Bennett or learning what he could about sheep, Mr Shepherd found reasons to employ him in commissions about town. Meanwhile, Alice and Nellie worked together on the Bouscognes' other needs. Shirts, trousers, linen: Nellie had made a list, and each time the two of them crossed something off, they would discover something else that must be added. Of an evening, together about the Barratts' fire (they were both boarding with the Barratts— more coins into Richard's emigration fund), the men would read, talk, write, while the women held their work to the firelight and carried on, sewing for Italy.

Richard was inclined to tease. "There are shops in Italy, I'm sure, Mrs Clay."

"Oh Richard!" exclaimed his sister. "Don't mock us!"

"Shops, with cloth in them, too, I shouldn't wonder."

"Not as good, Mr Barratt, as our English cloth."

"—And you know what Hannibal said, after he'd crossed the Alps, with all those laden elephants groaning, poor beasts; 'If only I'd known I could buy so many household necessities in Capua!'"

A snort of laughter from behind Mr Shepherd's newspaper.

"But this–! This is how you prepare if you are packing for Australia!" She paused in her work a moment to shoot him a sarcastic smirk, and he smiled back at her.

Papa had lowered his paper.... He was smiling at them, too.

*

It is a clear winter's day, sunny and still, and they are walking by the cliffs to the west of Plymouth. A day off, a day *out*; sunshine and air for everyone! Mr Shepherd had insisted. He had even hired a carriage (a cart), so that the Countess could come. And Jessie too: Mrs Threadgold, forsooth.

Now the Countess sits upon the cart bench, breathing with delight the clear air. Nellie and Alice and Jessie stroll close at hand, gazing over a sparkling pale-blue sea, and talking: there is much for them to discuss, the two older women and the young married lady. Mr Shepherd and Mr Barratt have strode right out to the cliff-top.

It is nice to see them getting on so well. Nice, of papa, to give his time to the Barratts, when he has so much to do in these final weeks in England.

Nice of Richard too, of course, to take time off from his plans.

But they do like each other. Papa, especially, took to Richard from the first.

And as the days pass, and evidence and judgement support intuition, Mr Shepherd likes him more and more.

The women spread out the rug, the little picnic. Alice and Nellie wave and halloo to the menfolk. Richard waves his hat in response, and the two start back— hale Richard Barratt, broad-shouldered and deep-chested and tall... and papa; thin as ever (though that coat makes it look worse); a little more stooped, too, than Nellie remembers seeing him... He has taken his spectacles off, and is polishing them as he walks, still chatting, eagerly, to the bigger man... pushing his glasses back onto his nose, fumbling slightly...

Seeing him like this, exposed in the sunlight, Nellie is struck afresh by the scale of what she and her father are undertaking. She a woman, and he already of an age that—

Papa stumbles!

— and Richard catches him in a moment– has already steadied him.

They laugh together.

The pair of them stride on cheerfully, towards the waiting women, her father leaning secure, now, on Richard's arm. "What a prop and stay you have in your brother, Miss Barratt!" he calls gaily. "I can only pray, that in Italy we will be able to find ourselves a man-of-affairs with half his talents!" —and he fumbles once more at his glasses.

Papa does not normally wear his spectacles out of doors.

What the devil is he up to.

*

Mr Elliot sits at the head of the semicircle. To his left, Mrs Rathbone (the Hon. Miss Pettigrew that was), and then Mrs Southey, whose husband had done so extraordinarily well in the West Indies; to his right, the Dowager Viscountess Dalrymple, flanked by his own wife; facing him, a fire that burns with flameless intensity. Sir Walter is out, somewhere. It goes best when Sir Walter is out.

"—And my wife the only one of you with a husband yet living! Now, do not be giving her ideas, I beg you! I am afraid that, with so many rosy faces and lively forms here about her, you will be giving her a taste for widowhood!" The three visitors are tittering helplessly: they have been subjected to nearly an hour of Mr Elliot, and are by now putty in his neat, rather small hands.

*   *   *

"And Australia...! Why Australia? I can't *imagine* anywhere worse!"

In the privacy of the midday kitchen, Alice is expressing her opinion at last. Alice has called a family conference for this very purpose: just Alice, and Richard, and Mr Threadgold, who they owe so much. And who completely agrees with her:–

"It is to New England that a man goes; a man in your situation. At least, in New England, there is some civilisation. At least, there, you can hope to receive letters from home more than once in a year!"

Richard shrugged.

Alice took over again.

"But in *Italy*—well, you could be the steward!"

"Aye! Just as Mr Shepherd, himself, was steward once, to Sir Walter Elliot's family. At their magnificent estate in Kellynch Place."

"Me a housekeeper even!"

"Where else could you hope for such a step?"

"...but..."

He had managed little more than that monosyllable for most of the discussion. If you're the strong, silent type, with moments only of mirth, it can be difficult to argue your case when women, and so forth, start to go on at you. They'd been going on at him for nearly half an hour.

"But." At last, though, something serious was making its way out of the depths of Richard's heart to his mouth..

Alice, who recognised the symptoms, waited attentively this time.

"But..."

They waited some more.

"— Do you not want, ever, to just— To be a free man."

"We *are* free!"

"The freest nation in Europe!" Mr Threadgold is emphatic about this. He is a member of the parish council, and feels such things strongly.

"No but I mean— Imagine, Alice. *Imagine*...."

"Imagine what, Richard dear?"

Richard Barratt leant forward. "Hundreds of acres..." He held out both hands, towards something. "Bennett once went twenty-seven days without touching his hat to anyone. He counted."

A short silence.

It was the silence of people who do not for a moment see the household member before them going twenty-seven days without touching his hat—it's just ridiculous!— but who do not know if it is wise, while he still breathes heavily like this, to burst his bubble.

After a decent interval, Mr Threadgold resumed: "What, though, of your duty to Mr Shepherd? To his widowed daughter?"

"I don't have any duty to them."

"Richard!–"

"*Mr Barratt!*" Mr Threadgold is older than Richard Barratt, as well as richer. "No I *must* say this Mr Barratt—late events in France!— the carnage!— violation of all that is!–"

He feels, too, that people must remember that Richard Barratt is not in fact his, Mr Threadgold's, father-in-law.

"I take my leave."

He stood up and strode to the door. Alice scrambled to be quick enough to open it for him.

At the threshold he spun on his heel; "The Bouscogne family unites three estates!"— and left.

Alice closed the door quietly behind him.

Then she spent silent fifteen minutes, hemming a Bouscogne chemise.

Then, finally:

"We cannot be thinking always only of ourselves, Richard."

Chapter   25

"— bevy of British beauty, to support the spirits of this old married man!"

Mr Elliot had been first out of the dining room again today, but his time he had not immediately approached the nest of dowagers in which his wife sat. He'd been waylaid, apparently, by a mixed gaggle of younger women, and carried off by them to the instrument. He spread his charm around, she had to say that for him...

But he was flashing her a glance. Elizabeth jerked upright in her chair– "*So*, Mrs Rathbone— do– will– er... *Are* we to meet you, at the concert tomorrow? I do hope so!

"For I know it would be such a pleasure for my husband to see you there, and to speak to you afterwards. Of the performance. To see you, *both*", and she bowed politely towards Lady Dalrymple, who sat beyond the richer widow. "Your observations after the Mozart last week– well! Mr Elliot was quite in raptures! '*Taste, judgement, memory*'; let me see if I can recall his exact words!... '*Mrs Rathbone unites, in one mind, such command of the theory of music, together with an exquisite sensibility to its effects, such as are not often met with separately, let alone united, as they are, within that one girlish form.*' I assure you, I felt quite jealous! But Mr Elliot does love his music."

"Oh yes *wasn't* that Mozart *so* lovely..."

This was Lady Dalrymple, commencing. You will recall that in Bath, Lady Dalrymple— the Dowager Viscountess Dalrymple— had been famously musical.

In London the standards are rather higher. While Mrs Rathbone descants, in a voice both fluent and piercing, on whether *Don Giovanni* should be classed as *opera buffa* or *dramma giocoso*, Lady Dalrymple subsides again; is silent, pleating the edge of her fichu.

And yet, there could be no doubt; she was the nicer of the two, was old Lady D.

He has sent her another look.

"– *Well!* You and my husband are really *two* of a kind, Mrs Rathbone! And Lady Dalrymple too. This is the kind of conversation that I know, in his heart, poor Mr Elliot would like to come home to, after a concert, and suchlike. He says, that he simply *must* have a musical companion, at home! He calls me an *ignorant child,* if you please; and has commanded me to read— oh, I don't know what books, about music and opera, and acting and so forth— he has handed me the most enormous pile, my head reels—! He quite misses it, at home... a *musical* companion—" and so on, and so on... and at long last he called out, from his place at the fire:

"I do indeed!— you speak of music?— I do indeed, my dear Mrs Rathbone; Lady Dalrymple! I tell my wife, that if she cannot learn to take the subject of music with the passionate seriousness that it so clearly deserves, I will *set* her aside, and marry *you*, Mrs Rathbone–" A delighted roar of laughter from the room drowned the rest of his speech; and Mr Elliot, throwing up his hands in mock-despair, has left British beauty, and is heading towards them. ("Take my chair, Mr Elliot, I believe I must speak to...") "*Now*, Mrs Rathbone! Now, that I fairly have the two of you to myself!..."

Thank God...

Elizabeth drifted away.

*

Mr Barratt is down by the docks. He has been talking, again, to old Bennett, and now he is alone, seated on a bollard, gazing out across the water. Beneath him are wind ropes as thick as his own muscular arm, that then swing off out, aslant, across a gulf of water before him, away and up... to the towering bowsprit of a magnificent ship of the line. To which the unwieldy cables attach, looking by this time as insignificant as gossamer.

But the colossus is pinned to the quay by hundreds of these spidery tethers; pinned, like Gulliver, asleep in Lilliput. She will never wake. She is here to be broken up for scrap.

It is the same in every port in England. Beautiful ships. Beautiful rigging; blocks, shackles, fittings; all a chandlers' business; which is in turn a mere tracery over the spars and the hull itself, skin upon skin, frame within frame, down to the massive beams fluted together with a skill to make you weep. Each ship, in turn, is taken, and bound to a quay— like this, any old how— ripped apart, and sold off in gobbets.

The needs of the nation have changed.

A murmuring along the waterfront breaks in on his thoughts. Men are calling out, laughing, swearing.

Gapes and stares direct his gaze.

Richard Barratt cranes his neck too; running his eye up the mainmast of the shackled giant, and then up the topmast that surmounts it, and then, the topgallant mast above *that*, which has been left fixed and bare for no discernible reason, and surmounting them all... against the sun... someone is standing on his hands.

Some topman, showing off his skills, one last time.

"...clown!"

"...bloody fool kill hisseln..." He won't, though. That the distant exclamation mark honed this trick of his, on this very mast-tip, while both of them traced crazy loops among the constellations of the South Pacific... But a distant roar intrudes:

"YOU! BACK TO WORK IF YOU HOPE FOR YOUR PAY!"

The tiny figure flips itself upright, loops itself onto a backstay, and in a stomach-churning moment slides the whole great fall to the deck.

Picks up a crowbar and disappears, into the demolition gang.

*   *   *

Mrs Rathbone is laying down the law, about how to order dinner when on the road; to the amusement of the whole table. Mrs Rathbone, the Honourable Miss Pettigrew-as-was.

Which means, really, that she is one of those girls who have gone down, not up.

Her skin *is* lovely, though. Lady Dalrymple could not but admit it. This evening she did look quite lovely. She looked quite young.

Too, Mrs Rathbone was grown marvellously confident these days. She held her head with a new tilt, and talked airily, like this, a lot.

Lady Dalrymple sat silent. She had sat silent through most of dinner so far, and they were now at the cheese. She was beginning to feel that it had been a mistake, to come up to London. Fiona was... She crumpled– no she *smoothed out* her plain fichu; she smoothed it out...

"A glass of wine with you, Lady Dalrymple?"

The dear Baronet.

It was so nice of him. "Why thank you, Sir Walter!" Mrs Elliot, though, was whispering, audibly; *"Papa isn't that your fifth?"*

"Helps me sleep, m'dear."

Now *here* was topic that... "Do you have trouble sleeping too, Sir Walter? London is so very... I find it so hard to drop off, myself, these days."

"You should try laudanum, Lady Dalrymple!" It was Mr Elliot, calling across from the other side of the table.

He seemed waiting, too, for her reply; and she hastened to acquiesce — oh yes indeed I *always*– But instantly, that fluting voice:

"No no, I cannot allow it! A foul tincture, and a fouler habit! Mr Rathbone's attachment to it, in our early married days– oh!– how often I wished the whole medical profession *au diable!* In the end, I forbade it from the house!"

"Really? Mrs Rathbone? What a dragon the poor man must have thought he'd married."

"Oh he did indeed!"

*   *   *

Mr Shepherd, being such a fussy and precise old man, has made everything quite formal and plain. Now all Mr Barratt has to do is sign.

His hand engulfs the quill.

Richard Barratt's hands are huge, the right two glove sizes larger than the left, as is common in men who have laboured mightily from childhood. It makes dipping a tiny nib in a tiny inkpot a perilous undertaking for most of them.

But Mr Barratt, ex-ship's-chandler, can handle it. He has handled so many things. ("My brother is a *very* superior man, Mr Shepherd, I can promise, you would *never* regret—")

Yet he hesitates...

Mr Shepherd's slim fingers slip forward to guide him. "So, just *here*, Mr Barratt— and here."

He signs.

Did he miss pipping Macarthur at the post, and himself laying the foundations of the Australian wool industry?

Or maybe he missed drowning; alone, in some nameless creek, found on no map, trying to rescue a lamb from floodwaters; the caramel torrent about him swiftly darkening to black.

Or waiting out his days behind yet another shop-counter. Mr Barratt, of Sydney Town: Chandlery and Hardware.

Who knows.

*

Snowflakes, soft, and huge, and slow, and hypnotic, are gently drifting in loops and spirals beyond the glass of the window-seat. Behind them, the Cossington's library is empty; the fire, only, crackling softly, the music and the bustle of the ball muted, through fifty yards of warm stone, to a quiet rumble.

"... my respect for you, and my desire, above all— let me admit the soft impeachment!— to secure a— well!... a well-informed, a *like*-minded companion... a mature and womanly presence, to transform those long, empty evening hours that I find hang so heavily upon me, in Somerset! Which is otherwise so lovely. If you could, then, find it in your heart—"

He looks, hopefully, at her.

She looked back in some confusion.

He resumes... "if you *could* submit, to new duties, and consent to make Kellynch Hall your home, you would–"

"— Oh! but but– but well– well but I *was* intending... Of course since Arthur died I– one is devastated of course but—"

"(Of course! Of course!)"

"— but, I *have* been very happy in Bath and- and— and my music and so on, and I *was* thinking of..."

"Naturally Lady Dalrymple; *Bath*. That you should bury yourself forever in rural retirement is out of the question: Bath must and shall be your final home."

"Oh that's good", murmured Lady Dalrymple weakly.

"We shall all be together often, I hope, in Bath. *But...*" and he leant in so close that the fire flooded the room with a swooning heat and a light of flickering rose; "*If you could*, as I was saying, find it, in your heart, to submit to new duties, and consent to- *consent*, that is; you would not only honour our family inexpressibly; but also, dare I say it, make more than one soul within its walls *truly* happy I mean—" He fumbled with his gloves, blushing visibly, to the roots of his hair, and right on cue the snowflakes zipped about like mad. "... I should say..." — and he reached forward, and took her hands in his.

"Oh!...

"Oh– well then... really... I– I *suppose* that–"

A sharp intake of breath —! and those neat hands carried her own with all swiftness to his lips. "*How* happy you make me, Lady Dalrymple, *how* inexpressibly happy! Through me, all the House of Elliot welcomes you!– and with such joy!

"... Curse it—" and he kissed her hands again... which was really very nice of him, obviously... and he laughed, shortly; and frowned; and looked a little aside; and then it burst from him —

"I find I almost envy Sir Walter his good fortune!"

Lady Dalrymple with furtive diffidence extracted one of her hands. It flew up to the edge of her fichu, and began to pleat frantically.

*

"It is such a relief! Oh I'm *so* glad! Oh it takes away *all* my fears almost."

Her father only nodded, but his face was deep with satisfaction.

"It takes away *all* my fears", Nellie repeated. The agitation of her happiness would not let her sit– "And even Alice too!– for the children. Oh yes papa we can take the children now, I quite agree! I mean it doubles their security, that some one or another of us will always be... why it multiplies it by four!"

Mr Shepherd did not dispute her mathematics (though he could have): instead he said, rather quietly under the elating circumstances, "I share your satisfaction, Nellie dear."

After a bit more joyful pacing about the room, Nellie added, "And we cannot be *too grateful*, to Mr Barratt, for consenting to take such a step."

Mr Shepherd nodded soberly.

"— But papa when did he tell you? Did they ask you? or did you ask them? Why did he change his mind?"

"It came utterly out of the blue. But, Nellie dear, don't look a gift horse in the mouth. Don't probe, my dear."

*

That night, the Elliots returned to their fashionable street even later than usual. Mrs Elliot went straight up to her room. She seemed quite fagged out. Her husband, though, popped into the Baronet's bedroom; just to apprise the old man of the night's events, and outline the alterations that he could expect, now, in his mode of life.

The bedchamber was fusty with a middle-aged fustiness; its curtains tightly

drawn, the fire apparently quite burned out. Old-fashioned hangings fes-
tooned the bedstead, confusing the issue still further— so it was only when
Mr Elliot had flung the last of the covers on the floor that he was forced to
believe it.

The room was empty.

He raged about the house, shouting orders at a tumble of terrified half-
dressed servants. Every lantern and every candlestick in the place was pressed
into service to search the house from cellar to attic. They searched until dawn;
but Sir Walter was nowhere to be found.

Chapter 26

Sir Walter was in a fair way to never being found, for his appearance right now
differed on almost all points from the description that his son-in-law quickly
circulated to every coach inn and posting house within fifty miles of London.
The fashionable morning coat, the breeches of latest cut, the yellow boots and
the shining hat; nay, the very hair powder that his son-in-law had not scrupled
to suggest he might be wearing: all had been carefully folded into a satchel—
and lost, when his exhausted horse fell while wading a particularly muddy
stream. Sir Walter had fallen too.

No need, now, to worry that the lack of wear on this hideously outmoded
coat and pre-war set of breeches would attract attention; no concern that this
hat of 1812– worn twice, and sitting in camphor ever since– had too sleek a
nap to have knocked about on anybody's head for three or four years. The
cottagers with whom he had taken refuge were unable to appreciate how brilliantly ill-matched his outfit was, how convincingly secondhand it must appear
to anyone who had glanced, even in the most casual way, into *Ackermann's
Repository,* but the old woman added to his credibility by mending the great slit
in his coat-sleeve with a gratifying degree of imperfection. That ragged darn
had added the final, elusive touch which suddenly makes an outfit come to
life. Sir Walter had been pleased to perceive its dramatic effect: pleased, even
through his pain.

The pain, let us confess, was considerable. The Baronet and the superannuated carriage-horse were alike unaccustomed to riding, and the brutal
mutual pounding of the last two days had inflicted such agonies, such damage
indeed, as to compel an unscheduled halt. They were laid up in this remote
cottage, in bed and paddock respectively, getting their strength back. Yes;
there it was, down there, the horse, the... the beast. Under the three apple
trees that the old couple here called their orchard. Stuffing its face.

The sight was unavoidable, for the attic room he occupied was so small that when Sir Walter used the chamber pot, as he was forced to now (and merciful Heavens, the torment of his inner thighs), he must steady himself with the door jamb in one hand, and the bedhead in the other, meanwhile facing straight out of the window.

And now he lowered– bracing himself for the cruel chill of porcelain pressing into his raw buttocks— *O sweet mother of God!!!*

... A long, long... moment.

At last, the agony abated. Sir Walter was able, slowly, to lean forward... and, resting his arms on the windowsill, and his chin on his arms, let Nature take Her course.

In the yard below, the cottager, toothless and potato-faced, pottered about whistling *Lillibullero*. He had been pottering about, since dawn, whistling *Lillibullero*. A groan escaped Sir Walter.

The horse looked up.

Met his eye.

They gazed at each other with loathing.

*   *   *

Everyone is delighted by the astonishing, the *wonderful* news, that Richard and Alice Barratt are to receive such an elevation! After so much undeserved ill-fortune, to be appointed a steward, *and* a housekeeper–

And of the Bouscogne estates, no less!

Everybody has a visit owing, and congratulations to give; everybody has their tale to tell, as to how they were dumbfounded by the news, or had suspected it all along, or had thought of it themselves some time ago but had not like to say. Practically everybody has an opinion too on the wisdom of the move, and many a suggestion or three as to how best it all might be done, while other people exchange intuitions as to how it will all turn out.

It was a pity, perhaps, that it must be Italy.

But Lord!– it had so nearly been Australia!— and Miss Barratt and Mr Barratt are showered with handshakes and kisses and slaps upon the shoulder: on all sides it is joy, and it is relief.

The rumble of preparations rises in an instant to a deafening roar. Barely two weeks remain until the *Bernadette* sails, and everything still to be done! The full sibling flock, with friends and neighbours too, are in and out of the house all day, helping and advising, questioning and talking, sewing and carpentering and packing—and then unpacking again in search of items suddenly needed immediately, while nieces and nephews in varying stages of development do all that lies in their power to help, the older girls making cups of tea with china thought to have been dealt with by now, the younger ones wrapping up small but crucial household items safely inside towels and linen, while those infants too young to contribute in any other way tumble about underfoot laughing and screaming and wetting themselves.

Through and among them, all the long day, Miss Alice Barratt hurries about her work. Busy as a bee, tidy and neat-handed, she does that which has been left undone, and undoes that which should not have been done, and re-does that which has been undone again when her back was turned, all with a cheerful face and a right good will!

Mr Barratt, only, was composed. Mr Barratt is known about town to be a man of deep inner feeling: handsome men always are. Yet his deep waters ran, on this occasion, particularly still. The gleams that had lit his dark eyes these few weeks past— as when he spoke, for example, of meat sheep versus wool sheep, or of lambing schedules, and their integration with shearing schedules, or of the rumours (scarcely creditable, surely?) that there was, in the southern colonies, simply no foot-rot— they were gone. Alice sang about the house like a lark, but Mr Barratt's self-control was almost invariable.

Almost. Not quite.

Nellie, in the ebullience of her feeling, chose one evening to wind an arm boldly about his neck and to tell him— smiling into his face the while— that in Italy, when they got there, he would have to stop calling her 'Mrs Clay' and start calling her *Senora*. "Senora *Bouscogne*– or *Madame*— what do you think?"

He looked back at her glowing face, inches from his own— and for a second, some great emotion seemed the heave below the tight-stretched surface of his countenance.

"I shall call you *ma'am,* of course. That is what stewards do."

For some moments Nellie hovered, unable to credit her ears. Then, as his meaning dawned on her, with exquisite mortification she steadily blushed scarlet all the way to her toes.

Mr Barratt unwound her arm and gave it politely back to her.

"Let us start now."

*

"... nor coffee houses, nor brothels nor mortuaries."

The quiet man tapped the papers of his report together with an air of finality, and pushed them across the desk. "It is as I thought from the beginning: he has left London. We must scour the roads, Mr Harolde."

"Then he could be bloody anywhere! Ten days— he could be at Land's End, he could be at John O'Groats by now!"

"I very much doubt it. A non-rider, at his age. No groom. And on that horse. Fifty miles, I'd say. Though, barring accidents, he'll make better time in the coming days."

*

Sir Walter was starting to make better time these days! Today, too, he had felt it safe to assume the main road and all its amenities: there could be no danger, surely, fully fifty miles from London. The day had dawned fine, and he had re-arranged many little things about his clothing and the saddle and so on, and had set out in good spirits, and virtually pain-free.

Rain had closed in around noon, however, and he was once more in no little discomfort. Three hours ago, the wet had worked its way through the last of the capes of his greatcoat where he sat on them. "Nay, ye mun spread the capes out, sir, like a lady's riding habit, so as they falls on aeither side like great black wings. Not sit on 'em like a chook." To which Sir Walter had replied, with some hauteur: "I think I know my own comfort best, my good man."

Now, though, the cloth, this morning so dry and delightfully springy to sit upon, was wet and hard, compacted lumpily beneath his– his nether regions.

But suffering, endured, will have its end. They were creeping up to a coaching inn, at last. The yard was empty... no— a lounging boy sauntered forward to take the bridle. Cheeky young cad. Why did not his master put a rocket under him.

Sir Walter pointed dumbly to a mounting block; worked his feet from the stirrups; eased himself, at last, from a saddle of granite. *Zounds...*

Gad-*zooks*.

... God's blood.

*

"So how many do you have on the job?"

"Some dozen, at the moment, Mr Harolde."

"'*Some dozen*'?" mimicked Mr Elliot. "How many would that be exactly?"

"Twelve", the man replied.

"Then double it. How quickly can you double it?"

"It will be no more than calling upon the O'Kevins. They can be on the roads by nightfall."

*

Dinner was disappointing, as usual; nothing on offer but fried beef; but the inn was warm, the fire in the public room, delightful. And though that very first action, of sitting down in front of it, was still a painful and protracted process... he found that today, once fairly seated, he could already move his limbs with some freedom. Which was excellent. Excellent progress. Tomorrow, he might have a shot at fifteen miles!

The post, travelling day and night and changing teams in under two hundred seconds, covered fifteen miles in ninety minutes. Luckily, Sir Walter did not reflect on this. Instead he flexed his limbs systematically, and thought of his goal, and felt hopeful, and proud, and determined, all at once.

"Rheumatics, that would be."

The confident statement came from an old man on the opposite settle, who had watched the business of his sitting with a sympathetic interest. Sir Walter had at first expected that the air of a gentleman would protect him from casual conversations on the road— had feared, too, that it would betray him— but the truth had soon forced itself upon him that it is impossible to have much air when your arse hurts like hell.

"Ah— yes. Yes my val- my good wife, ah, usually has an embrocation for it but..."

"Borage!"

"Pardon me?"

"Borage– In a tincture. Applied *to* the leg but not when it's heated, no no, *elevate* the leg and then..." It was odd: Sir Walter found that he needed scarcely to nod, and go 'mm', and these self-important old men would go on and on indefinitely— while he himself could slide into a pleasant semi-doze. Where had such people been, all his life?

*

"Alright double it then. I'll send you a sliding scale of what I'm prepared to pay, depending on how quickly you find Sir Walter."

"I look forward to reading it, Mr Harolde"; and the man bowed his head again. He was always scrupulous about pronouncing the final 'e'.

*

Soothed by the voices about him, Sir Walter was in the last stages of nodding off when the landlady bustled in to show him to his room.

The usual dark kennel.

"I've put you in with only just Mr Braidley, his lordship's valet. I'm that sorry to be so late with it but you know how it is when great folk swoop down on you unexpected— though his lordship is certainly the *kindest, easiest* gentleman to deal with, so affable about his meal though we had but beef and partridges and a fricandos of veal and a *scrap* of fish in the house, yet it's always so with the truly great, we see so many of them here, *so* affable and easy, and I thought– you, perhaps, being in the secondhand clothes line...?... that you might like to have a word with Mr Braidley yourself, Mr —?"

"Anderson", replied Sir Walter, sinking weakly onto the bed.

Once, he had prepared another name. In the weeks that had led up to his flight from London, one sleepless night in two had been devoted to the issue of his pseudonym: he had searched childhood memories for his old nurse's ancient lays; had combed Scott and Byron and the social columns for a name both noble, and mysterious; a name that, like the best lingerie, simultaneously concealed, and– well– strongly suggested.

But what came out, every cursed time, was "Anderson. Mr John Anderson". He reached stiffly to take off his boots.

The landlady hurried forward to oblige.

"Thank you. You are most kind."

"Ah, Mr Anderson, a day on the road always knots up my good man just the same."

"Most kind... And—" For she had turned to leave. "Madame, I beg you—"

"Yes?"

"— to tell your daughters– and, perhaps– your good self..."

"Yes?"

"...that waists—" Sir Walter eased his legs up onto the bed. "Waists–" falling backwards gratefully— "are *lower* this year."

He sighed deeply.

"The expectation is, that next year, they will be lower still."

*

The tribe of O'Kevin has celebrated its windfall in gin. Now the men are dispersed through a dozen different night coaches, and as Sir Walter sleeps, these radiate, apart and out, a slow-motion explosion across the map of England.

Chapter 27

Richard Barratt and Mr Shepherd are settling into harness. Tandem harness.

Every day they go out, to do this and that. The business of Nellie and Alice keeps them close about the house, mending and making and cleaning and packing, while the men, ranging the town about their wider affairs, return only at dinner-time— that is, if some one or another of their new associates does not urge them to stay and dine. Each evening, their return shows Mr Shepherd more and more pleased with Richard Barratt.

And Richard with him. Nellie could see.

"Do you know, Nellie, that Mr Barratt has a brother actually in *Turin*? Can you imagine!"

"Yes: Tom, the eldest of the boys; yes I know. He went there in seventeen... seventeen ninety two he said–" Mr Shepherd tossed his muffler across the back of his armchair and sat down— "*Isn't* that amazing Nellie? A brother in Turin! And he speaks– well, whatever they speak there– but Mr Barratt himself has a little proper *Italian*, can you believe that Nellie!"

"Yes Mr Barratt and Alice both; we used to–"

"And French! We were talking with a man off the *Etoile* today and Mr Barratt was talking to him in French!"

"... just vocabulary..."

"—yes that's the part to start with– Gets you in the door. And then, with time, the rest follows—... Oh! I am more and more impressed with this Mr Barratt of yours, Nellie!"

"He's not my Mr Barratt."

Mr Shepherd finally looked at her.

"Oh. Ah, I suppose yes he's all our Mr Barratt."

Said Mr Barratt then entering, bearing a jug and two tankards, this nascent conversation was suspended. "Here you are, sir— *As* the doctor ordered. This'll put the flesh on your bones."

"Ah; porter! That's right, Mr Barratt. I feel stronger already, stronger, and younger, under your ministrations! Now, Nellie has been telling me that you and she—"

But Nellie is closing the door behind her.

With a click.

"Of course I'm annoyed with him Alice. He– he keeps on calling me *ma'am.*"

"Nonsense Nellie!"

"He does!"

"Well I've never heard him do it. He calls you Mrs Clay, doesn't he?– or Mrs *Bouscogne!* I must practice that one myself! What do you think *we* should call ourselves? Will people there be able to say 'Barratt'?"

"Oh he doesn't do it in front of you or papa. He does it when we're alone."

"Oh." This did silence Alice, for a moment.

But then she resumed her energetic attack upon the glass: they were cleaning windows. "Oh well I'm sure he'll get over it. I mean he doesn't mean anything by it. After all nobody's really sure *what* to call you these days! And he does like you Nellie– he always has."

Well I don't like him.

*

"It's certain? Plymouth?"

"The Plymouth road. Asking the distance remaining to Plymouth."

"Ah." Mr Elliot sat silent.

After a while, he was seen to be smiling a little.

"I rejoice for you, Mr Harolde. It must be an inexpressible relief for the family."

"Eh? Oh– oh yes; yes absolutely!—*Plymouth!* Well well. The old dog."

*

It was unreasonable of her, she knew, to be upset by such a trifle. For every moment of resentful indulgence, there were twenty preceding, in which she endeavoured to reason with herself; to persuade herself to feel less.

—but it was so *mean* of him! She hadn't meant it like that!

For *once* things were going well for her. Why shouldn't she be happy?– just for a teeny tiny moment! Things would all be difficult enough soon enough God knows.

And why shouldn't she be Senora Bouscogne?— To him, as well as to everybody else.

Why wouldn't he just be happy for her?

She damn well was Madame Bouscogne. They wouldn't be doing any of this, without her money.

∗

"We mustn't have any scenes, Nell."

"I haven't made any scenes!"

"Barratt is a find, Nellie. He's an absolute jewel. We are extraordinarily lucky to have persuaded him to join our party."

"It's not *me* who is being difficult!"

"But it is up to you to ease the difficulty. I'm sure you understand."

"No I don't!"

"If you will put aside thoughts of pride, Nell. Get down off your high horse. Mm?

"A little womanly yielding, a little deference— and he will perk up again.

"Mmm?

"Nell: just do whatever it takes."

∗   ∗   ∗

"Mr Barratt"

"Ma'am?"

— Nellie walked out of the room.

Then she walked back in. "*Why* are you being so horrible?"

Mr Barratt looked at her with every appearance of calm wonder. "Ma'am?"

"Mr Barratt, you know none of this is my fault. I didn't know anything about it. Papa knew, Alice knew, everybody it seems was talking about this arrangement except me. I was probably the last person to find out. So why on earth am I the *one* person you seem to be taking it out on, I just don't under-stand."

Now Richard did seem sincerely baffled. "What are you talking about?"

"Australia! You not going to Australia! Coming with us instead! I know it's not what you dreamed of but it's hardly my fault. Did I do a *single thing* to persuade you?"

He did not answer.

She answered for him.

"No!"

She struck her fist upon her breast. "I would never, ever have done such a thing!"

Mr Barratt went extremely red. He looked away.

Then he put his face in his hands.

Nellie rushed forward to comfort him. Somehow, after a confused half-minute– it ended up with her sobbing into the shelter of her handkerchief – or no, not even that, for Richard had hold of both her hands, and was patting them as he had done, on a few particularly bad days, long ago when she was a child– leaving her confused and smeary countenance open to his gaze; "...there there; it will be alright, girlie. It will indeed..."

— and no doubt she was more over-wrought than she had realised— the hurry and bustle of the last several weeks— "I'm so sorry, Mr Barratt..." It was all very hard to make sense of. Richard thank Heavens seemed to feel himself on solid ground though; she sniffled some more, and he rubbed her hands reassuringly. "Everything will be alright, you'll see..."

Once she managed to reclaim her handkerchief, and wiped her face, they withdrew into their own chairs.

She blew her nose.

"But you mustn't call me ma'am. I won't *have* it—"...and the tears spurted out again, making Richard smile: "What must I call you then?"

"The same that you used to!"

"What? Mam'zelle Shepherd?" His voice was teasing, his smile indulgent.

"No! Just... Mrs— Mrs Clay I suppose or— Nellie. Why can't you call me Nellie, like Alice does."

Richard raised his eyebrows to himself.

"And I'll have to call you Richard."

"Alright, you fussy girl. It is as you wish."

*

"Just my best man, then?"

"Of course send your *best man,* you–" A calm eye caught his own.

Mr Elliot made do with a snort. "—Do you think I want your worst?"

"It is as suits your intentions."

The answer gave him pause.

"Ah— Well! Then. Your best– er– *or* your worst– as the man may happen to be."

"If that's your wish, Mr Harolde, I'll send O'Kevin."

"Oh! Oh you'll send *O'Kevin*, will you? — glad to have that cleared up! Such a load off my mind!"

"Indeed sir. It will be."

∗   ∗   ∗

At last! In the lofty privacy of the best room in the best coaching-inn in Plymouth, Sir Walter flung his satchel triumphantly on the bed, turned and — stared. Aghast. The rugged stranger looming before him seemed to tower to the ceiling. Thin. A thing of angles. Yet somehow, menacingly powerful.

Sir Walter was hypnotised.

Greasy, grizzled hair clung flat to a bony skull. Untamed eyebrows beetled crazily, over eyes framed by deep carvings of crows-feet. The shoulders were broad, the figure, in contrast to the devastation of the face, eerily athletic and upright. But– the clothes!... Sir Walter's guts dissolved.

That sorry coat, worn to a poor man's shine.

Those clownish, sagging breeches.

The boots!...cracked, at every crease, by the action of mud, sun, rain, sun, mud. At best, this is an active gentleman-farmer, off to direct a day's hedging and ditching among his men. At worst...

Sir Walter lifted an appalled hand to his jaw. The figure in the mirror did the same.

There was no doubt.

Where once had been a fine, firm, creamy double chin, there now hung– turkey wattles.

∗

Sir Walter sat on the hotel bed, his head in his hands. He had been so sitting for a hour by the town clock, while a wan morning light made success-iveslow discoveries on the dusty floor, and people came and went in the corridor beyond, and voices rose in the street below his window; rose, and drifted away. Now the clock struck eleven.

Sir Walter sighed massively; lifted his head at last... ouch... sore neck... Stared hopelessly about him.

Here was his riding gear, freshly washed and pressed.

Listless, he drew it over. The maid had turned the cuffs for him, to hide the frayed edges.

I suppose I could wear that.

Propose, in shabby, worn-out riding breeches, and a coat with turned cuffs — *No!* It was an intolerable slight! One which he must not, *cannot* offer to any woman—

His heart lurched, his throat grew strangely thick.

There was a horrid prickling pressure behind his eyes.

*   *   *

They are doing all the last-minute packing. It is incredible, how much last-minute packing there is. The last boxes must be at the dock by six bells in the afternoon watch. "What the devil does that mean?" Mr Shepherd snarls.

"Grandpapa it means three o'clock."

"Then why cannot they say so? What is wrong with everybody else's way of telling the time? Why this parade of *bells!*"

Nellie is trying to suppress her smile. So is Richard. They catch each other's eye.

"Bells, for all love!—"

*

The westering winter sun, at once glaring and cold, inched up the counterpane, slipped across Sir Walter's hair where it straggled over the pillow, glided across his cheek, and stuck a finger in his eye. He flinched: shifted his head, with fractious lethargy, into shadow.

The sun, undeterred, crept higher still— until, again, a chilly beam pierced the despondent man's sight.

This time Sir Walter lacked the will even to turn his head. He closed his eyes, and lay limply. Black dots drifted across a yellow world.

Something hot slithered slowly down his cheek, and then dropped, cold, on his ear.

*   *   *

"But they are so *tiny!* Such tiny beds!"

"Bunks", corrected her brother. "Bunks are always tiny, don't you even know *that?*"

"And I must share it with you, Auntie— *Tante* Bouscogne? How ever will we manage?"

"—and what are *you* wailing about, I have to share with grandpapa and all his smells!"

"And why do we have to sleep aboard *already?* Why can't we spent one more night ashore?"

"Yes why do we have to—"

"Perhaps, children, you might both prefer to go back to school."

— The children silently got on with it.

Auntie Clay was such a Tartar, these days.

*   *   *

Moonlight lay on the counterpane. Sir Walter had crept beneath it two

hours ago. Now the clocks were striking three, in tones as pure and imper-
sonal as the frosty air. He sleeps.

In the *Bernadette* Nellie sleeps, her arms around a sleeping Josephine.

Mr Shepherd sleeps.

Alice Barratt sleeps. She is dreaming of white marble hills.

Richard Barratt dreams of sheep, that run away and away, and he can't
catch them.

Ariosto lies awake, thinking about how he is a Count.

O'Kevin sleeps like a log, wedged securely in the corner of the posting
coach that rushes and thunders and shouts all through the night, towards Plymouth.

Chapter 28

Dawn and Sir Walter rose together. Clear in its bleak light, he saw his path and
made his plans.

He must return to his family estate. Somehow, the road north must be
traced, to Somerset, and the rooms and galleries and closets of Kellynch Hall.

There, were clothes in abundance! There, too, was jewellery; rings, fob
chains, fob-watches to go with them. Snuffboxes!— he had more snuffboxes
than he knew what to do with! It was all portable property. He would port it
to Bath, and convert it to cash. And then he would try again.

To see a way forward was of great benefit to his spirits. He called for
water, dressed easily in his riding clothes, put himself on the right side of a
large breakfast, paid his bill with his last full crown, waited for the change, and
strode out to the stables. The weather on the return journey south would be
even worse of course; later in the year. But if necessary he would take— *yes*, by
God in His Heaven!— *The public coach!*

Good Lord above, why had he not thought of that before? Absolutely
everybody travelled by the stage coach! It must be tremendously cheap!

Chapter 29

"'Way, lady— 'Way, you silly c-!"

Mrs Penelope Bouscogne shot the carter a look which silenced him,
hitched her bulging reticule higher, and sprang across the cobbles to the far
side. The Bouscogne establishment was out in force. At the first light of

winter dawn they had swarmed up from the docks, and now they were hurry-ing, severally, about the streets of Plymouth one last time, in pursuit of those last-minute essentials which a night aboard brings so sharply to mind. Nellie has given them each a list.

And she will pick up, while she is about it, a memorial cream cake; they should eat it *en famille,* with the dear Countess, this afternoon. Before they finally took ship.

She scanned the street for a baker's sign.

On the pavement she had just left, another, towering head and shoulders above the crowd, was also scanning the street– Richard!

The man turned. Not Richard.

  Not Richard, but surely...

Nellie's guts did a quick uneasy jig: just a caper or two. She knew that face. That spade-shaped chin, those tiny eyes. Afternoons in the park with the Tory gentleman; one of his men. Or, not his *man* exactly, but... O'Kevin, wasn't it?

Yes. *Kevin* O'Kevin.

She stared.

The man turned full about. Complete mutual recognition. Those hole-in-the-snow eyes. Touched his cap... no.

No.

His reaching hand had pulled the brim hard down over his face– and he turned away.

  She'd always found him utterly repellent.

She spun on her heel, doubled a corner and strode on — Just the cream cake, and then straight back to the ship to off-load– she was overtaking people now, jostling them with her laden basket– fell in, at last, behind another tall figure walking almost as fast as herself. Let him carve a path.

Which he did, perfectly straight and confident as a flagship among its fleet. Shabby coat and cracked boots, upright back and assured air: a perfect English gentleman-farmer. They didn't have that type, Nellie knew, in France; in Italy. Over there, a man couldn't...

—But– good Lord man, this was nonsense!

They could be sailing any moment! And here he was, leaving! *For a change of bloody clothes!*

He stopped dead.

Nellie ran violently into the back of him.

Sir Walter turned, and caught her.

Chapter 30

The eating-house into which he drew her roared with the lunchtime trade. The Baronet seemed as unselfconscious in its workaday surroundings as herself: claimed a space for them both at the long trestle without any aristocratic flourishes of manner, ordered briskly and sensibly; exchanged, even, the standard enquiries: health, yes, thank you, family yes very well and yours?– London, Kellynch, a Continental tour this summer how nice, and what brings you, Sir Walter, to Plymouth–?

... and Sir Walter had fallen silent. *(And what on earth, Sir Walter, are you doing in those clothes?)* Apparently from not knowing what to do, he had pulled out his pen knife, and was spoiling both it and its sheath by cutting the latter to pieces. Her eyes were fixed on him in impatient wonder... though soon, in spite of the wild originality of the situation, a tiny part of Nellie strayed back to those crucial last-minute purchases... She did have them all. Yes. She did.

Except!– the dear Countess's farewell cream cake, oh!— But the sheath being reduced to shavings, Sir Walter looked towards her in an agitated manner, and thus began; "In vain have I struggled. It will not do. My feelings will not be repressed. You must allow me to tell you how ardently I admire and love you."

Nellie's astonishment was beyond expression. She stared, coloured, doubted, and was silent:– only the certainty that the bakery would close within the hour dashed, rabbit-like, through her head.

This he considered sufficient encouragement, and the avowal of all that he felt, and had long felt for her, immediately followed. As the waiter placed their bubbling plates before them with a flourish, and then, came back with the porter, and then with the black pepper, and then hung about at the next table eavesdropping shamelessly, Nellie listened. "Do not imagine for a moment, my dear Mrs Clay, that my affection originates in nothing better than gratitude..."

"...felt, that I *admired* you— but I told myself it was only friendship...

"...began to make comparisons between yourself and– well– others—

"...and what do I not owe *you*, who showed me how insufficient are all my pretensions, to please a woman worthy of being pleased!"

Nellie smiled at this, really quite tenderly. Sir Walter blushed, and gabbled on: "... whether it might not be a possible, an hopeful undertaking, to persuade you...

"...foundation enough...

"...cannot fix on the hour, or the spot, or the look, or the words... was in the middle before I knew that I had begun..." ...It sounded like a book, but it couldn't be, because Sir Walter never read any.

"Tell me, then, have I no chance of ever succeeding?"

He stopped in his earnestness to look the question, and Nellie lifted her eyes to his– but she could really say nothing– or at any rate not quickly enough–

"You are silent!" he cried, with great animation; "absolutely silent! At present I ask no more..."

Nellie lowered her eyes again. The waiter gave up, and wandered away.

..."For I cannot make speeches, Mrs Clay", Sir Walter had resumed; and in a tone of such sincere, decided, intelligible tenderness as was tolerably convincing. "Odysseus, returning to his Penelope– though I quite recognise that you are not *my* Penelope at all, and I cannot presume..." (It does not occur to Sir Walter that she also differs from the archetype in having been someone else's Penelope since last they parted; but let it pass.) "...You alone have brought me to Plymouth! For you alone I think and plan..." (And I mean! Sitting about weaving? Methinks not!)

"... half *agony*, half hope!..."

(Though there is a school of thought that Odysseus' wife had a relatively pleasant time in his absence, and wasn't totally delighted to see him back.)

"...happier than I deserve!"

(They offer some convincing arguments.)

And he looked at her;

"...?"

She spoke, then, on being so entreated.

What did she say?

Just what she ought, of course. A lady always does.

Chapter 31

For those of you who are not ladies, and who thus remain completely in the dark and agog with curiosity, I sympathise: and here is the exact dialogue.

"I am honoured, Sir Walter, that you could desire me to be your wife; deeply honoured. I know what your standards are, and that you could consider me to fulfil them is such proof of the warmth of your attachment, as almost overwhelms me—" and Nellie stopped, to wipe away a tear.

A perfectly genuine one.

"And, for my own part, as I was privileged to share your family life in Camden Place— all those happy months!—and grew to know you all so well, almost every day brought reason to increase my regard for you; until I became convinced, from all my knowledge of your head and heart, that nothing could

make me happier than to be Lady Elliot, provided our finances were in reasonable shape.

"But are they? Forgive me, but you know it is important. The London
house cannot have come cheap, nor London clothes and London habits– and
I am dreadfully afraid that you have secured carriage horses again, with all that
they entail by way of grooms and tack and stabling expenses. How exactly
does the debt stand at the moment?"

Sir Walter sighed— almost groaned— and wiped his face with his hand.
"Well my dear, it cannot be good— at least, it cannot be as good as it was get-
ting under your guidance in Bath. It is true– I confess, it is true– that once in
London, certain expenses presented themselves as inevitable–"

"— oh Sir Walter—"

"I know my dear I *know*. But... without your steady hand, and without your
foresight, and without your clever suggestions as to how to do things more
efficiently and... and economically... well I am afraid neither Elizabeth nor I
are terribly good at organising a household and–

"and oh, Mrs Clay!" He seized her hand, almost reproachfully. "We missed
you terribly! What a *blessing* it was when you joined us! and how happy we
were together in Bath! And, what a *dreadful, pointless mess* my life has been since
you left!"

Nellie could only murmur sympathetically, and press his hand with hers.
She preferred to be honest, where possible, and so she did not say that the
same period had been, for her, similarly a blank. She found, though, that she
could honestly assure a damp-eyed Sir Walter that there had scarcely been a
day of it when she would not have been heartily glad to find herself back in
Camden Place. "Has the house there been quite given up?"

"No— At least– we found we could not break the lease..."

Oh dear! Two lots of rent at once.

Sir Walter read the thought in her eyes, and blushed miserably. "Putting it
like that, I do realise I have been terribly silly. Oh, what *will* your father say?" –
and he seemed ready to give way to despair.

Now if anything is pointless, it is despair.

"Come! It cannot be as bad as all that. The blessing of the entail is, that
there will always be the income from the estate. And the estate is good. Let us
call for pen and paper, and do some sums, and make some plans."

Sir Walter sighed some more— quite shuddered at the sight of the pen and
the paper— but he acquiesced.

There was another hurdle, though, to be faced. Nellie was looking at it, out
of the corner of her eye so to speak, even as she and Sir Walter worked — first
with trepidation, then with increasing optimism— through the calculations of
debt, interest, income and expenses that soon covered the emptying table and
swiftly began to acquire porter pot rings... You see, in the position in which

she found herself, Nellie wished above all to be open. It feels so much more comfortable. You feel so much better about yourself.

However.

With only nine thousand pounds in the family, and an unknown but confessedly dilapidated estate to resuscitate, which would absolutely drink money for the first few years, ... well. As all the nineteenth century working class knew, as all who have lived at length in really hairy financial circumstances, with no rescue in sight, come, in a cold dawn, to discover– there is such a thing as being honest beyond one's means.

It is an extravagance, a moral self-indulgence, even, of which Mrs Clay, Madame Bouscogne.... Nellie... could none of them wish to be guilty.

Yet she found, as she patted the sheets of paper together, Sir Walter wiping the pen meanwhile, that the words spoke themselves.

"You do remember, do you not, that in ten years of marriage I never had a child."

Sir Walter glanced up from his pen-wiping, saw her set face, and addressed himself to the pen once more. "Of course, my dearest Penelope. That has always been perfectly obvious between us."

"Not even— Not even so much as a— as an accident. You know?"

"A sailor's life…"

"A sailor's life had nothing to do with it. Of this I feel certain. All my acquaintance managed it, and their husbands were ashore less than mine."

Sir Walter put a last polish on the pen.

"Yes well."

He held it up to the light and peered at it, just as though he were not hopelessly short-sighted.

"I have lived, you know, for such a long time, with the understanding that I shall never have a son. So it is nothing new. And now, too, with the marriage of Elizabeth and Mr Elliot–" Nellie grimaced very slightly; so did Sir Walter "—I can hope, in any case, to see a grandson take up the entail. I assure you, Penelope. I do not marry in the hope of an heir. A son is nothing to me, compared with the very great happiness of calling you my wife."

At this, Nellie beamed... melted...

– well she should have. Instead she has suddenly put her head in her hands. She seems to be staring down at the table— at the papers?

What we can see of her face is inscrutable.

Maybe she is comparing the figures on the paper before her, to another set of figures? Setting her hypothetical worst balance sheet in Italy, against the steady predictability here?

Probably, then, she would be adding the two balances together.

If so, she will definitely be coming out with a positive figure — some of which must, obviously, then depart England, to offset that red ink in Italy.

There to mingle with it, as deep and soothing sepia.

... washing the strain from the faces of those she loves best.

Does she see them?

Gathered there, together, beneath the ancient walls of the Manor of Bouscogne. That fabled place; that Arcadia of her childhood fancies.

They all live there now; it is home, to them. She sees the adults lazing, perhaps, on a picnic rug. Under an olive tree. Eating strange Italian food; talking, smiling... and surely, too, in the golden fields about them, splashed with poppies, the children are playing, their happy cries rising, faintly (at this great distance from her), high up. Into sunnier skies.

She lowers her hands. Looks at Sir Walter.

After the strain of prolonged mathematics, his face is loose, exhausted; weak.

Perhaps she compares it with another face, that is none of those things.

But I'm just guessing.

I know this is a critical juncture, but I'm not risking another poke in the eye.

All that I can definitely report is that at this point, she smiled at him — and held out her hand.

Beaming... speechless... he clasped it in both of his...

And on the other side of the street, Kevin O'Kevin shrugged, and walked away.

*   *   *

It was upon Anne Elliot that it fell, therefore, to utter that monstrous something which a lot of our characters were thinking, at this point, yet none but Anne has resolve to frame and state.

"Mrs *Clay?*"

Her words rang about the drawing room of Kellynch: rang, and rang again. She drew out the final vowel with extraordinarily unpleasant length; more, really, like this: 'Mrs *Klaaaeeeiii?*'

"Father— Father you will recall– perhaps– that *Mrs Klaaaeeiii* is a poor widow, barely able to live–"

"No no!" interrupted Sir Walter eagerly, "they have money now! Lots! or– an estate– any number of properties– needing only a *little* work– And her nephew! Her nephew is a Count!"

At this Lady Russell presses her hands to her temples... but, racked between opposing imperatives of deference and veracity, she finds herself too oppressed to even properly breathe, let alone give utterance.

Nor need she. Anne is speaking still.

"A widow, between thirty and forty!—"

She speaks at length, while Sir Walter shrinks visibly before them.

"... nothing to live on... no surname of dignity..."

Sir Walter has retreated to the fireplace.

"...of all the people in all the world..." He gazes into the hissing depths. It looks nice in there. "...a mere Mrs *Clay*..."

Elizabeth's battened face suddenly explodes too into speech— "Mrs *Clay!* Mrs *Clay,* to be the chosen wife of Sir Walter Elliot! Preferred, by him, to his own family connections! For you can be sure that my husband and I will not visit at Kellynch when such a woman—"

"Oh don't mind us, Sir Walter. *We* shan't object in the least!"

It was Mr Elliot, carolling happily from a window-seat.

"On the contrary! We shall visit frequently. I quite long to make the acquaintance of the new Lady Elliot!" He leaps to his feet, slapping the day's newspaper into a neat roll. "I do so wonder, what kind of person she will be. Don't you, Lady Russell?"

The old lady clasps her hands— suddenly frail, suddenly elderly— beneath her chin, and squeezes shut her eyes... shakes her head. Her jaw trembles.

Mr Elliot smacks her lightly on the back with the folded newspaper "You're a dear old thing, Lady Russell; did I ever tell you that?"— and walks from the room.

One by one, the women follow him.

Only Anne, the last to depart, at the very threshold turns back. She has one last volley of duty to discharge.

"You know, Father, that after this, people will laugh at you."

Sir Walter by now is clinging to the chimney piece. His face is pressed against the backs of his hands. He does not look up— he does not *want* to look up— but he finds himself rolling, at her slight, dark, savage figure, just quickly, one white-rimmed eye.

"Ah well, my— my dear. I think we both know: they always have."

Chapter 32

The day Sir Walter Elliot married Mrs Penelope Clay was the happiest day of his life to date. His second Lady Elliot promised all that the first had promised: beautiful, accomplished, clever; already the aunt, or something, of a baronetish something; and blessed, above all, with vast and comforting organisational powers; the first Lady Elliot indeed, in all but that first Lady's soul-destroying capacity for noble endurance.

Nellie had a lovely day too. Stuff which had been missing at her first wedding was here in scads. There were hothouse flowers by the bucket, acres of silk, furlongs of lace, an excellent carriage at the church door; and the church itself was beautiful, and packed to the choir-stalls with affected guests.

Chief among these latter is the massive tribe of Musgrove cousins, all in varying degrees of pleasurable distress. Captain Wentworth and Mrs Wentworth are there too, naturally; but they maintain, behind expressions as cold as Arctic seawater, a dignified reserve. Mary Musgrove, however — the youngest Elliot sister, we met her briefly in Bath, at the corner of Belmont and Camden, remember? — went so far as to cling to her husband's shoulder and cry buckets. She felt the indignity of the relationship so keenly that she could not bear to look away the whole ceremony, and could no more have boycotted it, as her exasperated husband had suggested, than she could resist squeezing a pimple.

"Do you, Walter Elliot..."

"I do!"

Mary whimpers, and sinks her nails into her husband's arm.

"Do you, Penelope Clay..."

"I do."

"Who giveth this woman to this man?"

Mr Elliot titters soundlessly, and mouths *'I do!'* It is noticeable that, of the immediate family, only Mr Elliot looks to be in a truly festive mood.

Mr Hardcastle is the man who speaks the words aloud, though. He is deputising for Mr Shepherd. On this beautiful day, Papa and the children are a thousand miles away. They are in Italy. Safe from this giggling maniac. Nellie had insisted.

... but here is that awkward moment, of silence, during which the groom fits the ring onto the bride's finger...

...and she smiles serenely.

And if the smile is blossoming from the certainty of family preserved and security achieved, rather than from the joyful visions of young love's dream, well, let's just say it here: Love's young dream always vanishes. Uncertainty, on this point, is limited strictly to the question of what will take its place. The loveliness of entailed landed estates, at least, is amaranth.

As for her husband — and he is beaming from ear to ear, for the deed is done and they are sweeping down the aisle (and oh!– there is Lady Russell, bearing up with fortitude): yes he is old, and no he is not terribly bright, but he is sober, he is rich, or soon will be again, and he's an old sweetie really, as long as you always take care to brush him up the right way.

He is handing her into the carriage; the barouche-landau. She will have to arrange for its sale. Still: for now, how nice to sit down at last; and in such dignity. Someone calls "a stirrup cup for the bride!", and a silver goblet is thrust into her hand. She drinks it off with an inscrutable smile, and hands it back to Mr Elliot, who instantly fills it again for Sir Walter—

but the happy groom is throwing largesse to the crowd. His tenantry have stood in wait outside the church door all morning for this moment, and now they are cheering and capering, from genuine high spirits, of some sort. There are calls of "God bless the Baronet!" and then a child's voice is heard: "God bless her ladyship!" And the call is taken up, around the church, and all down the street, as the barouche-landau spanks away from the church door...

Yes, Nellie's second wedding day was in truth a day of joy, as well as a day of satisfaction, deep and abiding. She had been the victim of romance in her youth; she had learned prudence as she grew older: the natural sequel of an only too natural beginning.

Chapter 33

Dear Papa,

You will excuse I know my dreadfull writing, it is the first time in five months that I have been able to hold a pen, and even now Sir W. will allow me only a few lines. We read, however, in your latest, that Mr & Mrs E. plan to take you in on their way through to Italy, and I feel <u>very very strongly</u> that above <u>all else</u> ...

[A short section has been elided, as it is in a cipher still unbroken.]

Heartening, though, to hear the olives so v. promising— your news from Turin, wonderful!— Ariosto's progress quite marvellous — I will secure a proper English governess for Josephine immediately.

As for me, do not be concerned, everyone assures me the worst is over, and that I will soon feel quite well—

but dear Walter presses me to rest now.

So I will only add, that the doctor came <u>again</u> today, and after doing all his usual etc etc, said, that he <u>thinks</u> now that it may be twins, while Mrs Collier, by simply dangling a ring over my enormous figure, has determined that they will both be boys.

*

And they were.

*

Chapter 34

It is now my pleasant duty to round off the fates of those whom the reader has followed— with interest, I hope; with patience, certainly— through the length of these volumes. It is for me a joyful occasion, seeing as pretty much every character finishes the tale with their just deserts; the good happily, the bad, unhappily. 'That is what '*fiction*' means.'

First, the minor characters.

As Austen courteously assures us, Lady Russell soon overcame her aversion to Captain Wentworth, and learned to love him as a mother a son. Not every son is without fault, but while he was ashore she humoured, softened or concealed his failings as best she could, and the memory of a duty done then formed another satisfaction in his absence. And in any case the Wentworths were absent a lot, leaving to Lady Russell the important business of forming the minds of their little girls and boys, so she had her hands really very full, and her time very much taken up, especially for her time of life; of course, she would do anything, for dearest Anne.

From this you can see that Anne's husband was *not* thrown ashore by the final crushing of the Corsican Fiend. On the contrary, he almost immediately got employ, in the form of an independent command in South American waters, where he did remarkably well. (After the Napoleonic wars ended, the waters of South America became quite thick with fictional naval heroes, *all* doing remarkably well: it's amazing that Spain managed to hang on to any of her colonies as long as she did.)

Anne accompanied him on most of his postings, which more than made up for all those missed trips to London when her father and sister used to go off and leave her behind at Kellynch, the beasts. Under her gentle influence, Captain Wentworth expanded his reading to encompass Johnson and the Lake poets, became a model captain in the reformed post-war navy, and began grinding his teeth at night, and when he did indeed come into honours, being made, not just a Baronet, as sister Mary had rather feared, but Lord Wentworth and a peer by GAD, his wife became Lady Anne *in sensu propre,* and everyone in the Elliot family had to give place to her. Her father was ecstatic! her sisters, less so: but the chance for Lady Anne to purse her delicate lips, and sigh over the spiritual grossness of her closest kin, was now quite wasted — on her, for whom a happy marriage had restored all that was best in the Elliot spirit.

Mm.

Who else?
Ah: Mr Elliot! ...
Mr Elliot.

It is rare for the Mr Elliots of this world to meet the sticky end that they deserve. Unshackled by conscience, they do well wherever a series of fleeting encounters typifies social life (as for example now), and in some societies, even better– as when surrounded by conscientious elders who clean up the damage they leave in their wake. Meanwhile they skip on, lighthearted, down the decades, unburdened by guilts or cares, and this is very good for their health.

Feelings they certainly have — as may be, of triumph or chagrin, according to the success of their schemes — but where they will beg our assistance under reversals, and receive it too, they experience no obligation to return the favour. Plenty of them, too, have sense enough to skirt outright criminal activity, or at least its debilitating consequents; discovery, and punishment. Withal, these parasites upon the social order of mutual trust and mutual assistance, which characterises civilisation in its truest sense, tend to make old and cheerful bones.

It is with quiet satisfaction, therefore, that I record the death of young Mr Elliot.

It happened on the very Continental tour we saw mentioned in Nellie's letter. Our villain had been sitting in his rooms somewhere in the south of France, lightheartedly essaying, by means purely *manual*, the asphyxiation of the hotel cat. It was only a very small cat, and his enthusiasm for once outstripped his sense of self-preservation: he allowed its hinder legs sufficient play to scratch him.

A full bulletin of Mr Elliot's symptoms, treatment, and demise (written in a hand comprehensively unlike any that anyone had ever clapped eyes on), was provided to his widow by the attending physician; a certain Dr Moulin. It is evident from this sad document that a *posse* of pathogens must have leapt from the beast's claws into Mr Elliot's bloodstream, and thence to his liver, heart, spleen, kidneys, lungs and finally, and very slowly, his brain — after which we will enquire no further. This is the final chapter, after all.

— Just, I have to say. Among the billions of sentient creatures who have endured this dreadful death, very few have been as deserving of it as Mr Elliot.

For his widow— for Elizabeth— what a release! She arrived back in
Somerset already half a dozen years younger than she had been on leaving it,
for a good bank balance is the most potent rejuvenator known to Man: what
miracles cannot be wrought, then, by the acquisition of such wealth as is now
Elizabeth's? She can probably fool about in happy independence for another
ten years, and still look forward to being a child bride.

In short, she is back where we first met her: only, where previously her
term of joy was perilously close to its end, she now has an indefinite lease on
her understanding of happiness.

Alice and Richard Barratt remained all their lives in Italy, where the climate
gave them, too, a fresh lease of youthful energy. Under their combined care
the Bouscogne establishment flourished so rapidly, and so well, that the Barratts were soon free to branch out on their own account. Alice married a wine-
merchant,– a kind, energetic man, well-endowed with Nature's choicest gifts–
while Mr Barratt went on to make a very decent fortune as a dealer in building
supplies and marble, and in the district is celebrated, to this day, for being the
first to publish poetry written in the local dialect. His own idol being Burns,
rather than Byron, it was a cycle of the most frightfully hokey love sonnets
ever written, in honour of a fat little black-eyed convent girl, whom he subsequently wed. So perhaps he was never cut out to be a hero, anyway.

Let us hope so.

What of *our* children: what of Josephine, and her brother?

The young Senor Ariosto went on to make an excellent thing of his Italian
estate. Another pen than mine will have to tell of his leading role in the mech-
anisation of olive oil production: if we peep into the future, though, we may
discern him, a wealthy nineteenth century industrialist and innovator, taking in
Kellynch almost yearly on his trips to Scotland and the North. At such times,
his Italian brood and their blond cousins run about together in the summer
gardens of Kellynch, re-enacting the Napoleonic wars, often with surprise
endings, while the even tenor of Mr Shepherd's days are galvanised by learning
from Ariosto more than he had ever imagined there was to be known about
manufactories, and by discussions with Ariosto's almost intimidatingly clever
wife on the role of the higher mathematics as applied to ciphers.

From this it will be evident that Mr Shepherd held out for many years
mor e against his life-long foes, pneumonia and debilitation. It was often
touch-and-go– but on young Ariosto finally coming to man's estate, the frail
old gentleman was able gratefully to retire, at last, to England, to spend his
twilight years at Kellynch Hall. There, he lived in the greatest harmony with
his daughter and his son-in-law; lived to teach history, geography and creative
accounting to a new crop of Elliots, and also of Cumberlands. (Josephine married a Cumberland and— well— she had a lovely time.) In Mr Shepherd's

actual twilight years, he even grew a few roses in his cheeks, as old people sometimes do— and few would have believed that the calm, keen-eyed old gentleman, translating *Moliere* before the smouldering wreck of the library fire, could ever have spent so many dreary years in a French prison. It is true, though, that he never could abide a pigeon.

Sir Walter had, with his new wife, two more children, both girls, and was in the end as happy as a man can be whose marriage is, at bottom, based on little more than mutual affection, a shared solicitude for the well-being of their family, estate, and dependents, a respectful recognition of each other's strengths, and a fond accommodation of each other's weaknesses. Unqualified submission suits some personalities, but very few: Sir Walter exercised complete dominion over his wardrobe. All else was deferred to his wife's clear head and firm hand.

And that Lady?

She found, as time went on, that she indeed gained all on which she had calculated: no more, and no less.

*

EPILOGUE

On one point only did she remain, for a time, in suspense.

You see, Lady Elliot could not forget that her first husband had also had a child.

George Clay had loved that boy with all his heart: he had sent its mother money once. And on his very deathbed he had begged his dry-eyed wife to seek out the boy, and make of him an Englishman; not a sorry Mediterranean salami-chewer.

At the time, Nellie had not felt very sympathetic. Ah well: those who can barely live, and who live perforce in a very small, and generally very inferior, society, may well be illiberal and cross. But if a very narrow income has a tendency to contract the mind, and sour the temper, an expansion of that income will enable a naturally broad mind to expand, in its turn, to something closer to its native proportions.

"Sir Walter, my dear..."

Sir Walter concurred. They must find the lad, and bring him to Kellynch.

It took some searching, and some negotiations. His mother at first wanted more than she could get— protested that, at ten, the boy was just becoming useful to her (a slur, by the way: he'd been useful for years, his good nature and his dexterity with everything from a leaking window frame to a dirty nappy having long rendered him invaluable in his mother's chaotic household); asserted that not even another fifty-four pounds— no, nor guineas neither— could tempt her...

Finally, however, she was persuaded to be reasonable: and it was a dreary, wet, thoroughly English winter's day when the shivering child arrived at the gates of Kellynch Hall. He was short for his age, and their grey stone and black iron, towering above him— tall, awful, dripping— nearly proved (for a moment) the last straw on his youthful spirits.

He had kept those spirits up in the first week of his journey by applying, to its frequent bewildering changes of direction, all his small stock of navigational knowledge— and, when this had finally failed him, by seizing on rare sightings of the sun, as adjusted for time of day by the coachmen's clocks. Right now, he reminded himself that here, at Kellents Hall, he would at last learn navigation properly: so well that, as a man, he would always know exactly where he was. Thus, too, he would take his first steps along the path that would make him a real sailor, like his father: *un capità*.

— And oh, what a pity that his trousers were wet with this English wetness!— his shoes, soaked— his hat, in spite of all his endeavours, still visibly crushed; for his mother, pressing him into that first coach, had assured him that long ago, as a mid, Sir Walter Elliot had sailed with Cook!

He must pull himself together, and make a good impression.

With this determination in his heart, the boy squelched stoutly behind the butler along a nautical mile of marble corridor into, confusingly and suddenly, a truly enormous room. High above him someone was intoning "Master George Clay". Strange though the words were, he could detect in them an introduction, so he swept off his dripping hat with a manly, childish flourish, to bow low:

"La benedicció de Déu sobre vostès!"

For many horrible moments, nobody answered him. They just stared.

He breathed deeply, and tried again:

"The God- wit... *God-be-wit-you!*"

Still they stared.

So he bowed again, for good measure — and stood; twisting his hat.

His flaxen infant's hair had long ago darkened to ruddy brown. In this, as in every other respect, there stood before the astonished Elliots a small, bedraggled Captain Wentworth.

The End.

Endnotes

1. Regarding Vol I, Ch 3; the error about the date of Lady Elliot's death:

As *Mrs Clay* is for genuine Austen aficionados, I will leave you the fun of working this out for yourself: start from the year of her death as given in the Baronetage, and do the sums relative to the other dates and ages in Chapter 1 of *Persuasion*.

And if you feel you are getting nowhere, don't give up, reflect: in none of her previous mature novels has Austen given us even a single specific year. By the end of that first chapter, though, Austen has specified the calendar year in which the *Persuasion* opens, Anne's and Elizabeth's age at this time, their respective ages at the time of their mother's death, and the fact that the death took place thirteen years ago— all this even to the point of repetitiousness. It's a thoroughly uncharacteristic proceeding, which alerts us to spot something hidden within it.

That something delivers such a savage final blow to Sir Walter's character that, for a while, it seemed impossible to rescue him.

2. A third interpretation of Anne's words is easily deduced from the Narrator's own footnotes of Volume 1, Chapters 8 and 10, *viz*: that Austen's two naval brothers had some eighteen children between them (two wives dying in the process) and that a naval commander's pay at this time was about £176 a twelve-month; £143 if peace were declared. As we also learn in *Mrs Clay*, promotion and higher pay is assured once an officer is made *post*-captain. Before then, though, his future lacks any such certainty.

Further information which may be useful: although, afloat, all sailors had free accommodation and basic food, a captain had what was then the significant expense of his clothing (both informal, and gold-bullion-embellished), and of following the inflexible naval tradition by which he must invite his officers regularly to dine at the captain's cabin; dinners and wines, the excellence of which reflected the honour of his position and (in the case of visitors), that of the ship.

Wentworth, then, was in this position: a fresh-made commander, at the most junior level of the pay-grade, with no private income, and little in the way of the connections needed to secure the key promotion he needed to change all this; the promotion to post-captain. A family— potentially expanding, nine months after every shore leave, to goodness knows what proportions— can become a worry, a distraction from his duty, and a very significant financial obstacle to maintaining the dignity of his position. George Clay's self-pity about being burdened with a wife does not negate the reality of the problem, or the validity of Anne's scruples.

Quotes & References

Parker, Keiko. (2001) 'What part of Bath do you think they will settle in?' *Persuasions, 23,* 166-176.

Parkinson, C. Northcote. (2005) *The Life and Times of Horatio Hornblower: A Biography of C S Forster's Famous Naval Hero.* McBooks Press; Ithaca, N.Y.

Sutherland,Kathryn. (2005). *Jane Austen's Textual Lives: From Aeschylus to Bollywood.* Oxford University Press; Oxford.

"To travel hopefully...[is a better thing than to arrive]": the line is often attributed to Buddha, but was in fact to be Kipling.

The end of Chapter 20, Vol II, mangles the beautiful ending of *A High Wind in Jamaica* (1929) by Richard Hughes.

The much-quoted description of Jane Austen as "an old maid (I beg her pardon – I mean a young lady)... no more regarded in society than a poker or a fire-screen" is from Mary Russell Mitford's letters. It can be found in context in *The Life of Mary Russell Mitford: Told By Herself in Letters to Her Friends,* published in 1870 and edited by Alfred Guy Kingan L'Estrange— who felt compelled to append to her remarks the footnote: "Every other account of Jane Austen, from whatever quarter, represents her as handsome, graceful, amiable, and shy."

The Narrator appears to share the common belief (Vol III, Ch 19) that Austen objected to characters plunging into a 'vortex of dissipation'. In a letter to her niece Anna (September 28th, 1814), Austen clearly states that she does not object to the thing itself; it is the expression alone that she cannot bear.

The three direct quotes from Austen are from two successive letters to Austen's niece, Fanny Knight. (Note these comments were written in 1817 and not, as given in the early publications of the Brabourne letters, 1816), thus:

Writing of matrimony: "Single women have a dreadful propensity for being poor." March 13th, 1817;

Ten days later (March 23rd, 1817), writing of heroines generally: "Pictures of perfection, as you know, make me sick and wicked"...— and then, only a few lines on, she writes o f *Persuasion* specifically: "You may *perhaps* like the heroine, as she is almost too good for me."

If you have enjoyed **Mrs Clay**...

...you are part of a tiny minority. Please, recommend the book to all the like-minded acquaintance you have, as God knows it will never sell in any other way.